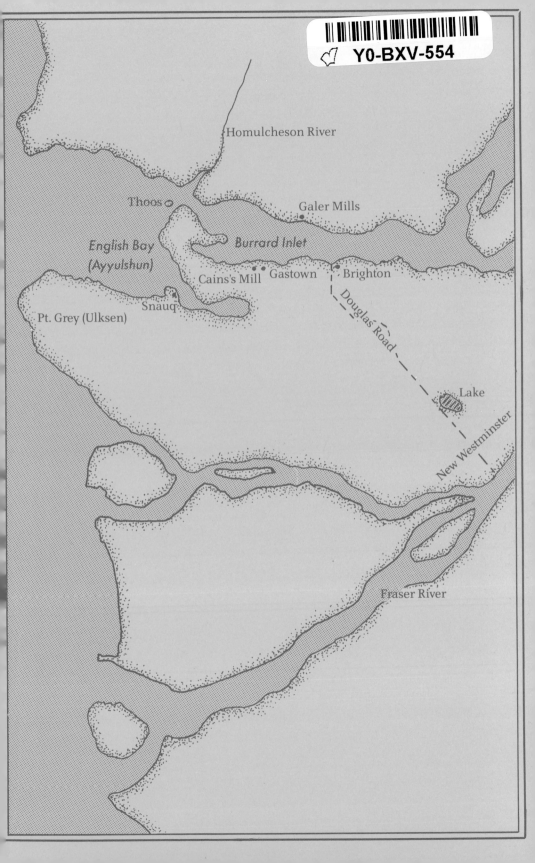

Homulcheson River

Thoos ○   Galer Mills
                             •

English Bay   Burrard Inlet
(Ayyulshun)

                      • • Gastown • Brighton
                 Cains's Mill
Snauq   Douglas Road

Pt. Grey (Ulksen)

                                                Lake

                                           New Westminster

                                    Fraser River

THE WEST COASTERS

A sweeping saga of the men and women who settled Canada's Pacific Coast

A Novel by

David Corcoran

Macmillan of Canada
A Division of Canada Publishing Corporation
Toronto, Ontario, Canada

Canadian Cataloguing in Publication Data

Corcoran, David, date.
　　The West Coasters : a novel

ISBN 0-7715-9683-9

I. Title.

PS8555.O72W47 1986　　C813'.54　　C85-098864-0
PR9199.3.C67W47 1986

Designed by NewtonFrank　　　50,833

Macmillan of Canada
A Division of Canada Publishing Corporation
Toronto, Ontario, Canada

Printed in Canada

CONTENTS

for Charles

PREFACE

The West Coasters is a novel, a work of fiction. Although the majority of the events in the book did really happen, I have frequently altered dates, locations, or minor details. Many of the historic and political figures (such as Amor De Cosmos, Gassy Jack, Sir James Douglas, etc.) have been presented as accurately as the distance of time and the vagaries of history allow, but the major characters (the Cainses and the Galers, Sitka, and Mei-fu) are fictional.

Ultimately, this is a story, intended to portray the spirit and flavour of life on Canada's Pacific Coast before the turn of the century, and should not be taken as an accurate history.

I would like to express my gratitude to the Explorations Program of the Canada Council for their support during the writing of a portion of this book. I would also like to thank both Jerry Newman and Cherie Smith for the countless hours they spent reading various drafts of the manuscript and discussing them with me.

Vancouver
July 1985

CHAPTER ONE

1857

SITKA WAVES. HUGE WAVES. PUSHED BY THE WIND. Rolling, cresting, crashing, and foaming up to the beach; they were higher than a man, higher than two men, louder than a hundred, stronger than a thousand.

Sitka sat strongly before them, cross-legged on a grassy bank. She was of the sea, born of a dead woman, with the sound of the surf in her ears. Her real name, the name she had been given during the ceremony for her twelfth birthday, was Sitakala-noughtun, but the people of her tribe simply called her Sitka. She had been raised on the mainland behind Vancouver Island, and she had loved the ocean and the gentle swelling of its life. Even during storms it had never been more than a little worrisome. Now it terrified her. Here on the island's unknown western shore she faced the real ocean, the killing ocean, impossibly huge and unknowably angry. Without taking her eyes from the waves she worked deftly at the bird net, feeling with her fingertips and tying quick knots in the thin strips of intestine. It was a fine net; the tribe would praise her.

The tribe. Since she had been taken slave they had treated her well, but no amount of kindness could compensate for the pain they had caused her. She spat into the cedar box at her side, "Murderers," and scooped another handful of salmon roe into her mouth; the eggs popped and squirted bitterly against her tongue.

She would never fit in. At home she had been a giantess, here she was merely tall; but there were other differences. Their hair was auburn, hers raven, their skin bronze, hers brown sepia, their noses were fine, hers hawkish, their eyes angled and half-lidded, hers round and open — and they were murderers, she was not.

The tap-tapping of elkhorn mallet on jade celt stopped and Sitka turned to see what had interrupted the work behind her. Ouhiliu laid his tools on the totem and rubbed his chest. His face was troubled. Ouhiliu. *Heekw*, important man. He had been good to her; unlike her husband, who had run away in her time of need. Tcaga: spoon, lazy one, drifter, trader, spoon, eater, fat Tcaga.

Ouhiliu had not come with the raiding party; he was old, too old for killing. He had bought her from the chief and now it was for him she chewed salmon eggs into tempera to be made into paint for his totem poles. Countless times he had consoled her and apologized for the actions of his people. Time would cure her, he had said. She knew time would not cure Ouhiliu. She was sorry for him. At home she would have paid much for a shaman to dispossess such a friend as Ouhiliu. She spat. Here she could do nothing.

"Is it painful today, Ouhiliu?"

His eyes opened and he stopped rubbing. "It is nothing," he said. "A little tightness, that is all."

"Perhaps you should rest."

"Rest is for the old," he said, stooping and picking up a cedar rain hat from the ground.

"Of course, Ouhiliu, but still—"

"Here. Cover your head, for it is beginning to rain."

"Please, Ouhiliu, if you will not rest, at least wear the hat yourself. It is only a drizzle and I don't mind the rain."

He scowled at her, then placed the cap on his head and smiled. "You only abide the rain because it hides your tears, Sitka."

She whirled back to the awesome waves and shut her eyes until the tap-tapping resumed. He had seen.

Whipped by the wind, the drizzle and the spray from the salt sea stung her face but her eyes remained open, black and un-blinking, with tears rolling down from them.

While her fingers worked independently, Sitka counted the waves, again, and again, and again, and in her mind each one carried a child floating on its crest towards her. Then she was back on the mainland in her corner of the longhouse next to fat Tcaga, with her children sleeping quietly around her.

In the dream she was running, running from the cliff where she had been talking to the ocean, admiring its serenity. She had seen stars floating up through the water like phosphorous bones loosed from the bottom and had been filled with foreboding. Running, she could hear a great beast; then she tripped, fell, and in the falling could smell its foul odour. Scrambling, running, crashing, and running again she could feel its evil gnawing at her and thought it was behind her, then ahead, or maybe above, winging blackly to her village, a malevolent demon intent on some great horror and filling her with dread.

The blackness descended on her and she struggled, gasping and inundated, up, up from the depths, up from sleep, awaking to the sounds of screams and the sight of war clubs slashing at the night.

"Run! Children: Cutick, Tumas, Skoail." Vicious faces, slashed longitudinally in red and black, rolled down the longhouse in waves towards her family's corner. Those nearest the door were taken, or dying, or dead. Fat Tcaga shoved her from the sleeping platform as he puffed to his feet and sought escape. She rolled over the coals of the cooking fire and sparks swirled through the blackness like a signal; the faces turned. Sitka pushed herself up while her daughters, Tumas, ten—The Moon—and younger Skoail—Daylight—beat the fire from her clothes. The knives were reaping closer; Sitka's two sisters, clubbed and hoisted limply onto warriors' shoulders, were whisked into the night. Tcaga escaped through the rear exit.

Run, run. Cutick. The baby, her son, her baby, Cutick. With one arm she grabbed the cradle and crushed it to her breast while with the other she herded Moon and Daylight, sweeping, pushing, shoving, don't trip, run, run. Too late: blocked. Daylight at her skirt, screaming at the flashing knives. Backed into a corner, Sitka shrieked and hissed and clawed at the faces. They toyed with her, slashing little rents in her fighting arm, which flowed with blood.

A warrior shouted orders and two more flanked her, one left, one right. The left one lunged at Daylight, and as Sitka defended her, unprotected Moon was snatched crying away and lanced high overhead, where her shrieks died and her blood flowed. Then Daylight, silent, stoic Daylight, was gone and gutted on the floor. Lastly, Cutick was ripped from her breast, the cradle splintered open, and then, only then, as the slave club swung and struck her back into the black horror-dream, did she see his blood and know that he had been dead all along.

She awoke in the grey pre-dawn, rolling and heaving on the open ocean, lying in a pool of pink water at the bottom of a canoe. Around her the members of her tribe lay scattered like a catch of salmon, some unconscious but most awake and grim-faced, staring out at the ocean. Her sisters were not among them. Sitka pushed herself up and fell towards the side of the canoe, intending to jump and vaguely believing she would swim to shore and search for her dead children. A rough hand grabbed her and threw her down, and she felt the shooting pain from the cuts in her arm. The club rose and she shut her eyes, ready for the blow, but it did not come; the chief stopped it, concerned about his damaged property, and ordered her tied with cedar-bark rope. For hours she sat, trussed hand to foot, counting the wounds on her arm—twenty-four, eight for each child she had not saved.

The trip to the west shore of the island took seven days, with nightly stops in wildwood clearings, cold splashes into shallow water to haul the canoes ashore, gather firewood, cook meals, and piece together fragments of victory stories boasted about in a language Sitka scarcely understood. She knew that most of the bragging was done by the shaman. He was a loud, wispy man with a tweezed beard, a daintily carved bone in his nose, cedar-rope braids in his hair, and a necklace of whale's teeth. During his firelight ravings one word recurred over and over: Toxwid, Spirit of War, Self-Destroying One.

From one of the slaves who spoke the language, Sitka learned of the shaman's dream. For three nights Toxwid had appeared to him in the form of a giant raven with a woman's head. She had flown south, then north, then east, winging in the moonlight close to the water with the shaman on her back. As he told the story, warriors tapped slowly on logs or knocked pieces of driftwood together, beating out the rhythm of the spirit bird's wings. The shaman told of skimming the silhouette of the mainland treetops, soaring into the night and plummeting to the roofs of the enemies' longhouses, which shattered and burst into flame.

Once she knew of the story, Sitka pulled her cape tighter round her throat to shut out the rhythm of the spirit-bird's wings.

Fog. Stiff-armed and cold, Sitka creaked into the morning, blowing ashes and smoke out of the fire and coaxing it to life. Northbound geese honked unseen through the mist while gulls and canvasbacks strutted the beach and wrens and thrushes rustled in the undergrowth. Spring robins. Spring.

On the third day the canoes rounded the southern tip of the island and Sitka glimpsed the white man's fort called Victoria, lurking in the trees. Grey smoke curled into white fog and the sounds of machines and occasional shouts echoed out over the still water. But the men themselves remained hidden, like wolves slinking through the night, there but concealed, dangerous but unseen. Sitka hated them. The iron and the Hudson's Bay blankets were not worth the hell they brought. She knew of their diseases: smallpox, measles, venereal disease; their justice and their religion: hypocritical, ravaging; their firewater: mind-stealing; their lust for otter: dying with the animals; for land: just begun; for women: constant and cruel. She felt guilty that Tcaga traded with them at their mainland fort, Langley, on the Fraser River. He did not fish and hunt with the rest of the tribe but paddled the river between the settlement and the inland tribes, exchanging scrap iron and trinkets for furs, and furs for blankets, and blankets for more furs until he had enough to last him through a lazy winter of eating and sleeping.

Sitka had not expected a better husband; she was not of an important family, nor was she pretty. Even as a child she was big-boned and man-like, with a thin face on a strong body, thick lips, and coarse hair. Now, at thirty-one, wrinkles were already etching into her skin and her breasts were sagging. No, Tcaga had not been such a bad catch: he rarely struck her, and he had given her children. At the birth of their first son she had been elated. Sitka, mother of children. Children: two dead of smallpox, one drowned, two stillborn, three murdered, all gone, all dead, all lost; Sitka, mother of dead children.

As the canoe rolled in with the surf, Sitka watched the women and children running to the beach while the elderly plodded carefully behind. The big canoes were hauled out of the water, overturned, and covered with mats to protect them from the sun. In the wake of the celebration Sitka climbed the grassy bank to the village. It was much like hers but larger and richer; the longhouses were bigger and their posts more intricately carved, the totems were taller and more numerous, there was more salmon drying in the sun, more people, and more finery. That night there was feasting and the dividing up of spoils. Sitka and three others were claimed by the chief. Her sisters had disappeared.

Saskwalah was a fine man, old but still strong and wise. His longhouse held ten families and the lower third of it was partitioned off by a carved cedar wall. The central crest was a bear's head which was five feet across and towered up to the rafters. Sitka did not enter. Like all slaves she slept in the main part of the house near the front entrance so that in case of attack the least important would be the first to die. From her sleeping mat she watched Saskwalah's family pass through the bear's mouth. He had two wives: Yanahook, young, beautiful, and pregnant, and Hupal—Sunshine—a woman of laughter. She was thirty-eight and still attractive, if not beautiful. The creases at her eyes and mouth swept her skin upwards over fine bones, giving her the impression of a constant smile. She was dainty, round-faced, and graceful.

It was Hupal who treated and bandaged Sitka's arm, who gave her a sleeping mat and a goat's-wool blanket, who told jokes and tried to make her laugh. It was Hupal who was sorry.

Sun burned into summer. The robins moved back to the prehistoric coolness of the deepwoods and were replaced by hummingbirds and dragonflies hovering low over the water lilies. The summer wore on through bluebells, columbine, shooting stars, fields of buttercups and purple iris, primrose, snatches of violets, and finally fireweed—brilliant, crimson, and heavy with hornets. Sitka staggered through the summer, empty-headed, gathering berries: blueberries, red elderberries, salmonberries, and currants, unaware of the swarming mosquitoes, which gave way to deerflies; she trudged the upper slopes of the hills behind the village bent under the weight of her burden basket, mechanically picking and gathering, unconscious of bears, unconscious of life. The sun sucked her dry till she was hard and brittle.

In the autumn she began to soften. Hupal's jokes dredged up ripples and traces of smiles from her depths, but it was Mowitch who truly touched her heart. He was ten, named after the deer, and, like the deer, was shy, secretive, skittish, and quick on his feet. Mowitch was Hupal's son, but with three stronger and older brothers he was not likely to become chief, nor did he want to.

One cool autumn night after food and firelight storytelling he crossed the smoky room to Sitka's mat and timidly offered a knotted loop of string. Sitka sat cross-legged and blank-eyed, automatically weaving a basket, lost in thought, not seeing. Carefully, Mowitch tugged at her hand and looped the string around it. Then slowly, painfully, thawing slowly, Sitka began the game. Cat's cradle, cat's cradle; she knew how to play, of course she knew it. She had taught it to Moon and Daylight and the others, but her fingers fumbled and she forgot the moves. The boy sat gravely, patiently, and instructed her. He began to talk. Few of the words made sense but they were a child's words and they poured over Sitka like warm water and melted her. Her fingers limbered and she played faster, more surely, until, finally, she grinned and the entire house stopped, shocked, and watched while she hugged the child to her breast. Sitka was laughing.

In the late autumn the chief ordered a totem pole carved to commemorate the birth of the child expected by Yanahook. It was to be sixty feet, ten sections of six feet each, and Sitka was the price paid for one section. She rolled up her sleeping mat without comment and moved to the next longhouse.

Her new master was Ouhiliu, an old and important man with many slaves. He was a recorder of legends. At night Sitka would lie frozen on her mat and listen as he thrashed in his dreams and called for his dead wife.

Ouhiliu was good to her. He spoke her language and delighted in practising it on her. Sitka became his constant daylight companion. While the others laboured at their separate tasks, she sat by the totem-to-be and worked and talked and watched as the wood fell away from her section of the pole to reveal the face of a deer: thin-boned, wide-eyed, fine and precise.

Nightly, Mowitch appeared, string in hand, standing tentatively in her doorway. She told him stories in a rough-hewn version of his language while Ouhiliu elaborated on the subtleties.

As the first heavy rains of winter drummed on the roof and the wind clattered the boards and jiggled the night fire, Sitka wrapped herself in fur and contemplated her future. She could marry. The tribe would allow it; indeed, they encouraged it. But she would marry a slave and her children would be slave children; like her they would pass through the village barely noticed, with no past and no future. Her children must have a future she could fret over and plan for. Slowly, like the gathering of dawn, the idea came to her: she must escape.

Her movements became guarded as she watched Ouhiliu and the rest of the tribe, planning, watching, anticipating her freedom. She played less frequently with Mowitch and spoke little to Ouhiliu. Day in, day out, she worked at her tasks and waited, chewing salmon eggs into tempera to be made into paint, sitting cross-legged, watching the ocean for clues, tying quick knots in the bird net with her fingertips, and counting the waves again, and again, and again.

"It is raining harder," Ouhiliu said as he stretched bow-like with his fists knotted in the small of his back and his face up-turned to the storm. He rubbed his chest. "That is enough. Let us return." Sitka spat in the cedar box and folded the bird net into her lap. "Look. The boy has been waiting under the spruce trees." Sitka glanced at Mowitch running towards her, then drifted back to her work.

Ouhiliu knelt beside her. "You are thinking of escape?"

She turned on him angrily. "Escape?"

"You do not play with him any more. A woman who loves children so does not neglect them without a reason. You want children of your own but you will not marry a slave. Am I correct?" Sitka continued working. "You do not have to run. You are a hard worker. Since my wife died I have not enjoyed talking and laughing with anyone as much as you."

Sitka stared. What was he saying? A noble marry a slave? Ridiculous. Or was it? Things were so different here. Was Ouhiliu *hegus* enough to convince the tribe? Could it be done?

As Mowitch raced up to her, rain-wet and panting, Ouhiliu placed his hand gently on her shoulder. "I will give you children," he said. As Sitka readied the first volley of her questions, Ouhiliu's hand flew from her shoulder and clutched at his chest. He fell back and sprawled in the grass. Sitka leapt to his side. Frantically her fingers fumbled at the knot in his cape and her own heart raced erratically.

What to do? What to do? "Shaman? Shaman!" she shrieked. "Mowitch, get the shaman!" She clutched his arm and shoved him towards the village. "Get the shaman!" Mowitch raced over the ground, rain streaming in his wake.

Sitka tore the cape from her shoulders and punched it into a pillow for Ouhiliu's head. Kneeling, she blocked the rain from his face and listened to the shallowness of his breathing. His eyes drifted, unfocussed, roving inwards on a voyage of their own, and his lips quivered, parted, and shaped themselves into words. But there was no sound except the hiss of the rain and the push of the wind. Sitka cried.

Ouhiliu. Important man. Carver of totems, recorder of legends. Selfless Ouhiliu, who would humiliate himself in the eyes of his tribe for her. Ouhiliu the kind. Ouhiliu, bringer of hope.

The ground echoed with the footsteps of the tribe running from the village to the beach; first a warrior, then three, a young woman, Hupal, the shaman, Saskwalah, Yanahook, the others, all jostling to glimpse the *beekw*. Mowitch clung to the fringes.

Sitka pushed herself up from the ground, clenching her fists. "Ouhiliu is dead." Her voice was flinty and cold. "Ouhiliu is dead." Those closest to the body moved back, uncertain and afraid of danger. Some pushed closer, while others drifted back to the village singly or in groups, arms around each other, blending with the rain, consoling, reflective.

Slowly, wraith-like, the shaman raised his hand and pointed at Sitka. "Sorceress," he cried. She began to deny his charge but the shaman's eyes were wild and she knew there was no defence. "Sorceress." Sitka ran, but someone grabbed her heel and she slipped on the wet grass. Frantically, she struggled for footing but the men were upon her. Twisting, tugging, and frenzied, she was pinned to the ground, then dragged to her feet.

Mowitch threw himself at her attackers in a flurry of ten-year-old limbs, but he was thrown roughly away.

Hupal, avoiding Sitka, eyes carefully on the ground, helped Mowitch up and led him back to the village, steering his shoulders lightly with her fingertips.

Sitka grew quiet and let herself be carried while the rain splashed across her face and the low clouds churned and circled overhead.

Inside Saskwalah's longhouse she was made to kneel in a corner on the hard earth floor and her hands were tied behind her with cedar-bark rope. The shaman worked roughly at her hair, combing, patting, and sweeping it upwards until he had pulled it all tight round the edges and piled it high on her crown.

With spit on his hands he worked the topknot into a loop, inserted an arm-thickness of devil's club, and tied it round with rope.

"Admit you are a sorceress," he said.

Sitka shook her head. "I am not."

The shaman took the stick in his hands and twisted it round like a tourniquet. Sitka's eyes opened wider as her scalp pulled tight.

"You killed Ouhiliu."

"Ouhiliu was my friend."

The stick jerked round again and the tightest strands snapped and pulled out their roots.

"The boy told us Ouhiliu touched you and fell to the ground."

"I am not a sorceress."

Again the devil's club turned and wrenched Sitka's head over her left shoulder. She pulled back to keep her neck from snapping, and out of the corner of her eyes she could see a blurred image of the shaman, grave and intent, and wondered if he really believed what he accused her of.

"Sorceress!"

"No! I am not. I . . . am . . . not." The words came strangling out of her, her jaw almost paralysed.

As hard as the shaman twisted, Sitka fought back until her throat trembled and her head shook. She could feel something warm and wet trickling over her shoulders and down her breasts and wondered if it was sweat or blood. Moisture seeped from her eyes and the corners of her mouth, and she thought her neck would break. "I am not." The stick swung free and her head flopped limply onto her chest. A length of rope was tied to her hands, looped round the devil's club, and jerked tight. Her head was slashed back and her hands were yanked up until her body was jack-knifed backwards, and in this position, with her throat constricted and her arms straining at their sockets, she listened to the planks being moved behind her. The shaman dragged her by the devil's-club stick, folded her into a shallow pit in the earth, and replaced the boards. In the darkness she fainted.

"Don't go up the mountain again," her father yells. His face is close and the three finger-length welts which stretch from his forehead to his cheek where a black bear clawed him long ago redden. The puckered flap of skin over his right eye shakes with anger. "Or the Wild-Woman-of-the-Woods will get you." Sitka, a child of eight, wide-eyed and fat-cheeked, hangs her head.

Ah, the woods. There is no Wild-Woman. Her forests are peaceful, enchanting, soft green, cool, still — when the sunset hits the leaves from underneath the colours are vibrant — and she enters them quickly, a child, ducking under brush and looking guiltily over her shoulder at the women picking berries near the shore.

Sunlight filters through openings in the branches, raising pillars of steam from rotting logs. Moss springs underfoot, covering everything in pads of rolling green, and soft lichen hangs in shreds from the trees. Enormous trunks — fir, cedar, pine, and spruce — rise like dinosaurs out of the ground, their branches forming a tight canopy which blocks out the light. In places no sun has reached the forest floor since before the time of the First People.

Sitka climbs quickly, the hard pads of her small bare feet digging firmly into the loose gravel of the foothills. It is summer. Bluejays screech and dart along the path ahead of her. Hummingbirds hover over a field of purple honeysuckle. The trees thin and the trail steepens. Halfway up the mountain she stops and stretches out her arms to the first warm tickle of wind rushing up the hillside. It is late afternoon. She turns and scrambles along the rocky path, up, up past the last stand of poplar and birch, up through the damp granite canyon which rises like a giant staircase, up over the field of smooth round boulders left by an ancient glacier, until at last she is in a vast meadow of yellow lilies. Ahead is the whispering tree, her tree, her safe and secret place, and she runs towards it, pushing her way through the tall stalks of fluffy white bear grass which rustle and sway over her head. The ancient lone cedar clings stubbornly to the edge of a sheer bluff which drops six hundred feet to the foaming Homulcheson River. Wind from the southern lowlands sweeps across the inlet, collides with the rock wall, and rushes upwards, gathering speed until it whistles over the lip of the cliff and into the arms of the dancing tree.

She stands at the base of the trunk, peers up through the branches, and smiles. The small burial box containing the bones of her dead mother is still where she and her father lashed it the summer before, safe and untouched, rocking gently in the wind, its small peephole facing south so the dead woman can gaze out over the inlet below. Around it, half hidden in the swaying branches, are more bentwood boxes, their red-and-black crests faded by sunlight — aunts, uncles, cousins, relatives she has never known. Above them are her grandparents, then her great-grandparents, and finally, at the top of the tree, Skwinatqa, her great-great-grandfather, who led the tribe south from the Skomishoath River countless winters before.

Sitka rummages in the tall bear grass for the long pole she has notched into a rude ladder and props it against the lowest branch, twenty feet above the edge of the cliff. She climbs up and settles herself in the crook of a thick limb which bobs in the wind like a canoe in a gently rolling swell. "Yes," she says, "this is my tree." She pats its smooth trunk and looks out at the panoramic view.

Below her the silvery Homulcheson tumbles down the granite mountain, threading its way through the lush green rain forest, and empties into the long blue finger of water which pokes far into the eastern woods. Across from it, seagulls whirl around the rocky ledges of Thoos, the high bank, which pinches the mighty ocean into a narrow channel, and at its base is Slahkayulsh, the man who was turned to stone for defying the spirits; the great column of rock towers up from the seabed, guarding the entrance to the inlet beyond. Inside the passage the gulf broadens. Thin wisps of smoke curl up from the *lumlam* of Whoi-whoi, her village, which stands parallel to the thin strip of gravelly beach. Behind it is the marshy lake where the beaver live. To the south and east, the wilderness, dark green with hints of yellow and brown, rolls endlessly, limitlessly, over the far horizon. To the west, the sea, blue-grey, crisscrossed with silver lines where the currents run, curves towards the hazy outline of the great island where the enemy live. Sitka watches it, shading her eyes with her hand, as she recalls the gruesome stories she has heard in the village of war canoes, battle songs, and stone clubs.

The wind blows, the ancient cedar sways, and, as Sitka watches the distant island, the whispering tree begins to sing. Long, long ago, before the days of Skwinatqa and the great trek south to the fertile inlet, it had been struck by lightning and its top sheared off. A new shoot had begun at its base and, as it grew, the two trunks had crossed and the branches intertwined. Centuries of rubbing together, tossed in the wind, had worn the bark from the numerous places where the limbs touched, and the golden wood underneath has become polished to a hard, smooth amber.

Sitka smiles as the wind increases and the shattered trunks grind together in a vibrant, plaintive moan. She sits through the afternoon, riding the updrafts high above the inlet, safe and secure in her secret place, coaxing the squirrels and watching a family of grouse squatting turnip-like below. She plays house with cedar cones, arranging them on the branch in order of size and assigning them names. She scolds the youngest, while for the older ones she arranges propitious marriages. She sings to them and tells them stories that her father has told her. Stories of the original people, the legend of the trees:

> Long ago, before the pinkman came and before the Indian, when the earth was new and still, the great god Tetl was looking for a place where his people might dwell and prosper. With the help of a magic butterfly who could cover half the earth with a single beat of his wings he found the very best land, here at this spot.
>
> Tetl placed his people on the earth and for a time they were happy among the bear and the salmon. But they were a wasteful people and soon they became greedy. They killed more bear than they could eat, they picked the berry bushes clean and stockpiled huge quantities of salmon, and then complained that there was no longer enough.
>
> Tetl came down from the skies and told them to behave or they would be punished. The First People were horrified and for a time they were less greedy, but soon they went back to their old ways; killing and eating and wasting, and always complaining they did not have enough. Finally, darkness descended and lasted for many days. When it lifted, all of Tetl's people had been turned into cedar trees and a voice was heard to say: "You will remain in the trees until men come who will use my land better. They will eat your cones and boil your needles for tea, they will strip your bark to clothe themselves and cut your wood to build their homes."

Sitka had asked her father why there were not men or bones inside a tree when it was cut and he had replied that it was the spirits of their ancestors inside the trees and not their bodies.

"What is a spirit?" she asked. Her father thought for a long time, then said that a spirit was the breath of life.

"Can I see one?" she asked.

"Can you see your breath?" he answered.

"On a cold day I can."

"So, under certain circumstances, you can see a spirit," he said.

"What does one look like?"

Again he thought. "Spirits can be many different things. To some they are the sound of the wind or the movement of fire, while to others they are ripples in water or a shadow seen out the corner of an eye. Also, spirits can appear in many different forms. In the case of the trees, more practical men may hear their magic in the splitting of wood to be used for houses, but for myself they are more wondrous than that. I like to think of the spirits as butterflies.

In the arms of the cedar tree, Sitka daydreams and sings to the cones until the wind grows cold and the orange sun hovers low over the great island to the west. It is time to go. Feeling for the ladder with her bare foot, she glimpses a shadow sliding behind a tree in the distance and freezes. She watches for a long time but nothing moves, so she reaches for the ladder again, and again the shadow slides closer to her tree. Motionless and frightened, she strains to see what it is, but while she watches, the forest is still, and when she moves to go, the shadow creeps closer, always just out of sight, always ducking behind the trees just as she looks, working its way closer and closer to her.

The shadow is below her. She twists on the branch to see it but it moves around the tree. She can hear its heavy breathing. Panicked, she begins to cry and scream for her father. Then it is at the bottom of the ladder.

The Wild-Woman-of-the-Woods, naked and bony, shards of lichen for hair, green-glass eyes, a bone in her nose, and bear-claw teeth; she shakes the ladder and howls like a wolf. Sitka claws the bark, desperate for escape, but the other branches are too high and she clings to the tree trunk trapped and crying.

The Wild-Woman is halfway up the ladder when the tree begins to tremble. The base of the trunk swells, rippling upwards, and through her arms Sitka can feel something inside shooting up from the roots and quivering out to the branches. The woman stops, wild-eyed and hissing, staring at the branches, which are bulging and sprouting. The needles turn to buds and the buds to white flowers, and out of the flowers come butterflies. Butterflies by the hundreds, butterflies by the thousands, golden, tangerine, and auburn; crimson, ochre, and scarlet; speckled, multi-coloured, and stippled, they swarm and pirouette, brush Sitka's face like snowflakes, and fall upon the ladder. Buried in a cloud of butterflies, the Wild-Woman-of-the-Woods is plucked from her perch and carried aloft; she crashes up through the branches in a trail of cedar shards, hissing and spitting, up over the field of swaying bear grass, past the craggy mountain summit to the snowy ranges beyond, where peak after peak rolls in the distance like whitecaps on the ocean, harsh and bright and dazzling in the sun, each slightly taller than the one before, stretching back to the horizon and vanishing in haze. The Wild-Woman is gone.

The forest edges back to stillness, the squirrels scuttle and scurry, and the turnip-like grouse waddle back to their places while Sitka sits on and stares at the last stirrings of the place where the butterflies have gone.

She awoke painfully, throat parched and shoulders searing. With her head wrenched back, unable to swallow, she was lifted, kinked and hurting, out of her dreams and back to torture. The house was empty except for a man tying ropes in the rafters, a woman singing softly as she hung cedar boughs from the walls, and two men digging a trench which began a few feet from her pit, wandered erratically about the lower half of the house, and exited through a side door.

As a child she had seen these preparations many times and knew the house was being readied for Toxwid, Spirit of War, Self-Destroying One. She would not be a part of this ceremony.

Again the shaman twisted the devil's-club stick until her neck shuddered and her mind drifted back to the pit, back to the safety of her dreams and the protection of her forests.

She awoke to the steady, rhythmical beat of drums — hollow logs, upturned cedar boxes, stretched animal skins — the hiss of rattles and the murmur of chanting, low and resonant. Firelit faces lined the walls of the longhouse; the people stood, crouched, sat cross-legged: young men painted red and black, women with eagle's-down hair, elders, grey and wrinkled, hiding frightened children under their ceremonial blankets. Only one fire burned, but it burned fiercely. Pockets of pitch exploded in showers of sparks which spiralled up through the shadows to the opening in the roof. The air was thick and redolent with cedar.

Sitka groaned and tried to focus, but the ceremonial masks which hung from branches on the walls spun in her head: cannibals, *hamatsa*, wolf masks, skull faces — abalone-eyed, shrill-faced, fang-toothed — a panoply of demons. She shut her eyes.

When she opened them again Toxwid, the Spirit of War, stood in the distance by the fire, pointing at her. She was a young woman in an elaborately woven blanket, wearing a gentle yellow mask with round cheeks and smiling lips. A carved wooden bowl next to Sitka's face quivered, leapt from the ground, and glided to Toxwid's hand. The woman released it, and again it danced through the shadows, floated shakily, hovered, and returned to its place. Toxwid's face cocked coyly, cracked, and split apart to reveal her true nature in a second mask: the face of a raven, demonic, savage and cruel. Again Sitka groaned and shut her eyes.

The next time she opened them something caught her attention in the direction of the pit — her pit. Something was in her pit. She twisted on the ground to get a better view. A pointed stick was wriggling up through the ground, then another. Slowly the double heads of Sisiutl, the horned serpent, rose from the earth. The heads were inlaid with mica scales and carved with hollow eyes, blunted snouts, flaring nostrils, and thin red lips. The jaws dropped open to reveal split tongues of cedar bark flapping over rows of teeth.

The drums stopped beating and Toxwid ran to the pit and grabbed the monster by the horns. The serpent fought back and dragged the woman to her knees and into the pit up to her elbows. The Indians shouted encouragement and several strong men rushed to help. They wrapped their arms around her waist, dug in their heels, and strained to pull her back. Sisiutl fought harder, and slowly, inch by inch, the young woman was dragged under the ground while the crowd roared and the dust rose.

As her feet disappeared into the earth, only one man still hung on. He shouted and cursed and his body convulsed with the struggle, but he too began to slip. When he was elbow deep in the pit the monster suddenly roared and the man was dragged along the ground, stumbling and falling and ploughing up furrows of dirt with his arms. He zigzagged around the lower half of the house, fighting the underground monster, and was finally dragged out the side exit. Again Sitka groaned and shut her eyes.

Hours passed. The fire compacted, folded in on itself, and glowed with coals, the storytellers reviewed their exhausted repertories, the drummers' hands grew numb and the singers hoarse. Sleeping children were carried gingerly to their beds, reluctant good-byes were whispered in the drowsing house, and Hupal, Mowitch, and Yanahook returned to their quarters through the bear's mouth. The shaman left, but as an afterthought he returned, rolled Sitka into her pit, and replaced the planks.

In the darkness Sitka listened. The dying remnants of chatter grew weaker, faltered, and faded into snores. Night owls hooted in the forest. Dirt trickled down from the sides of her pit and she counted her heartbeats and listened to the rasps of her breath. Somewhere in the mists between waking and sleeping a cedar plank shifted and a small, nervous hand darted into the pit and was gone.

Sitka was awake — wide awake — alert, ecstatic, and frenzied. Something was in her pit, something long and thin and sharp. A knife. A knife was in her pit and she wriggled and thrashed and wrenched herself around painfully to grasp it. Working in the darkness behind her back she sawed and fumbled and clutched and sawed again. Her hands were numb and her wrists so painful she could not tell if she was cutting rope or flesh, but at last her head snapped forward and she bit her tongue to keep from weeping.

As she rolled on her back, her leg bumped something soft and it sloshed. A goat-skin bag. Water. Water. Her hands shook as she undid the knot, and water, cold and sweet, gurgled from her mouth and bubbled down her chest. Reluctantly, she tied the bag. Then she rubbed her neck and thought. How long till daylight? She wanted to rest, gather strength, and exult in her reprieve, but the face of the shaman spun in her mind and she would not risk facing him again for anything.

Cautiously she lifted the edge of a cedar plank just wide enough to see out. An unknown man lay inches away, and as he rolled in his sleep his arm sprawled out and clamped the board shut again. Sitka slumped in the darkness, fingering her knife, and wondered if she could kill him, silently. She noticed a piece of rope by her foot and kicked at it angrily, but it flopped back to the same place. She reached for it and tugged. It was anchored in the dirt. Feeling along the rope, she traced it to the wall of her pit, where the dirt was soft. The ceremony, the trench, the double-headed serpent, the man ploughing furrows, the trickles of dirt falling in the night — this was her escape. She pushed at the earth and it shifted like powder till she was in it up to her elbows. She nudged her head against the wall and winced. Devil's club. The needles stuck in her hands as she tried to untangle the stick, but her hair was knotted and matted with blood. Quickly she reached for the knife and hacked. The club ripped free and the tattered remnants of her hair fell loose about her shoulders.

She dropped the knotted club, jammed the knife in her belt, considered the water bag and the narrowness of the tunnel, abandoned it, and burrowed into the earth.

The trench was shallow — only two feet deep — and just wide enough for her body if she kept her arms stretched ahead. The rope was anchored to the bottom of the trench, and by pulling on it with both hands and pushing with her toes she inched through the soft dirt. As she reached for the next pull she raised her head just slightly and breathed in the tiny pocket of rarefied air. It tasted stale and dusty and the earth gritted in her teeth. Again she pulled. Her breaths were short and shallow. She dug into the ground with her fingernails and hauled herself forward. The air pocket filled in with powder and she panicked at the thought of suffocation, but she pulled back her hand, cupped it round her mouth, and sucked the air through her fingers. She pulled and burrowed, eyes clenched, pushing with her feet and gouging with her nails, digging, dredging, and boring into the earth; the dirt caked at her mouth and sifted through her hair and clothes, clamping solidly around her.

Sitka tried to recall the zigzag maze followed by the serpent-fighter, but her memory was vague and blurred with painted masks and flying bowls. Another of her precious air pockets silted over, her body shuddered with claustrophobia, and frantically she pushed her head through the surface. Rolling on her back she lay gasping, her face level with the ground, like a ghoulish woman in a shallow grave.

The house was still. Thin filaments of smoke curled up through the hole in the roof where early-morning chickadees darted in the greying light, scavenging for scraps. Sitka rose up out of the earth, only ten feet from the side exit, and knew that eyes were upon her. From the mouth of the bear Hupal smiled and encircled Mowitch in her arms. As he waved, silent tears rolled down his cheeks. Sitka was gone.

Forest or ocean? Forest or ocean? Either could save her and either could kill her. The sea was calm. She ran to the beach, to the smallest canoe, and, wading deep in the water, shoved the empty boat into the ebbing tide. With luck the ocean would take it far enough away so that if the tribe found it they would presume her drowned. She ran back past the village and fled into the forest.

The ground was cold and the underbrush thick, but she hacked with her knife and worked her way uphill. Before long she found a game trail winding up into the mountains and she loped along it, homing in on the dawn, east towards home. When she was above the lowland thickets she abandoned the trail and trusted in the deepwoods. The morning was fresh and brilliant and the forest alive. She sidestepped a spider web stretching across her path, geometric and impeccable, beaded with dew and dazzling with sun. Bluejays chattered at her from the trees above, and below her she saw the hindquarters of a bear disappearing down the hill to the north. At noon the wind began to blow.

She staggered through the day, resting little, drinking from streams, grubbing for roots, and by nightfall she was dizzy and near exhaustion. The wind whistled and the trees hummed with it, their branches swaying and their tops striking at the stars. The forest was black and full of silhouettes, movement, and sound.

Sitka selected a young spruce tree with layers of branches fanning to the ground like petticoats and slipped under them, straightening the skirts behind her. Under the tree the ground was thick with needles and she scraped them into a spongy mattress and stretched out luxuriously. Around her the forest tossed in the wind. Ancient tree trunks rubbed together, groaning and whispering, and Sitka was pleased because she knew the spirits of her ancestors were welcoming her back.

BURRARD INLET

MADELINE CAREFULLY LOCKED the store behind her and set off down the hill towards the fort, tapping the boardwalk with her cane. The morning air was still and chilly. She squinted her eyes against the sun and glared at the sluggish village below. Victoria. At the centre was the fort, fanning sparsely around it were whitewashed cottages, and everywhere there was vegetation — oak and maple, salal and swamp grass, yew, ivy, cedar, and cypress; it rolled down the hills, encroached on pathways, twined round house posts, straddled rooftops, and scaled the fortress walls. The settlement was a miniature English village perched tentatively on the edge of a vast primeval rain forest. Beyond it the ocean stretched to the horizon, flat, foreboding, gunmetal grey. Madeline shuddered. How she longed to return to the civilization of England.

She looked nervously down the length of the path, scanning the underbrush for Indians, then picked up the hem of her heavy black dress and dug her cane into the mud. This wilderness is destroying me, she thought. In the five short years she had been on the island, age lines had eaten into the corners of her eyes and mouth, and the perpetual dampness had cramped her hands with arthritis. She was forty-six, but she felt much older. Even her long black hair had faded to a dull iron-grey. She patted the tight bun at the back of her head. The pain in her fingers made it difficult to dress her hair, but each morning she rose religiously at five o'clock and winced and grunted before the mirror until the offensive strands were bound and trussed into a severe, tidy ball. After all, she thought, even at the edge of the world one must maintain a degree of dignity. She slashed angrily at a salal bush stretched across her path, hurried gratefully through the fort gates, and snorted with satisfaction. She had made it without encountering a single savage.

Inside the high log walls the settlement was hushed and slug-gish. A water wagon rumbled over the ruts in Fort Street. Dogs sprawled lazily in the morning sun, thumping their tails on the damp earth as she marched by. Flies buzzed over steaming piles of horse manure. Madeline nodded slightly as she swept past a group of idle men who tipped their hats and stared after her in surprise. She seldom ventured out of the store. When something needed tending outside, she sent her husband, or one of her daughters, but today the trip was necessary. Jonas was not yet back from San Francisco and her daughters could not be let in on the secret.

The bell over the entrance to the Hudson's Bay trading post jangled as Madeline stepped inside and leaned against the wall, waiting for her eyes to adjust to the darkness; the only light came from two small holes cut into the log walls and covered with oiled paper. The shop interior was like a cave: dingy, sunless, grey-brown. Animal traps, blue pots, lengths of chain, and dou-ble-bitted axes twisted slowly in the shadows, suspended from the rafters on wire hooks. Her own shop was much superior: it was bigger, cleaner, and brighter. She polished the floors and counters daily, she had installed two large plate-glass windows which Jonas had brought all the way from England for their twenty-fifth wedding anniversary, and she certainly did not hang goods from the ceiling where customers were certain to walk into them.

She ducked her head and hobbled to a counter at the back. Except for a dusty-looking clerk, who stared at her over his spectacles as he fiddled with a button on his waistcoat, the store was empty. "Good morning, Mrs. Cains. It's a strange day that sees you at the Hudson's Bay."

"A strange day indeed, Mr. Timmons."

"How's business up on the hill?"

Madeline sniffed. "It would be better, Mr. Timmons, if the Hudson's Bay would stop paying its employees in promissory notes which can only be redeemed at the Company store."

Mr. Timmons smiled slyly. "Yes. Yes, I suppose it would," he said. "Well, you'll have to talk to Governor Douglas about that, won't you?"

"I wish to purchase some land," Madeline said abruptly.

"Eh? What?" Mr. Timmons dropped the button and his eyes widened. "Land?"

"Yes, land. Lots 18, 34, and 126."

The clerk continued to stare; he made no move to produce the register. "Well, indeed. It's been a long time since I've sold any land about here."

"Well, you are selling some now. Hop to it, man."

Mr. Timmons routed among the shelves for the ledger. "Thinking of expanding your store, Mrs. Cains?" He snickered.

Madeline shut her eyes. Oh, how she wanted to tell him. Tell him everything: about the soda-water bottle half full of scaly gold Jonas had seen on the North Thompson; about the argument they had had when she learned he wanted to mine the metal himself—it was bad enough they were in trade, she would not have him mucking about in the dirt like a common labourer; about Jonas's trip to San Francisco and the prospectors who would be here at any moment; about the new sawmill they would build on the mainland—and about the death of the Hudson's Bay. She wanted to tell him that the monopoly was about to end and that the country (which the Company was supposed to develop but had kept such a dark secret) was about to be discovered and flooded with free-enterprising immigrants, who would demand land, roads, sewers, running water, free trade—and lumber. Because of Jonas's discovery the Hudson's Bay Company was about to join the dinosaurs, and Madeline was elated. How she wanted to rub his nose in it, not just the singular nose of Mr. Timmons, but the smug, monopolizing, collective nose of the almighty Hudson's Bay, and how she wanted to watch the Company squirm.

"No. We are not expanding yet, Mr. Timmons. These lots are to be registered in my daughters' names: Sarah, Mariah, and Caroline."

"Ah. Sort of like a dowry, eh? Or maybe an investment? Great future here in Victoria." The last was spoken sarcastically, through curled lips.

Madeline knew he thought her a fool, but she refused to be goaded into explanations. After all, she thought, he's only a clerk. She was certain the Company had sent him to Victoria as punishment for some unknown crime and contented herself with wishing he would never be paroled back to civilization.

"Yes, Mr. Timmons. Sort of an investment. The Hudson's Bay Company won't rule forever."

The clerk chuckled. "I wouldn't know about that, Mrs. Cains." He spread a map of the townsite on the counter, pinned it with his elbows, and cupped his chin in his hands. "Let's see now. Lots 18 and 34 are commercial properties, prime land, four acres, at five dollars per acre: that's twenty dollars apiece."

"And lot 126."

"126, 126 . . . I don't see it here. Are you sure you have the number correct?"

"Of course I do," Madeline snapped. "There." She jabbed her finger at the edge of the map.

"What? Way off in the sticks? Now what would you be wanting with twenty acres of forest way up in the hills? The town will never reach that far, Mrs. Cains."

"Just register it, Mr. Timmons."

"Very well. Twenty acres at one dollar per acre . . ." A mob of children stampeded past the oilpaper window, their excited voices fading in the distance. "That comes to a total of . . . sixty dollars, Mrs. Cains."

Madeline counted the money onto the counter. The forest lot would be ideal for Sarah. She was a pensive girl with a crabbed face and vinegary eyes, who had fashioned herself an old maid at twenty-four. Madeline's grey-haired grim-girl. In defiance of her warnings about wild animals, drunken men, and savage Indians, Sarah insisted on lingering in the night forest, perched on moonlit stumps, mentally stalking wolves and night owls. She was an impossible child.

Madeline never entered the forest; to her all of nature was dangerous and vengeful. Even the thought of Jonas striding through the trees, axe in hand, armed and ready to do battle, made her uneasy.

The shrill clamour of voices came again, echoing off the hills to the north and ringing with excitement, as the children puffed and tumbled up from the wharf. "Ship's in! Ship's in!" The clerk dropped his pen and scurried around the counter, but Madeline grabbed the buckle at the back of his waistcoat and held him firm. "Finish the deed, Mr. Timmons."

"But, Mrs. Cains, there's a ship in. First one in six months."

"And it will be there for many an hour yet. Finish the deed."

Mr. Timmons scuttled back to his place and scribbled furiously, while Madeline squinted her eyes and leaned over the counter, watching him. She had acted none too soon. The ship would contain prospectors. Jonas had spread the word in San Francisco. Everything was progressing according to plan. In fact, she had managed to improve on the scheme. The land purchase was her own idea and she had arranged it with money she had scrimped from two years of household expenses. Even Jonas didn't know about it, but she knew he would approve. By the end of the week the land would, at the very least, quadruple in value.

"Sign here, Mrs. Cains." Madeline dipped the pen in the inkpot and meticulously wrote her name in an elaborate, flowing script. Before she could finish, Mr. Timmons was gone in a flurry of dust, leaving the door ajar and the money on the counter. Madeline picked it up and turned it over in her hand. Careless of Mr. Timmons, she thought. It was tempting. She turned and looked at the open door, then smacked the money back on the counter and marched out of the store. She was *not* that kind of lady.

Outside, the town was in a furor. Men and women raced along the street and crammed through the gate to the wharf, laughing, pushing, shouting. Houses were left empty and doors ajar as people ran to the beach, drawn by the unexpected ship. Madeline eased into the crowd and let herself be swept along, carefully avoiding the galloping horses and occasionally stabbing her cane at excited dogs. Ahead, she could see the crowds thickening as hundreds of people pressed onto the wharf. Already the magic, intoxicating word was spreading from neighbour to incredulous neighbour, up from the beach along the human telegraph, increasing in volume and meaning:

"Gold. It's gold."

The dust thickened. Madeline extricated herself from the crowd and leaned against a tree, her eyes sparkling with delight. Behind her the bells of St. Andrew's echoed off the inland hills and mingled with the roar of the people. She rummaged in her purse, feeling for the new land deeds, then raised her face to the sky and laughed.

"It's gold."

Madeline shouldered her way through the crowd on the dock. Four hundred prospectors, many drunk, swirled around her, shouting and pushing as they grabbed at the bundles thudding onto the planks at their feet. A bony dun-coloured mule, trussed in a belly strap, brayed frantically as it swung over the heads of the mob. Bundles of provisions, tattered tents and tarps, rifles, pickaxes, and the precious saucer-shaped pans, were piled high on the wharf. Madeline dodged to the side as a fight broke out behind her over a small skiff the crew were unloading. She chuckled. There would be precious little transportation to the Fraser until Jonas returned with the *Orpheus*. His was the only ship large enough to take such a mob across the strait to the mainland. She shook her head and sniffed indignantly as a swarthy old man pushed by her, dragging a pair of snowshoes. It was obvious, she thought; they had no idea what to expect of the colony.

Madeline stared at the big three-masted schooner, the *Commodore*, as it creaked and groaned, tugging at its moorings, rocking gently on the black waters of James Bay, and she shuddered. It was not the pandemonium that had lured her onto the wharf. It was the ship itself. Since her arrival in Victoria in 1854 she had not set foot on a boat. The sea terrified her.

"Chelsea," she whispered. "God, how I wish they had never driven us from you." Shortly after her parents died, Madeline had insisted that she and Jonas move into her father's beautiful old home in Chelsea. She had spent most of her life there, and it felt secure to her; but, more than that, she worried about Jonas's disreputable background and how easily he still fell into coarse manners. Indeed, she hadn't even wanted to marry him at first, but he was attentive . . . and she was getting older. . . . She thought the respectability of a Chelsea home would improve his standing in society. But it was not to last.

Her head jerked to the side as the ship creaked at the wharf. She thought of her son, Jeremiah — gentle, handsome Jeremiah — drifting alone, deep in the grey waters of the Atlantic, and again she felt the infuriating, persistent lump in her throat. "Damn the Crimean War," she snapped.

When Russia had moved into Moldavia and Walachia in 1853, Jonas had begun selling guns to the Russians. His personal sympathies lay with the Turks, but they had no money and Jonas was not a man to confuse politics with business. When England had entered the fray on the Turkish side to protect her middle-eastern interests, Jonas had volunteered his services and been given a commission in the navy. By day he had fought the Russians. By night he had sold them guns. It had been a lucrative business.

When the English discovered his scheme they stripped him of his command, but could do no more. It was the newspapers that had destroyed them. Day after day the ugly story was splattered across the front page. The public was outraged. Madeline's friends from the elegant homes of Chelsea shunned her. Her servants left. Her children were pelted with stones in the park. Jonas had raged against the injustices of an ignorant public. "My business interests in no way affect my political loyalties," he shouted over and over. But it had done no good. There were no more shipping contracts.

Late one night Jonas had leaned across their big mahogany bed and announced that they were leaving for the New World, where he was certain politics and business would be kept in proper perspective.

In the weeks that followed, Madeline had moved slowly through the big house, packing the precious belongings they would take with them, fingering the portraits of her parents as she removed them from the walls, watching quietly as strangers loaded her furniture into wagons destined for the auction house. She had tried to hate Jonas, but couldn't; she knew that everything he had done, he had done for love of his family.

On a rainy winter day, at the age of forty-one, with one son and three daughters, Madeline had boarded the *Orpheus* and watched as their Chelsea home vanished behind a bend in the Thames.

A week out of London a black cloud had appeared on the horizon and the crew had watched it nervously, waiting for it to move. The next day the winds had come and the storm howled in from the northwest, pelting the ship with rain and churning the sea into a mountain range of white-veined waves. Madeline gathered up her daughters and herded them into Jonas's cabin on the aft deck. From the doorway she turned and watched as Jeremiah scrambled up the ratlines with the rest of the crew and was flattened against the shrouds by the powerful gusts as he struggled to reef the mizen topsail. Jonas stood braced against the weather-rail, his eyes fixed on the horizon.

Inside the cabin Madeline's daughters huddled around her, whimpering with every sudden lurch of the ship. She extinguished the lamps for fear of fire, and they sat through the night in darkness, listening to the shriek of the wind, the crash of the ocean breaking over the main deck, and the clatter of chains thundering against the yard-arms like distant drums. Over it all was the bark of Jonas's powerful voice: "Furl the main topgallants. Keep to fore and mizen topsails. Yo there, Carky! She's drifting abeam; bring her round!"

In the morning the rain stopped but the wind increased. Madeline picked her way over the broken furniture, which had tumbled in the night, opened the cabin door, and stared down the long length of the narrow deck. The *Orpheus* laboured up a towering wall of green glass, her bow ploughing deep in the water, breached the crest in a spray of white foam, and slid headlong down the other side, her spars groaning and her timbers creaking. Madeline glanced at Jonas — he still clung to the weather-rail, his black oilskin sparkling with dried salt — then she shut the door and returned to her daughters.

The day ground on through bone-jarring thumps and howling winds as the clipper banged through the heavy seas. Then, in the grey mists of twilight, as the *Orpheus* twisted on the peak of a thirty-foot wave, the wind shifted suddenly and struck her abeam. Slowly, irrevocably, she heeled over, her weather yard-arms dipping towards the water.

Inside, the children screamed as they tumbled against the cabin wall. A porthole smashed open and the wind whistled through. Madeline pulled away from the panicked girls and stumbled over the debris to shut out the gale, but before she could reach it, the cabin door shattered and the ocean flooded in. As the wave receded, it carried Sarah, her eldest daughter, with it.

Madeline dived out the door and caught the young woman by the foot, and together they rolled down the slanting main deck towards the foaming sea, tumbling over broken rigging and tangling themselves in a snarl of rope and chain and flapping wet canvas. They thudded to a stop against the binnacle-stand a few feet from where the water swirled over the iron rail. The lower dead-eyes dipped below the water. The *Orpheus* was on its side.

The mizen-mast yard-arm dragged through a wave and the spar snapped at its doubling. The topsail sheet flew off; its heavy chain racketed across the deck in a shower of red sparks and struck Madeline below the knees. Her left leg snapped. "Jonas!" she screamed. The wind gusted and the water surged higher, swirling round the two women as they clung to the binnacle-stand. "For the love of God—Jonas!" Madeline shrieked. She tried to shove Sarah up the deck, which slanted as steeply as a rooftop. "Get back to the cabin," she yelled. The gathered sleeves of the young woman's dress burst in the wind and flapped around her like wings. "Hurry!"

It was Madeline's son, Jeremiah, who saw them first. He grabbed an axe from the cabin entrance and slid down the deck. Long white whiskers of salt spray streamed from his coat as he braced his legs against the binnacle-stand and hacked at the tangle of ropes trapping his mother and sister. Another wave broke over the rail and Madeline held her breath as it surged up around her neck.

Jeremiah caught hold of a broken lanyard as it flapped across the deck and tugged on it. It was secure. He pushed Sarah to-wards it and she climbed quickly, pulling herself hand over hand up the sloping deck.

Madeline slapped at his hands as he tried to lift her. "You can't carry me up there," she shouted. She grabbed the lanyard and began to drag herself up, pushing with her good leg, clutching at ring-bolts and broken cables, her eyes slitted against the wind and the pain. A piece of tattered canvas flew over her head. She heard a muffled cry behind her and looked over her shoulder.

The sailcloth had wrapped around Jeremiah's head. He was on his feet, staggering drunkenly. The green-white sea surged over the rail and sucked at his legs. "Jeremiah!" Madeline screamed. He fell and slid back down the deck. "Jeremiah . . ." Still clawing at the wet canvas, he slammed against the iron stanchion. White water swirled round him and he slipped over the rail.

Later that night the storm vanished as quickly as it had come. The wind hushed to a whisper, the sea settled to a rolling swell, black clouds shredded across the cold white moon, and the stars shone through, bright and silent. Jeremiah was gone.

The crew manned the capstan and ran up the fore-topmast staysail. "Square the main yard" Jonas shouted. The slip of cloth unfurled and filled with wind. Slowly, painfully, with creaks and shudders, the *Orpheus* rose up out of the sea. Water streamed from her sides, exposing the tangle of chains and broken rigging on deck. The mizen-mast was gone. The lee braces had snapped, leaving the yard-arms to swing limply from side to side, flapping shreds of tattered cloth and broken gear. The cargo had shifted in the hold so that the ship listed badly to port.

Spare canvas was dragged up from the 'tween-decks. Makeshift repairs were made, and the *Orpheus* limped on towards New York, but Madeline's leg could not wait. Jonas set it as best he could, with nervous, gentle fingers, fussing over her constantly, crying out himself when he pulled on the bone and her face turned white and she bit through her lower lip.

But the leg had not mended properly. As soon as the *Orpheus* touched the East River wharf, Jonas rushed her from one doctor to the next, but the result was always the same: Madeline would walk with a cane for the rest of her life. She grew listless, silent, and bitter. Jonas tried to cheer her with coarse jokes, but she snapped at him. While they waited for the *Orpheus* to be repaired for the long trip around the Cape, Madeline brooded in their New York hotel room, staring for hours at her damaged leg, mourning the loss of Jeremiah — gentle, handsome Jeremiah — who had been her favourite.

"God save us from this savage place," Madeline muttered. She shut her eyes tightly, then opened them again and stared at the prospectors' ship tied to the Victoria wharf, creaking and straining at its ropes, its tall spars swaying gently as it rocked on the black waters of James Bay, and she shuddered. The painful lump in her throat would not go away. She turned quickly and pushed her way through the crowd on the dock.

And now Caroline was out on the ocean, somewhere between San Francisco and Victoria. Madeline had grudgingly accepted the dangers Jonas lived with daily, but Caroline was a child, and the thought of her sailing the Pacific coast was terrifying. When Jonas had asked what she wanted for her ninth birthday, Caroline had pleaded to go to San Francisco with him. At the time Madeline had dropped the dinner plate she was holding and quashed the idea immediately, but, unknown to her, Caroline had continued scheming behind her back, fetching her father's slippers, dropping hints, pleading, cajoling, and making deals until, finally, one sleepy, defenceless night, Jonas had announced she was going. There would be no appeal.

Madeline took a deep breath. They must have arrived safely in San Francisco and spread the word or the prospectors would not be here. They would be speeding up the coast now, or perhaps they were already at anchor in Burrard Inlet on the mainland, racing to install the machinery and cut the first boards before the gold-seekers arrived on the Fraser River.

She watched the noisy procession stumbling off the wharf and swarming through the fort. Already there was a crowd around the Hudson's Bay and another mob in front of the saloon, where a fight was in progress. Up on the hill, saplings were falling and tents blossoming up out of the empty spaces like giant mushrooms. Occasional sharp gunshots echoed over the water. Thanks to Jonas, Victoria would never be the same, Madeline thought. She smiled and headed for home. Her daughters would be frantic in the store. Oh, what a glorious day for business.

The clipper *Orpheus* — 265 feet in length, 25 feet deep, 2,100 tons, with 31 sails — thundered past Slahkayulsh Rock and slashed at the waves of Burrard Inlet. The sun caught the fine spray from the bow, transforming it into tiny twin rainbows, while the sails ballooned like a bank of tight white clouds and a British flag crackled from the mainmast. She was sleek and long and low in the water, rolling with the waves and singing in the wind.

Deep in the hold, below the waterline, Caroline held her breath and listened to the rumble of the ocean as it swirled under her, around her, and above her, slapping at the planks wanting in. She was nine years old, with thick orange hair, freckles, and moss-green eyes, and she stood with her hands on her hips in a cross-hatch of shadows from the iron grate above, her head cocked to one side, taking in the secret sights and sounds of the forbidden hold. Planks creaked and groaned around her. Oxen lowed and rustled in the shadows, bracing their legs against the roll of the ship. Overhead, sails crackled in the distance like starched linen on her mother's line. It was wonderful.

For weeks she had wanted to explore this place, but only now, as the voyage was almost ended, had she managed to sneak down the stairs unnoticed. She braced her hand against a bale of hay and tiptoed forwards. Ahead, the great circular saw blade, destined for her father's mill, sliced through the shadows, suspended from a beam by a leather strap which passed through a hole in its centre. It was ten feet in diameter. The ropes which had held it in place had broken just hours before in a sudden squall off the coast, and now the blade swung free, swaying with the roll of the ship, first far to port, where it stopped, motionless, then whoosh, slicing to starboard, whistling through the darkness, missing the floor by two feet. As it passed, Caroline brushed her hand against its surface. It was cold, hard, and smooth.

On the next pass she touched it again and decided she liked it. Somehow it seemed self-contained—whooshhh—with a life of its own—whooshhh—and it reminded her of an advertisement she had seen in a London magazine of a cat perched delicately on the edge of a self-emptying bathtub with its tail wrapped around its feet, watching the drain—whooshhh—holding itself in—whooshhh—ready to pounce—whooshhh, whooshhh—as soon as the water was gone.

She removed her hat and carefully lay down under the blade, just out of its reach, and pretended she was the heroine of a melodrama, tied to a log destined for the sawmill's teeth. The ship groaned and the leather strap creaked. In the darkness Caroline sucked in her tummy, watched the blade swing over her, and waited for the handsome stranger who would surely rescue her.

From this position she closed her eyes and concentrated on the odours around her. Mostly the hold smelled of oxen, the pungent ammonia-sharp odour of manure and moist straw, but there was a plethora of minor smells: apples from Oregon, coffee from South America, spices from the Spice Islands, the acrid scent of gunpowder, the tang of metal and machine oil, and the sweet smell of leather and burlap. The hold was a cornucopia of carefully selected treasures, and the best of them all was hers— the peacocks.

As the saw blade swung like a hypnotic pendulum, Caroline daydreamed about her recent trip. San Francisco. Never had she imagined such a place. Her father had told her that 370,000 people lived there, but it wasn't until she had bounced down the gangplank, wide-eyed and breathless, onto the bustling pier, and had seen the sprawling city beyond, that the number had any meaning. Truly, her mother was right: Victoria was a tiny mud-hole, a bad and stinking joke.

With her hand in her father's she had walked cobbled streets and seen buildings made of real stone, manicured parks, smoking factories, hundreds of wondrous shops, specialized to bizarre extremes, and restaurants—one had desserts that burned with blue flames, and crystal goblets with a gold rim for where the lips went—restaurants in such abundance that selecting one from the directory became a day-long ordeal that reduced Caroline to tears for fear she should fail to choose the very best.

And then there was Chinatown: smelly, crowded, bewitching Chinatown, where men scooped live lobsters out of huge vats and curls of cooking steam swirled through narrow doorways and sniffed at the hem of her dress. Much of it consisted of scrap-wood shanties stacked one against the other like playing-card houses, but the richer buildings had winged red roofs with carved yellow dragons. The Chinese were a mystery; she thought them comical, with their musical chattering, their snaky pigtails, and their staccato shuffling, but she knew by the way her father wrinkled his face, as he did when her mother boiled cabbage, that there was something wrong with them.

Soon she was marching haughtily beside him with her nose thrust up in the air, making faces at the people she passed. She was so engrossed in the game that she almost missed them. Peacocks. They strutted and primped in the centre window of a small store, their feathers extended, halo-like, around them. In the sunlight they were iridescent—blue, green, and gold—and they shivered and shimmered, dazzling, tufted, crowned, and haughty. Their rows of feathered eyes winked at her.

It was dark in the bird shop; the front window was partitioned off so that only a sliver of sunlight penetrated. Everywhere there were birds, hundreds of different kinds of birds: in cages, flying free about the store, leg-ironed to perches; chirping, singing, shrilling, talking; canaries, finches, macaws, budgies, hawks, cockatoos, and silver pheasants. There was even a large stuffed emu with red eyes hunched menacingly in a corner. None of the other birds went near it. "Watch out for the emu. Watch out. Watch out," shrieked a parrot. All of them were tended by a dwarfish Chinaman whom Caroline guessed to be a hundred and fifteen.

Her father had fancied a plain-Jane parrot, boasting only two colours and a ratty tail, and devoid of speech. Caroline demanded a peacock and got four. Her father explained that it required two to make a third—something she had vague notions about but had given up all hope of fully understanding—and that the others were extras in case one died on the long voyage up the coast.

"How do you keep the birds from flying out the door when people come in?" Caroline had asked.

The old man bent down close to her face. He smelled of sweet, fragrant smoke. "Well, little missee," he whispered, "I tells 'em street's full of emus." He chuckled. "Emus, see, plenty emus, all hungry fo' little birds."

"And they believe you?"

The Chinaman straightened. He wasn't much taller than Caroline. "Not always. Little dove once not believe; just little dove. He wait by door alla time, see, and watch it open, close, open, close. Then one day lady come in and, whoosh, he gone."

"What happened to him?"

"Why, emus get him, of course."

"I don't believe you," Caroline said.

Again the man bent and whispered. "Well, truly it was dog. Dove fly like winged dragon, up, down, this way, that way. But it do no good. A block away dog jumps it; grabs it right out of the air. I run after dog to get dove back but it's dead, little missee, oh yes, plenty dead. I puts it on top of emu's head until it smells, see. No birds ever fly out again."

"Watch out. Watch out," the parrot had screamed.

When the blade was far to port, Caroline jumped up and watched it rush to starboard. No one had come to rescue her.

At the bow the hold tapered to a point where the purl of the ocean rumbled into thunder. Two cages, with a pair of peacocks in each, nestled amongst bales of straw. In one, two limp, blue-green bundles lay on their sides, dangling flaccid necks through the coarse wire mesh and undulating helplessly with the swell of the ship.

In the second cage there was dancing. Caroline watched as the male unfurled his feathers to the limits of the bars and shook them at his mate. She cowered and backed away, her tiny black eyes watching him intently. He was persistent. Though his feathers snagged on the bars, his feet tripped on the wire, and his steps had to be choreographed to the rocking of the ship, he wobbled after her. She dodged, but there was no escape, and eventually he cornered her and pinned her from behind in a flurry of feathers and outraged screams.

Caroline was intrigued. She reached into the cage, grabbed a knot of tail feathers, and pulled. The male protested but dug in his spurs and continued the assault. Caroline tugged harder.

"Stop it. Stop it," she yelled. The feathers yanked loose, Caroline catapulted backwards and the peacocks screamed and jumped apart. The female scuttled to another corner of the cage, huffing and blinking indignantly, while her attacker lowered his topsails and pecked at the missing plumage.

Sprawled on the floor, Caroline stared at the handful of feathers and began to giggle. She removed the hat that Father had bought her in San Francisco, ripped out its silk flowers, and inserted a peacock feather. By winding it round the brim and tucking it under a ribbon she was able to fasten the remaining feathers to it and arrange them so they hung down her back. She strutted down the length of the hold. Now she was really a lady. True, she still had to wear calf-length flounces with silk drawers billowing underneath, but how many nine-year-olds had their very own peacocks and a feathered hat?

Towards the stern Caroline stopped and stared sulkily at three wire crinolines queued along the wall in gradations of size like a family of lady-shaped skeletons. The largest was for her mother, the next for plain Sarah, and the smallest for Mariah; there was not one for her. She pouted at the largest one and tugged its silk waist ribbon. The wire cage hinged open. She stepped in, fastened the ribbon behind her and squatted on the floor. How she had wanted one of her own. She had asked politely, pleaded, begged, cajoled, threatened, and sulked, but her father would not buy her one. He was old-fashioned; he thought her a baby.

She stared moodily through the metal wires, listening to the creak of the boards, the jangle of swaying chain and harness bits, and the whoosh of the sawmill blade. "What does Mother care for crinolines?" she muttered. "And they won't do Sarah any good; she's going to be an old maid and no amount of frippery will change that. Mariah," she conceded, "is sort of pretty, what with her passable face and big . . . well . . ." — Caroline looked guiltily around her — "bosom." There, she had said it. "Bosom, bosom, bosom." She laughed nervously and her cheeks flushed. "Well, mine will be bigger, and I am already much prettier than Mariah, so if anyone deserves a crinoline, it's me." She knew her finest asset was her hair; it was thick and orange — some called it strawberry blonde — but to her it was orange and it hung to her shoulders in a mass of curls. Her features were fine and small, with a nose that was barely more than a bump, and she was already tall for her age. She ran her tongue over her one small defect: there was a tooth on the right side of her mouth that was rather longer and sharper than all the rest. It worried her. Without that one flaw she would be perfect. But Caroline was resourceful. For months she had practised at home in front of the mirror until she had mastered a smile that displayed all of her teeth except the defective one. The result was a sly, almost lascivious grin, which gave the effect that she knew much more than a nine-year-old should.

Captain Jonas Cains, forty-nine years old, barrel-chested, hard and angular, sat at a small mahogany table in his cabin and tugged thoughtfully at his tangle of flint-coloured mutton-chop whiskers as he studied a copy of a request he had sent to Governor Douglas the previous year.

Captain Jonas Cains, Esquire,
24 September, 1857.

Governor Douglas
Fort Victoria

Your Excellency:

It is with great pleasure that I am able to inform you of a rare opportunity for enhancing the development of our mainland colony.

Providing a suitable location can be found, I propose to establish a first-class sawmill capable of delivering 50,000 feet of lumber per diem and employing 200 labourers, plus a patent slip to accommodate vessels of up to 2,000 tons burthen. For said mill I will require:

1) a seacoast tract for living and cultivation for the accommodation of two to three hundred people (say, 100 acres) to be purchased at the customary price of $1 per acre.
2) a much larger tract with exclusive rights of timber cutting on it (say about 15,000 acres) on Burrard Inlet, the Fraser River, Howe Sound and the adjoining coast, and that such land shall be held by myself on lease of 21 years at one cent per acre.

As Your Excellency can certainly appreciate, such a tremendous investment of capital will greatly enrich the economy of our burgeoning colony by providing innumerable jobs, both directly and in allied businesses, by supplying much-needed timber and, most important of all, by establishing a stable industry based on an inexhaustible resource which will, in turn, attract further investment and generally bode well for the future of the mainland colony.

At the same time I feel it my duty to stress the importance of settling on a fair price. Although, as an Englishman, I would regret to be compelled to invest my capital and industry in the United States, yet the advantages and facilities in that country are, as Your Excellency is aware, so generous that unless the land system of this colony presents somewhat equal advantages, I shall be compelled, however reluctantly, in justice to my pecuniary interests, to decide upon some point on the opposite coast in, say, Washington Territory.

As I have only the best interests of the colony at heart I pray that such a move will not become necessary, for I fear that a refusal of my request would greatly discourage the further investment of British capital from the colony.

I have the honour to be Your Excellency's

Humble Obedient Servant,

Captain Jonas Cains.

Jonas picked up Governor Douglas's succinct reply. It said, "Land question not settled. Proceed as planned. When prices are fixed the tract will not be sold without your prior refusal. P.S.: Do not interfere with Indians."

He threw down the letter; it was better than he had hoped for. He chuckled as he pictured the prim old governor wringing his manicured hands and wagging a knobby finger. "Do not interfere with the Indians indeed," he muttered. What was the old boy going to do? Slap his wrists? "Damn the Christly Bloody Indians."

Douglas would not be in power much longer, anyway. While the governor was away on one of his many business trips, Jonas had circulated a petition complaining to the British government that Douglas's dual appointment as governor of Vancouver Island and Chief Factor of the Hudson's Bay Company represented a conflict of interests detrimental to the colony's development.

Since 1849 the Hudson's Bay Company had enjoyed a royal charter giving it a monopoly on trade with the Indians and a right to all land and its mineral resources in return for seven shillings per annum and a promise to establish a settlement. Settlers had not come to Victoria. They refused to purchase land from the Company at a dollar per acre when they could get free grants of 640 acres per person in Washington or Oregon. The few that did buy were banned from the lucrative fur trade and forced to share their business profits with the Hudson's Bay. In return they received little: lumber was in short supply and most of it had to be imported from Puget Sound at high prices; food was scarce and expensive; there were few streets and no public lighting, no sewers, and no fire department. Water cost twenty-five cents a bucket.

Jonas was certain the Hudson's Bay charter would not be renewed next year. Already the first shipload of prospectors would have reached Victoria and the Hudson's Bay Company would be crumbling under the responsibility. Soon the country would be flooded with thousands of immigrants, all demanding more than the Company could afford to provide. Hudson's Bay was doomed.

Jonas laughed. What a difference from the days when he had inherited his father's slaver and run blacks from the Portuguese barracoons on the west coast of Africa to the swamps of Havana. Those were glorious days, he thought. But he had sold the slaver to buy the *Orpheus* and marry Madeline, the aging only daughter of an old family. And now he was a respectable merchant and the settlers were going to make him rich. Very rich. They would buy goods from his store in Victoria and lumber from his mill on the mainland. Lumber for houses, shops, ships, wharves, and wagons.

He strode to the porthole and gazed out at the vast tangled rain forest. Fir, cedar, hemlock, and spruce grew thick and heavy, right to the water's edge, their dark-green reflection rippling in the small waves of Burrard Inlet. The forest is endless, he thought. A hundred men could spend a lifetime chopping through this wilderness and still never make a dent in the supply.

He grinned as a slim dugout skimmed around a point in the shoreline and headed for the *Orpheus*. Yes, things were well in hand.

"Indians!" The shout came from the poop-deck.

Jonas hitched up his pants and flung open the door of his cabin.

"Indians!"

"Damn the Christly Bloody Indians," he shouted.

He clattered onto the deck and bellowed at the sailors who crammed the rail, peering up the inlet at the approaching canoe and the thin wisps of smoke curling over the trees from the village of Whoi-whoi. More dugouts rounded the point and swarmed towards the ship. "Lower the sails," Jonas shouted. "Prepare to drop anchor. Furl main and mizen —" He stopped suddenly and stared at the broad tablelands on the north shore of the inlet. Black smoke billowed from a slash fire in a small, freshly cut clearing, and through the thick tangle of forest in the foothills he caught glimpses of a narrow water flume snaking through the treetops like an aerial highway. It had not been there the last time he visited the inlet. "Carky," he shouted. Men's voices and the sharp clang of a hammer on metal drifted over the water.

Carky, an old Scotsman who had been with him since the Crimea, hurried along the deck. "Aye, Cap'n?"

Jonas pointed a stubby, outraged finger at the north shore. "What the hell is that?"

Carky leaned against the rail and squinted his eyes. "I dinna ken, Mr. Cains. Could be a water-powered mill, I suppose."

"Jeesus," Jonas snarled. "I'll be damned if—"

"Siwashes to starboard," a man shouted from the bow.

Carky whistled, a low warning sound. "It's that damned 'Queer-cotton' fellow again. Slipperier'n spit, he is."

Jonas glanced at the long, slim dugout as it pulled away from the flotilla and skimmed towards the ship. Kweahkultun sat in the stern on a raised platform, swathed in a red Hudson's Bay blanket, smiling and nodding grandly. Men in the centre of the canoe pounded on wooden drums while others scattered eagle's down on the still blue water.

"Fetch the interpreter," Jonas snapped. He took a last glaring look at the new clearing on the north shore, then moved to the starboard rail.

Though he knew what the outcome would be, he was obliged to bargain again. Last year he had offered Kweahkultun one hundred pounds of iron, ten sheets of copper, and twenty Hudson's Bay blankets for the land around Whoi-whoi, but the brazen old mugwump had refused. "It's the only spot with water deep enough for our ships," Jonas had railed. It was a fair price. More than even the Hudson's Bay would demand. He wouldn't have offered that much except he was willing to concede that moving an entire village—even a village of savages—was a bit of an inconvenience. Kweahkultun was adamant. Jonas was outraged. He swore and threatened, then bristled down the inlet, promising revenge. "Think it over," he had warned. "I'll be back."

"Get on those sails," Jonas shouted. "Furl fore and main royals. Move it."

The ship blossomed with sailors. They clambered through the rigging and over the ratlines, up through the shrouds, up to the foretop, on to the topgallants, and up to the skysails. Below, they sang, yarding on the reef tackle, furling the sails, and securing

the bunt whips. The canvas crackled and flapped in the wind—
some sails curled up and others shrivelled, like deflating balloons
peeling off skeleton spars—and the bright blue sky shone
through.

The *Orpheus* shuddered as its bow settled in the gentle swell
and it coasted round the point. Jonas shaded his eyes against the
afternoon sun and scanned the south shore. The Indian village
was in chaos. Dozens of savages crowded the gravel beach, chattering excitedly and pointing at the great ship. Behind them the
longhouses of Whoi-whoi squatted on a large grassy bench which
merged into low round hills tangled with berry bushes and
poplar.

"Drop bower and kedge," Jonas shouted.

The chains rattled as the anchors slid over the side and the
clipper wallowed to a stop twenty yards offshore. Canoes
swarmed over the bay, but only one came close, a trail of white
eagle's down fanning behind it. "Lower the Jacob," Jonas yelled.

As the rope ladder flopped over the side, the slim dugout
darted towards it. Four Indians clambered up, followed by
Kweahkultun, a stooped, leathery old man who smelled of smoke
and fish. Under his red Hudson's Bay blanket he wore a tunic of
shredded cedar bark.

Jonas did not invite him to his cabin; he leaned on the rail,
facing the village, and squinted at him out the corner of his eye.
"You're looking old, you overblown, fossilized fart," he said.
Kweahkultun smiled and nodded. "So you're back again, you
greedy, foul-smelling copulator of dogs," he said in his own
language.

The interpreter—a young Salish boy who had been trained by
the missionaries in Victoria—scurried to the rail and stood
awaiting direction. "Ask him if he's changed his mind," Jonas
snapped.

Kweahkultun laughed and rattled away at the interpreter. Indeed he had. He had thought it over carefully and realized what
prosperity a mill would bring to his tribe, and after much delib-
eration he had convinced the heads of all the leading families
that land should be sold to the pushy pinkmen. Warriors had
been dispatched by canoe and, after much searching, had selected a prime location, a summer fishing camp ten miles distant,
which could be purchased for two hundred pounds of iron and
twenty sheets of copper. No blankets necessary.

Jonas stiffened and shook his head. "You're a fool," he growled. The interpreter hesitated. "Tell him!" The boy relayed the message falteringly. Kweahkultun glared at him. "I scoured this coast for a year," Jonas said, "and this is the only spot with plenty of trees and deep-water access for big ships."

Kweahkultun smiled benignly and pointed at the small clearing on the north shore. "He seems to have found another place."

"Who?"

The chief paused, concentrating, while he formed the white-man's awkward name. "Mattew Galuh. He too admired our snug *lumlam* and the pretty setting of our village, but when I told him Whoi-whoi could not be sold, he simply found another place to cut trees. Perhaps you too were to look again. . . . There is so much forest, so many trees."

Jonas jabbed his finger at the village. "I want that land," he yelled. "No substitutes. No deals. No stalling. I'm in a hurry. Get those people off or I'll blast them off."

Kweahkultun's men moved forwards as Jonas drew his pistol. "Now look," he said. "I'm taking this land whether you like it or not. So you may as well accept my offer." The boy relayed the message quickly, but before he could finish, Kweahkultun had started over the rail. Jonas grabbed his arm. "All right, you miserable thief. I'll make it one hundred and fifty pounds of iron, twenty sheets of copper, and twenty blankets. But for this village. No more."

Kweahkultun shook his head.

"You idiot!" Jonas screamed. "You want your people killed?"

Kweahkultun sneered, curling withered lips back over a full set of teeth, and spit on the deck of the ship.

Caroline bounded out of her father's cabin, trailing her feathered hat behind her, and ran to the bow, leaning far out over the rail so she could watch the Indians as they paddled furiously for shore. They looked savage: long-haired, brown-skinned men with bare chests—the one at the front even had a bone pierced through his nose — and they shouted in thick, guttural sounds as they paddled their carved red-and-black canoes towards the beach.

What Caroline liked best about the village was the totem poles; one was as tall as a ship's spar, carved and painted in bright colours, showing animals with round, startled eyes and fat, blunted teeth. There were smaller, unsettling ones too; ten-foot men with their arms outstretched to the ocean. Shrubs grew from the tops of their heads and creeping vines rooted their stout legs to the ground.

"Position fore-cannons!" her father bellowed.

Caroline clung to the railing excitedly as the two iron barrels were hauled to the bow, stationed between the balustrades, jammed on their gudgeons, and pointed at the village. She had never seen them fired before. The canoes sped up in a confusion of paddles and shouts as the Indians raced for shore. Men lined the starboard rail of the *Orpheus* to watch. As the heavy balls were rolled down the iron gullets and tamped into place, Kweah-kultun's dugout scraped onto the gravel beach of Whoi-whoi.

The ship grew silent, until the only sound was the click of Jonas's boots as he paced the wooden deck behind the guns. The cannoneer stood ready, torch in hand. On shore, the Indians ran to their houses. The waves lapped at the waterline and a brisk breeze gusted at the trees, while seagulls hung suspended and sleek, motionless in the air, riding the wind.

"Fire!" Jonas shouted.

The silence shattered. Seagulls screamed and the ship shuddered. The shots fell short: one in the water, exploding in spray, the other on shore, splintering canoes and throwing up sand.

"Two points higher," Jonas barked. "Fire! Fire!"

The second volley lodged in wood. The totem with the baleful eyes and outstretched arms snapped off at the base, hovered a moment, then crashed through the trees and slumped onto the ground in a swirl of dust. The other ball splintered through the roof of a cedar house; its rafters quivered and groaned, and the structure collapsed.

The deckhands cheered.

The blasts echoed like thunder off the mountains to the north. The Indians wailed and ran, confused and panicked, knocking one another down as they fled to the woods. A handful hung on, groping desperately through the debris of the shattered *lumlam*, searching for their relatives, but as the rumble of thunder faded, the only other movement left in Whoi-whoi was the slow curl of dust swirling up through the treetops at the edge of the village. The seagulls returned in wary silence, sleek and motionless, to ride the currents over Burrard Inlet.

"Lower the boat. We're going ashore."

Caroline stood by the rail, shifting excitedly from one foot to the other. "Can I go too?"

"No," her father said. "You stay here."

She pleaded and begged, then threatened, and finally wound herself around his leg and cried. "All right," Jonas said. "But stay in the lifeboat. Carky, keep an eye on her. See she doesn't go ashore."

Caroline sat primly in the stern, clutching her peacock hat with one hand, trailing the other languidly in the cold blue water. Ten feet from shore the inlet shallowed quickly and the bow stuck on the bottom. The men splashed out, hauled the boat to within a few feet of the beach, and scrambled up the grassy bank behind it.

Carky waited until they were gone, then waded out to the stern, running his hand along the gunwale, until he was inches from Caroline's face. "D'ya no think I'm gettin' a squint old for baby-minding, m'lady?" Caroline nodded slowly and seriously. Carky glanced over his shoulder but could see little because of the high bank. "Would you be doin' me a wee favour then, lassie, and stay in the boat like your da' said, so's I can be helpin' the men?" Again Caroline nodded. "That's a good girl, and dinna budge now; the water's terrible deep here, terrible deep." Caroline peered into the water. "And I've heard nasty things can happen when wee lassies dinna do as they're told." He rubbed his index finger slowly, thoughtfully, against the smooth wood of the gunwale. "Like them peacocks, now; we wouldna want anything happenin' to your precious peacocks, would we?" Caroline pursed her lips and glared sternly at the grizzled old face from under her eyebrows. He twisted his closed fists together and made a grinding, crackling noise with his mouth. She winced. Then he winked at her, turned, and scrambled up the bank, leaving her alone in the stern of the big empty rowboat.

She fidgeted with the feathers in her hat and watched the shifting animal shapes of the clouds billowing over the inlet. Occasionally she could hear her father's voice shouting orders — "You there, start digging a pit. Bloody savages. The mill will go here. You four, clear away this debris. The rest of you start on a raft, and make it sturdy. I'll keel-haul the man who dumps my oxen in the ocean" — but the bank was too high for her to see over. She moved to the bow and stared into the water. It didn't look so very deep, and there was only a small surf. "Perhaps..."

She lowered a tentative foot, but the ocean swelled over the top of her leather boot and she jerked it back. The water was cold.

She twisted on the bench and puffed out her cheeks. If only she had stayed on the ship. At least she could have seen what was happening. The lifeboat was so boring. Again she straddled the gunwale and lowered her boot into the water. It was deeper than she expected. She frowned and leaned further over the side, reaching for the bottom with her toe. The water was up to her knee, and she was about to give up when the boat shifted on its keel and, with one foot still hooked over the gunwale, she pitched broadside into the surf. When she righted herself, the water was up to her waist. She wrung out her hat and marched up to the beach, dripping and indignant, while the insulting waves chased after her.

Further along the shore she sneaked into the woods and struggled up a small bank, slashing angrily at the bushes which snagged in her hair, and carefully skirted the grassy bench until she came to a clearing on a low rise at the back of the village where she could see everything. She settled down to watch.

The ramshackle village was in chaos as her father's men ripped boards from the walls of the longhouses and stacked them for use in the construction of the mill. Others were digging up the large house posts and totem poles and lashing them together to make a raft. Far to the right, Carky was digging a hole; next to it three bodies were piled neatly on the ground.

Directly below her and set slightly apart from the rest of the village was the house that had been shattered by the cannonball. Three of its walls had been demolished, but the one closest to her stood upright and there was a hand sticking out from behind it. As she watched, the fingers moved. She pushed herself up, walked to the wall, and peeked around the corner.

An Indian man lay in the pile of rubble with heavy boards across his chest. She knelt down beside him and looked into his face. He was old, brown, and wrinkled. Three scars raked across the left side of his face from forehead to cheek. Caroline thought it looked as if an animal had clawed him. Flies buzzed around a thin trickle of blood congealing on his chin, and his chest made a shallow, bubbling sound.

She backed away as the right eye suddenly fluttered open and stared at her. Slowly, the old man smiled, then the eye fell shut and the shallow bubbling stopped, but the smile remained.

Caroline was only nine but she knew what death meant, and this man was certainly dead. She pushed herself wearily up from the ground and trundled across the grassy field towards her father. She doubted that Carky would dare to touch her peacocks, and if he did she would ask her father to keel-haul him; she was curious to see what that was like. Besides, she couldn't possibly hide the fact that she was drenched. And then there was the dead man. Someone had to tell.

She was surprised no one yelled at her. Her father merely patted her wet hair, and, while the smiling dead man was being pulled out of the shattered longhouse and stacked with the rest, Caroline was bundled into coats and whisked back to the ship, where she towelled herself dry in her father's cabin and snuggled into clean, warm clothes.

Late in the afternoon, when the raft was ready, she watched as the oxen were dragged onto the deck, bellowing and blinking stupidly at the bright sun. One by one they were wrestled into belly straps and winched over the side of the ship, where their eyes went white and wild and their legs dangled pitifully under them.

At sunset the saw blade was carried reverently to the rail, trussed, and carefully, slowly, solemnly lowered to its waiting bed of burlap. It covered most of the raft. Caroline held her hands to her face to block out the men until she could see just the blade, a jagged gleaming disc, floating over the bay, slicing its way to shore.

On the beach, twenty men spaced themselves evenly around it, hoisted it to their shoulders, and, with Jonas in the lead, carried it in procession to two notched pillars. An iron bar was passed through its core and the men lifted it onto the pedestal. The blade stood parallel to the beach, four feet off the ground, and, as the sun set behind the great island in the hazy distance, it began to glow.

Caroline looked behind her and saw that the sky was a deep, even crimson. When she turned back to the blade, it was blood red. The ship grew silent. The men on board gravitated to the rail.

On shore, Jonas stepped forward and struck the blade with his fist. As the sun set, the blood-red disc rang like a church bell, then the colours flickered, faded, winked, and dissolved into darkness.

CHAPTER THREE

1859-60

RIVER OF BLOOD

THUNDER. FOR TWENTY-ONE DAYS the storm had been building; black clouds scudded in from the Fraser and brooded over the treetops, pressing down on the silent land, blacking out the sky. The echoes dwindled to an oppressive stillness. The forest held its breath. Then, at last, the upper branches rustled with the hiss of drizzle. The drizzle swelled to a downpour and roared through the woodland, churning the Fraser River into a rolling ribbon of puckered mud.

Gustaf Biggörn ran his fingers through his beard and smiled. He was glad of the rain. For weeks now the impending storm had made his oxen edgy and skittish; with each thunderclap they lurched against their yokes, bellowing, lashing their tails, and flashing the whites of their eyes at the sky. They would work better now.

He retrieved his double-bitted axe from a stump on the river bank and strode into the forest. The trees were colossal, and grew so close together it would take a day of solid rain for the moisture to reach the ground. Around him the woods were dark, soft, and dry; great trunks towered pillar-like into the gloom, and a thin white mist percolated through the open spaces.

He swung his springboard overhead, wedged its metal lip into the notch of a tree, and hoisted his bulk up onto it. His shoulders ached and his legs were stiff. It would be noon before the grimace melted from his face and his arms swung freely. With the first chop the tree shuddered and groaned. He had been working on it for three days and had expected last night's wind to tear it down, but there it was, stubborn and defiant, clinging spitefully to the last shreds of its thousand-year-old core. It was a two-hundred-forty-foot Douglas fir, six feet in diameter and one hundred feet to the first branch. It weighed six hundred tons.

Alone in the forest Gustaf swung his axe in a steady rhythm and squinted his eyes against the flying chips. He was glad to be free from the religious oppression of Sweden, secluded here in the empty woods of the New World. He had given up logging and fled his shack on the Umealven River in 1850 after the death of his wife, Eva. Eva . . . He tightened his grip on the axe and swung it harder as the image of her face, made more lovely by the distance of time and the vagaries of memory, floated through his mind. When they first married he had thought of her as a hummingbird, she was so small, frail, and capricious, but over the years her fiery eyes dimmed in the isolation of the Swedish forest. She began to read the Bible constantly. She shrivelled, became wasted and intense.

Driven by boredom she had travelled to Lycksele and defied the state Lutheran church by attending a Methodist gathering. She became obsessed. Despite the fact that the preaching of any religion except Lutheranism had been banned, Eva became a self-appointed missionary ablaze with the truth, skimming down the Umealven in Gustaf's punt, searching the banks for potential converts in lonely cabins, organizing meetings, and recklessly denouncing predestination. She offered salvation for all.

At Gunnarn she was surrounded by the authorities in midstream, capsized, and whisked off to Umea for public confession and reaffirmation in the Lutheran faith. She would not submit and was jailed on rations of bread and water.

Gustaf had tried desperately to support her. He even became a Methodist — not so much out of true conviction as out of a belief in religious freedom — but it had done no good.

After her fourth imprisonment, the fire was permanently extinguished and Eva returned meekly to Gustaf's shack, where she sat in a chair by the river, day after day, silent and withdrawn, watching the dull water roll by, eating little and saying nothing.

She withered impassively. One day Gustaf found the chair empty and Eva gone; her body was recovered two miles downstream.

Sweden had become intolerable for him, so, in 1850, he sailed for the empty lands of the New World.

Gustaf was so engrossed in his memories that he didn't notice the first groans and tears as the tree began to topple, but when it crackled explosively and dodged away from his axe he leapt from the springboard and fled. Branches and debris rained around him. The descent was awesome: as its core severed, the tree screamed and ripped a path through the forest, snapping off branches and shattering smaller growth in a thunderclap of rage which died in a whoosh and a shudder of earth as the trunk hit ground, recoiled, shivered, and settled in a flurry of needles and shards. The great fir lay still and huge, stretched along the dirt, shrouded in dust, its head bowed in the river. Soon the only sound was the rustle of rain high overhead.

Gustaf chopped a notch into the side of the fallen tree, three feet off the ground, and wedged in the springboard so that, when he stood on it, his chest would be level with the top of the trunk. His crosscut saw skidded and bounced over the bark, gripped with its teeth, and dug into the wood, spewing sawdust like snow. He grunted over the saw, periodically shaking his head and spraying a shower of sweat around him. His arms swung freely now.

The saw jammed. As he yanked it out and sprinkled it with kerosene, he saw the silhouette of a tall, mannish woman in a calico dress trudging up from the riverbank, and he grinned. She moved slowly, with a rolling motion, placing her feet carefully, swinging a bundle from one hand and holding the other to her stomach.

Sitka placed the package on the ground and smiled up at him. Two years ago she had been a slave, creaking over the hills behind Alberni Inlet, stooped under the weight of a burden basket, but now she arched backwards with her face thrust up at the treetops and her belly swelling in front. Gustaf carefully helped her up onto the giant trunk, and together they untied the cloth bundle and pegged its corners with chunks of venison, bread, a can of tea, biscuits, and honey.

Far above them the storm raged, but tucked snugly in the folds of the woodland they watched spring birds flickering through the stillness. A woodpecker hammered on a dead cedar, his head a red blur as he grubbed for beetles. Bluejays ricocheted through the pine branches, hovering over the picnic lunch, shrieking and diving after the scraps Sitka tossed to them. Her dark eyes sparkled. She was radiant.

From the moment she had escaped, she had gravitated eastwards, leaching strength from the forest and safety at night from the clotted branches of low-slung trees. She had slogged up mountains, shivered through streams, and scudded down valleys, trapping rabbits in the lowlands, thinking only of Tcaga and home.

Three weeks later she had stood on the island's eastern shore, facing the broad strip of ocean which separated her from the mainland. She wandered north until she found a small village displaying the crests of her clan. The tribe was sympathetic, but the canoes had left a month before to trade fish and cedar boxes for the meat and goat's wool of the mainland tribes. No one would be travelling to her village again till next summer.

Sitka spent an uneasy winter, weaving blankets and cloaks for the chief in return for food and a place in his longhouse, until finally, a month ahead of schedule, she coaxed the traders into their canoes and set off across the straits for home.

They arrived with the dawn. Sitka sat in the centre of the dugout and held onto the gunwale as they glided past the long finger of Slahkayulsh Rock and slid through the narrows. Seagulls screeched overhead, the pale orange light of sunrise gleaming on their white wings as they twisted and darted around the rocky ledges of Thoos. The inlet opened before them and Sitka smiled at the familiar silver lines criss-crossing the water where the currents ran. The same brown, barnacle-encrusted rocks she had always known lined the shore, and the air still smelled of salt and cedar. Her heart beat faster as she pointed the way.

They rounded an outcrop of rock, and the paddlers faltered to a stop. The village was gone. In its place, perched on the high, grassy bank, were the squat, gangling buildings of a sawmill. A log boom floated a few feet from the narrow gravel beach, and a wharf jutted out into the water. White men moved slowly through the clearing. Sitka was shocked and bewildered. She looked wildly around her, searching for landmarks. How was it possible?

Then, as she watched from the canoe, white smoke puffed through the roof of the new structure and from inside came a deep rumbling sound which changed to a low howl, then quickly ascended the scale to a shrill, full-throated scream. The air shattered. Ducks churned across the inlet and a large blue heron lifted his bulk from the shallow water and sailed over their heads, his long, stick-like legs dangling behind him. A few seconds later, from the opposite shore, came the answering shriek of a second mill. The paddlers turned the canoe quickly and headed for the open ocean.

On the still, green waters of Ayyulshun Bay they encountered a lone young man returning from a night of duck-hunting. He told them the story of "Kweahkultun and the Greedy Pinkman", then offered to lead them to the new village site at Snauq, half an hour's walk away from the sawmill.

Sitka's heart sank as they paddled up the shallow, marshy inlet and the houses of her people appeared on the right bank. The water smelled foul. She stared into it and watched the shadow of a ten-foot sturgeon moving slowly, turgidly, through the brackish water.

She strode through the village, drawing clusters of excited early risers in her wake, but as she approached the *lumlam* which bore the crests of her husband's family, they hushed and drifted nervously off. In the dark she found Tcaga's familiar round shape sprawled on the sleeping platform with his back to her. She placed her hand on his shoulder and he puffed and grunted up from sleep, rolled over, and uncovered a young woman snuggled against the wall.

He was not happy to see her. "You're back." He said it indifferently, blinking up at her, a statement of fact, devoid of emotion.

The woman's name was Homana, but secretly Sitka called her Slug. She had a several-months-old baby — Tcaga had wasted no time taking a new wife — which was sick and neglected. The Slug cheerfully unburdened herself of it and Sitka took over. She was given a cramped sleeping area a short distance from the new couple where the noise of their love-making wounded her dreams.

From Matchakawillee, the plump, friendly old wife of Kweahkultun, who fussed in the affairs of every household, Sitka learned of her father's death. Tcaga had been away trading with the whites at Fort Langley at the time the village was destroyed. It was Matchakawillee herself who had gone to the greedy pinkmen and stopped them before they could bury the bodies of her

people in the ground. And it was Matchakawillee who had supervised the painting of Sitka's father's face and the folding of his
body into its small bentwood burial box; then she had ordered
her sons to carry it to the whispering tree.

The next day Sitka rose early and walked up the mountain to
the field of swaying bear grass where the ancient cedar hugged
the edge of the rocky cliff. She climbed up to the new box and
settled herself next to her dead father. The air was still, the tree
silent. She carefully swept the broken cedar shards from the lid,
shifted the box closer to her mother's, and retied the lashings
with her own hands. Then she sat through the rest of the day,
staring out over the silver-blue water. She was the last survivor of
her father's line.

Sitka withdrew into herself and tended the child. She watched
Homana carefully: the woman was young and pretty and must
have cost Tcaga a great many blankets, but she was aging rapidly
and smelled of dead meat. She shared all of Tcaga's worst habits:
they ate like dogs, stayed in bed most of the day, and drank
continuously. Together they railed at her cooking, throwing un-
satisfactory bits into the fire, jeering at her protests and making
jokes behind her back, but when Tcaga was alone, he lowered
his head, avoided her stare, and sulked out of the house. She was
a silent reproach to him, an ugly reminder of how he had fled the
longhouse on the night of the raid, abandoning his family to the
warriors' clubs, and he grew bitter and hateful towards her. Like
sunburned snakes, the awkward threesome smouldered painfully
through the hot summer.

In the autumn her tormentors left on a trading expedition up
the Fraser, but they returned a week later and ordered Sitka into
the canoe. She paddled from the bow, while Tcaga steered and
Homana lounged in the centre shouting advice. They had nudged
their way upriver for fifteen miles when Tcaga turned the boat
and guided it towards a solitary cabin of peeled pine logs perched
on the bank at the edge of the forest. On the gravel beach was a
heavy, barrel-chested pinkman, with a woolly black beard, wild
hair, and ape-like hands, cradling a case of whisky. Sitka was
ordered out of the canoe.

She stood on the beach, awkward and confused, while the
ape-man loaded the whisky in her place and slid the canoe back
into the river. Sitka glared, but Tcaga did not look up from his
paddle. The canoe drifted downstream and Homana's jeering

laughter echoed over the river, accompanied by the clink of bottles.

Gustaf had terrified her in the same way a bear would. He was massive and awkward, he talked to her in rumbling bass noises she could not understand — and, worst of all, he was white. For the first week she huddled in a corner of the cabin, cringing from his touch, expecting to be struck dead with syphilis. But Gustaf was patient. He treated her kindly, and gradually her fear disappeared. She warmed to his tenderness and was soon alive with the prospect of children. She was suspicious of his motives: there were no beatings, harsh words, or insults, and very little was expected of her. She cooked and did light cleaning but was not allowed to cut firewood, and when Gustaf caught her hauling water from the river he had swooped down the bank, snatched the pails out of her hands, and carried them himself. Sitka was mystified.

When the winter rains had shrouded the river, chilled and crystallized into snow, Sitka trudged daily to a deep, narrow trench in the forest where Gustaf worked, crouched under a log that was propped up over his head. He heaved down on one end of the saw from the bottom of the pit, while a hired miner pulled up from above. The cut moved slowly, painfully, down the length of the log; then they removed the board and began again. She knew Gustaf got the worst of it: within minutes his arms would be numb and his eyes and nostrils caked with sawdust, but he pumped on like a tireless machine, sending clouds of hot steam puffing up out of the deep black pit into the chill winter air until the sun set and she helped him out of the trench and walked him home.

After dinner the miner would leave for his own shack off in the woods, and she and Gustaf would laze in front of their small stove for hours, decoding each other's language, unravelling past histories, talking, listening, confiding, and sympathizing. By December Sitka was pregnant.

When the snow melted, trickled away, and brewed into mud, the miner left for the gold-fields and Gustaf returned to the business of chopping trees. Sitka made daily pilgrimages to the nearby hills with her bundle of food, and together they sat under the giant Douglas firs while spring birds flickered through the shadows around them.

"Matthew'll be 'round next week," Gustaf said as he drained

the last of the tea from his tin mug. "We should have enough logs by then."

Sitka nodded enthusiastically. She liked the handsome young man who always smiled at her and paid Gustaf such large sums for his booms of cut logs. She had listened many times while he talked with Gustaf and she knew that he had come from the south, from a place called Maine, and that he had left his home as a young man and travelled a great distance to build his sawmill. He lived there now, across the inlet from Jonas Cains's mill, where the village of Whoi-whoi had stood, and he worked in the forest at the base of the mountain which contained her whispering tree. He had no wife, this she also knew, but then few of the pinkmen did, and this was a great puzzle to her. Why did they not bring their women with them?

Sitka smiled. She looked forward to Matthew Galer's visit. He would come round to their cabin in his noisy great ship, the *Cariboo Fly*, hook onto the floating raft, and tow it back to his mill, while he and Gustaf talked and laughed on the deck. Sitka would go too; she always did. Once they had tried to get her to board the floating monster with them, but she shook her head firmly and took up her usual position on the raft, sitting cross-legged at the front of the log boom.

She loved the short trip down the slow, rusty Fraser, round Ulksen Point, and over to Burrard Inlet. As they chugged past the canoes darting over Ayyulshun Bay the people of Snauq would stop paddling and gape at her, sitting proudly on her enormous raft of floating logs, looking straight ahead, pretending not to notice their envious stares.

Sitka packed up the remains of lunch, while Gustaf sprinkled his crosscut saw with kerosene. He lifted her carefully from the top of the great log and set her firmly on the ground. "Thank you," he said. Sitka shook her head in confusion. He was still a great mystery to her.

Gustaf eased the saw back into the tree's wound and resumed his work. Sitka watched from the ground. Already he was breathing heavily, and sweat beaded his forehead. She lifted her bundle and trundled down the narrow forest path towards their small log house on the bank of the Fraser, her bare feet padding softly on the thick carpet of dead needles. The rasp of the saw faded behind her, blending with the wind and the lap of the river.

At the cabin door she stopped abruptly, cocked her head to

one side, and held her breath. The bundle slipped from her fingertips. Filtering through the budding poplars lining the river bank came the shouts of men and a loud chugging sound she could not identify. She crept closer to the water, instinctively crouching low to the ground, and peered through the under-brush.

Anchored in midstream was H.M.S. *Plumper*. It was similar to Matthew's ship—there were no paddles or sails, and black smoke churned from a long, fat pipe which rose totem-like from its centre—but it was much larger. Even at rest it made a frightening rumbling noise.

Since the beginning of the gold-rush, Sitka had watched count-less boats ferrying thousands of prospectors up and down the Fraser: rough and wild-looking men. During the first summer they had pried all the gold from the river's mouth, then bounded northward, leapfrogging from one creek to the next, past the cabin, shouting, cursing, and bragging their luck from one leaky boat to the next. They wormed their way northward to nearby Fort Langley and beyond to boom towns Sitka could not imagine like Hope, Van Winkle, Soda Creek, and Richfield. She had watched silently from the cabin door as they paddled north, strong, excited, and hopeful, only to see the river spit them out again, weak, dispirited, and bitter.

Few of them became rich. Many died. Sitka herself had found the lean and battered corpse of a red-headed prospector snagged in the bushes at the river's edge with an arrow lodged in his throat, and shuddered at the implications. Without telling Gustaf, she had removed the arrow and fed the body back into the river for the ocean to deal with.

This ship was obviously different: it swarmed with red-uniformed men who lowered axes, saws, chains, poles, and other tools into a rowboat. As the boat jerked free and pulled across the current, another took its place. Soon there were four skiffs lined along the shore five hundred yards below the cabin and the narrow beach was crowded with soldiers shouting, jostling, and clambering up the bank and into the woods. Sitka waited ner-vously in the underbrush while Gustaf hacked his way through the salmonberry bushes to the string of boats and hurried into the forest after them.

Late summer. Sitka lingered on the trail, brushing leaves from her dress, while Gustaf forged ahead. She was terrified. In the four months since the uniformed men had arrived, a settlement had grown out of the forest to the west of their cabin. During the winter she had prowled furtively through the woods like a wolf on the fringes of civilization, tempted, but afraid to approach. Occasionally, as she spied on the workmen from the bushes, one would point in her direction and call to the others while she slunk off into the forest, flushed and angry at her own cowardice. She was certain she had earned a ludicrous reputation among the new townsfolk.

Gustaf waited for her to catch up. "Are you sure you want to go? We won't if you don't want to."

"Of course I do," she said.

"Well, come on then."

She picked up the hem of her dress and trudged through the shadows, straining her eyes, feeling with her feet, and pacing off intricate dance steps in her head. What was the fun in dancing when it was all so complicated?

Gustaf hadn't exactly asked her to go. Two months ago he had sat solemnly at the dinner table and explained that Queen Victoria had named the settlement New Westminster and that there would be a dance to celebrate. "What a shame you're pregnant," he had said. "Otherwise I would like to go." Sitka had wondered if he was ashamed of her. "Then we'll go," she said. Gustaf had beamed, and they sat up late into the night talking, laughing, and making plans: they would buy dress material from Fort Langley and new pants for Gustaf. He would teach her to dance.

In the Hudson's Bay store she had stood, mystified, before pyramids of cloth bolts stacked like stubby corpses waiting to be stitched into life, and tried to imagine what they would look like in the form of a dress on a whiteman's dance floor. She wanted something bright. Something startling. Something that would stand out and make people point and say, "There goes Gustaf's wife." Her hand melted into a thick crimson velvet. She bought yellow gingham for a petticoat and orange ribbons for trim.

By day, in secret, she had cut and measured and stitched: a yellow underdress, a matching turban with trailing scarves, and a red overskirt trimmed in orange, scalloped, looped up, and pinned like bunting with canary bows so that the bright lemon petticoat glared through. To camouflage the fact she was eight months pregnant, she padded out the waist with rolls of canvas, then chopped away the abdomen of a crinoline so that her belly poked through and lay flush against the red velvet. She looked fat but symmetrical. Without showing Gustaf, she hid the dress away till the night of the dance.

In the evenings, after dinner, they had pushed aside the table and chairs, up-ended the bed, and waltzed around the tiny dirt floor, stirring up dust, while Gustaf hummed and Sitka pursed her lips, wading through the intricate steps until their feet tangled and Gustaf dissolved into laughter. Sitka was undaunted. She plodded doggedly about the room from dawn till dinner, until she could waltz perfectly by herself and almost as well with Gustaf.

Finally, on the day of the dance she had carefully lifted her dress out of its hiding place, struggled into it, and practised all morning. During the afternoon she fidgeted at the table, periodically opening the door and checking the progress of the sun across the sky. When she saw Gustaf coming, she flung the yellow scarf ends of the turban over her shoulders and sailed out to greet him like a red flagship on an angry yellow sea.

His jaw dropped. He said nothing. Sitka paraded proudly before him, taking his gaping mouth as a sign of great admiration.

She could not eat dinner. She sat at the table and smiled into Gustaf's staring eyes. "Do you like it?" she had asked. Gustaf nodded weakly.

Sitka edged off the trail and stepped onto the scar of hillside that was now New Westminster. She hesitated. Her stomach snarled. Everywhere there was carnage: stumps, shadows of stumps, silhouettes of stumps and shattered trees, broken branches and jumbled logs; the ghosts of the forest cluttered the ground in silent recrimination, and over it all the syrupy music of a fiddle floated down from Government Hall at the top of the hill.

The sunset seeped across the sky like maroon smoke. The river looked frozen and bloody. She felt doomed: maybe her dress was a little too bright, perhaps she had cut it all wrong, what if she tripped and made fools of them both, or, worse yet, maybe no waltz would be played.

They floundered through the debris until they found the main street, a narrow path studded with boulders and precipitous drops that wound erratically up the hillside. Sitka was amazed at how much had been done in four months; everywhere the skeleton frames of half-constructed homes rose up around them, glowing gold and orange in the sunset. She counted forty dwellings, ranging from miners' tents and a hollowed-out stump with a roof and a door to the cavernous, shingled, and whitewashed government building perched on stilts and built over snags.

At the top of the steps, the glare from the hall flooded out the door. Sitka hesitated. She was about to change her mind when Gustaf's arm circled her waist. She turned and smiled at him, and let herself be led into the room. Seventy pairs of eyes turned to stare. There was a buzz and a twitter among the ladies. At the far end of the hall, Governor and Lady Douglas sat by an open fire. A sombre tableau of businessmen dressed in black and white, their ladies dressed in varying shades of grey, ranged down the left wall in gradations of wealth, while across from them the red-coated Royal Engineers and shirt-sleeved miners squeezed around a pine counter which had been converted to a bar. The hall smelled of freshly cut cedar. An ancient fiddler creaked up from his chair and began a jig which sent the miners whooping and the floorboards bouncing.

They sat on a small bench by the door. Sitka eyed a group of ladies near by; they were all drinking a dark liquor from fine carved glasses. "Let's have some whisky," she said.

Gustaf frowned. "But you don't drink."

She glanced again at the women across from her, then stared at the floor.

"All right," Gustaf said. "I'll go to the bar and be right back."

When she was alone, Sitka twisted the ribbons dangling from the neck of her dress and tried to find a comfortable position. The music started again and there was a thundering of boots as the men rushed to find partners. The couples formed two long lines down the centre of the hall, their faces glowing orange from the coal-oil lamps, and marched forward and back like colliding waves. Sitka was amazed.

As she watched the intricate manoeuvres and tried to relate them to the orders the fiddler was shouting, she noticed someone standing beside her and looked up into the wizened face of a plump half-breed woman in a coal-black dress. "How do you do?" she said. "My name is Amelia Douglas." Sitka smiled as Lady Douglas settled herself on the bench beside her.

"What are they doing?" Sitka asked.

"It's called the Virginia Reel."

"It's . . . silly."

Lady Douglas laughed. "Yes, I've always thought so myself." They watched the dancers ducking under upraised arms and trotting round in circles by themselves.

"You're pregnant," Lady Douglas stated. Sitka stammered. "No need to blush, dear. This is the frontier. They don't care. Is that your man? Biggörn?"

"You know him?"

"I've heard of him. He cut most of the timber for this hall, didn't he?"

Sitka nodded. She liked the directness of this blunt old woman.

"Will you be bringing the child up Indian or white?"

"I hadn't thought about it," Sitka said.

"Take my advice and raise him white. That was my big mistake. See my daughters over there?" She pointed at two tall girls standing by the fire. "I sloped their foreheads when they were babies to make them beautiful, and now they carry their heads like curses. White men sneer at them. They are lost." Sitka stared at the deformed girls; their foreheads sloped sharply back from their eyebrows to a point at the crown. She had heard of this practice among the northern coastal tribes and, although she was willing to concede that it did attract attention, she did not think it beautiful.

"Have you heard of Queen Victoria?" Lady Douglas asked.

Sitka nodded.

"She's a very powerful woman. All this land is hers now — and I don't just mean New Westminster, but all of it: from the coast to the Rockies and north to the Tlingit lands. The Indians will never get it back; the tribes are too scattered to resist. If our children are to prosper, we must acknowledge that and raise them as whites."

As Gustaf squeezed away from the bar and up to the bench, Lady Douglas rose and whispered, "Take my advice. Raise them white." She nodded to Gustaf, then to Sitka, and waddled off down the hall, nodding and smiling.

"You're making friends in high places," Gustaf said as he handed her a metal cup. Sitka took it and noticed that the people on the wealthy side of the room were drinking from glasses.

"I've not been doing too badly myself," Gustaf said. "I met a Mr. Connolly at the bar. He has a gang saw for sale in Fort Langley that he got from an old logger down at Puget Sound."

"A gang saw?"

"It's a small steam-powered saw with six blades. It'll cut an entire log into boards in about ten minutes. Think of the time it will save."

"You're going to buy it?"

"I certainly am. He's going to ship it down on the next stern-wheeler. We'll have it running in three weeks." Sitka was not impressed by the money, and she hated the clamour and confusion of machinery, but she would welcome anything that could uproot Gustaf from that oppressive pit. She raised her tin mug in salute the way she had seen others doing. "To the gang saw."

The fiddler was joined by a young harmonica player and the mellifluous strains of a waltz breezed through the hall. Sitka blanched. Her feet seemed rooted to the floor. Then Gustaf's hand pressed warmly on hers and she felt herself rise and move into the crowd. The heat of his body radiated through the hole she had cut in the crinoline, and her nerves thawed. The patterns, the numbers, the counting, all melted from her head and she coasted through the hall, content and pleased. The room hushed. the faces of other dancers glided in and out of her field of vision, making a collage of placid smiles, and among them she glimpsed Lady Douglas, sitting amidst her daughters, beaming and nodding towards her. She floated peacefully and her eyes drifted shut. When the music ended, she and Gustaf lingered on the dance floor, swaying gently, heads bent, eyes closed.

Sitka sat next to Gustaf and cradled the last of the whisky in her hands as a scrawny man in a red uniform swaggered up to them. "No drinking for you, miss. You'll have to get rid of that."

"I beg your pardon," Gustaf said.

"I said she can't drink it. We don't sell whisky to Indians."

"This lady is my wife."

"Makes no difference, sir. That's the law. You know what they're like when they're drunk."

"No, I don't," Gustaf shouted.

Sitka placed her hand on his arm. "It's all right, Gustaf. I didn't want it anyway." She held the cup out to the soldier.

"I'm not a waiter," he snapped, turning on his heel and swaggering away from them.

Gustaf grabbed the tin mug and was about to fling it at the soldier's back when Sitka stopped him. "Gustaf, please. Don't spoil it. Let's go home." He placed the cup on the bench, folded his arms across his chest, and glowered at the floor.

"It doesn't matter," Sitka said. "Can we go now?"

"Just a minute. I want to remind Connolly about the saw." He heaved himself up and disappeared into the throng.

Sitka sat stiffly, her back aching, her face flushed from the embarrassing confrontation, and watched the shifting crowd in the lull between dances.

Abruptly the fiddle erupted into the raucous strains of a polka. The men cheered and thundered through the room. Sitka jumped. A red-eyed, sweating miner grabbed her hand and yanked her to her feet. She pulled back. "I don't know how," she pleaded.

"No *klootchman* ever turn me down afore," the man sneered. He grabbed her waist. Sitka tried to move her right foot back into the first step of the waltz, but he jerked her to the left and then to the right. He hopped and spun, charging down the floor and dragging Sitka with him. Her feet tangled. She lunged to the left. The miner squeezed her tighter — he reeked of whisky and sweat — and they lurched around the hall, scuffling and struggling.

Her stomach churned and she tried to keep up, shuffling her feet erratically, but his moves were violent and unpredictable. The room flashed sickeningly around her. She felt dizzy and nauseated. On the second circuit her womb clenched and shuddered. She struggled. Her feet locked and she fell to her knees, gashing her chin on the man's belt buckle.

"Gustaf!" she cried.

The miner released her, the music stopped. As she fumbled at the dress tangled around her feet, she glimpsed Gustaf charging through the crowd towards the frightened man. She pushed herself up and fled from the hall, clutching her belly and gasping for air.

Outside, she slumped against a strut supporting the hall and tried to calm herself. The sky was black, starless, windy. Again her womb contracted and she felt the child wriggling inside her. Her knotted fists pressed to her stomach and she clenched her thighs, trying to hold it in. A thin trickle of blood fell from the cut on her chin and splattered across the yellow petticoat. "No. Not yet," she whispered.

A woman darted down the steps and rushed towards her. "Have your pains begun?" Lady Douglas demanded.

Sitka doubled over and shook her head angrily. "No. It isn't time."

The old woman ran to the steps and shouted at the crowd gathering round the door, "Fetch Dr. Jones. Quickly!" She darted back to Sitka. "Put your arm around my shoulder. We're going to the barracks. The doctor will meet us there."

"But it's not time," Sitka wailed. Hunched forward and huddled together, the two women staggered down the dark trail. Behind them the crowd erupted in shouts and confusion, and Sitka looked back to see the foul-smelling miner hurled down the stairs. He thudded against a stump, and Gustaf dived on top of him.

"It's all right, Mrs. Biggörn," Lady Douglas said. "Everything will be all right now."

A small room at the back of the barracks was partitioned off from the rest by a canvas tarp and behind it were four cots. An officer with splints on his leg was propped up on one, reading a book by a kerosene lamp. "What's going on?" he demanded.

Lady Douglas ignored him. She lowered Sitka onto a bed and was unfastening her dress as Dr. Jones and two men arrived. The men picked up the officer's bed and carried him, protesting, out of the room.

"When is it due?" the doctor asked.

"Not for a month," Sitka said.

He turned to Lady Douglas. "We'll need to keep the baby warm if it's to live. Build the fire. There's clean towels in the cupboard." As he clattered through the utensils in a drawer Sitka watched him carefully. He was old and lean, with a fringe of fluffy white hair, but he moved calmly and probed her abdomen with gentle fingers. At his touch her waters broke and the contractions began again, flooding down from her stomach in waves. She gripped the edges of the bed and shut her eyes, remembering the day on the beach when the waves rolled towards her, and each bore the face of a child on its crest. She swore that this one would live.

As the hours passed, Sitka sank into pain, surfacing occasionally in the lull between contractions. Fiddle music floated through the open window and the image of white men and women dancing the Virginia Reel, rushing forward and back in two long lines like colliding waves, gyroscoped through her mind. Once, she opened her eyes and saw the worried face of Gustaf staring down at her. She thought of her age, of Cutick, and Moon, and Daylight, until she began to cry for fear of losing the baby.

As the first rays of dawn seeped up the Fraser and Sitka lay exhausted, sweat-drenched and grunting, the child squeezed painfully out of her on a river of blood, and the cord was cut. Red and hairless, it was upended and slapped into life, crying bitterly.

The excited face of Lady Douglas hovered over her. "It's a girl. She'll live." Her heart leapt at the words and she imagined the child racing through its life: waddling excitedly into the forest behind Gustaf, circling over his head as he tossed her in the air, learning cat's cradle, disdaining dolls in favour of long dresses, courting, and growing old with a family of her own. She would call her Eva.

Two days later she was placed on a stretcher and Gustaf and another man carried her through the woods and back to the cabin as she clutched Eva to her breast. At first the child was shrunken, with shiny red skin stretched tight over stick-like bones, but Sitka nursed her constantly and she fattened and thrived. Gustaf moved a chair outside the hut and Sitka rocked the child in the summer sun and watched her grow.

As the final days of August smouldered through the forest, baking the ground into a parched crust of burnt needles, Sitka walked to the beach and watched the flat-bottomed stern-wheeler nose up to the shore and disgorge the gang saw. It was a squat, brutal contraption with jagged teeth, and it sprawled insolently on the gravel. Gustaf pampered it; he sweated over the parts, bathed them in oil, and coaxed them into life. Finally, the boiler was fired, a head of steam built up, and the machine belched into life. The blades churned and the saw waited hungrily for the first log.

"Hump! You—Buck. Git on! Ye-ow-ow-ow! Brin! Brolin! Hump! Hump!" Gustaf swaggered down the line of four bulls, bellowing and jabbing at their flanks with his goad. "Move it, Buck! Hi-ee-ee!" Each of the animals weighed eighteen hundred pounds, but the train of logs they were pulling totalled three hundred tons. Their yokes crackled and the chains shivered and hummed as they thrashed forwards, churning up dust, straining and wrenching, while their tails lashed and their muscles bulged. Again the goad-stick stung, piercing a rear bull's flank, and he danced sideways, lunging wildly at his harness and throwing the others into confusion. "Whoa-oa-oa," Gustaf crooned. He flung the stick on the ground, cursed, and stormed back to the lead log.

The day was hot. He crouched behind the bulls' hooves, slapping fish oil on the small logs he had laid crossways as skids. The air was cloying, and thick with deerflies; he raked his fingers through his beard, clawed at the bugs sucking on his chin, and arched his back as tiny rivulets of sweat criss-crossed down his spine.

He rose slowly and moved down the log train, running his hand along the chains and checking the dog spikes. As soon as he slopped on the fetid oil, the log swarmed with insects. He moved to the next log, and the next, and the next, baking in the sun, mopping his forehead with his damp shirt-sleeve and scanning the trail expectantly for Sitka.

"All right you lazy sons-a-bitches," he growled. "No excuse now." He took a deep breath. "Hiy-ee-ee! Git on! Hyah! Move it, Buck, or I'll cut your balls off! Hump! Hyah!" He raced around the team, slapping and jabbing with his stick and barking curses. The bulls lunged solidly, shifted their weight, dug in, and strained against their yokes with their heads lowered and their eyes wide. At last the lead log jerked ahead, the bulls stumbled, jolted forwards, and yanked again, prying the second log loose, then the third, and the fourth, until the whole train shuddered into motion with the quiver of chains and the screech of timber. "Hiy-ee-ee! Hump, you bastards! Hump!"

As the first log crested the slope that led to the river, Gustaf slackened his pace and strolled beside the bulls, encouraging them softly. They relaxed and eased the timber down the grade with little strain. Ahead, through a tunnel of poplar leaves, the muddy Fraser shimmered in the hot sun. At the foot of the hill the gang saw waited impassively in the shade.

Crack! Halfway down, the lead log rolled over, wedged behind a stump, and slammed to a stop. The bulls snorted and backed up painfully, shaking their heads in confusion, while Gustaf stormed down the trail to fetch the peavey.

The log butted flush against the uphill side of the stump. He jabbed and swore but the peavey would not wedge in, so he moved to the downhill side, jammed the point into a gap, hooked the cant over the log, and heaved. The huge block groaned and shifted a few inches towards him, ripping part of the stump away, then stopped. Again he jabbed, hooked the lever, and strained down until his neck muscles quivered and one foot lifted off the ground. The stump split in half, shattered, and exploded in a spray of dry pulp. The log sprang forward, cracking Gustaf's shins, knocking him down and rolling up his legs. Startled by his shouts and the sudden movement behind them, the bulls lunged forward and again the log rolled, crushing and grinding up to his groin and then his waist. He screamed and hammered the bark with his fists. It stopped and he slumped back unconscious.

He awoke slowly, groggily, to the feel of moisture on his face; his eyes fluttered in shadow, slitted open, and focused on Sitka. Her face shimmered in front of him like a mirage and behind it the log loomed up from his stomach, stretching endlessly out of his field of vision like an enormous wall. He was cold. The sun burned hotly down and he shivered. His legs were numb and his chest icy. He rolled his head to the side: the team had been unhooked and were foraging contentedly in the underbrush. Eva lay cradled in a stump near by. He tried to push himself up and was instantly flattened by a searing pain that flooded up his spine, exploded at the base of his skull, and receded in waves, leaving him chilled and dazed.

Sitka lowered her ear to his lips. His breath was shallow, erratic. "Finish me," he whispered.

She jerked her head away and screwed up her eyes. "I'll get help," she said.

"I'm dying."

She knew it was true. The log had devoured his body up to the ribs, and the dirt around him was sodden with blood.

"Finish me."

"How?"

She pushed herself up and staggered around the log, desperately searching for a solution; then she stooped over a large rock and clawed around it with her fingers. She could barely lift it; stooped, straining, and shaking, she carried it to Gustaf and held it over his head.

He smiled up at her and they stared silently at each other while Eva slept, bluejays skimmed down the trail darting low under branches, and the Fraser River, clotted with rust, pumped monotonously, indifferently, on to the ocean.

"Now," Gustaf said. She raised herself up, grasped the boulder, heaved it overhead, and wavered unsteadily. His voice grew in intensity — "Now!"

Sitka wailed and drove the rock down.

The cabin door clicked firmly behind her. She scooped Eva up from the ground, and the child's face snuggled sleepily against her old cedar-bark cloak. With her free hand she fitted the strap of a burden basket over her forehead and hoisted the bundle of provisions onto her back. At the edge of the forest she looked back at the prim little cabin nestled on the bank of the river; then she ducked under the branches and hurried into the woods, away from the town.

BLACK~DROP FOG

"I-AM-I-AM-I-AM-I-AM-I" The engine of the side-wheeler chugged and Matthew drummed his fingers on the rail in time with its rhythm. The water was black and pocked with drizzle; his reflection buckled and warped. "Damn." Fear: He was twenty-eight years old and had crossed a continent from Maine to the gold-fields of San Francisco, then north to the steep ledges and giant cedars of British Columbia — all without fear. But the water terrified him.

In his dreams he thrashed helplessly a foot below the surface; then the sun flickered and he sank into darkness. The water was a live thing which could suck him down to hell.

Cold sweat trickled down his forehead and gathered at the corners of his eyes. His knuckles whitened. The ship's whistle blew and Matthew whirled away from the water and relaxed back into the chug of the engine: "I-am-I-am-I-am-I-am-I".

He watched the men from his mill who had come to meet the bride-ship in Victoria. They lined the starboard rail, passing a jug of whisky from hand to hand, shouting, joking, laughing. Production would be down this month. It would take two weeks of solid drinking before they would begin to drift back to the mill — woebegone, penniless, dreaming of the next blow-up — and some, he knew, would simply disappear to God-knows-where. He had been lucky to maintain a skeleton crew at the mill. He smiled. It was unavoidable: they were bushed, stakey, and the newspaper had promised women—white women. He wasn't interested in a bride for himself, but, still, it would be a novelty to see them.

Smoke. As the ship rounded Laurel Point and eased into Victoria Harbour, ashes drifted over the bow and settled on the deck like autumn leaves. Across the bay from the Fort dozens of Indians clustered on the beach and watched as their village burned. Uniformed constables with white handkerchiefs tied bandit-like across their faces shimmered in waves of heat as the last cedar shack ignited like kindling. Flames curled skywards and sparks spiralled up into black clouds. The ship's engine stopped and the air was silent except for the crackle of fire.

"'Bout time they burned the bastards out."

Matthew glanced at the speaker leaning on the rail next to him and guessed he was a Victoria businessman. "What's going on?" he asked.

"Smallpox. No more room at the Injun hospital, and they just spread it around among the whites. Burn 'em out and drive 'em north, that's what I say."

Dugouts skimmed past the side-wheeler and headed for the open ocean. Matthew watched an unconscious man with open, white eyes sprawled in the bottom of a slim canoe paddled by two women; his hand dangled over the edge, tracing a delicate "V" in the black water. He turned away.

Before the gangplank was in place, he leapt to the dock and strode along Wharf Street. It had been a year since he'd seen Victoria, and the change dazzled him: brick and stone buildings stood where canvas tents had flapped in the wind; he passed theatres, shops, banks, businesses. On Government Street he stopped to watch a group of men testing the gas pressure in the city's first street lamp. Granted, there were still problems, like the gaping holes in the boardwalks or the stagnant water flowing out of the Gipsey House Baths into a scummy pool on the paving stones, but the town was fast becoming a city.

He noticed passersby moving out of his way as he clomped along the boardwalk, the rough planks crackling under his caulk boots, but he was used to it. Most of his life people had given him a wide berth. It was partly his appearance—he was six foot four, broad-shouldered, with an axeman's muscular arms and large hands; his dark-brown hair was wiry and tangled, streaked with blond from the summer sun, and it curled into thick brown sideburns and a bushy moustache — but it was his presence people avoided. There was an intensity to his stride, a drive, a single-mindedness of purpose, which parted a crowd as the bow of a ship parted water.

The office of the *Daily Colonist* was a narrow clapboard building, weathered grey and bleeding rust from its nailholes. A large sign in slashing script covered most of the window:

Vancouver Island & British Columbia
— UNITE OR PERISH —
Two Colonies are a Surplus of One

Matthew opened the door and stepped into a small, dark room that smelled of dust and printer's ink. A gaunt, bloodless man jumped up from the clutter of tools at the foot of a hand-driven rotary press and darted to the back of the room, so that the machine stood between them; he was tall and gangly, with an enormous wiry beard that lengthened his face.

"Are you the editor?" Matthew asked.

"Might be. Then again, I might not. You armed?" Matthew shook his head and the man relaxed visibly. "Amor De Cosmos. Editor."

"Matthew Galer."

There was an awkward pause while the two men stared at each other. "Well, what do you want?"

"I came to place an ad for my mill." Matthew pulled a sheet of paper from his shirt pocket and unfolded it, while De Cosmos darted around the press inspecting its rollers. "'Galer Mills'," Matthew read. "'Lumber For Sale. Fir, Spruce, Cedar, Tongue and Groove Flooring' . . . ; it's all here."

De Cosmos looked up from his inspection. "Damn machines. Never trust 'em. Insufferable, beef-witted monsters; less dependable than the Governor himself. Look at this thing. The roller axle's broken. Look at it."

Matthew looked.

"I've got a paper to run today. Where am I supposed to get another axle?"

"'Bout the same size as a common nail, isn't it?"

The editor stared at Matthew, looked at the roller, then stared at Matthew again. "What did you say you wanted?"

"I came to —"

"You signed the petition yet?"

"What petition?"

"What petition?! Plan on advertising in a paper you've never read? It's in every issue. How many British colonies on the Pacific Coast?"

"Two."

"Right. How many should there be?"

"Look, I'm a —"

"This is a reform paper. We don't take ads from our enemies."

"One."

"So sign the petition." De Cosmos darted across the room and riffled through the drawers of his desk. "The union of the two colonies is an economic necessity," he said. "If we join the commercial possibilities of Victoria with the agricultural and industrial possibilities of the mainland we will raise the British possessions on the Pacific Coast from the level of frontier culture to the high standard of England's civilization. Here it is. Sign."

Matthew took the pen and wrote his name.

"We destroyed the archaic monopoly of the Hudson's Bay Company with a petition to the Colonial Office, and now we'll unite British Columbia and Vancouver Island the same way. Then it will be Douglas's turn. Representational government is —"

"And now you will take my advertisement."

"Two dollars a month. Run it every issue."

Matthew counted out the bills while De Cosmos unfolded the paper gingerly. "Galer Mills ... Burrard Inlet, eh? Didn't know anyone lived out there. Takes a man of conviction to —" He glanced at the press, dropped the paper on his desk, and scuttled back to his work. "A common nail ..." He twisted the roller brutally.

"Do you know when the *Tynemouth* will dock?" Matthew asked.

De Cosmos smirked. "Petticoat-chaser, eh?"

Matthew shook his head. "Not interested for myself, but half the men from my mill come all the way across the straits just to catch a glance of a white woman."

The editor shook his head woefully. "Foolish notion, sending bits of fluff halfway round the world without prospects. Should have arranged husbands for 'em first. But they'll be grabbed up quick enough, I suppose. Treacherous bloody ornaments; worse than machines. . . . I wrote that story up yesterday. Paper's by the door; it's on the house."

Matthew grabbed a news-sheet from the top of the pile and plunked a nickel onto the counter.

"I'll have to make a trip to Burrard Inlet and inspect this Galer Mills of yours," De Cosmos said. " 'Progress in the Wilds'. Human-interest stuff, you understand."

Matthew stepped out into the grey drizzle and riffled through the paper.

The Petticoats Have Arrived!

September 17, 1862.

Today we boarded the steamer *Tynemouth* at Esquimalt Harbour and inspected the cargo. The ladies are mostly cleanly, well-built, pretty looking young women—ages varying from fourteen to an uncertain fig- ure. Taken altogether, we are highly pleased with the appearance of the invoice. They will be brought to Victoria and quartered in the Marine Barracks, James Bay, tomorrow at noon.

It's mine . . . give it back.

Water. Please?

How can I wear this?

Can't anyone spare some water?

The rats have chewed it.

It's so dark.

I'm scared.

Rain and rain and rain.

We'll all be raped.

Mamma—

Stop whimpering.

. . . so dark.

Abby curled into the shadows of her bunk and listened to the clamour billowing around her. The pain in her head was building fast, and the effect was like knitting needles sliding under her right eyelid and up into her skull. She shuddered and her eye drooped and turned, aiming itself grotesquely at her upper lip. She reached under her pallet, pulled out a flask of Black Drop — laudanum — and carefully measured eighty drops into a tin mug. The liquid quivered in her cup with the roll of the ship; it was dark crimson, the colour of blood, and it slithered down her throat like syrup.

Escape. Abby drifted peacefully, wrapped in the dry softness of cotton wool, lulled by ocean waves, snug and serene, on the last leg of her journey to the New World. The New World. The words tripped off her tongue bright and clean like polished silver, and she smiled. They were pregnant words and they conjured an image of men and women sprouting full-grown from the earth with no past and an unlimited future. She thought of her mother, a prostitute, who had died of syphilis, propped against the wall of a roofless cubicle in Spitalfield Street, dreaming of escape from London's slums, when Abby was only six. How she had hated the woman. It was only now, twelve years later, with London an ocean and a continent away, that she could forgive her mother for the countless groggy hours she had spent on her knee sewing fingers for gloves, the back of her dress pinned to the old woman's apron, the reek of gin wafting over her shoulder, jumping in fear at the sudden slaps across her ear when she began nodding off to sleep. There would be no Spitalfield in the New World; of that she was certain.

Slowly Abby pushed herself up from the bunk and gripped the floor with her toes to keep from floating up to the ceiling. The portholes were wide open, but still the air was rank with the smell of sixty women who had been locked in the dark for one hundred days. She edged down the narrow passageway; everywhere there seemed to be elbows, breasts, and feet dangling from upper berths; corsets, crinolines, oval hoops, and open trunks blocked her path. The chatter and shrieks of the girls surged through her head like the swell of the sea. At the end of the cabin she found a washtub and manoeuvred it back to her bunk. As she bent to place it on the floor someone bumped her from behind, and the tub slipped from her fingers, clattered to the ground, and rolled at her feet. Abby screamed.

The recollection was instantaneous and hellish. One night, a week after they had rounded Cape Horn, she had taken her nightly dose of laudanum and snuggled into her bunk as the ship began to roll. In the hold beneath her a five-hundred-gallon water tank had been stored on top of a load of iron rails. The storm worsened. The huge metal drum broke free from its moorings, clattered across the rails, and slammed into the bulkhead with a hollow boom that reverberated throughout the ship like thunder. All night Abby had lain, limp and pale, staring into the blackness, paralysed, mesmerized, obsessed. She held her breath, anticipating each explosion of sound, until she was gasping for air.

The noise stopped. The ship vanished and Abby stepped out onto a vast plain of pure white sand. She was alone. In every direction an indistinct horizon blended into white sky. Then the sound began again, distant and muted. It increased in volume, each blast louder than the one before, until the plain shook and Abby fell to her knees and covered her ears. Time stretched endlessly. She could taste the sound—it tasted of metal—she could smell it—it smelled of smoke—but nothing appeared. The horror of it was the anticipation, the expectation, the waiting.

Abby had awoken with a scream that was choked off by a flood of vomit. The ship was still.

Matthew stalked onto the wharf, thumbs hooked in his belt, planks crackling under caulk boots. People moved out of his way. He turned and scanned the scene. Thousands of men stood staring out to Laurel Point. They were from Victoria, Esquimalt, and Nanaimo, and from the mainland: New Westminster, Fort Langley, Boston Bar, Hope, Yale, the Cariboo; some had travelled for weeks, tramping from the headwaters of unnamed creeks, sliding down mountains, and funnelling into the Fraser, abandoning their gold to vie for the rarest commodity of all—women.

Matthew saw only three ladies, their arms hitched tightly round their husbands'. The rest of the crowd was men; they clogged the beaches, the roads, the wharf; they clung to trees and to rooftops, and filled the length of Government Street with a sea of anxious faces. The crowd was hushed. Members of the Victoria Band lined the wharf with their instruments dangling absently from their fingertips. Everyone stood silently, shoulder to shoulder, lips parted, faces wet in the light drizzle, holding their breaths, staring at the grey horizon.

Abby peeled off her underclothes. She had worn them for a

hundred days and they stuck to her skin, leaving bits of white cotton. The chaperone, an ugly old widow named Mrs. Robb, held up a grey blanket while Abby stepped into the tub, anchoring herself to the edge of a bunk with one hand. Hot water slithered soapily over her body. She was eighteen, tall and shapely, with large breasts and pale skin. Her hair was light blonde and it hung about her shoulders in thick curls.

She peeked over the edge of the blanket and looked at Mrs. Robb. The woman fascinated her; her face was a complex cluster of fleshy pads criss-crossed by purple veins. Her nose was an inverted turnip and her ears stuck out from her bonnet like large raw slices of red ham. Mrs. Robb smiled up at her and Abby ducked back behind the blanket. "Hurry up, dear; my arms are getting tired."

Abby scrubbed her face vigorously. She was not vain but she was grateful for her face, particularly in her present circumstances. She had delicate cheekbones, a small mouth and nose, and a high, broad forehead. Her eyes were by far her most striking feature; they were large and oval, black with a thin iris of green, and the laudanum gave them a lustre. Mrs. Robb had simperingly called them bedroom eyes.

"Abigail, dear," the old woman whispered.

"Yes, Mrs. Robb?"

"Lately I have been thinking of what will become of you in this savage wilderness. There are so few women and you are such a pretty girl I'm certain you will be married straight off, and there's something I've been wanting to warn you about, about . . . well, about your wedding night."

Abby stopped scrubbing.

Mrs. Robb lowered her voice even more. "You see, dear, as a wife you will have certain duties, certain obligations, which may at first seem disagreeable, even distasteful, but you must prepare yourself to bear these inconveniences with decorum."

"Like what?" Abby asked.

"Well, for one thing"—Abby strained to hear Mrs. Robb's whisper—"your handsome young man (and I'm certain he will be handsome) will insist that you remove *all* of your clothing."

"No!" Abby peeked over the blanket.

Mrs. Robb blushed, but Abby noted the twinkle in her eye. "Yes," she said, shaking her head sadly. "It's true. And there's more. Hurry up, dear, there are other girls to instruct besides yourself."

Abby ducked back behind the blanket and strained to keep the laughter out of her voice. "What more?"

"Well" — Mrs. Robb's voice rose in pitch — "then he too will remove his clothes, *all* of them, and both of you will be, so to speak, in the pink."

Abby snickered.

"What, dear?"

"Nothing, Mrs. Robb." She bent double and clasped her sides to keep from laughing out loud. Though still a virgin, she had heard countless versions of this tale whispered by the orphanage girls late at night amid snickers and giggles, but never had she heard it related with such gravity.

"Then he will do certain things to your body — to your *naked* body — which of course I am not at liberty to discuss in detail." Mrs. Robb sniffed piously. "But rest assured that, although his treatment of you may at first seem unpleasant and vulgar, such is the common lot of a married woman. At such times it is often a good idea to think of other things: perhaps the household chores you will do the next day, or your needlework. In time his demands, his *lusty* demands" — Mrs. Robb paused to savour the word — "will grow less distasteful to you. Indeed, some women even grow to take a mild pleasure in these nightly pressings of flesh against flesh, or so I am told. All finished, dear?"

Abby was disappointed. This was not how it had been described in the lewd French novels Audrey had smuggled into the orphanage and read in hushed whispers to the wide-eyed girls in the dormitory. There the heroine inevitably "panted and thrashed joyously as her voluptuous bosom heaved in ecstasy". Needlework indeed!

The towel rubbed hotly over her skin, sending sparks shooting up her arms and legs. Abby shrugged. She would disregard Mrs. Robb's version. The French novels seemed much preferable. As she wrapped the towel around her breasts, she wondered how some of the younger, more impressionable girls would take the old woman's warning. Melissa, for example, would be terrified by such a tale. "Have you told Melissa this?"

"Oh yes. Yes, of course." Mrs. Robb whipped the blanket over her arm. "But I haven't told Trudy yet. I must do so right away."

And she hurried down the dark passageway, anxious to tell the tale yet again.

Abby unwrapped the new shift and bloomers, donated tearfully by the headmistress of the orphanage, and slipped them on. It hadn't been a bad place, she thought. Not a bit like the scandalous orphanages Dickens wrote about; and the headmistress had been truly fond of her. Granted, it was there her headaches had begun and she had started to take her daily doses of laudanum, but this hadn't stopped her from ingratiating herself quickly by tending the smaller children, doing extra jobs, and studying late into the night, until she knew more about English and art than her teacher. By the time she was old enough to be sent to work at a milliner's, she had become indispensable and the headmistress refused to let her go. And there she probably would have stayed, dreaming of a real home, growing into stultifying, bespectacled spinsterhood — respectable young men simply did not search for wives in an orphanage, as Audrey was continually pointing out — had it not been for the visit of Baroness Burdett-Coutts.

Abby had considered hiring herself out as a governess to a good family, but a week before the Baroness had come she received a woeful letter from Audrey, who had done exactly that, complaining she was a mindless slave without a minute to herself. When she wasn't tending the children or washing their clothes, she was forever attacking the endless mountain of needlework her mistress set before her, sewing nightcaps, day-dresses, play-clothes, dolls' dresses, bloomers, shifts, handkerchiefs, and tiny gloves, with never a single man in sight. At the mention of gloves, Abby dismissed any notions of becoming a governess.

And then the Baroness had arrived, sweeping through the orphanage in a rustle of black silk, on a wave of lilac perfume, her tireless voice like a silver bell ringing out the promises, the opportunities, the wonders of the New World: bountiful nature, fresh air, open spaces, burgeoning industry, equal opportunity, a new start — and men, plenty of handsome, young, ambitious, single men who didn't care two hoots if a woman was an orphan or a princess. Abby could not wait to leave.

Everyone had hated to see her go. During her last weeks the orphan girls had watched her with awe, as though she were already dead, a ghost, a mere body lingering stubbornly on, awaiting shipment to another world.

Mrs. Robb trundled back, looking angry and disappointed as Abby pulled her new whalebone corset out of its box. "Brazen strumpet," she muttered huffily. "Couldn't tell *her* a thing. Said she knew all about it. Here, give me that." She took the corset and wrapped it around Abby's middle.

While the old woman yanked mercilessly on the laces, Abby held onto a post and thought of the orphanage. She had drifted through the endless corridors — "Suck in your stomach, now" — teaching English and art — "Hold it" — hearing voices flitting out of half-open doors — "Breathe in" — "Yes, she's the one. Our Abby. Living among the savages" — "And out" — stumbling between a dream and reality, tighter and tighter, until the ship had come — "Once more" — and the voyage had begun — "There now. Thin as a pin."

Pinched and unable to bend, Abby prepared the great oval hoop and stepped into it. It was a portable fortress, formidable and inhibiting, which no man could breach unbidden. Petticoats: one, two, three. Then the best, the dress, unlike any she had ever known; it had been given to her by the Baroness herself. Each of the girls had received one, but Abby's was the nicest — maroon silk — and it rustled over her head, crisp and new. She gathered up the remaining charcoal sketches which she had done on the long voyage and stuffed them into her satchel. The portraits she had given away, but the anonymous drawings — gaunt, shadowy faces peering from the rabbit-warren of darkened bunks, a disembodied hand illuminated by the porthole light, the Reverend's back ascending into daylight — she had kept. She punched her old underwear into a ball and shoved it quickly out the porthole.

Moments before the *Tynemouth* passed Laurel Point, the sound of its engines filtered over the silent crowd and the shout went up from the men on the rooftops. "They're coming!" Hats flew into the rain. The cannon at the fort boomed. The men roared and the mob surged forward, sending those at the edge of the dock tumbling into the cold harbour, while the band blasted out a marching song. On the beach a mare panicked at the explosion of noise and ploughed through the crowd, churning men in her wake. Flowers appeared from everywhere; they were hurled forward, scooped up, and hurled again until the air rained colour and the black water was thick with a gaudy floating carpet.

Matthew watched the figurehead, a young woman with arched

back, vacant eyes, and wooden tresses curled over uplifted breasts, as it glided serenely, implacably, towards the bed of flowers. He smiled as a white ball popped out of a porthole, billowed, unfurled into bloomers, and bobbed in the wake of the ship.

The young women cowered from the rain, pulling themselves into the folds of their cloaks. They stood in pairs lined down the length of the deck, with Mrs. Robb and the Reverend in the lead. Some muttered prayers like incantations, others wept openly in great heaving sobs, their faces thrust up to the black clouds and rain, tears washing down their cheeks, while the rest stared, wide-eyed and pale, at the mob on the dock. Abby stood behind Mrs. Robb, snug and serene in her black velvet cloak and laudanum haze, feeling light and buoyant despite her fifty pounds of clothing, and smiled out at the New World. As the procession moved slowly towards the gangplank, Melissa began to scream.

Matthew and his neighbours pushed back, sending more men toppling into the ocean, and a narrow passageway opened up down the length of the wharf. At the end of it, steam wafted up from the tubs which had been set out in front of the Marine Barracks for the women to wash their clothes in. They started down the gangplank like a funeral procession. Fights erupted sporadically as the bachelors jockeyed for position, and Matthew braced himself against the shoving. As Abby stepped onto the dock, a chorus of men whistled. He watched her carefully. She was beautiful. And she was the only woman smiling.

Abby stared down the length of the gauntlet, amazed. They were actually waving fistfuls of money in front of the frightened girls. Grizzled faces with open, shouting mouths swam in her head. Hands reached at her out of the crowd. They'd gone mad. She laughed, reassured that there were plenty of potential husbands.

Which one to choose? Ahead, she saw a handsome, broad-shouldered man, standing half a foot above the rest, watching her intently, and she slowed her step. He stood firm and quiet in the frenzied crowd, his lips parted, smiling, smiling at her. She could not stop staring. Melissa shoved her anxiously from behind and she hurried ahead.

When she reached him, she pretended to stumble and fell against his chest.

He placed his hand on her arm.

She looked up into bright-green eyes and Matthew smiled down at her. "Willing?" she asked.

"Willing," he said.

With their hands clasped, Abby and Matthew stepped from the line and together they ran past a shocked Mrs. Robb and down the gauntlet to the sound of cheers and shouts. Those who had flowers left threw them at the fleeing couple. Abby's cloak whipped back as she ran, and the rain spotted the maroon silk and bled it to crimson.

Rain drummed on the deck of the ship, obscuring the planks in a wet, white haze. Abby felt her husband's arm circle round her waist. "Does it always rain like this?" she asked.

Matthew chuckled. "No. Only eight or nine months of the year."

Abby smiled. She liked the rain. It made her think of the snug homes of London and how, as a child, she had peered through dripping windows at cozy fires flickering over mahogany mantelpieces. She remembered the exhilarating smell of cool, damp air as she ran home after a shower, the heels of her shoes clicking over clean, slick cobblestones, and the delicious sensation of curling into a ball under her patchwork quilt in the orphanage and listening to the thrum of the storm on the roof. On sunny days she felt exposed, vulnerable. But she could lose herself in the rain.

The ship coasted slowly past Slahkayulsh Rock and poked her prow into the narrows, hugging the sheer rock face of Thoos. Seagulls plummeted out of nests wedged in the rocky ledges and swarmed around the ship. To the north the cold granite peaks of Sheba's Breasts jutted six thousand feet into the dark grey clouds.

The channel widened into Burrard Inlet and Matthew smiled with pride. This was his home: fold after fold of dark-green mountains, pleated like a rumpled accordion; iron-grey water ringed with the flame colours of autumn leaves; the rain; the sound of the saw, muted in the distance; and now Abby.

Just yesterday he had been single, walking the streets of Victoria, the hand of the beautiful stranger in maroon silk resting lightly in the crook of his arm. She had asked countless questions about his business, his past, his dreams, and he had answered her easily, comfortably, as if he had known her all his life. They had visited a chemist's shop where Abby had purchased laudanum from a plump, cheerful man behind the counter.

Early in the evening, as they passed the offices of Southwell and Honeybee, Matthew remembered why he had come to Victoria and hurried inside just as the doors were being locked. He arranged for the firm to act as his agent, bidding on overseas contracts through their office in San Francisco and selling his lumber at their warehouse in Victoria. Then they had walked to the harbour, where Matthew chartered a three-masted schooner to take them to Burrard Inlet after the ceremony the next day and return with his first load of lumber for general sale in Victoria. None of the men from his mill had found brides yet. They would make the trip alone.

In the evening they had dined off white linen at the Royal York. She had smiled at him through the glow of candlelight. Her laughter had sounded like the ring of fine crystal.

The rain had stopped. They walked through the cool evening air, savouring the scent of early autumn. To the west the sun hung low over the open ocean, turning the undersides of black rain clouds pale pink and deep orange. They had followed a brook upstream into the forest and watched fat raindrops collect on the rim of ochre-tinged leaves and plop into clear, still pools. Overhead, the orange harvest moon was plump and full. He had kissed her on the lips, there by the brook, and her mouth was cool and soft, and encouraging. But as he reached for the buttons at the back of her dress, old Mrs. Robb, who had followed them from the Royal York, had rushed around a bush, clucking like a mother hen, and whisked Abby away. "Time enough for that after you're proper wed," she threw back over her shoulder, and Matthew was alone, red-faced and blushing, the sound of the brook chuckling at his feet.

They had been married in the morning in a mass ceremony with thirteen other couples. The minister who had accompanied the brides officiated, Governor Douglas acted as a sort of congregational best man, and Mrs. Robb, shocked and bewildered because it was all happening so fast, diddled in the aisle, straightening dresses and doling out handkerchiefs. Even she was being courted; a toothless old Mexican who worked in the northern gold-fields had tried to pinch her bottom three times, despite her enormous bustle, and she was seriously considering his proposal.

At the last moment someone had suggested that thirteen couples might be an unlucky number to marry at once, so an additional pair, caught in the excitement of the moment, jumped up from their pew and joined the line at the altar. The congregation had cheered and stamped their feet under the pews, drowning out the sound of the rain on the roof. The ceremony proceeded: vows were exchanged *en masse*, rings were produced — some donated by spectators on the spur of the moment — and everyone had adjourned to the Governor's residence for a grand reception hosted by the city.

Matthew and Abby had slipped away early and run through the downpour to their ship at the dock, where they stood on the deck, shivering in the rain, waving at the few revellers who had braved the torrent to shower them with flowers and rice. The schooner cast off, glided over the black waters of James Bay, and turned towards the mountains of the mainland and the lush rain forests of Burrard Inlet.

"What's that?" Abby pointed at the south shore of the inlet.

"Cains's mill," Matthew said. "Jonas Cains. He's British. Never met him myself. I've gone over a few times to say hello, but he's always off on the island. Carky says he's got a store over in Victoria."

"Carky?"

"He's my foreman — a crabby old Scot. You'll meet him soon enough. He used to work for Cains, till he came over to my mill last year. Half my men used to work over there, but the old buzzard doesn't pay them near what they're worth and the living conditions aren't fit for animals, so sooner or later they all come to Galer Mills. Saves me a lot of trouble finding loggers."

Abby held her hand over her eyes to block out the rain and squinted at Cains's mill. A low wall of mud-brown brick hunched on the small rise at the back of the grassy bank. "Is that a house they're building?"

Matthew glanced at the southern shore. "Reckon."

"Then they'll be moving here permanently."

Matthew nodded and stared straight ahead.

Abby watched the south shore in silence. Neighbours. She hadn't expected it. Here, at the end of the world, in the middle of the wild rain forest, almost a full day's sail from the tiny village of Victoria, they were going to have neighbours.

"Hey!" Matthew's hand jerked against her waist. "You're supposed to be interested in the north side of the inlet. This is where we're going to live." He smiled as the ship slipped past the mouth of the Homulcheson and the mill-site spread before them. There it was, Galer Mills, *his* mill, perched on a narrow tidal flat at the foot of the mountains, a small spot of brown in the vast greenness of the mainland forest. A collection of cedar buildings—storage sheds, bunkhouses, a cook-shack, and an office—ranged around the huge two-storey saw-house. The flume entered the clearing from the northeastern mountains and raced down to the water-wheel. One by one the flotilla of logs corralled in the shallow water were grabbed by steel teeth and jerked brutally up the ramp and into the mouth of the sawmill. Over it all was the sound of the saw, screaming, screaming.

As the schooner approached, a bell on the wharf clanged. Men hurried out of the mill, out of the forest, and clustered on the dock. They stood motionless, hats in hand, mouths gaping, staring at the first white woman to arrive at Burrard Inlet.

Matthew waved and Abby did the same. The men cheered. Money changed hands. Most of it went to a grizzled old man who stood cackling on the dock in his shirt-sleeves, rain dripping from the coarse grey stubble crusting his face. Matthew chuckled to himself as the old magpie stuffed the bills into his shirt and looked furtively up at the docking ship. "You been makin' money off my wife, you old maggot?" Matthew yelled over the rail as the ship lurched and creaked against the timbers of the dock. The men roared.

" 'Tis you yourself and no your wife who's made me a rich man today, Matthew Galer. I've been tellin' 'em you'd be comin' back with a braw bonnie lassie for a wife, but they'd no believe me."

The gangplank was lowered and Matthew escorted Abby to the dock. "May I present the first lady of Burrard Inlet: Mrs. Abigail Galer." The men cheered as Abby made an exaggerated curtsey. "Well, what do you think, Carky?"

The old man appraised her as though she were a load of lumber. "A bit pinched around the middle . . ."

"I'll warn you," Abby said. "I've a nasty right hook."

". . . but a bonny enough lass, I'll reckon." Carky bowed and again Abby curtseyed.

"The show's over," Matthew bellowed. "I want this ship loaded by tomorrow."

The men drifted back to their jobs, but Carky remained. "There's been a wee problem while you were away," he said.

"What?"

"Rustlin'. We've lost a hundred logs."

"Jeesus," Matthew swore. "Place a twenty-four-hour guard on the pen. I'll see you in the office after dinner." He grabbed Abby's wrist and led her up the hill.

"Would you like to see the mill?" he asked.

Abby raised her eyebrows. She had expected to be shown her new home first, but Matthew was rushing ahead.

"Over here's the bull pen." The sound of water drowned out his voice as they passed under the flume which towered thirty feet above them, supported on wooden struts. "I've got two teams of eight bulls working in the eastern hills today, plus these four spares."

Abby stared at the great black beasts, their hides slick and shiny in the rain, as they wallowed through a sticky gumbo of mud and manure behind their stout log fence. "That's wonderful," she said drily.

Matthew nodded. "Over there's the bunkhouses." Abby wiped the rain from her face as she trudged behind him. He pointed to a row of small weathered-grey cabins tucked in a grove of poplar at the western edge of the clearing. "There's a potbelly in each one," he said proudly. "Four men to a bunkhouse and each one's got his own bed. No muzzle-loading here."

Abby nodded wisely. "What's that?" She pointed at thin wisps of smoke curling up out of a circle of stovepipes set in the ground.

"Coal pit," Matthew said. "It's a hole about eight feet deep and twelve across. We load it with wood, set it on fire, then cover it with a half-foot of dirt, except for a couple of these smoke-holes, so's the wood inside just smoulders; then in eight or ten days we'll have coal for the blacksmith's shop. Come on, I want to show you the cook-shack."

And so he led her through the complex assortment of buildings: from the narrow dining hall, with its long row of rough plank tables, to the steamy blacksmith shop, where the bellows wheezed and home-made coals glowed fiercely in the darkness, past steel saw blades stacked like rows of crocodile teeth against the walls of the filing room, through workshops where pitch stumps burned under upturned kettles and long strips of beef-hide, the hair still on one side, were stitched into belts to run the pulleys and drums, to his own small office cluttered with damp paper and an open cash box, and the small company store where his men could buy anything from straight razors to tin pants. He led her through the muddy compound, oblivious to the pouring rain and her drenched clothing, which now weighed close to one hundred pounds.

Finally they came to the saw-house itself. Abby stared up at the torrent of water flooding from the open end of the flume into the buckets of the huge wooden water-wheel. "She's twenty-four feet in diameter," Matthew shouted over the roar, "and supplies enough power for two muley-rigged sash saws and an edger. We're cutting five thousand feet a day right now." The water-wheel thundered and groaned as it ground in its slow, steady circle. "Come on, I'll show you."

Inside, the mill was dark. Men moved through the shadows, watching from the corners of their eyes as Abby studied the complex network of cogs and gears which meshed like the inside of a giant clock. Matthew explained the workings to her, but the meaningless words washed over her like the rumble of water in the buckets outside as she stared in awe at the gears. Each one was made of wood and every cog — hundreds of them — had been carved by hand and inserted into holes drilled along the edges of the wheels. "Did you make all this yourself?" she asked.

Matthew grinned. "Mostly. Come here; I want you to meet some of the men. Bull Thompson there's my edger-off. Al Carson sets fractions on the carriage. Chino's off-bearer and slabman and Scotty runs the dolly." As Matthew pointed out each man, he glanced shyly in her direction, then turned back to his work. "Now then, would you like to see the shingle saw? It's down in the basement —"

Abby placed her hand on Matthew's arm. "Could we see it later? I'd really like to get out of these wet clothes."

Matthew glanced down at her soggy, mud-spattered dress and nodded. He could put it off no longer. "Sure," he muttered. He led her out of the mill and across the yard, his feet dragging through layers of wet sawdust, and onto a steep trail that led into the eastern woods. They walked hand in hand, uphill, past the smooth, straight trunks of cedar trees. The ground was dry under the tangled canopy of branches. Abby's shoes slipped on the thick carpet of sheddings.

As they crested the hill, a tiny log structure appeared, tucked in a small clearing overlooking the inlet. In the distance black clouds scudded over the grey water. The cabin was low and squat, with a sloping, moss-covered roof. There were no windows.

Abby bit her tongue and tried to smile as Matthew pushed open the narrow door. "Course, I wasn't expecting company; it's a bit of a mess."

His voice sounded light, flippant, but Abby noted the nervous quaver. "Will you carry me across the threshold?"

"Of course, of course," he said. He bent down and scooped her up in his arms, straining under the weight of her rain-drenched clothing. The metal hem of her enormous hoop skirt sprang up around her legs like a tent. Matthew stepped forward but the wire frame wedged against the narrow door. He twisted her sideways, his face serious and intent, but her dress snagged on a nail. Abby began to giggle. Awkwardly, Matthew balanced her on his knee and unhooked the skirt with his free hand. He tried again, backing through the door and easing her body into the small room until only the bottom of the great metal cage remained outside, sprung tight against the door frame. They were stuck. Abby was shaking with laughter and Matthew too began to chuckle. He started to pull. "Wait!" Abby cried. She released her arms from around his neck, leaned forward, and squeezed the hoop into a narrow oval. Matthew tugged, and together they popped into the cabin, laughing uncontrollably.

Gently he set her on her feet in the centre of the small, dark room and hurried to light a coal-oil lantern. Her laughter dissolved as orange light flickered over the log walls. Matthew stood nervously in a corner, stooped at the shoulders so his head wouldn't bump against the low ceiling, and studied Abby's face as she looked around. The floor was hard-packed dirt, and the single room was so small her enormous hoop skirt filled half of it. Rain dripped through a hole in the roof, plopping noisily into a tin bucket. There were two pieces of furniture: a small pine table and a narrow rope-frame bed with a straw mattress. The room smelled of sweat and mildew, and Abby decided the source of the odour was the heap of dirty clothes on the rickety table.

She stared at the dark, windowless log walls and strained to keep her voice light. "Well," she said, "at least I won't have to worry about making curtains."

Matthew rushed to her and took her hands in his. "I'm so sorry, Abby." The words flooded out of him. "I wasn't expecting a wife, truly I wasn't. I only went along with the other men, but when I saw you ... I'll build you a fine house, a grand house. You'll want for nothing. I'll put it up on the hill with — "

Abby placed a finger lightly on his lips and watched his face until the furrows faded from his brow. She wrapped her arms around him. His lips pressed against her mouth, his tongue soft and warm against hers, and his hands fumbled over the long string of buttons down her back. The maroon silk slipped easily over her head. Her hands moved under his shirt, over the fine brown hair of his chest, round to the hard muscles of his back.

He removed all three of her petticoats in one motion and pressed against the wire cage as his fingers searched for the clasp at her waist. He could not work it. She eased herself away and unhooked the tiny lock. The wire hoop hinged open. Abby stepped out.

"You're beautiful," Matthew said.

She turned her back to him and lifted her heavy blonde hair as he unlaced the long whalebone corset. His hands slid underneath and encountered more cloth. His mouth moved along her neck and the soft hairs of his moustache tickled her ear. She turned and kissed him again, peeking through half-closed eyes at the soft light glowing on his long lashes. She slid the damp shirt from his shoulders and traced the muscles tapering down his sides to the buttons of his pants. The chemise slipped over her head and she shivered as the rough calluses of his hands moved gently over her bare breasts. He eased her drawers down her legs and she held his shoulders while he unbuttoned her kid leather boots and pulled them off. Then she was in his arms again and he eased her onto the narrow rope bed, balancing precariously above her while he removed her garters and slowly rolled the white silk stockings down her legs.

She watched him as he stood to remove his pants. "The bed's lice-free," he said stupidly. She studied the shocking tan line as he peeled off his trousers. His legs were white, streaked with soft brown hair.

At last they were naked on the narrow straw mattress and she felt his soft-hard body, warm and gentle against hers. She closed her eyes and breathed deeply. He smelled of summer, of rich black earth, of cedar and freshly mowed hay. When she opened them again he was watching her; she saw the look of wonder, of awe, on his face as he studied her, and she knew that she loved him.

Out of the corner of her eye she saw the dull orange glow of the coal-oil lamp reflecting in the shiny bands of the great open crinoline. It's not like Mrs. Robb said at all, she thought. She reached up, hugged him tight against her, and sank back into the hushed comforting sound of rain drumming on the roof.

The rustling of logs stopped; the guard was disbanded. The men drifted back from Victoria; three of them had landed brides from the *Tynemouth*. Matthew built three trim cottages, spaced in a wide arc around the edge of the clearing, and leased them to the married men.

Snow appeared on the upper slopes and slowly inched down the mountains week by week, until it hovered a few hundred feet above the mill. The rain was incessant.

The Galers settled into a routine. Every morning at four-thirty they slipped through the muck, Matthew to his office and Abby to the cook-shack. She hadn't been asked to work, but it made her feel a part of the mill. At a quarter to six the mob descended, vulture-like, silent, bleary-eyed, and sullen; they did not speak but ate furiously — fresh bread, eggs and bacon, flapjacks, coffee — and when the first scream of the saw began at six they were gone in a rush, leaving Abby and the cook with the carnage of another meal.

At nine she walked to Matthew's office and spent the morning writing in the ledger, counting cash, and putting the mill's books in order. She quickly realized that the enormous house Matthew was building on the hill was devouring more than the small profit they were making from the local lumber trade. Matthew had taken out a loan on his ship the *Cariboo Fly*. When she protested, he had laughed and refused to discuss it. Although Abby dearly loved the house, she did not want it to ruin them, but Matthew was obsessed with fulfilling her dream of a home of her own. Indeed, one evening, when she had asked which of the rooms she could use for her painting, he had leaned back in his chair and looked at her quizzically. "I hadn't thought of that," he

had said. The next day construction began on a two-storey hex-
agonal tower, which would rise up the western side of the house.
The top floor of the tower would be glass all round — "So you'll
have proper light and a decent view," he had said — and there
she would paint.

Abby understood why Matthew had begun talking of expanding the mill; they would need the money.

At noon she would slam the ledger shut and rush up the hill
for the precious half-hour when the men working on the house
would lay down their hammers and she was free to roam, undisturbed, through the myriad of half-built rooms: parlour, drawing
room, dining room, library, bedrooms, storage rooms, kitchen,
sewing room, sunroom. A verandah stretched around three sides
of the house, and on the slope of the roof was the skeleton frame
of an "observation deck" — Abby hated the term widow's walk —
facing the open sea. She would climb the stairs to the western
tower and there she would stand, with the wind whistling
through the eyeless sockets where the windows would go, and
gaze out at the grey inlet and the wild black clouds. Across the
water, the brick house of Jonas Cains was nearly complete.

In the afternoon, when the bang of the hammers jangled her
nerves, she would gather up her sketch pad and her bottle of
Black Drop and slip into the forest to search for a quiet dry spot
under the dripping trees.

Sometimes, in the evenings, they walked along the shore, warm
in each other's arms, watching the stars, listening to the rasp of
the ocean. When the rain was too heavy, they huddled in their
small cabin, propped on straw pillows on the new rope bed
which Matthew had made, and read old newspapers by lamplight:
"Smallpox Kills 20,000 Indians", "General Lee Routed at Poto-
mac", "Camels Used on Fraser Canyon Road Construction",
"Indians Murder Whites on Saturna Island", "Lincoln Frees
Slaves", "Union of Vancouver Island and British Columbia
Blocked by Governor", "Amor De Cosmos Elected to Assembly",
"Transcontinental Railway — Possibility or Pipe Dream?"

In the spring they sailed to Victoria on the *Cariboo Fly*. While
Abby visited the chemist's shop, Matthew ordered a steam engine, boiler, and circular-saw blade from Southwell and Honeybee. When they returned, two hundred logs were missing.

Matthew ordered a brand made and as each tree was felled it
was emblazoned with the initials GM. Again a guard was posted

on the pen and again the rustling stopped. Matthew fumed.

When the first heat of summer began, the steam engine arrived. The saw-house was widened, the new blade was installed, and nine more men were hired to tend it. Production doubled. Lumber began to accumulate unsold on the dock. By winter the wharf pilings were creaking and the beaches were lined with stacks of timber.

"We've got to develop export markets." Matthew paced the office. "San Francisco, Hawaii, Australia; they need our lumber."

Carky shrugged. "Well, I dinna see 'em beatin' at the door to get it."

"Because they don't know we're here."

"What about that Sopwell and Honeytree — "

"Southwell and Honeybee," Matthew snapped. "They say we're a bad risk. The first captain they sent couldn't find the entrance to the inlet for fog and the second claimed it was too shallow."

"The channel's plenty deep enough by the southern shore."

"You and I know that, and the local sailors know it, but now we've got to convince the world's ship captains."

"And how will you be doin' that, Matthew Galer?"

Matthew stared out the office window at the neat stacks of freshly cut timber being loaded onto a ship across the inlet. "How does Cains do it? He's got one there now all the way from damn China; last month it was Argentina. How the hell does *he* do it?"

"Went and got himself an agent in San Francisco last spring," Carky replied.

"How do you know that?"

"Well, I dinna ken for sure, laddie. Just a wee bit of scuttlebutt I been hearin' by-and-by — from some a them men what quit him last month to hire on here. Makes sense though. He's been a-sailin' most a his damn nasty life and oughta be in thicker'n spit with dozens a them smart agentin' fellas what works for them big shippin' lines and can be sendin' a ship near anywheres they damn well please."

Matthew stared across the water at the ship from China and looked at his own stacks of unsold lumber shimmering in heat waves on his dock. "I'm going to San Francisco," he said. "I'll meet with these shipping agents myself, and the presidents of the major lines too. I'll need a dozen charts of the area and I want soundings done on the narrows."

"Aye," Carky said. "And when will you be goin'?"

"Not till next month. Southwell has promised us another try — a schooner out of Chile called the *Valparaiso* — and I want to be here to see it loaded. Pray it makes it through the narrows, Carky, or it can do us more harm than good."

Carky moved towards the door.

"One more thing," Matthew said.

"Aye?"

"I'll be going to Victoria tomorrow on the *Cariboo Fly*."

Carky stood thoughtfully in the doorway. "And is it a long time you'll be gone?"

"About a week." Still Carky did not move. "Mrs. Galer will be going too."

"Aye, sir." The door closed silently.

Matthew turned back to the window and the piles of greying timber stretched along his beach, and smiled. Everything was going according to plan.

He hurried out of the office and down to the shore, where a stone-faced Indian woman, cloaked in cedar, sat silently in a canoe, bobbing in the lee of the wharf. He leaned over and whispered, "Tomorrow at sunset," then pushed the dugout back into the inlet.

Early the next morning, Abby and the three other brides from the *Tynemouth* chattered excitedly about the long shopping lists tucked in their dress pockets as they tilted their big hoop skirts and squeezed down the narrow passage between the piles of sawn lumber on the wharf. The light drizzle stopped, and the women pushed back the hoods of their cloaks and applauded a delicate spot of blue that had appeared in the southern sky. Matthew helped them aboard and waved to the captain in the wheelhouse. The steam whistle shrieked and, as the faint spot of blue spread slowly across the sky and the bright yellow sun glared through, the *Cariboo Fly* eased away from the dock and aimed her bow at the high rocky ledges of Thoos.

Instead of crossing directly to Victoria, the ship swung wide across Ayyulshun Bay, skirted the shore to the wide, silty mouth of the Fraser Delta, then chugged upriver to New Westminster.

Matthew kissed Abby full on the lips, amid snickers and giggles from the other young wives, and leapt to the wharf. He stood on the dock and waved until the *Cariboo Fly* had turned in the current, coasted downriver, and vanished around a bend.

He hurried through the town; it was early afternoon. The English fashions and courtly manners of the ladies clogging the boardwalks looked incongruous in the wild and muddy clearing of New Westminster — Stump Town. Everything — sidewalks, houses, hotels, saloons — had been thrown up in a rush over the butts and trunks of fallen trees. There were no streets, just irregular open spaces potted with holes and barbed with the scrag ends of trees jutting up from the mud. There was no order; sporadic spots of graded road suddenly dropped six feet to the next level, boardwalks ended in the middle of a block, saloons obstructed what should have been thoroughfares.

He looked to the east, at the spot where Gustaf's cabin had stood. The town now covered it. He smiled sadly as he thought of the rusty gang saw he had found abandoned on the banks of the Fraser and how he had restored it and used it to cut the timber for the three small cottages he leased to the married men.

The raucous sounds of Stump Town faded as Matthew strode through the woods along Douglas Road. It was early afternoon. Occasional sightseers returning from Deer Lake cantered by on horseback, waving and splashing mud in their wake. The wind blew down from his mountains and the forest rustled, shaking summer rain from its upper branches; clouds shredded and scudded southwards. He was glad the night sky would be clear.

The road ended at a shallow, swampy lake. Matthew skirted it and continued north on a trail overgrown with salmonberry and skunk cabbage. Shortly before sunset he slid down a bank near to Cains's mill and crouched on the southern shore of Burrard Inlet.

Across the water his mill rumbled and screamed as logs banged up out of the pen and into the saw-house. To the west the remaining shards of cloud glowed pink, then orange, then red behind the silhouette of trees. The saw stopped. Men filed out of the woods and the mill, their tired voices floating over the water on the wind. Lamplight glowed faintly from the cook-shack. The inlet was dark.

Matthew did not see the canoe until it was almost on shore; the stone-faced Indian seemed to loom up from the water, black against black, and paddled to the beach in silence.

Matthew crouched in the bow as they glided quietly across the inlet. The water was black, like ink, and it flickered in the moonlight, wind-chopped, lapping at the canoe, reflecting stars that blinked on and off in the waves. He gripped the edge of the shallow dugout as it rolled sickeningly and water splashed over his knuckles. He could not unclasp his hands; he shut his eyes and bit into his tongue. The wind dried the sweat from his face.

On the northern shore he splashed into the shallow water a short distance from the log boom and took the rifle the Indian handed him. He smiled and nodded his thanks, but there was no reply. The canoe eased away from shore and disappeared in the blackness.

Matthew waited. About midnight he heard the faint chug of a steamship west of the mill. It stopped. The wind whistled through the silence. A rowboat appeared, grey in the moonlight, and pitched its way toward the mill. When he looked back to the pen, the silhouette of a man stood on the boom. He had unfastened the chains and was herding logs through an opening with a peavey. Matthew crept closer, his eyes wide with anger. While the man bent over his work, Matthew sprang onto the boom, darted over the logs to the deep end, and aimed his rifle.

The rowboat stopped. Matthew sighted down the barrel. Two iron points centred on the man's back. "Don't move," he shouted. The man whirled around. Matthew flinched and his gun lowered. It was Carky.

The Scotsman cursed and hobbled over the boom, ducking his head and darting left and right. Matthew snapped the gun back to his shoulder.

A shot rang out from the rowboat and thudded into the log between Matthew's feet as Carky jumped to the beach and disappeared into the underbrush at the edge of the inlet. He crouched. A second shot ripped through his right arm in a spray of blood and bone, slamming him backwards and into the water.

The salt water, cold and black, seared his arm and flowed into his mouth. He thrashed, reaching for the log boom with his left arm. "Abby!" he screamed. He could hear the fading rustle of bushes as Carky fled through the forest, then the chug of the steamship as the engines turned over and the rustlers raced away from the mill. "Abbyyy!" His heavy caulk boots sucked him down as he strained and twisted, craning his head backwards, eyes wide and white, pleading, pleading for air. The inlet closed quietly over him.

Dream-like, Matthew ascended, rushing up through the blackness with a ringing in his ears. He felt cold and numb and drowsy. The ocean lapped at his body, stars whirled overhead, hands strained to pull him up. Air. He shivered and looked into the stone face and black eyes of Sitka.

Fog. Abby squirmed on the moss-covered log and straightened up from the picture on her lap. It was hopeless. She could not draw herself. Whenever she tried, grotesque lines stuttered across the paper. She had found the perfect location, a thin fragment of the inlet framed by cedar and salal with the far shore misty in the background, and in her imagination she could see herself clearly, in stern profile, blending with the trees, hands folded, face immutable, staring out at the water.

The woman on the paper was not her; it was not anyone she knew. The eyes were all wrong. She tried to fix them but the damp paper dissolved under the charcoal and left a gaping hole across her brow. She folded the sketch carefully, tucked it into her satchel, and wiped her fingers across her apron. With her hands clasped around her knees she pressed her cheek to the ugly black smudges and rocked back and forth.

Why must everything be a competition? Last night Matthew had told her about the trip to San Francisco and suggested she take her drawings to a gallery there. Until then she had enjoyed them, she was proud of them. Now they were a threat to her. He had turned her art into a contest which she was afraid to enter and afraid to lose.

The first twinges of pain flickered across her forehead. She pulled the Black Drop from her satchel, measured out the eighty drops, and stared into the cup at the deep-red liquid. Matthew didn't approve; he didn't nag her, but it was obvious from his stern looks and the way he tried to distract her whenever she reached for her medicine. Perhaps he's right, she thought. Her headaches had become less frequent, less severe. But still ... it was so comforting. She sipped the laudanum slowly, rocking on the log and humming softly.

The twinge of pain vanished. She grew light and drowsy as the warmth radiated down her arms and legs. Fog billowed in off the inlet, rolled over the ground, and curled around the tree trunks. She smiled and listened to the rush of water behind her from the flume which floated above the fog, supported on struts—struts built by Matthew—like the ghost of a railway track laid up the side of the mountain.

The forest was dank and dripping. It smelled of damp earth and rotting leaves. Slippery-looking ferns grew wetly up over decaying stumps, lichen hung like bunting from the branches around her, and trees crumbled under the sucking roots of their parasitic young. She sat with her head cradled in her hands, lost in a laudanum haze, and listened to the soft, spongy sound of growing moss. In the distance the gentle sigh of the ocean rose and fell in rhythm with her breathing. Over it all rolled the fog.

Twigs snapped behind her, then off to the side. Abby turned slowly and thought she saw a faint flicker of something duck behind a log on the far side of the clearing. A pine bough quivered next to it, though there was no wind. "Hello?" No one answered.

The faint snickering sound of a child's laughter echoed through the forest surrounding her, then slowly the fat, round face of a little girl rose up from behind the log.

Abby stared at the vision; the head floated free, disembodied, over the soft blanket of fog. "What's your name?" she asked.

The vision didn't answer. The little girl cupped her chin in her hands, propped her elbows on the log, and stared back at Abby, smiling like a forest elf, her large black eyes sparkling with mischief.

"Where did you come from?" The head began to sink back into the mist. A sharp guttural command came from somewhere near by, and Abby turned. A hazy figure stood at the edge of the woods. It drifted into the clearing, its legs obscured by fog. The twinkle vanished from the little girl's eye and she darted from behind the log and ran to the side of a tall, stern-looking Indian woman in a cedar-bark cloak.

Abby was shocked by the incongruity of the pair as they walked towards her. The woman looked big-boned, awkward, and homely, as though her features had been carved from old clay, but the child, whom Abby guessed to be about four, was beautiful. She had the big black eyes of the older woman but her complexion was fairer and her bone structure fine and delicate. The biggest difference was in their hair: the woman's was heavy, black, and coarse, like dead lichen, but the girl's was like a sunset, a deep, rich copper, streaked with bronze, gold, and flame.

Abby stood up. Although she had never seen her before, she knew at once that this was the stone-faced woman Matthew had talked about. "You must be Sitka," she said.

The woman nodded and pulled the child out from behind her. She was small and shy, and twisted uncomfortably at the end of her mother's arm. "This is Eva. My daughter."

Abby bent over her. "Hello, Eva."

The little girl squirmed and bit her lower lip. "Hello, Mrs. Galer."

"How old are you?"

Eva smiled, not understanding, wriggled back behind her mother's legs, and peeked out from behind the skirt of shredded cedar bark.

Abby brushed her hand across her forehead. "Would you like to come up to the house?" she asked. "I could make some coffee…"

Sitka shook her head and they stood in silence, looking at each other.

"I've been wanting to meet you," Abby said, "to thank you for saving my husband."

Sitka stared at the thick carpet of pine needles.

"Is there anything I can do for you?"

"You like children." It was a statement of fact.

Abby nodded. She hadn't really thought about it. Most of her life she had been surrounded by children and had taken them for granted. It was only now, in the isolation of the New World, that she had begun to miss them.

"Matthew said you are a teacher. Can you teach Eva to read and write?"

"Of course. I'd be delighted," Abby said. "Oh, we're leaving for San Francisco in a couple of days; we'll be gone a month, but we can start as soon as I get back."

"I will pay you," Sitka said.

"Oh no. Really. It's the least I can do."

Sitka reached into a basket hanging from her shoulder, pulled out a large piece of stone, and handed it to Abby.

It was a small, primitive rock carving, about three pounds in weight, rough and stained with age, of a crouching man with broad, flat features. An enormous phallus rose up to his chin. His lips were parted and his eyes large and vacant. Abby lifted it carefully with both hands. She turned it sideways and smiled.

Thin arms grew out the side of the penis and reached towards the man, and tiny fingers clasped him round the middle; it was a child sitting on his lap. She turned it again to the front; the child, as seen from this angle, was unquestionably meant to represent a very large male organ. The carving was old and spotted with lichen. The head was thrust back, neckless, stretching the lips into a thin, painful "O". The nostrils flared and oversized eyes bugged out of their sockets and stared blankly skywards.

"What is it?" Abby asked.

Sitka shrugged. "Stone Man."

Abby looked at it again, and as she studied it, it seemed to quiver in her hands and grow lighter. Her eyes widened, her lips parted, and she felt a strange sensation, not quite fear, but a tightening of the stomach. "It's beautiful," she said. "What does it mean?"

Again Sitka shrugged and shook her head, but her thick lips pressed into a small, sly smile.

"It's so old," Abby said. "Where did you find it?"

"Up there." Sitka pointed in the direction where the flume entered the forest. "On the mountain there is a place where the women of our tribe used to go — " She stopped. The bell at the end of the Galer Mills wharf clanged loudly. Sitka began to back across the clearing.

"It's just a ship," Abby said. The shouts of men echoed through the forest to the east as they ran unseen towards the mill. "Wait," Abby said. But it was too late.

Sitka grabbed Eva's hand and hurried across the clearing, pulling her daughter behind her, and the pair vanished into the forest. The fog curled in, blotting out the vacant green spot where they had disappeared.

Abby shook her head, cradled the rock statue in her arm and drifted through the woods, back towards the mill.

The saw had stopped. The clearing was silent and white with fog, the mill deserted. She noticed the office door swinging on its hinges and ran to it. "Matthew?" she called. No answer. Papers fluttered across his desk in the draft. She placed the Stone Man absently on top of them and closed the door behind her.

Abby stood on the wharf and peered into the fog, listening, listening. To the west she heard a muted crunch like a tree falling in the distance and ran along the shore towards it. Rocks forced her off the beach and she splashed through the shallow water towards the narrows.

As she rounded a point, the dim outline of a large schooner, grounded, tilted partly on its side, loomed up out of the fog in the shallow water at the mouth of the Homulcheson. Canoes and rowboats swarmed around it. Matthew appeared on the tilted deck, one arm in a sling, the other clutching the rail as he called to a man below, "We'll need a ship to get her off. Tell Johann to bring round the *Cariboo Fly*." His voice was low, venomous, brittle. The man hurried off along the beach.

Abby picked her way over the rocks towards a group of men on shore, dreading her first question. She asked the cook, "What ship?"

"The *Valparaiso*," he said. "Captain's drunk."

Abby folded the maroon silk dress — it was still her favourite — onto the pile of clothes in her trunk and ran her hands over its seams, smiling at the crisp, delicate feel of the material rustling under her fingertips, sending a delicious tickling sensation shivering up her arm. She poked at the lid and it fell with a heavy thud, then she turned and sat on the trunk to rest. San Francisco . . .

She wasn't sure they should be going at all. Matthew's arm was still raw and stiff; just yesterday he had presented her with a splinter of bone which he'd pulled out himself after it had worked its way to the surface. He'd placed it in her lap and smiled, like a cat bringing home a dead bird.

She thought of the rustling and of Carky, and the anger welled up in her again, hot and raging, making her heart thump against the tight walls of her corset. Carky was back across the inlet, working for Jonas Cains, who had paid him to spy on Galer Mills and rustle the logs, or so the gossip of the inlet went. God, how she wanted revenge, how she wanted him to pay for the pain in Matthew's arm, and for the terror she had felt when she heard how he had almost drowned, but Matthew would not hear of it. "It's over," he had said. "There'll be no more rustling. Besides," he had added, as if it explained everything, "Cains is British."

Shortly after her return from Victoria, Abby had travelled to New Westminster. She had told Matthew she was going shopping, but secretly she had gone to see the Chief Justice.

"And whom, exactly, do you accuse of shooting your husband?" he had asked.

"I don't know," Abby had said. "It was dark and the man was offshore in a boat, but we're certain he was hired by Jonas Cains."

"My dear Mrs. Galer," the Chief Justice chuckled, "we can hardly charge Captain Cains with hiring an unknown gunman to shoot your husband simply because you are certain it was so."

"All right," Abby snapped. "What about the rustler? We *know* who *he* is. My husband caught him pushing logs out of the pen. He's back working at Cains's mill now."

"And did anyone else see him steal these logs?"

"Yes," Abby said. "An Indian woman; she can identify him."

"An *Indian* woman?" The Chief Justice laughed out loud. "I am afraid, Mrs. Galer, that her testimony would not count for much. Indeed, I doubt that Judge Begbie would even allow her to take the stand. Why, they are savages, Mrs. Galer, and have no conception of truth or justice. They will say anything under oath. No, I am afraid it is out of the question. And so it is a stand-off — the word of your husband against that of this Carky fellow. Hardly a convincing case."

Abby glared at him and snatched her purse off his desk. The Chief Justice leaned forward, smiled sympathetically, and lowered his voice. "My dear Mrs. Galer," he said, "I don't doubt that a grave injustice has been committed against your husband — why, the wound in his arm is proof enough of that — but you must understand that, as you tell the story, a charge against this 'Carky fellow' would be tantamount to accusing Jonas Cains himself. Captain Cains is a wealthy and influential man, one of the most prominent of our frontier citizens, and his wife is said to be from an old and esteemed English family. Your case would require a great deal of proof, and all you can offer is the word of your husband — an honourable man I am sure, but not even a British subject — plus the testimony of a female savage who may or may not have seen something, from a great distance, in the dead of night, by the light of the moon. Hardly a watertight case." The Chief Justice shook his head sadly. "I am sorry, Mrs. Galer. But I can only recommend that you forget this unfortunate incident. Let it rest."

"Let it rest." Abby sighed. She pushed herself up from the trunk, walked to the bureau, and picked up her bottle of Black Drop. As she began to measure out the red-brown liquid, she glimpsed the rock carving Sitka had given her squatting on its haunches on a corner of her table and she stopped. Absently she replaced the glass stopper and set down the laudanum. She lifted the Stone Man carefully, the rough granite scraping her skin as she cradled him in both hands. She chuckled. How upset Matthew had been. He hadn't noticed it in the office until he reached for a piece of paper and it rolled across his desk. It had unnerved him. He had stormed up to the house, his face pale, and brandished it in front of her like a weapon. "What's this?" he had asked.

"It's a statue."

"Yes, I can see it's a statue, but what does it mean?"

"Well, I don't think it means anything. What's wrong?"

"Nothing. I just don't like ancient little men rolling across my desk unannounced. I don't like it."

"Are you offended?"

"No. No, of course not."

"Matthew. You're embarrassed by it."

He glanced at the floor. "No," he grumbled. "Well, I . . . no. I just don't want that thing in my office." And he had banged out of the house and down the hill to the sawmill.

Abby turned the statue sideways and looked at the little fingers clinging to the man's ribs. Her smile faded. She placed a hand lightly on her belly and wondered if she were pregnant. It was too early to be certain, but still . . . The thought unsettled her. She carefully returned the Stone Man to his corner of the bureau and stared at the bottle of Black Drop. She would have to give it up. I'll not have my child screaming day and night because of my folly, she thought. She had seen it often in the back alleys of London: gaunt creatures with exhausted cries, huddled in the arms of grim-faced women, and always they belonged to mothers who took laudanum. But, then, she also remembered old Mr. Gothroy of Spitalfield Street who had tried to give it up; she had peeked through the burlap curtain of his cubicle and seen him thrashing convulsively on his narrow cot in a puddle of excrement and vomit, howling in torment at demons only he could know. She picked up the bottle, then put it down again. Angrily she turned away from the bureau. I'll decide later, she thought, and hurried out of the room.

Upstairs, in the western tower, a pair of shrikes were nesting under the eaves, their bizarre calls drifting through the open

window as they imitated first a bluejay, then a robin. A dead
mouse quivered in the light breeze, impaled on a rusty nail on
the window ledge. "Butcher birds," Abby whispered.

She turned back to her stack of paintings beside the wooden
packing crate, lifted one from the top of the pile, and held it
critically between her thumb and forefinger, twisting the canvas
so the sunlight streaming through the open window glinted off
its surface. "Winter Rain Forest". It was a dark woodland of
sombre curves, brooding fungi, and rotting vegetation. Everywhere was the incessant rain of winter. She placed it in the slim
wooden crate Matthew had prepared, then pulled it out again.
She didn't really have to take them to San Francisco. It was
Matthew's idea; she'd never actually agreed. Abby fitted the lid in
place. She would just take these few, in case, and if they fell
overboard on the way . . .

The shrikes switched to their own true song, a clear, delicate
queedle, *queedle*, and Abby glanced out the window and smiled
at them. She stopped and looked again. There, in the centre of
the inlet, was an enormous clipper, her layers of billowing canvas,
stark white against the bright-blue sea, crackling in the breeze as
men scrambled over the ratlines furling the sails. She picked up
the telescope she kept by the window and focussed on the ship's
deck. Near the bow, a stern-looking barrel-chested man was
pointing at the brick house on the south shore. Next to him was
a matronly woman in a high-collared black dress and tight grey
bun. She was calling angrily to someone at the stern. Abby swept
the telescope along the length of the deck to a girl with red hair,
who was climbing the mizen-mast towards a peacock perched
on the futtock plate. The bird was watching her, its small black
eyes winking angrily, its green and blue feathers quivering around
it in a gaudy display. Abby swung the glass back to the bow and
read the name on the plate behind the figurehead. The *Orpheus*.
She snapped the telescope shut and glared at the ship. "So," she
muttered, "the mighty Jonas Cains is taking up residence at last."

A LITTLE PRESSURE

DAWN. THE CROWD SWIRLED AND pushed around the doorway of the tiny New Westminster telegraph office and overflowed into the open, huddling under umbrellas and straining to see past the heads in front. Inside, a small bald man, tired and sweating, made the final connection that would link the town by wire with San Francisco. The room was hot, muggy, and jammed. He squinted at the wires and his spectacles slid down his nose. "That should do it." Carefully he squeezed around the table and sat in front of the key.

"Quiet please." Everyone hushed as he bent over the transmitter and tapped rhythmically. The clicking stopped. Seconds passed. A minute. He wiped the sweat off his face and tried again. Silence. The crowd shuffled nervously and leaned closer, holding their breaths, willing it to work.

With the first clatter of the receiver the throng roared and the little man jumped, snatched his pencil, and bent over the striker until his ear almost touched it. MESSAGE RECEIVED STOP WELCOME NEW WESTMINSTER STOP SAN FRANCISCO.

Four boys sprinted out of the office shouting the news, while men and women crowded around the operator, waving slips of paper over their heads, calling out names and messages, anxious to know if their American relatives had survived the Civil War.

The receiver clattered again. The crowd grew so quiet that the scratch of the operator's pencil filled the room. He gasped. The clicking stopped. The little man was white and trembling. "What is it? Who's it for? Read it. Read it."

Jonas Cains snatched the paper off the table, glanced at the message, then read aloud: "PRESIDENT LINCOLN SHOT STOP DIED THIS MORNING STOP WILL KEEP INFORMED."

The crowd stood stunned and silent, then slowly a murmur started at the back, and swelled into an outcry. More people pushed out of the office to spread the news.

Again the receiver stuttered and clicked into life. "It's for you, Mr. Cains," the operator said. His pencil raced across the paper. "Sorry, sir. It doesn't make sense. Want me to confirm it?"

Jonas glanced at the message — "No. No, thank you" — folded it, and slipped it into his coat pocket. "But I wish to cable a Mr. Clarence Darby of San Francisco." The little man scribbled down the address. "The message is to read as follows: BEGIN AT ONCE STOP SEND PRAYER BOOK TO ARTHUR IMMEDIATELY STOP JONAS CAINS."

As soon as receipt of the cable was acknowledged, Jonas squeezed out of the tiny room, unhitched the gelding he had rented from Brighton, and cantered out of town along Douglas Road.

The morning was cool, grey, and wet, the trail empty and quiet except for the hiss of rain and the sucking noise of the horse's hooves. He fingered the message in his coat pocket and smiled. It had originated from Arthur in London, then been forwarded via Clarence Darby in San Francisco. So clever to have a man in the Colonial Office, he thought, even if communication is slow and second-hand. But that will soon change; the transatlantic cable will be complete in the fall. Then Arthur can be triggered in minutes.

He looped the reins over the saddle-horn and pulled a thin leather-bound volume from his pocket. The Prayer Book. He hunched forward to shield it from the rain, spread out the telegram, and quickly decoded it, leafing through the hand-written code for words he was unsure of. It was as he suspected. ENCOUNTERING OPPOSITION STOP STALEMATE STOP NEED CATALYST STOP BALL IN YOUR COURT STOP ARTHUR.

Jonas tucked the code book into his pocket and fumbled for a match. He flicked it with his thumbnail, lit a corner of the telegram, and held it until the flames curled round his fingers. Then he dropped the ash into the mud behind him and galloped ahead.

The Douglas Road was complete now, linking New Westminster with Brighton on Burrard Inlet, three miles east of Jonas's mill. Governor Seymour, with only a little prompting from Arthur in the Colonial Office, had ordered it punched through in a hurry. Jonas cursed the way it snaked drunkenly through the forest, curving around stumps and rocks, but there had been little time for digging or blasting; he would need immediate access to the telegraph office in Stump Town and refused to make the long trip by water round Gray's Point and up the Fraser River.

At the end of the trail was Brighton: a new resort hotel set in a grove of willow and poplar. With its enormous dance floor overlooking Burrard Inlet and the mountains, it was rapidly becoming a favourite weekend watering place for the citizens of New Westminster and a fashionable inn for people from Victoria and the United States who were visiting the mainland.

Jonas dismounted and paid the proprietor for the horse. "Where's Jimmy?"

"Down at the wharf, Mr. Cains."

Jonas nodded and walked brusquely down the long, narrow dock. At the end of it was Jimmy, fat and pale, sitting cross-legged in the rain with his thumb in his mouth, pulling on a length of cotton thread. He was thirty-five.

Jonas took a deep breath. "Hello, Jimmy." He tried to say it softly but still the man whirled around, startled, and stared up at him with wide, frightened eyes. He was drenched; his shirt stuck to his skin in translucent folds and his short hair was plastered to his head. "What you got there?"

Jimmy smiled. "Spider." He stood up and pulled the black thread hand over hand as though he were drawing water from a well until the spider dangled in front of Jonas's eyes. It was missing two legs and the remaining six quivered faintly, groping for the thread tied around its middle.

"Looks like it's almost dead," Jonas said.

Jimmy frowned and stared at the spider, his lower lip quivering.

"You can take me back now."

Jimmy dropped the spider into a small glass bottle, poked the thread in on top of it, screwed the lid tightly shut, and put it in his pants pocket. He held the rowboat still until Jonas was settled in the stern, then jumped in after him.

As they glided through the rain, Jimmy began to sing in a monotone.

> "Bird ate a fly,
> And fly ate a spider.
> I ate a fly,
> But I won't eat the spider."

Jonas shivered; the man was barely human, and would be better off dead. He glanced across the inlet at Galer Mills. "You make lots of trips over there, Jimmy?"

The boatman stopped singing and smiled. "Yes, Mr. Cains."

"How many men has Galer got working for him now?"

"Lots."

"And how many is lots, Jimmy?"

The fat man screwed up his face in concentration, then slowly relaxed as his mind wandered. He began humming the tuneless song again.

"Useless sod," Jonas muttered. He turned sideways in the boat and studied Galer Mills. The bark of the stevedore echoed over the water from the wharf where three schooners were loading lumber. He'd sent a man over just yesterday to sniff around, and found that two were bound for Australia and the third for Hawaii. Jonas had heard about Matthew's trip to San Francisco and how he had wooed half a dozen shipping magnates with his confident manner and promises of prime lumber at cut-rate prices. He'd watched with interest as buoys were set in the channel and the first of the foreign ships sailed timidly through, and he had noted how the huge stacks of unsold lumber lining Galer's beaches had dwindled to nothing. But he was not worried. Soon, he thought, Matthew Galer will be riding on my coat-tails — and a coat can be easily shed.

Jimmy heaved hard on the oars and dug the bow into the gravel on the south shore of the inlet, directly across from Galer Mills. Jonas jumped out, paid him, and climbed up the bank to his mill-site. He stopped by the wharf and leaned against a post to survey his domain: one hundred acres — which he had bought from the Crown for ninety-five dollars — on which stood the sawmill itself, two bunkhouses for his forty-three workers, the outbuildings, and his own home of solid brownstone brick. Madeline would be there now, in the backyard, despite the rain, tending her immaculate English garden, edging the sedate green lawn that framed her impeccable, geometric beds of roses — she had even cultivated a new hybrid, the Caroline Rose, which she had named after their third daughter. He kicked angrily at a peacock that had strutted across the grass to peck at the cuffs of his new trousers. The birds simply had to go. Yesterday he had even found one resting on his own bed and would have throttled it if Caroline had not burst into the room full of tears and imprecations. He still could not resist her.

Across the clearing he could see the hazy outline of men and oxen struggling through the driving rain with the giant trees. The bulls' heads swung slowly, rhythmically, from side to side as they dragged the huge blocks out of the forest towards the screaming saw. He owned the timber-cutting rights to twenty-three thousand acres, stretching south and east to the Fraser River, west to the ocean at Gray's Point, and scattered in pockets up the northern coast to the Squamish River on Howe Sound. For sixty dollars he had obtained a twenty-one-year lease; the colony had been desperate for industry and settlement.

Jonas motioned to Carky, who scurried over to him.

"Good day, Mr. Cains. We — "

"I've taken out a contract for Hawaii; I want an extra thirty thousand feet by the end of the month."

The foreman's mouth dropped open. "But we canna. We havena — " He stopped and shook his head quickly, his jowls quivering like a bulldog's. "We'll need more men. Do ye no see — "

"How many?"

The old Scotsman rocked back on his heels and sucked in his cheeks. "Och, I reckon twenty'd do it; but they'd have tae be swingin' their axes within a week, and we've no the bunks to sleep 'em in. You see, we still have — "

"You'll have them, and they can sleep in tents. The men I have in mind won't be too fussy, Mr. McShane. But get that lumber cut or you're finished. Understand?"

"Aye, Cap'n. No problem, sir. Now, if you've a wee minute, Mr.

Cains, we're just fetchin' to set off the domino and it's a grand sight it'll be, I'm sure." Carky hurried across the clearing, waving his arms and howling orders.

Jonas chuckled to himself. The fellow's really not half bad, he thought. Twenty extra men for thirty thousand feet? I'd have thought it would take forty. . . . As he walked into the forest to where the domino would take place he wiped the rain from his forehead and raked his fingers through his hair; grey strands stuck to his hand. He scowled. Tomorrow would be his fifty-sixth birthday.

"Timber-r-r-r. . . ." The air crackled with the sound of tearing wood as a two-hundred-foot Douglas fir quivered, hesitated, then plunged, gaining momentum. It slammed into a second tree and the two ripped on, smashing into a third, then a fourth, fifth, sixth. The undercuts had been made with precision to send each tree crashing into the next. Seven, eight, ten, twelve. The domino snaked violently through the forest, flattening smaller, uncut trees as a bonus. Twenty, twenty-five, thirty. The forest thundered. The ground shook. Huge logs flew up from the debris like matchsticks as the destruction spread out in a fan shape. Forty. Fifty. Carky threw his battered slouch hat on the ground and jumped up and down, the men howled, the oxen bellowed, but the only sound that could be heard was the roar of the domino. The last tree shattered and exploded into fragments, branches rained to the ground, and the roar echoed off the mountains like distant thunder. Sixty-five trees had fallen.

Jonas chuckled. Not bad. Not bad at all.

Chang Sun Lee crouched on the deck of the *Sierra Nevada* with his back against a cabin wall. Steam wafted up from his clothes. For three days he had sat in this spot, pelted by rain, unwilling to move for fear he should lose the slight protection of the wall, but now, at last, as the voyage was almost ended, the sun was out and he revelled in its warmth. He draped his queue over his shoulder to dry, hugged his chest, and smiled as he listened to the click of the Mah-Jongg tiles around him. He was thirty-four, small and bony, with a hooked nose, thin, sloping shoulders, and, as his mother had said, the hungry look of a stray cat in his eyes.

In 1849 he had left his wife and daughter in the small farming village of Sanshu on the Pearl River and travelled to the golden hills of San Francisco. There had been no point in staying. His mother and father, three brothers, their wives, twelve nieces and nephews, and four cousins all shared the same house — a sprawling, leaking, ramshackle affair with cloth partitions and tiny rooms built of sticks and scrap wood — and they all worked the same small plot of land. It was decided he should scoop up some of the great wealth everyone knew lay in the hills of the Golden Country and send it back to the family. When he left he had tried, unsuccessfully, to bring tears to his eyes.

For eight years he had patiently sifted through the tailings of abandoned gold mines, and twice a year, religiously, he had sent half of his earnings back to Sanshu; the other half he had hidden against a time when he might need them. Then, in 1857, he had met Mei-fu Sun, a woman of twenty, who worked in a vegetable store.

He had wooed her feverishly, but her Jade Gate would not open without the casting of horoscopes and a formal marriage. He had so longed to touch her fine white skin, which was as wondrous to him as a winter lotus or the delicate sheen of a spring sunrise on new rice-paper, that he finally consented, and, even though it was against Chinese law for a man to take two wives, they were wed that same year. Despite the guilt eating at his insides like a great hunger, he never told Mei-fu about his first wife on the Pearl River or the day when he would be expected to return, but he continued to send money home out of his secret savings. When his new wife bore him a son, Chang wept and blessed the gods. As the years went by they worked hard, she in the vegetable store and he at labouring jobs once the gold-mines dried up, and always he had tried to hide what little money he could, but Mei-fu's eyes were sharp and soon his savings were nearly depleted.

The day that the last of his money was sent to Sanshu, Chang made a decision. He would travel north to the British colonies in search of the fortune he was sure awaited him there. Mei-fu cried and pleaded to go with him, but he refused, though in his heart he wanted her with him.

Diligently they had saved enough money for the cheapest one-way ticket to Victoria. On the day of his departure he had walked to the waterfront, Mei-fu following a few paces behind, with the hand of their six-year-old son in hers. They had stared dully at the great wooden ship that would carry him to Gold Mountain, avoiding each other's gaze, until finally the gangplank was about to be raised.

Mei-fu had smiled and asked him again to send for her as soon as he was established. He had assured her he would. They had looked into each other's eyes until Chang began to shift his weight uncomfortably from foot to foot; then, shrugging his shoulders in his characteristic way, he scurried up the gangway to the *Sierra Nevada*.

Now Chang heaved himself up from the deck; his knees creaked. What to do about Mei-fu and number one wife? He must make his fortune quickly. By all the gods, he must do something.

The five hundred Chinese on board were stirring, gathering their bundles and shifting towards the gangplank. Chang forced himself to dismiss his problem and concentrate on the immediate task of pushing to the front of the line. He wanted to be first off the ship to greet the limitless possibilities he was certain awaited him in Gold Mountain. The sky over James Bay was clear and bright. Seagulls glided alongside the ship. A good omen.

As they approached the Victoria wharf a murmur of excitement rustled through the crowd and Chang had to brace himself to keep from being pushed over the railing. Halfway down the dock was a large banner in Chinese characters which read "JOBS" and under it were three tables. In front of each was a smaller sign describing the type of work offered. Chang squinted to read them. The first was road construction, the second stringing telegraph lines, and the third sawmill work. Which to choose? Perhaps the telegraph?

Before he could decide, the bars of the railing were slid aside and he was running, running down the wharf with the mob of howling Chinese pushing from behind. As he reached the telegraph table, puffing from the mad run, someone shoved him violently to the side and he found himself standing in front of the sawmill table. "Piss on you and all your ancestors for a thousand generations, you motherless, dog-eating turd!" he screamed in Cantonese. The offending man blanched. Chang composed himself, smiled, and looked into the cold, brittle face of Jonas Cains.

"What's your name, John?" To the whites all Chinese were John; it was easier than trying to pronounce the difficult foreign names.

"Chang Sun Lee, honoured sir."

Jonas wrote it down. "Ever work in a mill before?"

"Oh yes, many, many times," Chang lied.

"Your English is passable. Do you speak Cantonese?"

"Yes. Oh, very yes. Read and write both languages."

"Good. Sign here. I'll need an interpreter; you can start today. Thirty-five dollars a month. If you work hard and your languages are as good as you say, I'll raise it to forty. Your food will be provided and, for now, you are to sleep on the ground in a canvas tent; you will supply your own blankets and axe. Understood? Good. Stand over here. Next?"

Chang waited beside the table, elated, and blessed all the gods for his luck. Less than two minutes in Gold Mountain and already he had a job and a favoured position as interpreter. Who knows what opportunities might lie ahead, he thought. Truly, this is the land of winter rice.

"You, there," Jonas snapped. "This bastard doesn't speak English. Ask him if he's worked in a mill before."

Chang bowed slightly to the Chinese man. "Honoured sir," he began, "the barbarian wishes to know if you have ever worked in a sawmill. Truly he is ignorant and in a foul temper, but for a meagre ten per cent of your earnings I am certain I can assuage his fury and guarantee your employment."

Jonas pushed himself away from the table and gathered his papers, pleased with his morning's business. "That's all!" he roared. The crowd of Chinese in front of him groaned and screeched, cursing their luck and the steely-eyed barbarian. Quickly they shoved into line at the next station.

Jonas smiled. He had hired twenty Chinese at fifteen dollars a month less than he paid whites. A good bargain. He was aware of the ten per cent Chang had squeezed out of each man, but it didn't bother him. The fellow was clever, and it had amused him to watch the suspicious eyes darting from him to Chang and back again as the negotiations proceeded. He had acquired a smattering of Cantonese during the Opium War of 1840 from a mule-faced pearl-diver named Charlie Bo, who could hold his breath nearly four minutes while he drilled holes in the bottoms of the Chinese "scrambling dragons", but he didn't need the language to understand this transaction. The situation was clear enough. "Tell all the Johns I hired to be at the dock tomorrow at sunrise; we won't wait for stragglers."

Jonas turned to go, then whirled round to face his new inter-preter. "Oh, by the way, Chang," he purred. "You've made a good profit today. About an extra sixty dollars a month, isn't it?" The Chinaman blanched. "I figure a fifty-fifty split would be fair, don't you?"

Chang began to haggle but stopped; the cold grey eyes made him shiver. "More than fair, honoured sir."

"Good. I'll see you tomorrow."

Jonas walked up Government Street, smiling and confident, enjoying the warm sun, tapping his coat pocket; in it was an authorization for a $50,000 bank loan which he had negotiated the day before. He headed for the office of J. W. Trahey, ship-builder. With the money he would order a side-wheel steam tug, the finest on the coast — one hundred forty-five feet long, eighty horsepower — to guide ships through the Burrard Inlet narrows. He decided to name it the *Isabel* after the banker's wife; after all, he thought, business is business.

Ahead, a gaunt man dressed in black, with a cane dangling from his right arm, dashed across the street. Jonas hurried after him. "Mr. De Cosmos," he called.

The man whirled about, brandishing the cane like a sword. "What? What? Oh. Mr. Cains." He hooked the weapon back on his arm and sniffed. "How do you do?"

"Fine, thank you, Mr. De Cosmos. Lovely day."

"It's a ghastly day. Have you seen this?" He stabbed his cane at a poster fastened to a street lamp.

ANNEXATION MEETING
TONIGHT

Royal York Theatre
8:00 PM
All Welcome

"No. No, I hadn't," Jonas lied. "I've been at the dock all morn-ing. What a bloody bore."

"It's an aberration!" De Cosmos ripped the paper off the lamp-post in a fury and threw it to the ground. "Filthy, treasonous propaganda. The traitors should be caught and hanged. We'll never join the Yankees."

"Fancy," Jonas mumbled. "I must have been mistaken."

"What's that?"

"Well, forgive me if I'm wrong, but I was under the impression you were an American citizen. Were you not born in Maine?"

"I am a British subject!" De Cosmos shouted.

"Yes, yes, of course. Excuse me."

"This is an English colony and English we'll stay."

"Ah, but will England have us?"

"What do you mean?"

"I mean that a little pressure could go a long way." De Cosmos's eyes narrowed. "Is it not true," Jonas asked, "that Governor Kennedy blocked your petition to merge British Columbia with Vancouver Island?"

"The fool's a coward," De Cosmos railed. "He's afraid that when the two colonies unite, Seymour on the mainland will get the governorship and he'll be out on his ear, and rightly so; post him to Borneo, that's what I say. We've no use for stonewallers here."

"But the Crown supported him."

"The Crown is an ass," De Cosmos blurted. "Sometimes, that is."

"Mr. De Cosmos, I am a businessman, not a politician, and I am certain you are far better informed in these matters than myself. Indeed, perhaps I have already said too much."

Jonas turned to go, but De Cosmos grabbed him by the shoulder. "Wait. What did you mean about a little pressure going a long way?"

"Well," Jonas confided, glancing down the street to see if anyone could overhear, "it had occurred to me that this 'annexation business', if properly handled, could work to our advantage."

De Cosmos recoiled from him.

"Now, hear me out, Mr. De Cosmos. I was just thinking that British Columbia and Vancouver Island, though small and isolated outposts with little industry and less population, are in a strategic defence position. Yes, very strategic.

"There are rumours, or so I am told, that the eastern colonies will soon unite into a Canadian confederation — an admirable move — but they seem oblivious to their vulnerability; Americans to the south, and, if they don't do something about us soon, they may well have Americans to the west and north as well. The only way the British possessions in North America can remain secure against the threat of American invasion is to unite from the

Atlantic to the Pacific. The Canadians need us, yet the Colonial Office refuses to see it; indeed, they won't even allow the union of its two western possessions, which is surely the first step in a coast-to-coast confederation."

"Hear, hear," De Cosmos interjected.

"So, I was merely thinking that a little pressure might open their eyes, so to speak — force them to see the western colonies in their proper perspective. I'm sure they would not want the stars and bars flying over Victoria."

De Cosmos was silent for several moments, considering the possibilities. "Then perhaps the news is not all black," he muttered.

"The news, Mr. De Cosmos?"

"Yes, a most distressing cable has just arrived from San Francisco." He glanced over his shoulder and lowered his voice. "The Fenians are gathering. They've threatened to invade Victoria and New Westminster."

Jonas struggled to suppress a smile. "The Fenians?"

"Irish fanatics. They've already caused havoc back east. They're bent on creating war between England and the United States and now, it seems, they think they can do it by threatening the British colonies on the Pacific. But, as you suggest, Mr. Cains, perhaps this could be used to our advantage. A little pressure, eh? ... Providing it doesn't get out of control, of course." De Cosmos whisked the cane off his arm and stabbed it into the dust of Government Street. "I must see Governor Kennedy at once." He bobbed his head like a pigeon, touched his hand to his hat, and scurried off up the road, his coat flapping about him.

Jonas waited until he was out of sight; his lips curled into a grin. "God damn," he chuckled. "So Darby's begun already." He stooped, picked up the crumpled poster, smoothed it, and refastened it to the street lamp. "No need to waste a notice," he muttered. After all, he thought, I paid good money to have them printed.

It was actually Mr. Weitzel, a wiry little man from the Cariboo with a bald head and an enormous beard, devoted to the cause of annexation, who had arranged for the posters and passed Jonas's money on to the manager of the Royal York Theatre for the evening's rental. A useful man, Jonas thought. The only one I could find foolish enough to stand before a crowd of Britons and suggest they join the Yankees. He stepped back to study the notice, nodded with satisfaction, and continued up Government Street to the office of J. W. Trahey.

As the sun set and the last of the gas lamps were lit in the Royal York, the auditorium doors opened and the audience crowded in. A young and rowdy group pushed their way to the pit. The seats filled quickly. A half-dozen men with bulging coat pockets edged down the aisles and positioned themselves near the stage. A few elderly men looked cautiously about and chose seats near exits. Three women appeared—the schoolteacher, and two wives who were known by everyone to be nags and trouble-makers—but the men were surprised even they had been allowed in; this was, after all, a political meeting. The crowd was noisy and excited.

Jonas Cains sat in the back row, his chin resting on steepled fingers. The lights dimmed slightly. He glanced at the empty Governor's box and scowled. Amor De Cosmos, apologizing profusely, squeezed between the seats towards him, tapping with his cane like a blind man, looking nervously about. He glanced under the chair and flopped down next to Jonas, placed the cane across his lap like a shotgun, and stared grimly ahead.

"Will the Governor be attending?" Jonas asked.

"Of course not. That'd give too much credence to what is obviously a farce." De Cosmos pulled a flask from his coat pocket, swigged, and passed it to Jonas.

"No thank you. How did he take your news this afternoon?"

"What? The Fenian threat? He's scared to death and rightly so. Dangerous bloody business, despite your 'pressure notions'. He'll be recruiting a militia next week. Messages have been sent to London, but it will take months."

Jonas smiled slyly. Mr. Weitzel walked onto the stage; he was a small, timid-looking man. His bald head gleamed under the gas lamps as he stood at the lectern, shuffling papers. The crowd hissed. The lights dimmed. He introduced himself, and a low rumble of satisfaction rose up from the audience as an egg was lobbed over their heads and cracked against the lectern. The speaker looked nervously about. Steady, Mr. Weitzel, Jonas thought, you'll have to stand a lot more than that if you expect to earn your five hundred dollars.

"My friends," Mr. Weitzel began, his small blue eyes darting from one angry face to the next. "As you know, tonight's meeting has been called to discuss the possibility of annexing Vancouver Island and British Columbia to the United States." The young men in the pit applauded, but were quickly drowned out by the boos and hisses that rose up out of the seats behind them like a swarm of hornets. Mr. Weitzel wiped the sweat from his shiny forehead and stuffed his handkerchief back into his pocket.

"The colonies are in an economic depression; the gold-mines are failing; industry and agriculture are dependent upon local markets; our governments are operating at a deficit. We are isolated, depopulated, impoverished." His voice was thin and shrill. The audience shifted ominously in their seats.

"But to the south, to the south I say, is a young nation, a strong and prosperous nation, walking, nay leaping, into the future with a pride and confidence which we will never realize so long as we remain the pitiful backwater outpost of an empire so vast and distant that nine-tenths of its population has never even heard of Fort Victoria. But think for a moment, my friends, of the United States." Mr. Weitzel's voice dropped to a low, wistful reverie. "The *United* States of America ... does not the very name conjure an image of strength, unity, confidence—prosperity? And all of these wondrous and golden characteristics, these strong and promising qualities so vital to the life-blood of a burgeoning nation, lie within our grasp, my friends, just a few miles to the south, beckoning us, tempting us." His voice began rising to a crescendo. "Our future lies to the south, I say, in a young and mighty nation that is waiting patiently, sympathetically, waiting for us with open and bountiful arms to muster our courage and sever the chains which bind us to an old and crumbling empire whose ignorant, parochial, and *laissez-faire* attitudes twist like a knife in the very heart of our colony."

The men in the pit roared their approval, while the rest of the crowd shouted angrily. Amor De Cosmos jumped from his seat and shook his cane over his head. "Traitor!" he screamed. "Filthy, treasonous, bloody traitor!" The audience picked up the chant, shouting, "Traitor, traitor, traitor. . . ." The men in the pit yelled angrily over their shoulders. Jonas saw that De Cosmos was shaking; he pulled him back into his seat. The outburst subsided.

Mr. Weitzel gripped the edges of the lectern and spoke in a quiet, soothing voice. The audience strained to hear him. "Traitor? That does not offend me; indeed, it has been said of greater men than I. I am not a traitor; I am a Briton, like yourselves, with only the best interests of the English people at heart. But the sad truth, my friends, is that England does not want us." A nervous murmur rolled through the audience.

Mr. Weitzel's eyes narrowed as he sensed he had touched a real fear. He pressed on. "And why should she? England is a long, long way away, my friends. We are cut off even from the Canadas by thousands of miles and a colossal wall of rock and snow and ice which will never, never be penetrated. Canada will never attempt to breach this natural fortress so long as we have nothing to offer her but our debts."

"Lies!" Amor De Cosmos was on his feet, screaming, spittle running down his chin. "It's all lies!" He pushed his way to the aisle, careless of the toes he was treading on — "I'll put a stop to this" — and stormed out of the theatre. Another egg was lobbed up from the centre of the audience, struck the podium, and trickled down to the stage. The crowd roared. Mr. Weitzel did not flinch but he gripped the lectern fiercely, a sly, crooked smile showing through his wiry black beard. Jonas was impressed; the fellow was good, almost too good.

"To the south," he shouted, "is a powerful nation with the ambition, the population, and the wealth we so desperately need. Their continental railway is *already* in place; the Civil War is over; their government is strong, their economy booming. Everything we need is there and waiting for us — a vast orchard heavy with fruit, while we cringe against the fence like a starving man hugging our loyalty to our shrivelled bellies. A spur line could be driven north within months and settlers would flood our land, like the fountain of youth, bringing hope, money, and industry. Gentlemen of Victoria, our destiny lies in America!" An orange struck him in the forehead and he reeled back, stunned.

Eggs and fruit rained onto the stage, some landing in the pit. A man in the front row picked up a tomato and hurled it back into the audience. It hit the schoolteacher's cheek, burst, and splattered over her dress. She screamed.

Instantly the men around her were on their feet and charging down the aisles. Those in the pit leapt over the backs of seats, fists raised, and rushed to meet them. The two camps collided with a bellow of rage, and the theatre resounded with the smack of knuckles on skin. Men toppled over one another as everyone pushed and crowded into the aisles. The elderly hovered near the exits, shouting their support, ready to flee. Mr. Weitzel, beaming, his arms held out like a crucifix, descended from the podium and waded into the fray like a martyred saint. Instantly his nose was bloodied and he slumped to the floor.

Without warning, the gas lamps lining the walls of the Royal York flickered and went out. The theatre was dark. The sound of the fight shifted key from anger to alarm as the crowd began pushing towards the exits.

De Cosmos raced back into the hall, breathless, proudly slapping his hands together. "There! That'll put a stop to this treason," he bellowed. "I've shut the gas off."

Matches were struck; tiny dots of light appeared, scattered throughout the hall like fireflies. Jonas pushed himself angrily up from his chair. He had not planned on this; the situation was out of control. Behind him he noticed the hiss of gas from a lamp over his head.

"The gas is still on!" he bellowed. "Put your matches out or you'll blow us all to hell!" The pinpoints of light whizzed frantically and disappeared. The theatre was black again. Gas pumped into the hall from eighty-five lamps.

"But I thought —" De Cosmos began, but his voice was drowned out by the rising panic. Men shouted and pushed through the darkness, then a woman screamed as she lost her footing and fell in a tangle of crinolines; others tripped over her, some hitting their heads on the wooden armrests. They blocked the aisle and the crowd backed up behind the pile of bodies, pushing with their elbows to keep their footing as men jostled around them, vaulting over the seats and scrambling for the door. The air began to smell acrid and sickly.

"Don't panic," Jonas shouted. "I thought you claimed to be Britons." The crowd quietened. "Well, show it. You will kindly leave in a calm and orderly fashion." Someone helped the woman to her feet. Two unconscious men were grabbed by the arms and dragged slowly up the aisle as the crowd groped their way towards the foyer, which was packed with people streaming out the one door into the cold, fresh air of night. Faint rays of moonlight seeped into the theatre.

As the last man stepped out of the hall and into the lobby, Jonas rushed down the aisle, peering into the darkened rows of seats. He had not seen Mr. Weitzel leave, though it had been hard to tell. The man could still be useful, he thought.

In the silence the hiss of gas was loud. The air reeked. When he reached the pit, he stumbled over a body. He bent close and recognized the dim outline of Mr. Weitzel. Choking on the fumes, he hoisted the small man roughly over his shoulder and pushed himself up. Then he froze. At the back of the stage, off in the wings, he saw the orange flicker of a small coal-oil lantern.

Jonas ran, his heart pounding, his legs pumping, Mr. Weitzel's head bumping against his back as he hurried up the aisle and into the foyer. It was empty. His legs were shaking. He staggered across the lobby, buckling under the weight. As he stepped over the threshold and into the night, the theatre exploded.

Wiley Burgess touched a grey-gloved finger to the edge of his moustache and watched, chagrined, as a sweaty Irish labourer loaded his luggage onto a dolly and wheeled it down the length of the crowded dock. Seagulls shrieked alarmingly overhead, white against the dark London sky. The Irishman disappeared into a thick crowd of emigrant peasants — gaunt men, ragged children, tight-lipped women in black wool cloaks — who squeezed and jostled one another down the dark alleyway formed by the waiting ships.

Wiley turned round and thrust his head through the window of his father's carriage. "Now see here, Herbert, this has gone far enough, don't you think? A joke's a joke, and all that, but — you can't be serious."

Lord Herbert Burgess, the tenth Earl of Downsview, peer of the British realm and member of the House of Lords, stared stiffly ahead at the narrow strip of glass that separated him from the coachman. "Have a pleasant trip, Wiley."

The young man's hand tightened convulsively around the silver knob of his walking stick. How he hated that ruthlessly impersonal face, that aloof British profile with its trim grey beard like iron plating, locking his father in. "Well, what the hell am I supposed to do in Canada?" he sputtered.

"Make something of yourself," Lord Herbert replied coolly. "God knows you have been unable to do it in England."

"But the country's uncivilized."

"Then civilize it." The voice was a coiled spring.

"Now see here, Herbert, if it's about those gambling debts, I'm sure we can work something out. You could take it out of my allowance, in instalments, of course."

Lord Herbert sniffed contemptuously. "There would not be

enough years in your sordid life." A steam whistle shrieked at the
end of the pier, causing a flock of pigeons at Wiley's feet to rise
into the slate-grey sky. Lord Herbert continued to stare stiffly
ahead. "I suggest you board now. I have left your allowance with
the ship's captain and instructed him not to deliver it to you
until you are well at sea. If you fail to collect it, you will not see
another penny from me. Is that understood?"

Wiley pulled himself up to his full height and puffed out his
chest. "Very well,' he said. "Have your sport, Herbert. I had
planned to winter in Spain this year, but I suppose I shall have to
make do with fêting the colonial savages. Perhaps it would amuse
you if I were to learn Iroquois, or some such horseshit." There
was no reply. Wiley stooped to pick up a small leather carrying-
bag. "Very well then," he repeated. "I'll see you in the spring."

Lord Herbert shook his head slowly. "You are not to return."

Wiley's chest deflated as though he had been punched in the
stomach, and the leather bag slipped from his hand. "What?"

"I said, you are not to return; neither to Downsview Hall nor
to England. I have arranged with my solicitor that the earldom
shall pass to your brother. Upon my death you will acquire minor-
ity positions in two of the linen mills, plus some railway stock —
provided you remain in Canada. In the meantime you shall receive your usual annual allowance, again provided you remain in
Canada; you may cable me where to send the money upon your
arrival. Do I make myself clear?"

Wiley had turned white and gripped the door of Lord Herbert's
carriage. "You bastard," he screamed. "Why are you doing this to
me? Why?"

Lord Herbert turned to face his son, his blue eyes like ice, and
Wiley melted away from the edge of the carriage. "The girl is
dead," he said. "She died in hospital this morning."

For a moment Wiley was stunned, but the faint smile of satisfaction curling under Lord Herbert's moustache made him rally.
"But surely it can be fixed," he said desperately. "A little money
in the right hands — "

Lord Herbert snorted in exasperation, leaned forward, and
rapped sharply on the glass. "Downsview Hall," he barked, then
flung himself back on the plush velvet seat. As the carriage
lurched forward, he turned his cold blue eyes on his son for the
last time. "Stay out of England," he warned — then Wiley's handsome, stricken face vanished from the window.

"Wait," Wiley screamed. "You can't do this, you bastard." He snatched up a loose cobblestone and flung it furiously at the back of the retreating carriage, but it bounced off with a hollow thump, leaving a white scar on the polished wood, and the coach rumbled on. He noticed a constable sauntering towards him out of the crowd and quickly picked up his leather bag, brushed indignantly at the beaver collar of his heavy twill coat, and marched down the dock towards the iron-grey hulk of the waiting *Enterprise*.

Behind the cold granite peaks of Sheba's Breasts, thunder rumbled ominously. Jonas Cains carefully moved the glass jar of Caroline roses—the first of the new season—to the corner of his desk, propped up his feet, and gazed out the office window at the black storm clouds boiling over Burrard Inlet. It had been a long, tedious winter spent supervising the mill and training the Orientals. He now employed sixty Chinese and only fifteen whites; the Johns worked so much more cheaply, plus Chang inevitably scalped ten per cent off their meagre wages and religiously returned half to Jonas. By late winter, production stood at forty-two thousand feet per day. By summer it had reached fifty thousand.

True, it had been a boring, frustrating winter. Other than a brief trip to Victoria to dispose of the store on Yates Street and the last of their land holdings—at a delightful profit—he had spent the rainy season in his office, planning, plotting, waiting. Madeline had had the croup. Caroline had whined constantly about the endless grey mists and driving storms. Sarah, to the surprise of everyone, had come alive during the long winter, disappearing into the dank forest for hours at a time, returning in a mysteriously spritely mood. But inevitably the bounce in her step crumbled as soon as Jonas spoke to her. It made him shiver; he was still not convinced that Sarah was truly his.

Again the thunder rumbled, deep and ominous, behind the mountains to the north. Jonas smiled. At last the waiting was over; it was time to act.

Three pieces of paper were spread on the desk before him. He nudged one with the heel of his boot. It was from Arthur in London. What to do? The decoded cable read: FEAR OF INVASION WANING STOP DONE EVERYTHING POSSIBLE STOP CAN YOU GIVE PLAN A SHOVE STOP ARTHUR.

It was true. When Clarence Darby first wired the Fenian threat to the colonies there had been panic. A volunteer rifle corps had been recruited in Victoria. An artillery company had been formed in New Westminster, and the ranks of the militia swelled. The second cable had warned that forty thousand Fenians were ready to sail from San Francisco. The Royal Navy sent two steam sloops to Vancouver Island: the gunboat *Sparrowhawk* patrolled the mouth of the Fraser, and the iron-clad warship *Zealous*, a floating arsenal, anchored at Esquimalt. Rockets were set atop the government buildings to signal the naval base should the Fenians attack Victoria from within. While the islanders fretted through a fear-filled winter, Jonas waited in his office, scanning the local papers for the latest predictions of doom. Only he and Clarence Darby knew that the Fenian scare was mostly a fabrication.

But by early spring the tension had begun to ease. The threats continued, but not a Fenian had been seen. The rifle corps was disbanded. The artillery had stopped booming their cannon over the Fraser River and the militia had gone home. The rockets remained on the roofs of the government buildings, but there were few ships left to signal. Cables continued to arrive, but they were read with cautious scepticism.

Jonas lunged forward, snatched the cable off the desk, and read it again. He had made up his mind. It was a hard decision, regrettable—yes, very regrettable—but business was business. . . . More pressure would have to be applied. He jerked open the door, scanned the clearing, and signalled for Carky. "Tell Chang I want to see him at once."

He returned to his desk and picked up the second piece of paper. It was entitled: *Petition Requesting Admission of Vancouver Island and British Columbia into the United States of America*, and it was addressed to the President. Beside it was a second copy to be sent to the Colonial Office in London. The body of the letter complained of a lack of English interest in the floundering western colonies and a list of reasons why union with America was desirable. It ended with a request for annexation by the United States under any terms, and though it had been signed by only thirty colonists, mostly Americans, Jonas was pleased with it.

Before last year's meeting in the Royal York, annexation had been unheard of. Now it was discussed openly; at political rallies, on street corners, in saloons, wherever people met, in public or in private, it was a topic of conversation. Though the first meeting had been disastrous, it had planted seeds that were slowly germinating. Even the unplanned catastrophe and Jonas's act of heroism had proved extremely useful; he had been praised throughout both colonies and his reputation had skyrocketed. It fitted into his plan perfectly; he made sure the *Lillooet Colonist* carried the story.

The second meeting had been more sedate. Mr. Weitzel's proposal was seriously considered. Debate followed. The audience was overwhelmingly against annexation, but a resolution was passed requesting that London unite the two colonies immediately. Nothing happened. Jonas judged it was now time for the petition.

Chang knocked and poked his head through the office door. "You wanted me, honoured sir?"

"Sit down, Chang. There are a couple of matters I wish to discuss with you." To Jonas all Chinese labourers were Johns, except for Chang; he grudgingly admired him, as much as he could admire any Oriental, and appreciated the money he had saved him on wages. "You will please sign these documents and ensure that the other Johns do the same."

"What are they?"

"That, Chang, is of no importance to you or the others. It is strictly a political matter. Further, I wish them signed in proper English names. For yourself, Lee will do nicely, but I suggest you make it Mr. Charles Samuel Lee, or something of that ilk. You can help the others to make up decent names."

Chang winced. "And if they refuse?"

"I am not in the habit of making threats, Mr. Lee. This is not a request, it is an order. Are you not happy in your employment here?"

"Yes, honoured sir."

"Good. You have a steady job and receive an amazing salary, what with your extortion racket and all. . . . I'm sure you understand."

"Yes, honoured sir." Chang slipped the papers into the pocket of his tunic. "The documents will be returned tomorrow."

"Good." Now the second matter: I have a small job that needs to be done tonight, and I am willing to pay three thousand dollars."

Chang grew pale and Jonas looked out the window to hide his

smile. The clouds had grown blacker. The air was still. "That's a great deal of money, sir."

"Yes. Yes, it is. And so you can appreciate that the job, although not difficult, is of a . . . ticklish nature. Consequently I am not at liberty to disclose its details until I am certain of your convictions." Chang nodded slowly. "You see, if anyone were to know of my involvement in this matter, other than the person I hire, he would be in grave danger." Jonas pressed the tips of his fingers together. "Very grave danger, if you catch my meaning." Again Chang nodded. "I realize it is less than fair to ask for a commitment under these circumstances, Mr. Lee, but the sum *is* generous and the task most delicate." The silence grew. Jonas waited. "What about it, Chang? Three thousand dollars. Do you want it?"

The Chinese's hands were trembling. "Of course, honoured sir."

"You realize there will be no turning back?"

"You have my word. The job will be done."

"Good. Now this is what I want you to do. . . ."

Jonas leaned back in his chair and watched the Chinaman slip into the evening shadows. He was pleased with the bargain, very pleased. Naturally Chang had haggled; it was to be expected. He had resisted at first but finally allowed himself to be pressured up to four thousand dollars. Jonas chuckled. It was of no consequence. The money would never be paid.

Chang raced across the sawmill clearing, his heart pounding. Four thousand dollars. As he hurried towards the bunkhouse he calculated quickly: five hundred a year would be a vast sum to send back home . . . by all the gods, he would be safe for eight years. The thought staggered him. He could send for Mei-fu at once. They would build a small cabin in the woods near the mill. It was settled. Truly this was the land of opportunity.

The bunkhouse was dark and empty; the twenty Chinese who lived in the small log cabin were already at dinner. Smoke curled up from the open fire pit and wafted out the hole in the ceiling. The room stank of unwashed bodies and rotting clothes. Chang climbed quickly to his sleeping place and sat in the darkness, cross-legged. Thunder rumbled in the distance, drowning out the buzz of flies laying their eggs in foul-smelling socks dangling from the rafters. He shivered. How glad he would be to get out of this filthy place. His eyes followed the continuous rows of bunks lining the walls, stacked one above the other, like shelves in a pantry. Muzzle-loaded. For an entire year he had slept on this narrow ledge with the smelly feet of his friend Stinky Chung pressed against his head. One night, in a rage, he had slapped the little shit-reeking man awake and ordered him to turn around, but his foul breath and snoring were worse. Soon he would have a cabin of his own.

He thought about the job and for a moment considered going back to the office and refusing, but he forced the idea out of his head. If he reneged, he would have to give up his job and flee a great distance to escape the wrath of the devil barbarian. And four thousand dollars, eee . . . what happiness that would bring. Surely it was not too much to ask for such a great sum.

But could old steely-eyes be trusted? Of course not; there could be no written agreement, no witnesses, no chop, nothing but the word of a twisted, motherless, cold-hearted snake. He would have to take precautions.

Quickly Chang riffled through Stinky Chung's bedroll until he found the small brush, ink, and rice-paper he knew were hidden there. He wrote a short note in English and sealed it, and on the front he penned instructions in Chinese characters to his smelly friend. The second letter he wrote in Cantonese and stuffed into his shirt. He returned the writing materials, gathered the few things he would need, and hurried out of the bunkhouse.

The evening was dark and windy, the air electric. Chang ghosted across the quiet clearing to the stable, saddled the horse Cains had told him to take, and led it to the edge of the forest. Black clouds swarmed overhead, rolling higher and higher. Far to the east he saw the glint of lightning and heard the distant rumble of thunder echoing up the valley. He gritted his teeth, mounted the horse, then spurred it into the woods and cantered along the trail towards Brighton.

Sheet lightning glared over New Westminster. Governor Seymour turned restlessly in his bed as thunder shook the house. He had not been able to sleep. The grandfather clock in the hallway chimed 4 A.M. and he flipped back the quilt, slipped quietly out of bed, and stood by the window watching his wife. She looked frail and stick-like in the crumpled sheets with the lightning flashing over her.

He needed to go to the bathroom. Since his bout of Panama fever two years before, his bowels had never been the same. He considered the thunder mug under the bed but hated the smell it left in the room, so he decided to make the trek to the outhouse. "Can't sleep anyway," he muttered. He took his wife's shawl from a peg by the door, threw it over his nightshirt, and tiptoed out of the room.

Rain drummed on the roof. The hallway was dark. He clutched the banister and edged down the stairs, feeling with his bare feet. Again thunder shook the house.

At the front door Seymour pulled on a pair of galoshes and stared at his bony legs; they were trembling. He was too old for a wilderness posting. His health was poor. He felt tired and feeble. He sighed, pushed himself up, and prepared for the dash through the rain.

He flung open the door, darted through it, and collided with a solid lump. Shocked, he reeled back, his heart pounding, his legs buckling under him. It was a body, and it swayed in the wind, suspended from the verandah awning. The rope around its neck creaked. Seymour clutched the door-frame and held himself up- right. The lightning flashed and he saw the blood smeared on his nightshirt.

Shaking, he darted back into the house and found the coal-oil lantern on the sideboard. His fingers trembled as he struck match after match until one flared up and he touched it to the wick. The glass shade clattered into place and he ran back to the verandah.

The body hung three feet off the porch with its back to the door. The arms dangled free, fists clenched. Blood seeped through its shirt from several deep gashes and puddled on the floor. Sey- mour raised the lantern and stood on tiptoe to read a small note pinned to the left shoulder-blade with a knife.

> Many battles we have won,
> Along with the boys in blue.
> Now we'll come and take your land,
> For we've nothing else to do.
>
> *The Fenian Brotherhood.*

Gingerly, Seymour pushed the body with his index finger and it swung around to face him. There were more knife wounds in the chest. The head was tilted onto the right shoulder, the eyes were open, the lips closed and blue. Thunder crashed overhead. Seymour groped to the railing and vomited onto the ground. He had recognized the face instantly. It was the boatman, Jimmy.

The storm passed, but the clouds remained. At dawn Jonas stood in the doorway of the saw-house, the sky behind him fading from black to grey. Inside, it was dark and shadowy. The boilers hissed. The gauges fluttered, and when enough pressure was built, Chang flipped the switch that started the great blade turning. It gathered speed. The jagged teeth blurred and melted into a soft metallic haze. Only Jonas noticed the slight wobble as it spun. He quickly ducked out of the sawmill and hurried back towards his house.

Chang had woken him early, pounding on his door, standing in the rain, haggard and drawn. He had thrust the annexation petition at him — complete with the sixty signatures he had collected as the men filed out of the bunkhouse on their way to breakfast — and demanded his money for the job he had done last night. Jonas had stalled, insisting they must wait for confirmation from New Westminster. Firmly he had led the Chinaman across the compound and promised him the day off once the machinery was started and the workers had arrived. The fellow had not resisted.

Inside the mill, Chang moved mechanically through his daily routine: he levered a log into place, locked it firmly to the carriage, and started it moving. He had blocked the night out of his mind and now he felt tired, pensive, withdrawn. Listlessly he trudged around the saw, climbed down into a narrow walkway, and crouched in front of the spinning blade, lining up the cut with his eyeball. The log inched forward, then stopped just short of the saw. He shuffled back to the carriage, spun a wheel which edged the block a fraction to the left, then clambered back down into the narrow wooden trench. Again the carriage inched forward.

The instant the log touched the edge of the teeth, the machinery screeched. The saw buckled, flew off its axle, and tore through the walkway. Chang did not see it coming. Even if he had, there would have been no time to run; he was trapped in the narrow catwalk. The blade ripped through his torso, killing him instantly, smashed through the back wall of the saw-house, and finally came to rest embedded in a Douglas fir at the water's edge.

Jonas stopped on the front steps of his house as he heard the screeching crash from the mill. He glanced over his shoulder in time to see a jagged piece of steel smash through the saw-house wall; then he hurried up the stairs and closed the door behind him.

Indian summer. Jonas stretched out on the grassy bank overlooking Victoria Harbour and shielded his glass of champagne against the clouds of pollen wafting down the hillside from the red and purple fireweed ablaze at the edge of the forest. Groups of picnickers dotted the meadow and the sound of female laughter, civilized British laughter, drifted to him over the field, and he smiled. He was happy, delighted in fact, to have suggested a picnic on this, the most auspicious of days.

Caroline perched next to him amid the delicate folds of her robin's-egg-blue dress, her red hair glistening in the hot sun, chatting with De Cosmos, who lay sprawled on the grass, already drunk. Mariah, his middle daughter, sat across from him, flirting outrageously with the first officer of a British man-of-war she had met just yesterday. Sarah, of course, was gone, traipsing through the forest, pursuing her own unfathomable happiness. He glanced warily at Madeline, who was fussing over the wicker basket, busily repacking cold chicken and flinging uneaten bits of bread at the scolding bluejays. He gulped his champagne, knowing it was only a matter of minutes before she snatched the glass out of his hand and ordered him up.

He felt contented, amiable, and very pleased with himself. His plan had worked. When news of the Fenian murder was first cabled to England, warships had been rushed to the colonies from around the world and a special meeting of the Colonial Office convened in London. The importance of the western colonies as a strategic defence position against invasion by the Irish fanatics had been discussed; if the Pacific Coast was not secured, the possibility of a Canadian confederation would be aborted before it was born.

Arthur, in the Colonial Office, had announced that a petition of annexation was on its way to the White House. The officials were shocked: treachery from within and treason from without. He had suggested that the colonials were merely suffering a temporary loss of faith and all that was required was an indication of Britain's intentions towards her Pacific domain — a small gesture of support. Immediately the bill to unite the two colonies had been rushed through Parliament without debate. Arthur cabled the news to Jonas at once.

On August 6, 1866, Vancouver Island and British Columbia had been united. An embittered Governor Kennedy read the proclamation from the balcony of the government buildings; he was to be replaced by Seymour. The island would be absorbed by the mainland; the capital would be New Westminster. A new Legislative Council was to be formed consisting of twenty-three members — fourteen appointed and nine elected — and it was suggested by the Crown that they consider the possibility of uniting with Canada. The following day Jonas had announced his intention to run as member for Lillooet.

"Hurry on now, Jonas," Madeline said as she plucked the empty glass from his hand and packed it into the wicker basket. "We'd best get to the harbour." Mariah and Caroline were helping De Cosmos to his feet. As Jonas pushed himself up and slapped at the tiny white starbursts of pollen clinging to his black trousers, he tried to picture the little mining town of Lillooet perched somewhere on the Fraser in the distant wilderness interior, but the image would not focus. He could, however, see himself quite clearly in the Legislative Assembly, sitting stiff and erect on a leather-upholstered chair. True, he had never visited Lillooet — the thought of three days spent jostling, bumping, and bruising himself over the treacherous Cariboo Road on the Barnard Stage appalled him — but his opponent, a wharfinger from New Westminster named Henry Holbrook, had not made the trip either, so he was confident of victory. To compensate for his absence he had sent a large amount of money to his representative in Lillooet to be spent on his campaign, and he ensured that the local paper again carried the story of his heroism at the Royal York.

Madeline slipped her hand into the crook of his arm. "Don't fret over it," she said. "The voting is all done and we'll have the results by sunset." She smiled up at him and patted his hand. "I know you're going to win." Jonas grunted and let himself be led down the hillside.

The streets of Victoria swarmed with drunken men, pushing and lurching their way towards the harbour to witness the launching of the *Isabel*. Banks and businesses had closed for the election, but the saloons had remained open. The Cains party was swept along with them in the heat of Indian summer, Caroline and De Cosmos in the lead, Mariah and her officer lagging behind, engrossed in each other, Madeline clinging to Jonas's arm, occasionally flicking her cane at the ankles of anyone who jostled her.

At the harbour they made their way to the foot of the scaffolding, where a large crowd of dignitaries—political candidates, businessmen, and landowners—whom Jonas had invited on the inaugural voyage were waiting. Jonas removed his hat and stared up at the long white ship nestled in its bed of props, tilted bow to the water on a slipway next to the wharf. She was beautiful, one hundred and forty-five feet long, her polished-teak trim and brass fittings gleaming in the bright sun. For a moment he couldn't move.

From the wharf near by, the Victoria band blasted out a marching song. He felt a tug at his sleeve as Madeline pushed him towards the scaffolding at the stern of the ship. Slowly he climbed up and looked down at the carpet of faces below. The banker's wife, an overdressed, toothy woman in her early fifties, started up the ladder, smiling and nodding to everyone simultaneously. Her feet tangled in her enormous wire crinoline, which banged and snagged against each rung until finally, to the sound of guffaws and shouts from the drunken men, she hitched it up to her knees and scurried up to the platform. Red-faced and flustered, she took the bottle of champagne Jonas handed her and began fussing with her bonnet. The music stopped.

"Citizens of Victoria," Jonas shouted, "I dedicate this ship to the industry, prosperity, and economic health of our new colony, British Columbia. Ladies and gentlemen: the *Isabel!*" The band started up again, men charged down the slipway swinging sledgehammers at the supporting props, and the crowd cheered. The banker's wife, who was still fussing with her bonnet, let the bottle slip out of her fingers. It thudded onto the platform, unbroken, and rolled towards the edge. Quickly Jonas picked it up, thrust it into her hands, and pushed her to the railing, but the ship was already out of reach. She threw the bottle after it. It struck the stern, bounced off, and rolled down the ramp and into the water, still unbroken. The banker's wife scowled and the crowd roared.

The captain eased the ship alongside the wharf and the party filed up the gangway while the band played. There were one hundred and fifty guests, including the Governor and his wife, and they sauntered along the decks, waving at the crowd below, while liveried waiters bustled among them offering champagne, whisky, port, and sherry. Madeline scuttled to the galley to check on the cook.

Finally the band boarded and the gangplank was raised. The engines roared, the ship trembled, and the whistle hooted. Slowly the *Isabel* eased away from the wharf. Her side-wheel hummed into motion and she steamed out of Victoria Harbour and headed for the mainland.

Jonas stood in the wheelhouse next to the captain, admiring his ship. It was long and sleek, and purred like a cat. To his left, silver sprays of water spun in long, curving arcs from the bright-red blades of the paddle-wheel. "The fastest, strongest tug on the coast," he muttered. The captain looked at him. Jonas clapped him on the shoulder, handed him a glass of champagne, and stepped out onto the deck.

The sea breeze was cool and the water slightly choppy. Well-dressed men and women lounged in deck chairs or stood in groups around the rail. A poker game had started in the aft cabin.

Jonas noticed his eldest daughter, Sarah, standing alone at the bow, thin and pale, clutching the railing and confronting the ocean, with her brown hair whipped back in a long, straight line. He decided not to join her. Instead, he made his way to the back of the ship, where he found Caroline sitting next to Amor De Cosmos, the British flag fluttering from the stern behind them. Caroline always made him smile. She was sixteen, and with her red hair piled high on her head, she was stunning.

"Warm enough, pet?"

"Oh yes, quite." Jonas frowned at the glass of champagne in her hand. "Oh, Father . . . it's a special occasion. Amor tells me we'll get the election results at New Westminster."

Jonas glanced at De Cosmos. He was sprawled in a deck chair, oblivious to the whisky dribbling out of his glass and down his pant leg; he was obviously drunk. "Yes, yes, I should think so. The returns will all be in by sunset."

"Don't suppose you're much worried about it," De Cosmos mumbled. Jonas pretended not to hear as he took a glass of champagne from a passing waiter. "Clever of you to choose a backwater riding," De Cosmos continued. "Rather limits the competition, doesn't it?"

Jonas smiled. "Rather."

"Indeed, I'd say you're sitting rather pretty all the way round," De Cosmos said.

"How do you mean?"

"It just seems rather convenient to have New Westminster made the capital and British Columbia given the balance of power now that you have so much invested in the mainland." This too had been arranged through Arthur's influence. "Of course, I am certain your candidacy was prompted by strictly altruistic motives." De Cosmos guffawed and raised his glass. "To the good citizens of Lillooet."

Jonas turned his attention to Caroline. "Have you seen the Governor?"

"Seymour? Yes, I think he went starboard with that grumpy old furniture manufacturer Mr. Barnes."

"Thank you. If you'll excuse me, Mr. De Cosmos." Jonas stood up.

"One more question, Mr. Cains."

"Yes?"

"Do you know anything about an annexation petition?"

Jonas kept his face calm. "No. No, can't say that I do. Why do you ask?"

"Nothing. Rumours, just rumours."

At sunset the *Isabel* steamed up the Fraser River, red and orange sun-points dazzling in her wake. On board, the atmosphere was tense as the various candidates tried overly hard to appear unconcerned. The docks at New Westminster were jammed with people waiting to welcome the officials to the new capital of British Columbia. At the front of the crowd was the telegraph operator with the list of election results clutched in his hand. He was brought aboard and positioned in front of the flag. Everyone crowded to the stern to hear him announce the new government.

For every riding he read the candidates' names and the number of votes each had received, then paused for the cheers to subside before going on to the next. Instinctively the crowd gravitated away from the losers. Amor De Cosmos was returned as member for Victoria. He rose to give a speech, faltered, and slumped drunkenly back to his chair.

The last riding called was Lillooet. Madeline tightened her grip on Jonas's arm. "Mr. Henry Holbrook: forty-seven votes. Mr. Jonas Cains: one hundred sixty-one." The tipsy crowd cheered their host wildly. Madeline was overcome; despite her strict notions of propriety, she reached up on her toes and there, in front of everyone, kissed Jonas on the cheek.

CHAPTER SIX

1868

HEEKW SIEM

GOVERNOR SEYMOUR WAS TIRED. HE slumped in a high-backed wooden chair in the office of the New Westminster jail, his chin nodding towards his chest, lulled by the drone of rain on the roof. Scandalous place to hold a government meeting, he thought. He peered out from under his eyebrows at the members of the Legislative Council fanned around the table before him. It was Cains who was holding up adjournment; he wanted more timber rights. Seymour ground his hips into the cushion he had brought from home for the long session. I'm sure the citizens of Lillooet are mightily concerned about timber rights, he thought. He tried to ignore the churning in his bowels so he could concentrate on what De Cosmos was saying.

"According to the strict rule of international law, territory occupied by a barbarous or wholly uncivilized people may be rightfully appropriated by a civilized or Christian nation. Shall we allow a few red vagrants to prevent forever industrious settlers from improving upon unoccupied lands? Not at all. Locate reservations for them on which to earn their own living, and if they trespass on white settlers, punish them severely. A few lessons would soon enable them to form a correct estimation of their own inferiority, and settle the Indian title too."

Seymour glanced at Jonas Cains, who seemed oblivious to the discussion; he was toying with a large gold pocket watch. "Trutch. You're the Commissioner of Lands and Works," Seymour said. "What do you think?"

The small, anaemic man looked startled. His eyes flitted around the room and his fingers shuffled absently through a stack of papers. "The Indians really have no right to the lands they claim, sir," Trutch said. "Nor are they of any actual value or utility to them. It seems to me, therefore, both just and politic that they should be confirmed in the possession of only such extents of land as are sufficient for their probable requirements for the purposes of cultivation and pasturage, and that the remainder of the land now shut up in these reserves should be thrown open to pre-emption."

"What was the previous governor's policy on reserve allocations?"

Trutch studied the stack of papers flipping through his fingers as he spoke. "Douglas had no set policy, sir, but I believe he did mention the figure of ten acres per family."

Seymour could wait no longer; he needed to visit the outhouse at once. "Very well, Trutch, I will leave it in your hands. See that the Indians get something for their land; but we needn't be too extravagant. Gentlemen, it's late, let us adjourn." He jumped up and hurried out of the room.

Jonas stood on the boardwalk and breathed in the chill dark air of early winter. He had won. Cold rain streamed down the wall behind him and splashed up from the boards at his feet. The timber would be his, but not by force — the days of cannonading were gone. If the new government were to give him the land he wanted he must first placate the Indians. He would speak to Tcaga, a savage, to be sure, but influential and very useful when there was a profit to be made. Yes, it had all gone very well, better than he'd expected. Trutch had indeed earned his money.

The buckboard slithered to a stop and Jonas ducked under the canvas tarp and settled himself next to Carky. "Did you get all the supplies?" The Scotsman nodded without looking round as the wagon groaned and lurched forward with a sucking noise. "Did the *Anita* get loaded?" Again Carky nodded, the top of his balding head rocking slowly, his short, leathery neck buried in his slicker. "Good. Anything else?" The foreman turned to face him, and for the first time Jonas realized that the man hated him.

"Someone's lookin' for you."

Jonas could feel his good humour drain away like blood. "Who?"

"A woman. I told her you weren't there and she said she'd be back."

"Do I know her?"

Carky shook his head. "No. But you will. Says her name's Mei-fu Sun." The wagon banged over a corduroy bridge. Jonas braced his legs on the floorboards.

"What, Chinese? I don't know — "

"She's Chang's widow."

Sitka strode through the forest with Eva beside her. A pot of red ochre swung from her hand. She was happy. The air was cold, and over by the inlet it was raining, but here under the thick canopy of branches it was snug and serene and the carpet of needles under her feet was soft and dry. A raven swooped past them and she stopped to watch him glide along the wide channels between the huge tree trunks, his wings barely moving. She tried to take Eva's hand, but the little girl pulled away; she was still sulking.

For the hundredth time Sitka cursed herself for tearing up the bonnet. But it had been so unexpected. She had been sitting in their keekwilee, a small house scooped out of the dirt and covered with lodgepole pines, staring at the dark, dingy quarters in a silent rage when it happened. All summer she had been labouring to build them a house, a real house, a wooden house, but the job seemed endless. She needed one more tree, and it had taken her nearly a month to fell it. Today she had tried to split it and found the grain crooked and spiked with knots. Slab after slab had cracked off misshapen and useless—too short, too thin, crooked, warped, full of holes. It was getting too cold; the sap had stopped running. They would have to spend another winter in the cramped, cold, earthen house.

She had thrown down her tools and stormed back to the keekwilee to brood. What was the point in building a house anyway, she fumed? Indian boys do not go to lone wooden houses to search for wives who have been ostracized and have no family, no status. But then Eva would probably not consider an Indian anyway; the girl had grown strange to her. Each day she returned from her lesson with the white woman and Sitka sat quietly, studying the excitement in the young girl's face, straining to understand, as she chattered away about mathematics, history, geography: impossible villages far across the Great Sea, where cloth was made by machines, where men lived in stone houses, and women who couldn't even dry salmon painted their faces and rode through the streets in wooden boxes pulled by their husband's horses. And Sitka would shake her head sadly, unable to take it in, knowing that she had been left behind and that her daughter was lost to her forever. "Bring her up white," Lady Douglas had said. But what was the point, when the white men didn't marry half-breeds; they just lived with them and sat back and grinned while their friends ridiculed, calling them *klootch-man* and squaw, and then, after a while, they abandoned them. What was her daughter to do after she died: live out her life alone in a wooden house in the forest, talking English to the squirrels?

As Sitka stared at the cold dirt walls that must hold them for another winter and brooded, Eva had come home from her lesson. She popped through the hole in the roof, her bright face beaming, and scrambled down the ladder, chattering away in English and waving a bonnet — a white woman's bonnet. Abby had made it for her. Before she could stop herself, Sitka had snatched it away and torn it to shreds. "You are an Indian," she had yelled. "Do you hear? An Indian." But Eva was on the ground in tears.

That was four days ago, and still the child sulked. Sitka crouched down and wrapped her arms around the little girl. "I am sorry, Eva," she said. "Truly, I am sorry." Eva wriggled free of the embrace but took the big rough hand in hers, and they walked together down the broad path where the raven had gone.

At last they reached the black pond in the forest where the people of Whoi-whoi had come for generations to purify themselves and gather strength. Sitka removed Eva's cedar-bark cloak and dipped her fingers into the pot of red ochre; it reminded her of gutted fish. Slowly she spread it across her daughter's forehead, down her cheeks, and along her shoulders; then with both hands she painted broad streaks on the little girl's chest and stomach and legs. Eva did not squirm; she stood stoically, her black eyes wide and serious, her lips pressed into a thin line to keep her teeth from chattering.

The cold December drizzle burned Sitka's skin as she pulled

off her own cloak and placed it under a tree next to Eva's. She worked the paint over her skin methodically, thinking of last summer's hard climb high into the mountains in search of the special berries she needed to make the ritual paint.

Sitka placed the carved wooden pot next to their clothes and took Eva's hand. Together they walked to the edge of the pool and stopped for a moment to gather courage and watch the wisps of mist curl and twist over the black water.

The thin rim of ice at the edge of the pond cracked and splintered underfoot as they entered the pool. Sitka felt a shudder travel along Eva's arm as the water rose to her knees; the little fingers dug sharply into her hand. Feeling carefully with her feet, she crept forward over the rotting logs and debris until the water was up to Eva's shoulders. She motioned for her daughter to stay and pulled her hand away. With her back to her she pushed off and lunged towards the centre of the pond. The black water enveloped her. Her breath caught in her chest.

The pool was still and silent except for the hushed sound of the ripples fanning back from Sitka's hair and the whisper of drizzle over its surface. Her flesh numbed and her mind flooded with the recent news: the Slug was dead. Smallpox. Tcaga was without a wife.

She had heard it from Matchakawillee, the ancient white-haired crone who was Wife of Kweahkultun, headman of the most important family in her tribe, the *Heekw Siem*. The old woman had found her in the forest digging for camas bulbs and told her about the pinkman's pox, which had swept through the village of Snauq. So many were dead. Matchakawillee's three sons were dead. Kweahkultun was dead. The Slug was dead. That night Sitka had hurried to the gravesite, torch in hand, to see for herself.

The small, square box was where it should be, propped on short cedar posts and carved all round with Tcaga's crests. She had hastily pried open the lid and looked inside. There was the Slug, cramped and lifeless, her knees pressed against her fat breasts, her neck twisted back, her face painted red and black for the ritual of death, sneering up at the night sky, stinking. Sitka had slammed the lid shut and laughed. How she had hated her.

She arched her back, held her breath, and dived, fingers outstretched, sweeping the black water past her. Shivers trembled through her body. Tcaga had been cruel to her. He had fled the night her children were murdered. He had sold her for a case of whisky to feed the Slug. But he was an Indian, and Matchakawillee had said he would give a great potlatch to claim the title of *Heekw Siem*. If he would take her back, Eva would have great status. She would grow up in a position of respect. She would have her pick of husbands.

Deep in the water, Sitka could feel the magic of the pool seeping coldly into her. She had made up her mind. She would return to the tribe.

Sitka surfaced and filled her lungs. She felt pure and strong, and cold. As she turned to face the shore, her eyes widened. Eva was gone.

Panic. She twisted wildly from side to side, scanning the pool, and was about to scream the child's name when she saw the small copper head, nose-deep in the water, hiding behind a log, peering towards the shore. Someone was flailing through the underbrush.

Sitka swam underwater, surfaced next to Eva, and looked angrily over the log. The ritual had been interrupted. It was a bad omen. To be seen would spoil it completely. With her arm around her daughter and her teeth clenched to keep them from chattering, she crouched in the water and watched as a small Chinese woman and a boy of about nine staggered out of the bushes and into the clearing.

The woman wore men's pants and a knee-length tunic that buttoned to her chin. Her face was hidden by a large conical hat. Sitka was amazed at how tiny she was—the top of the boy's head was level with her shoulders—and how much noise she was making. She ran from tree to tree comparing each one to a piece of paper in her hand and chattered all the while in a high-pitched singsong. Sitka wondered if she was a shaman.

The boy marched quietly behind her, head bent, eyes focused on the ground. He seemed to be counting. Suddenly he stopped and raised his head, pointing at a dead cedar just a few feet from where Sitka had placed their cloaks. The woman scurried to the tree, and, kneeling, began to scoop away the layers of dead needles and cedar shards. She lifted a small steel box out of the earth and opened the lid.

"Aiee. . . ." The sound floated eerily over the water.

The box clanged shut and the woman jumped up and resumed her chatter. Suddenly she stopped and bent over Sitka's cedar-bark cloak. She lifted it with two fingers, then dropped it as though it had bitten her. Sitka and Eva sank behind the log as the little woman whirled around and stared out over the black pool.

When they surfaced again she was gone, and so was the steel box. They could hear her thrashing through the bushes in the distance. Sitka was furious. She lunged through the water, head bent, dragging her daughter by the arm. Eva began to giggle. Sitka slashed angrily at the pool and sent an arc of cold white water showering around them. Eva was silent.

On shore she ripped a handful of spruce branches from a small tree and rubbed them briskly over Eva's arms. The girl was blue. The ritual was spoiled. The pool was no more of a secret than New Westminster. She flung the spruce branches to the ground—they were stained red with ochre—and wrapped Eva in her cloak.

With a fresh handful of spruce she rubbed her own skin until it reddened with welts. To become pure and strong required privacy, concentration. The foolish woman had forced them to skulk in the frigid water like thieves. There was no telling what effect the interruption might have. No matter how careful Sitka was, no matter how exacting her plans were, there was always the unexpected, the impossible, to contend with. It was a bad omen.

Sitka rubbed fiercely. An old scar high on her right shoulder opened, welled with blood, and overflowed. Tcaga would never take her back. She leaned her forehead against the smooth bark of a cedar and watched the thin red line stretching down her arm as the spruce branches slipped softly from her fingertips.

As a child, Mei-fu stands in the dusty streets of Peking, by the red-brick wall of the inner city—the Forbidden City—begging copper cash from the rich merchants who swirl past in their brightly coloured robes like imperious butterflies. A man slows his pace and glances at the gaunt, naked baby tucked inside her tunic—it is her sister—but he shakes his head and hurries on. Her bowl is empty.

Behind her, trumpets blare and she turns and runs on painful bound feet, past the small hut of woven mats where her parents live in the shadow of the red-brick wall, to the Gate of Heavenly Peace, where she squats in the hot sand and peers through the spread legs of an Imperial guardsman who stands facing the road. He does not notice her. She stares in awe, trying not to blink in case she should miss something, at the splendid procession filing into the Forbidden City, bearing tributes from distant provinces for the birthday of the Emperor T'ao Kuang. There is a peach, the symbol of long life, larger than a man's head and all carved from gold, carried by six eunuchs on a platter of jade. She sees a chest of ebony inlaid with jewels, a water clock of marble seahorses with golden fins and ruby eyes, screens carved from ivory, coral, and amber; there is a necklace of imperial yellow pearl on a cushion of blue satin, and there are bracelets of rare red jade.

At the end of the line is a royal sedan chair, and Mei-fu knows by the curtains of gauzy yellow silk that it contains the Emperor's Consort. As the chair draws level with her, her child's heart beats fast, for the curtains part and the Imperial Lady looks out and sees her squatting in the dust between the guardsman's legs. Their eyes meet. She is more beautiful and splendid than Mei-fu has ever imagined. She wears a robe of red satin embroidered with dragons of every hue; gold sparkles at her ivory throat, and jade flowers gleam in her perfumed hair. Briefly the Chosen One smiles at her, then the curtains flutter shut and the sedan passes on.

Long after the procession is gone, Mei-fu stands in the shifting dust facing the Gate of Heavenly Peace through which the Royal Lady has passed into the Forbidden City. She is unaware of the child squirming angrily under her blue cotton tunic, for her eyes are shut tight and she is savouring the image of the Imperial Lady—the Chosen One—who has smiled at her, and she is swearing to herself that one day she will know such wealth.

At night she returns to the cramped woven hut and lies down between her younger sisters. The odour of manure is rank in her nostrils, for her father is a dung collector. An anger smoulders in her heart like fire, and she clamps her eyes shut to hold back the tears. In her dreams she sees him at dawn, waiting by the red-brick wall, basket in hand. Slowly the Gate of Heavenly Peace swings open and he rushes in, his sharp elbows battling the ribs of his competitors as he scoops up the choicest horse and donkey droppings from the sandy streets. He spreads them like treasures on the mats before their hut and turns them with his fingers as they dry in the hot sun. He will sell them to peasants for fuel.

Mei-fu prays to Kuan Yin, the Goddess of Mercy, to raise her up. She is certain this will happen, for she believes in the power of the Queen of Heaven. And has not the Chosen One smiled at her today? In her sleep she still sees the beautiful face, the curving red lips, the ivory teeth.

A drop of water splashes onto her neck and trickles down her back. It is cold, like ice. The image fades. Somewhere in the night an owl is hooting and twigs are snapping under the claws of night animals, but she will not acknowledge them. She is busy with her prayers.

It is her fourteenth birthday. She stands with her father on a summer evening by the Gate of Heavenly Peace. They are listening to the trumpets and drums. Merchants and labourers are rushing out of the Forbidden City, for it is sunset and no man save the Emperor may remain within the walls after dark. The goddess Kuan Yin is near, and Mei-fu knows this, for she is filled with foreboding, but she continues with her silent prayer, as she has always done, since the day the Chosen One smiled at her. She has hardened her heart and is determined to see it through.

On the first peal of the great bronze bell, her father spies a particularly splendid turd just inside the wall. On the second ring he darts forward. The gates begin to close. On the third and final blast his hand slips in and his fingers close about the rich brown dung. A soldier of the Imperial Guard spies the arm. Mei-fu sees him and knows that he is bored with his long, dull day at the wall. She sees him smile as he reaches for his scabbard, but she will not cry out, for the Goddess's hand is upon her mouth. The broadsword swings in a flashing silver arc and her father's hand, still holding the precious turd, falls limp and bloody onto the yellow sand.

She totters on her bound feet, struggling under the weight of her father as he leans on her shoulder. Blood is seeping through her blue cotton tunic, staining it black, but she doesn't mind, for a plan has come to her, full-blown, as though placed in her head by the Goddess of Mercy herself, and her black almond-shaped eyes are blazing with excitement. They will need money for medicine and a physician; she will sell herself to Kwung Low, who supplies concubines to the Manchu lords and the wealthy merchants. She knows her father will object — he is proud that he has never sold one of his daughters — but she is unconcerned, for she knows also that her chance will come.

She watches while her mother seals the bloody stump with an iron heated in a fire of dung. She announces her plan. "You will sell me to Kwung Low." Her voice is clear and hard like silver. The family stares at her, frightened by the strange voice and the fire burning in her great black eyes. "The Goddess of Mercy wishes it," she says. Her father shakes his head, but Mei-fu sits back, smiling, and watches and waits while the thin red stripe of poison inches up his arm to his shoulder and he slumps back unconscious. She turns her eyes upon her mother and says in the same brittle, silvery voice, "You will take me to Kwung Low now." The frightened woman glances from her daughter to her husband and back again, then nods her head and rises. They walk out into the drifting yellow sand and hurry through the shadow of the red-brick wall towards the Gate of Heavenly Peace.

Water splashes onto her neck and trickles down her back. It is hot, like blood. The owls are still hooting and the bushes rustle with anxious footsteps, footsteps heading her way, but she will not heed them, not yet. There is still the reward.

It is the Hour of the Tiger. Mei-fu's lips are upon the steaming stalk of her lord Huang Chi. He is old and feeble. Her eyes are open and she is watching the silver sheaths of her fingernails circled round the base of his limp worm; they are engraved with flying dragons, and the shields for her little fingers are of beaten gold. Her small hands are white and delicate from rubbing with scented mutton fat. The room is warm and the air fragrant with the scent of oil from the cassia tree with which she has anointed the seven orifices of her body. Her long black hair is plaited into two tight braids, looped over her ears and adorned with flowers of jade. She is beautiful.

From the corner of her eye she sees the light of oiled-paper lanterns shimmering on her robe of peach-coloured silk embroidered with phoenixes of every hue. The robe is on a chair by the red lacquer door. Beyond the door is the courtyard, and beyond the courtyard is the room of Lady Chi, Huang's wife. Mei-fu sees her, alone in this room, her viper face sour with jealousy, her golden nail sheaths drumming angrily on the arm of her blackwood chair. The worm slips out of her mouth and she giggles.

"What is it, my heart?" murmurs Huang Chi. His voice is thick and heavy with opium. He has grown rich selling this drug to foreign merchants.

"I was thinking of your audience with the devil barbarians today and how you covered your face with your perfumed fan and wrinkled your nose at their ghastly smell. They didn't even notice."

Huang Chi laughs. There is a bubbling noise in his chest. "You think too much of the West, my fragrant flower."

Mei-fu knows this; she is fascinated by the ugly barbarians, by their power, by their wealth — she has even wheedled a tutor out of her lord so she can learn their language — but she looks up at Huang with reproachful, pouting eyes. "If I do, it is only for you, my lord. I know it has long been like sand in your eyes that these giant-men-with-little-brains reap greater profits than you by selling your goods in the West. With your great wisdom, I am certain you are already planning to replace their ships with your own so you may keep all of the money which is rightfully yours. I only thought that if I knew their ways and language, I could be of service to you when you sail to Gold Mountain."

The clouds are gone from the old man's face. He is staring at her. Mei-fu lowers her eyes and returns her lips to the limp worm. She is confident her seed is planted within him.

It is dark and raining. Great white sails crackle over her head — the snapping wings of angry doves, she thinks. Her robe is soaked through. She stands before Huang's cabin, her small, bound feet braced against the roll of the ship, the barbarian ship, the ship of Gold Mountain. In the narrow crack of the doorway is the viper face of Lady Chi. She is smiling, but the effect is hideous, like the leer of a cat with a mouse between its paws. "His soul has gone to the Eternal Yellow Springs," say the sharp viper's teeth. Mei-fu looks over the hag's shoulder and sees her lord stretched on his bed of red satin sheets. His chest is still, his eyes open but sightless. The viper's hand darts through the door and plucks a jade flower from her hair. She turns and runs blindly, panicked, along the rolling deck of the dark ship, her wet robes flying about her, dove wings snapping at her head, but there is no escape. The rain weeps on and on, relentlessly, indefatigably, pursuing her to the shores of Gold Mountain.

The other three concubines are dragged to the dock at San Francisco by sailors with foul breaths and rough hands. They weep hysterically. Mei-fu will not be dragged. She walks daintily down the gangplank, her eyes lowered, and stands apart in her mourning robe of white satin. The sailors are disappointed. Her silver nail shields cut red crescents into the backs of her hands; at least she has saved these. Lady Chi leers at her from the deck of the ship as it moves slowly away from the wharf. Mei-fu turns her back on her. She will not cry.

Water splashed onto her neck and trickled down her back. It was warm, like tears. The claws of night animals rustling in the bushes had been replaced by the incessant hiss of rain. It was grey-dawn. She awoke with a start, a hand upon her shoulder, and sat up, knocking her head on the fallen log under which she and Wu Lee had slept for the last eight nights. Rain trickled down the collar of her blue cotton tunic and she shivered. They had been terrible nights. She had lain awake well past the Hour of the Tiger, her eyes wide as she watched the black trees thrashing in the wind, her heart pounding when the owls hooted in the wet forest, until at last exhaustion brought peace and she slipped into sleep.

"I can do no more." The hand belonged to Stinky Chung.

Mei-fu squinted her eyes and stared at the half cup of rice and the two eggs he pushed towards her. She was grateful that again he had brought food.

"The sly-eyed cook is on to me," he said. "You must see Cains. You must see him today. I can do no more." He dropped the food onto her lap and scurried off, leaving her groggy and bewildered, with the foul scent of his rancid body creeping like mist over her face. She shook her head and looked for Wu Lee. The child lay beside her in a shallow ditch, his head pillowed on a clump of wet moss, his mouth loose and open as he slept. "Wake up, my dragon," she said. "Today we snare the fox."

She sat throughout the day on a log at the edge of the sawmill clearing, her small hands folded in her lap, watching, waiting, thinking of Chang and the goddess Kuan Yin. It had been a year and a half since she had heard from her husband. For the first few months she had thought he was too busy with his new life in Gold Mountain to write. After that she decided he had forgotten her, or perhaps returned to China without her. It was only six months ago, when she had begun to save money for her passage to Victoria, that she began to suspect that perhaps he was dead.

Eight days ago she had arrived in this barbarous land. Eight days ago she had learned of Chang's death from the foul lips of Stinky Chung. He had given her the note in her husband's hand that had led her to the steel box by the black pond. For eight days she had sat on this log beside Wu Lee, plotting, planning. For eight days her fear and her fury had been building within her like the taut cable of a catapult aimed at the devil barbarian Jonas Cains.

She had first seen him the day he returned from New Westminster. He had gone directly to his ship in the harbour, where a second man had joined him. For three days she had sat on this log and watched as a fat old Indian paddled to the ship each dawn, puffed up the ladder, and entered the main cabin; then, each day at dusk, he lowered himself gingerly back to his canoe and paddled away towards the village of Snauq. When Cains had finally returned to shore, he had been careful to stay in the mill or with crowds of men. She knew he was watching her as she sat at the edge of the clearing, day after day, and he was avoiding her.

She glanced up at the black sky, shading her face against the downpour which fell like a grey veil from the brim of her conical hat, and winced; by the walls of the Forbidden City, where the summer sands of the Gobi Desert drifted like snow over her father's reed hut, men grew rich selling cups of precious water, but here the sky vomited rain, and a bucket forgotten outside would be filled in hours. She shook her head in disbelief. Eight days in this barbarous land and still she had not seen the sun.

A steam whistle shrieked at the edge of the clearing and she jumped. Men, huge men, barbarian men, filed out of the woods like an army of shaggy bears, their double-bitted axes slung casually over their shoulders, their enormous spiked boots skidding and sliding on the muddy paths, their coarse voices bellowing across the clearing as they cursed the weather, each other, their jobs. Some of them stopped, rain dripping from their bushy beards, and stared and pointed at her from a distance. Mei-fu lowered her eyes. So big. So impossibly big and noisy. Next came the log trains, groaning and crackling through the forest as the bulls heaved forwards, muscles bulging, eyes white with fear and rage, tails lashing at the roars of the bullwhacker. "Hiyeee ... !"

The great saw whined to a stop as the dinner bell clanged for the first shift and the Chinese marched quickly, quietly, out of the mill, their slight bodies blurred by the driving storm. At the end of the line was Stinky Chung. He was staring at her. Again Mei-fu lowered her eyes. The bulls bellowed and their chains clattered as they were unharnessed; logs thudded together, grindstones screeched, and over it all was the roar of the rain.

From under the brim of her woven hat Mei-fu watched the devil Cains hurry across the clearing and disappear into his office. Stinky Chung nodded in her direction.

"Wu Lee," she whispered. "The fox is in his lair. May the gods smile on us today."

She felt for Chang's letter in the secret pocket of her blue cotton tunic and her heart quivered like a bird in hand. Stinky Chung had warned her that the barbarian was like the Mount of Omei, never to be shaken, but still she must try, for she had spent the last of her savings on their passage to Gold Mountain and Chang had left them with nothing. She straightened her tunic, adjusted her hat, and headed across the clearing with Wu Lee's hand in hers.

A woman is a trinity of mind, heart, and spirit, she told herself. The devil barbarian is a man and has only the advantage of strength. The thought made her smile. She tucked it neatly into a compartment of her mind and closed it as though it were a cabinet drawer. She stood in the rain before the office door. Her heart was pounding. She held her breath and knocked. During the long silence she counted thirteen heartbeats.

"Come in."

Keeping her eyes lowered, she stepped into the small, cramped room and pulled the door shut behind her. Papers fluttered across a huge oak desk. Jonas Cains stood by the far wall with his back to her, bent over a drawing on a table. She removed her hat; her features were small and delicate, her cheekbones high and her eyes oval. An ornate golden butterfly was fastened to her black hair, which hung in loose coils. She cleared her throat. Cains turned to face her and she knew at once by the cold grey eyes which studied her like an abacus that the battle would be fierce. Modestly, she bowed her head and stared at the floor.

"Ah yes, my foreman said I should expect you. Chang's . . . widow?"

"It is a pleasure to meet you, Mr. Cains," she said in her best English. "My husband write so many letters in which he speak of you; I feel we are like old friends." She smiled up at the stern face and angry grey eyes.

"You have my profoundest sympathies over the death of your husband, miss. It was a regrettable accident. Most regrettable." He whisked across the room and pulled the door open.

Mei-fu was shocked, but she continued to smile and tried to ignore the cold wind sweeping through the open door and the papers falling like leaves from the oak desk behind her. "Such a cold and rainy country," she ventured. "I have just come from San Francisco, where it was so much — "

"Unfortunately," Jonas interrupted, "you've caught me at a very bad time, miss. Perhaps we could meet again tomorrow, or the day after."

Mei-fu stared at him, her eyes blinking in bewilderment. To-morrow? . . . The day after? . . . She could feel the anger building within her. How could business be conducted in a civilized manner without first exchanging pleasantries? It was disgusting. She shrugged her shoulders. Very well, she would play her open-ing gambit. "Ah, I not take much of your time, Mr. Cains. It is just a small matter of business."

"Business? Frankly, madam, I do not see what 'business' we could possibly have to discuss."

"It is a small matter. Very small. I simply come to collect the money you owe my husband."

The grey eyes did not flicker. "I owe your *husband* nothing, madam. What little money he had coming was used to send his body back to China at the insistence of his friends. What's more, if you had taken the trouble to check with them first, you would know that this extravagance was undertaken largely for the ben-efit of his wife, his *real* wife, who is at this moment mourning the death of her husband somewhere on the Pearl River."

Mei-fu lowered her eyes and blushed. She had long known of the other wife; indeed, she had suspected her existence from the beginning. The regular disappearance of small sums of money had made her suspicious. From there it had been a simple matter to trigger the assistance of the vast network of friends she had made in San Francisco's Chinatown. Questions had been asked and genealogies examined, and word had sped quickly back to her: Chang was married. The news had not bothered her; China was a world away. She had even admired his loyalty in continuing to send money.

Jonas slammed the door shut and towered angrily over her. "Which brings us to a very interesting point, miss. Who are you?"

Mei-fu stared at his shiny black boots and shrugged her shoulders. "My name is Mei-fu Sun. I am Chang's wife, his *second* wife. I have marriage document to prove it, as I have certificate of birth to prove this boy is Chang's son. But this is not . . . relevant." She smiled up at him, proud of the big English word. "What is relevant is the four thousand dollar you owe for what Chang do. Please read this." She pulled Chang's letter from her tunic and handed it to Jonas. "You will notice it is dated the day before Jimmy's death. The signature is Chang's. I can prove this with other papers."

She watched as Cains studied the page. When he had finished, he ceremoniously folded the letter in half and tore it to pieces. "There," he said. "So much for your scheme."

Mei-fu smiled and pulled a second letter from her tunic. "I may be a woman, Mr. Cains, but I not stupid. You destroyed only a copy. This is the original." She watched the abacus-eyes clicking off the options.

"Do you really think anyone will take this doggerel seriously? Why would *I* hire a Chinese thug to murder an insignificant, simple-minded boatman? It's ridiculous."

Aiyeee, Mei-fu thought. Stinky Chung was right; the barbarian is truly as stubborn as a stone. "Ah, I wonder this too," she said. She smiled up at him, her great black eyes wide and innocent. "And I think it have something to do with the note you have Chang put on the body from this Fenian Brotherhood. So I ask questions, plenty questions; I ask all the honourable men. They say the Fenians never want to come here," she said incredulously. "They never plan it at all. So then I wonder some more — why Tyee Cains want people to think this? — and I ask some more and the honourable men tell me how you make them all sign letter to President asking him to make Gold Mountain part of United States. 'We have to sign or Cains fire us,' they wail." She was warming to her story. "So I wonder: why he want Queen Victoria to think she lose this land to Americans? And I listen plenty and then I hear about this confederation — everyone talking about it — 'Gold Mountain better join with Canada,' they say, 'or she get et by Yankees.' And they talk about a railroad. 'Make it all one country,' they say, 'and stitch the land together with a railroad before it fall apart.' And then I know. Ah, then I understand."

She wagged a small finger at him. "You blackmailing Queen Victoria, Mr. Cains. You clever man. You want railroad to come to Gold Mountain so you make plenty money. And that's why you hire Chang to murder crazy boatman."

"Get out." Jonas's voice cut hard and sharp into her building confidence.

"Get out?" Mei-fu was stunned. "But the money. You must pay the money."

"That's blackmail."

"It's no blackmail." She stamped her small foot. "You agree to pay. Chang Sun Lee big fool to do what you say, but he did it, so you must pay," she snapped. "You have plenty and we have nothing because you murder my husband. You have fifty thousand dollar while we — "

"How do you know that?"

The cold grey eyes made her shiver. "I ask," she said petulantly. "You make me wait so long in this mouldy country, what you think I do? I ask plenty." She brushed at her tunic and studied the angry red face from the corner of her eye. "I ask and I find out plenty too. I find out you still owe money on your ship, the *Isabel*, and you owe plenty in back wages, so I make you deal. Good deal. Three thousand dollar and I give you Chang's letter."

Jonas lunged at her and grabbed her roughly by the arm. Wu Lee moved towards his mother but Cains shoved him aside. "Now you listen to me," he snarled. "You have no case, and you know it. There were no witnesses to the death of Chang or Jimmy. Your only evidence is this bloody letter and, as you have so graphically proved" — he flung the torn pieces of rice-paper in her face — "it can be easily forged. No judge will even give you a hearing. You haven't a hope in hell." He dragged her towards the door.

Mei-fu's heart was pounding against her chest as she pulled back, trying to dig her heels into the rough plank floor. "But you still have to answer plenty questions," she wailed. "Just a thousand dollar. Please. Or I make trouble for you."

He pulled her around to face him and yanked on her arm until she stood on her toes. Rain splashed across her face through the open door. "There will be no trouble and no questions," he said. "Do you know what they do to blackmailers in this country?" He shook her arm until she winced. "They hang them. They won't touch me but they'll put a rope around your nasty little neck and hang you from a bloody great tree for the crows to peck at." Mei-fu blanched.

"But even that won't happen because your case will never come to trial. And do you know why?" She could not answer. "This is a land of accidents, Miss . . . Lee, or whatever the hell your name is. Nasty accidents, like the one that happened to your husband and like the one that will happen to you if you cause me any more trouble. Do you understand that?"

Mei-fu nodded and opened her mouth, but before she could answer she was flying through the rain, her small feet skidding over the slippery clay as she scrambled to regain her balance. She fell backwards with a splash into the thick grey mud. A man who was crouched by the office window jumped up and ran across the clearing and into the woods. The door slammed behind her, rattling on its hinges and echoing in her ears like cold laughter. Wu Lee rushed to help her up but she slapped at his hands, lurched to her feet, and ran. "Pig-face," she hissed. It was humiliating. "God-damned, turd-licking, monkey-balled, dog-breath, shittee Cains." The rain slashed across her face. "Goat-fucker." The tears rolled down her cheeks. "Murderer . . . murderer."

She sat on a rock by the ocean, hugging her knees to her chest, and wept, until the grey clouds turned to ashes. Wu Lee sat quietly beside her and waited.

When she was done, she wiped her eyes with the sleeve of her tunic and got up. "Come," she said.

"Where are we going?" the boy asked.

She did not answer but plodded along the beach, her head bent, her eyes staring vacantly at the small slip of foam hurrying over the sand, Wu Lee's question whispering in the back of her mind with each roll of the surf. Where are we going . . . ? To the log in the forest, she supposed. What else was there? Where else to go?

". . . plenty for everyone. . . ." The words drifted to her through the black rain and she lifted her head. There were lanterns on the beach ahead, and clustered around them she could see the silhouettes of a large crowd of men. She quickened her pace.

"And yet another for the gentle timberbeast." They were loggers from Cains's mill and they stood with their backs to her, gathered around an obese middle-aged man with a muddy-purple face and a red-veined nose. He was filling tin cups from an up-turned whisky keg and haranguing the men like a quack at a medicine show. An enormous moose-hide coat hung tent-like around him, and each time he bent over the keg a small trickle of rainwater fell from the brim of his top hat into the cup he was filling. Mei-fu slipped tentatively into the fringes of the crowd.

Off to one side an Indian woman sat stonily on a weak-backed chair. Mei-fu whistled softly; the stone woman was the ugliest specimen she had ever seen. She was enormous, with fat breasts that rolled down to her lap, a pudgy, shapeless face, sunken eyes, and a lipless mouth that caved in over toothless gums. She sat with her legs spread wide to balance her weight on the flimsy chair. A skinny yellow dog huddled beside her with his snout burrowed in her lap.

"Drink it in health, my man," bellowed the quack. "Drink it in health — hey, quit pissin' on my canoe, you yahoo. . . . To Queen Victoria!" A Chinese tugged at his coat and held out a cup. The fat man leaned over him. "Hallo, little fellow. Didn't see you down there. Why, you're so small I'll bet that the good ladies of the night have to tie a rope round your middle so's you don't fall in." The crowd roared. "There you go, my good man, careful it don't stunt your growth." Again the men laughed but the of-fended Chinese refused the cup. The quack whisked off his top hat and bowed like a courtier. "My apologies if I have offended you, good sir. Surely I should not mock your size, for, as Gulliver so aptly said while in the land of Brobdingnag, 'nothing is great or little otherwise than by comparison.'" The laughter stopped. It was clear the Chinese did not understand, but he returned the bow and took the cup. The crowd buzzed.

"Drink up, my friends! 'Tis a fine night for washing away the pains of labour and what better cleanser than whisky? It gladdens the heart, lightens the mind, eases depression, and quickens the spirit; it slows age and strengthens youth; it keeps the teeth from chattering, the throat from rattling, the stomach from wambling, the heart from swelling, the sinews from shrinking, the hands from shivering, the veins from crumbling, the bones from aching, the marrow from soaking, and, if that's not enough, this particular elixir is guaranteed to put hair on your chest."

And so it went. For an hour and a half, spicy puns and lewd quips tumbled along the beach while cups passed furiously from hand to hand.

Mei-fu held her breath as a huge bear of a man sidled up to her and slipped a beefy arm around her waist. She turned to him; her eyes were level with his hairy chest. She looked up into a bushy black beard and dirty brown teeth. *Dew neh loh moh*, she thought with horror, tufts of hair grow even from his nose and ears, and he smells like the back end of a goat. She smiled up at him. The hand crept lower and squeezed her small buttocks. She pressed closer and accepted the cup of whisky he offered. His hands were red and puffy, the nails caked with dirt, but she was relieved to see that the sausage-like fingers, though fat and ugly, were very short. Perhaps his steaming stalk would not split me entirely in half, she thought.

She turned back to the crowd and noted the heads turning quickly away from her, the furtive winks, the anxious glances, the elbows jabbed in neighbouring ribs. She smiled slyly. Inside, her heart was pounding.

"It has just occurred to me," bellowed the quack with the barrel of whisky, "that we have already become fast friends, yet I have still not introduced myself. John Deighton is my name, born in Yorkshire; I've been a sailor, a miner, a prospector, captain, trader, proprietor, and general entrepreneur. My friends have saddled me with the somewhat odious appellation 'Gassy Jack', though I cannot understand why." The men chuckled. "And this stunning example of femininity" — he swept his hand towards the stone woman on the chair — "is Martha, a true Indian princess, and my wife." The men gaped at her, unsure of how to react. "See what a grace is seated on this throne: Aphrodite's curls; the front of Helen; an eye like Venus to capture and arouse. A combination, and a form, indeed, where every god did seem to set his seal, to give the world assurance, 'This is woman.' " The crowd hooted. Martha sat stoically, eyes glazed, staring straight ahead. The yellow dog looked balefully at Gassy Jack and thumped his tail on the sand.

"We have come to these virgin shores of paradise to start a small business — a pub. But alas, our means are limited — "

"Not on my land you don't." Mei-fu jumped; the shout had come from directly behind her. It was Cains. "You will not be building a saloon on my property."

"Property ends twenty yards the other side of that log," countered the bear-like man, still clutching Mei-fu's rump.

Cains's eyes darted from face to face as he searched for the man who had spoken.

"Certainly, sir," Gassy Jack interrupted. "I have no intention of building on your property. Twenty yards the other side of that log will do very nicely." He raised his cap a few inches from his balding head and tapped it back in place. "As I was saying, Martha and I are somewhat limited in our resources and would gladly accept any assistance in the way of building an edifice suitable to our proprietary interests." The men cheered. A pub next to the mill would save them the three-mile walk to Brighton and the jolting nine-mile ordeal on the New Westminster stage. They ran to get their saws and axes. "There's lumber at the back of the mill."

"You're not using my lumber," Jonas shouted.

"You can take it out of our back wages," said the belligerent voice.

"Yeah, what about our back wages, Cains?"

The men stopped and stared at Jonas. "He can't fire us all; it would take weeks to get new crews in here."

Jonas turned and stormed back to his office.

Mei-fu hurried along the beach, taking three quick steps for each long stride of the big bear-man, staring in awe at the white clam shells crunching under his enormous caulk boots. Lanterns swung drunkenly through the night as men darted about collecting boards, hammers, and nails. The beefy arm around her waist swept her implacably on like an eager broom. She glanced over her shoulder at Wu Lee; he trailed slowly, sullenly, far behind. The whisky keg rumbled past, pushed by two men. Gassy Jack appeared beside her, and slapped her back with an avuncular flourish. He whispered in her ear, "See me later, we could have a profitable relationship, most profitable." Before she could answer, he was gone, and still the arm propelled her forward, faster, more urgently, up from the beach and into the forest, her small feet tripping over roots and stones, until she stumbled into a clearing at a trot.

Lanterns had been spaced around the perimeter. Drunken men slashed at the underbrush with long machetes, exposing the blue-grey clay, while others smashed peaveys into the ground, loosening the earth for post holes. Beside her, rough planks from Cains's mill clattered onto a growing pile.

The whisky keg was rolled into place and propped on a plank straddling two stumps. The sausage fingers roamed, stroking and probing at Mei-fu's buttocks as Martha waddled up from the beach with her chair and lowered herself onto it. Gassy Jack presided over the whisky, filling cup after cup, shouting suggestions over his shoulder at the men shovelling dirt onto the base of the corner posts.

Mei-fu gasped as the fingers found the waistband of her blue cotton pants and darted under it. She looked up at the small red tongue protruding from the bear-man's lips. He was panting. "Money," she hissed. "I need money." The tongue retracted and the lips leered. As the arm dragged her towards the forest, she glanced over her shoulder at the great bulk of Gassy Jack silhouetted by the lanterns, his hands on his hips, supervising the construction. Beyond him the loggers built madly, wildly, shouting, pushing, laughing: two men were boosting up a third to nail on a cross-beam. The north wall lolled drunkenly.

Then she was deep in the forest, up against a tree, with a startled owl hooting in the branches over her head and the bear-man ripping at her blue cotton tunic. "Money," she hissed again, "I need money." The hands stopped for a moment and the man whispered in her ear, his breath hot and foul on her cheek. "How much?" Her mind raced. Gold Mountain . . . rich men . . . hungry men . . . no women . . . how much? "One dollar," she ventured. He laughed and pulled away, and Mei-fu's heart sank. She had asked too much. But then the bear-man's sausage fingers burrowed in his shirt and he folded *two* silver dollars into the palm of her hand and she stared and laughed and blessed the Goddess of Mercy thrice to the heavens.

"Oh . . . good . . . ," he crooned, his hands like a vise on her small round breasts, and "ahhh . . . ," as the fat red fingers tore at the buttons of his crotch, then "ohhh . . ." and "uhhh . . ." and "yesss . . ."

Mei-fu braced herself against the thick, coarse bark, hobbled like a horse with her pants about her ankles, and chuckled to herself while the owl hooted over her head, for it was as she had suspected: the great steaming stalk was a seedling yet. But still he cried out like the Emperor himself as he breached her gate and the worm slid in, and she looked up through the branches at the staring owl who hooted and blinked as the man slammed against her flesh, and she clenched the silver dollars in the palm of her hand, and she thought of Chang. *Who-whoo. . . .* Poor Chang, who had left her with nothing.

And the sharp bark bit into her naked rump. And the brown teeth bit into her cringing nipples. And the tears rolled down, and down, and down. She watched the black tufts of hair quivering in the barbarian's nose. "Bitch," he snarled. And she clenched the silver dollars in the palm of her hand. In the distance was the voice of Gassy Jack: ". . . a name to transport the blood and guts of old England to this primordial paradise. I name thee, the Globe Saloon."

Sitka lay on her stomach with Eva beside her and peered through the underbrush. Her heart beat quickly. They lay at the edge of a small gravel-field overlooking the *lumlam* and the dirty brown waters of Snauq. The rain had stopped the night before; the clouds had broken at dawn and piled up against the mountains to the north. The sky was clear and the sea in the distance a milky green, chopped by a cold wind blowing from the east.

Below her, four large dugouts were approaching the village. When she had first heard the drums and the rhythmic chant of the paddle song, she had run to the gravel clearing as fast as Eva could go and parted the underbrush in time to see the procession skim into view across Ayyulshun Bay. She had immediately recognized the emblems and imposing figure of Chief Chaythoos, from the east coast of the great island, seated on a raised platform in the centre of the lead canoe. He had waited until the last possible moment to make his dramatic entrance.

Sitka shifted uneasily and twisted a sprig of salal until it broke. It was the first day of the potlatch and still she had not shown herself. For three days now they had been running excitedly from one hidden lookout to another as group after group of guests had paddled up the marshy channel. Sitka was dazzled by their numbers. They had come from as far north as the Cheakamus, from Skagit and Nooksack to the south; they had travelled down from Copper Mountain and Chuchuwayha in the east and from Chemainus and the myriad of small islands to the west — until nearly two thousand Indians were camped on the beach in front of the great potlatch house. It was the largest gathering Sitka had ever seen.

The paddle song stopped and, as the chief's canoe drifted by the longhouses of Snauq, a dancer dressed in the costume of a grizzly climbed onto a platform at the bow. The animal's head was supported by a shoulder harness, so that the bear appeared to be eight feet tall. The drums began again, slowly at first, as the dancer swayed and worked his way up from a crouching position.

The tempo quickened. The paddlers began the song of the bear.

Dozens of canoes swarmed out to meet Chief Chaythoos. From all along the shore women waded into the cold water, anxious to greet relatives they had not seen since the last great potlatch.

Sitka pushed herself up and took Eva's hand. Her stomach knotted. What if the tribe turned their backs on them? What if the usher refused to seat them? What if Tcaga ordered them out? Eva tugged at her hand, and she began to walk down the path that led to the village.

The grizzly was at his full height, legs spread, arms outstretched; his claws were the size of a man's fingers. The drums pounded wildly. The bear rolled his head and roared; then the music stopped and the animal froze. The silence was intense after the frantic drums.

From her hiding place at the edge of the clearing, Sitka could feel the tension as everyone stared at the flotilla in the bay. Again the music exploded, faster and louder than before. The bear flailed his arms, swooped low over the water, and jumped up from the platform. Several times the singing and drumming broke off suddenly as the bear posed ferociously, and several times it began again in sharp staccato bursts that echoed like gunshot off the mountains to the north. At last the song crescendoed and stopped. The crowd buzzed with excitement as the dancer stepped down and took his seat.

Two columns of six men each filed into the water and fanned out in a "V" formation; half the men carried long, stout poles over their shoulders. The lead canoe, bearing Chief Chaythoos, slid silently into the V and whispered to a stop as the bow bit into sand. The paddlers climbed out while the men of Snauq slipped the poles under the canoe, then carefully raised them to their shoulders. Chief Chaythoos seemed oblivious to his change in elevation; he sat stiffly, swathed in red blankets, his face impassive, while he and his canoe were carried up the beach and lowered in front of the vast mound of food and gifts that had been donated by the guests. He remained seated while his men unpacked the baskets and cedar chests from his canoe and added them to the pile. The final addition, a small square of copper elaborately painted with a stylized eye surrounded by the chief's crests, was reverently placed at the top of the pile. Its name was Little-One-Eye, and its value was two thousand blankets. The crowd hummed in admiration.

From inside the potlatch house the sound of a deep-pitched drum boomed sonorously over the beach. Chief Chaythoos led the way to the door, where the head usher and his five assistants waited to direct each guest to a seat befitting his status.

As the crowd around the entrance dwindled, Eva tugged at Sitka's hand. Her eyes pleaded. "They will close the door in a moment and it will be too late," she said. Her mother stared blankly at the last of the host women filing into the lodge. Eva began to cry.

The sound yanked Sitka out of her trance, and she looked from Eva to the vacant entrance of the great potlatch house. She moved so swiftly, darting through the underbrush and striding across the village clearing, that Eva barely had time to wipe the tears from her face as they approached the massive doors. One was already closed and the other was being swung into place. They slipped through the narrow opening and the door thudded behind them.

A man halfway down the left side was making a speech. He had been seated incorrectly and felt it was his duty to his ancestors to bring the mistake to everyone's attention.

The usher, who stood just inside the door, looked at Sitka and groaned. He had been searching his memory for the lineage of the complainant, trying to unravel where he had gone wrong. Now this. The added dilemma of what to do with the host's first wife and her half-white child rattled him. He glanced down the length of the longhouse hoping for a sign, but Tcaga was engrossed in the slighted man's tale and had not noticed the late arrival. The usher thought quickly: second wife purchased after first wife taken slave, first wife returned miraculously then sold, second wife died. Did the sale of the problem-woman constitute divorce? Certainly it had not been formalized; she was still Tcaga's wife. But the child — it was not even of the First People. Perhaps he should ask her to leave it outside. . . . He could see the problem-woman glaring at him and quickly discarded the idea. No wonder she had been sold, he thought; such a headstrong woman would be a trial for any man. Why had she come, why had she done this to him? Perhaps she was a test sent to him by his protective spirit.

The problem began to edge past him. The usher was shocked. She was going to seat herself. He darted in front of her. Obviously she would not leave peacefully; he would have to wrestle her out of the house. It would be a bad omen. The best thing would be to seat her quietly and hope she was not noticed. He escorted her quickly to a small group of Snauq women seated near the door. The bench was full, and the usher was not certain she belonged on it anyway, so he found a clean cedar mat and spread it on the ground. Then he hurried away, shaking his head.

Eva and Sitka settled themselves at the feet of the curious villagers. They were grateful to be inside the great potlatch house.

The man who had been seated incorrectly finished his complaint and walked solemnly down the length of the lodge to Tcaga's chair. He pulled out his knife, cut a long strip from the Hudson's Bay blanket draped over his shoulders, and laid it ceremoniously across the host's lap. He was sorry for the disturbance. Tcaga picked two toy British flags tied to small sticks from the pile beside him and handed them to the man. He was sorry for the slight. Waving a flag in each hand the man strutted proudly down the hall, following the usher to his new seat, while the crowd murmured their admiration.

Crack! Crack! The speaker had stepped forward from his place next to Tcaga's chair and banged the heel of his talking stick on a cedar shake. The guests hushed.

> Many thanks are due for your presence in this house.
> Many thanks I offer for heeding our call.
> Many thanks I owe for the distance you have travelled,
> By paddle, by foot, you have come to our fires.
> For this I am grateful, for this I am humble.
> I am the voice of this house and I offer many thanks.
>
> Seven days past did some pack their gifts.
> Seven days past did some douse their fires.
> Seven days past did you leave your okwumuq,
> By paddle, by foot, you came from Mamukum,
> From Sqaqaiek, Kwanaken "hollow in the mountain",
> From Stamis and Sklau "home of the beaver",
> From Ekuks and Toktakamai "place of thimble-berries",
> From Yukuts and Slokoi did you travel seven days.

For hours the speaker droned on, giving thanks, listing villages that were represented, naming *siems*, the headmen, and their ancestors.

Sitka chuckled to herself as she watched her daughter gaping at the surroundings; Eva had never seen such an immense structure. The house was sixty feet wide and three hundred long. It smelled of fish and cedar and smoke. Three fires were spaced at equal intervals along its length, and each was tended by two men. Sunlight streamed through the chinks in the walls and the smoke-holes over the fires, slicing golden bars in the smoky darkness.

Sitka scanned the rows of shadowy faces, looking for Matcha-kawillee. She was not surprised by her absence; the old woman will be skulking in her house or the forest, she thought, refusing to acknowledge the ceremony or Tcaga's claim to be headman. Sitka could not blame her; the title had been in Matchakawillee's family for generations, and it would be painful to give it up, even though there were no men left to inherit it. She relaxed and settled her back against the bench; it would be a long wait for the first feast. The air was warm and comfortable. She felt at home among the rows of silent, patient faces watching the fires and listening to the speaker. It was good to be back.

Through the smoky rays she could see the dim outline of Tcaga seated at the far end of the house amongst the wealthiest of the visiting leaders. He looked older and fatter. His hair was greying, his face was pasty and etched with deep black lines. But she thought his eyes still looked young; they were bright black, glowing in the firelight. She jerked her head away. Don't be a fool, she told herself. He's much too far away to see his eyes.

Later she found herself admiring the sleek otter fur draped over Tcaga's shoulders. She was surprised to see that under it he wore the pinkman's uniform: black pants and jacket, loggers' boots, a collarless white shirt, and a misshapen hat. To dress like a white man on such an important occasion? But then, all of the men except those from the most isolated villages were dressed the same. Even the women wore blouses, petticoats, and shawls of brightly checked cloth. Only Eva, she herself, and the odd shaman wore the traditional cloak of woven cedar. She shifted uneasily. Tcaga had still not seen her.

The speaker's voice was flagging. He had talked well into the afternoon. The smells of the feast being prepared outside were drifting into the longhouse. Clouds had blotted out the sun, and the first drops of rain were sputtering into the fires. The attendants leaned forward and squirted streams of eulachon oil into the flames, which shot up through the smoke-hole with a whoosh. Surprised faces lit up in a bright-orange glow.

At last the speaker had come to the point. The purpose of the potlatch was to affirm Tcaga's claim to the most respected post in the village, *heekw siem*. The tribe had never recognized an omnipotent chief but each household had its own *siem*, or headman, who could trace his descent back to Skqomic, the first man. The *heekw siem* represented the largest and wealthiest house, so his status was greater, and when the council met to make a decision, his word carried the most weight. He would act as delegate in any dealings with the white man. To be *heekw siem* was the greatest honour any man could aspire to within the village.

Sitka listened carefully to the litany of ancestors. It was the same as she had always heard it until, fifteen generations back, the story took a peculiar turn.

> . . . who married Tciatmuq, daughter of owl,
> Descended from Tetketsen who defeated the bear. . . .

Tciatmuq, daughter of owl? Sitka blinked and tried to remember. Descended from Tetketsen? No. "Tciatmuq, daughter of owl, Descended from *Qautliwus*, son of Qoitcital." There it was: he had crossed genealogies only fifteen generations back. Of course, he had to do it if he was to claim descent from the first man, but why had he not chosen to do it forty generations back where the memory was murky and descent open to interpretation? Fifteen generations was not so long ago. Sitka looked warily around to see the reaction of her neighbours. She was grateful Matchakawillee had decided not to attend. The people near her were smiling and nodding at the speaker, enjoying the tale, others were dozing. Sitka was amazed. They had swallowed it.

Or had they? Perhaps they simply chose to ignore the lie. After all, Kweahkultun was dead. So many were dead. Who else was there? Because of his trading with the whites, Tcaga was by far the wealthiest man left. His family was old and the village did need a *heekw siem* to replace Kweahkultun. What else could they do?

> Brave Atsaian, son of Skqomic
>   — The first man —
> Who fell from the sky,
> At the dawn of the world.

The speaker thumped his talking stick on the cedar shake. A faint hum began at the far end of the house; it grew in intensity and flooded down the hall like a wave until the air shivered with the sound of the First People humming their acceptance of Tcaga's ancestral claim.

The doors swung open and two rows of men entered carrying huge feast dishes shaped like small canoes. The hall filled with the aroma of bear meat, smoked salmon, and roast duck. They took the food to the far end of the house and served the *siems* first, then the two rows split, one left, one right, and slowly worked their way around each side of the longhouse, cutting meat and heaping it onto tin plates. The procession continued: camas bulbs, steamed in an underground oven and flavoured with peppergrass and wild thyme, sap-bread made from the inner bark of maple and alder, fried mussels, wild beach peas, the crunchy roots of silverweed, acorn cakes, nettle soup, fiddlehead nuts, seaweed, white pine tea, and finally salmonberries. The feast lasted until dark.

When it was nearly over, children, restless from sitting all day, crept down from the benches to play on the packed dirt floor. Rain drummed on the roof, and the fire burned comfortingly. An old man stepped to the centre of the lodge and began a story.

"Once there was a wealthy *siem* whose wife had borne him five daughters. He wanted a son to inherit his name, so when the woman was pregnant for the sixth time he hired a shaman to work magic which would ensure the child was a boy. At last the time of birth came. As the shaman had promised, the wife bore him a healthy boy. The man was delighted and named his new son Whoi.

"But the woman did not recover from the ordeal. Three days later she died. The *siem* missed his wife greatly and grieved for a year.

"When the year had passed he married again. His second wife was a hard worker and pretty, but she was simple and very wicked. She hated the five daughters and was particularly jealous of Whoi because the *siem* doted on him constantly. One winter day she strapped Whoi to her back and set out in search of camas bulbs. The baby cried constantly at being taken from the warm house, but the woman believed he was crying for his father and she became very angry. She rocked Whoi and sang to him, but still the baby wailed. When she could stand it no longer she laid the child on a grassy slope and stuffed moss into his mouth. The crying stopped.

"The woman worked hard all day, digging further and further

afield with her stick until she was far away from the grassy slope. At dusk she hurried home with a full basket and an empty head.

" 'Where is my son?' thundered the *siem*.

"The woman blanched. 'I forgot him,' she whispered.

"The *siem* raised his fist and struck her across the mouth. 'Get out!' he yelled. 'And don't come back without him!'

"The woman fled the village in tears. She raced through the forest and back to the grassy slope. Whoi was gone. She searched the underbrush and found the tracks of a wolf near by.

"The second wife never returned. She lived alone in the forest, always in search of Whoi. She would snatch up young children who had strayed too far from the village, and they were never seen again, although sometimes their bones were found deep in the forest. She became the Wild-Woman-of-the-Woods."

The old man stopped and began to back away from the centre of the hall, but a distant sound stopped him. It was a soft, lamenting cry, like a loon, from the forest beyond the lodge. The audience hushed.

The sound came again, louder and closer than before. "Who-o-o-i-i-i!"

"The Wild-Woman-of-the-Woods," the old man whispered. "It's her." Children hurried back to the benches and climbed onto their parents' laps. "Bar the gate," he ordered.

When the cry sounded again it was loud and chilling and it came from just beyond the great double doors, rising from a moan to a high-pitched wail. The guests sat silently and stared at the entrance.

Sitka shuddered; she remembered the dreams she had had of the Wild-Woman-of-the-Woods. There was a sudden banging on the wall directly behind her. She jumped. It stopped, and began again on the far side of the hall.

"W-h-o-o-i-i!"

"The *swaihwe*!" shouted the old man. "Get the *swaihwe*!"

Sitka saw someone rush into a partitioned room at the far end of the longhouse. No one else moved. The rapid banging came again, this time from overhead. The creature was on the roof. The audience sat silently and watched the roof planks sag as the Wild-Woman-of-the-Woods made her way towards the smoke-hole.

A rattle hissed as the monster woman's head popped through the opening and hung upside down, her shards of lichen hair swaying far above the fire. Her face was streaked red and black — the colours of a corpse — and large white circles ringed her eyes. She peered around the walls of the longhouse, eyeing child after child, and each one snuggled deeper into its parents' arms.

On a signal from the old man, two hundred drummers began simultaneously to play a rhythm of one heavy beat followed by three short soft ones on cedar-box drums suspended from the rafters.

"W-h-o-o-i-i-i!" It was an inhuman shriek. The creature grabbed a rafter next to the opening, leaped through the hole, swung clear of the fire, and dropped to the floor. The Wild-Woman crouched on the beaten earth, scanning the children with her large white eyes. A curved bone pierced her nose, and long wooden claws hung from her fingers. She wore a short skirt of shredded cedar; her legs and torso were black, her arms and breasts blood-red.

She screamed and rushed at a young boy, then stopped a few feet short and whirled in a circle, her long lichen hair spinning around her. Again and again the creature shrieked and charged at different children, her claws outstretched, and each time she changed direction or turned away at the last moment. Finally she spotted Eva.

The Wild-Woman crouched in the firelight, her head tilted to one side, studying the little girl; her knees bounced in time to the drums, her claws opened and closed slowly. She made a low, gurgling noise in her throat, which flattened into a snake-like hiss.

Eva looked imploringly at her mother. "Close your eyes," Sitka whispered.

"W-h-o-o-i-i-i!" The Wild-Woman sprang into the air and darted at the little girl with the screwed-up eyes.

But before she could reach her, the rhythm of the drums changed abruptly and chanting began at the far end of the hall.

"Haiiii, hai, oh, o, o, o, o!
Haiiii, hai, oh, o, o, o, o!
Hai, ooooooh."

Six *swaihwe* dancers whirled out from behind the partition. Each wore a mask with a small upturned beak to represent the mythical bird that could sweep away evil spirits. Carved heads were perched on top of the masks, and long wands of eagle's down fanned around them like halos. The eye sockets were plugged with wooden pegs to look like protruding eyes. The dancers danced blind. A pair of attendants walked beside each *swaihwe* to guide him away from the fires and the walls.

The group split into two rows of three and moved down either side of the longhouse, spinning like tops. They wore goatskins shaped like inverted cones and decorated with tiers of white and black feathers. As the dancers spun, the feathers lifted and fanned around them. Their arms rose and fell in unison.

The Wild-Woman screeched and darted frantically around the farther end of the lodge, searching for a way to escape. She leaped at a smoke-hole but couldn't reach it; she climbed halfway up a roof support but fell back. The *swaihwe* were two-thirds of the way down the hall.

"Open the doors!" the old man shouted. Two ushers lifted the heavy bar from its locks and pushed. A cold wind sliced through the lodge. The air cleared of smoke and the fires kindled to a roar.

The Wild-Woman turned and hissed at the *swaihwe*, then fled into the rain.

"Whoi . . . whoi . . ." Her cries shrivelled and faded.

As the last of the dancers spun out the doors, leaving tufts of eagle's down floating in their wake, the chanting and drums crescendoed and stopped. The silence was startling, broken only by the crackling of the fires.

Sitka turned from the doors and looked down the length of the hall. Tcaga was standing in front of his chair, his hands on his hips. She could see him clearly in the clean, bright air. His small black eyes *were* bright and his mouth twisted into a half smile. He was looking directly at her.

Mei-fu could feel eyes on her, angry eyes. She turned over on her narrow cot, covering her bare breasts with her arm, and looked at Wu Lee, who stood defiantly in front of the burlap curtain that separated her small cubicle from the rest of the Globe Saloon. "Well, send the next one in."

"There are no more."

"What?"

"I sent them away."

Mei-fu snatched the flimsy dressing gown from the foot of her bed, swung her feet under her, and padded across the dirt floor to a small enamel bowl in the corner. She plucked a vinegar-soaked sponge from between her legs — may the gods forbid she should produce a barbarian child with tufts of hair growing from its nose and ears — and flung it into the basin. She stalked back to her bed and patted the straw mattress beside her. "Come here."

As soon as the boy was within reach, her hand darted up and slapped him hard across the face. "Fool," she shrieked. There was a lull in the talk and laughter on the other side of the curtain. Mei-fu lowered her voice. "I labour on my back day and night to coax these filthy barbarians to their little deaths," she hissed, "and now my own pale worm feels he has grown to a righteous dragon who must guard his mother's Jade Gate." She spat on the hard dirt floor. "*Dew neh loh moh.*" Her yellow robe fell open as she slid Chang's steel cashbox from under the bed and dropped in the two silver dollars she had received from her last customer.

Wu Lee sat beside her, his face stinging, his eyes smarting, and folded his hands on his lap. He stared blankly, full of shame, as she began counting the coins for the fourth time that day. The incessant rumble of the drums from the nearby potlatch filled the silence.

"Why did you do it?" she asked coldly.

"You dishonour my ancestors," Wu Lee said.

Mei-fu laughed. "Your ancestors were peasants. But we will be much more."

"You dishonour my father," the boy persisted.

"Your father rests comfortably with your ancestors on the other side of the world, and I am certain his wife, his *real* wife, tends his shrine daily and puts red paper robes on his goddess of mercy; she will need to if . . ." her voice trailed off. "But I will not speak ill of Chang Sun Lee. Our hearts were close." Mei-fu stopped her counting for a moment, then quickly resumed.

"So, my fiery dragon, what would you have me do? Sit in the street and beg for rice?"

"I could get a job at the sawmill," Wu Lee ventured.

Mei-fu smiled. "There are too many strong and hungry men who failed in the gold-fields. The mill is not desperate enough to hire children."

"We could wash laundry then."

Mei-fu chuckled. "It is true these filthy men must have a great many dirty clothes, but still I would die poor — and with wrinkled hands. How much money is in this box, dragon?"

Wu Lee shook his head.

"Nearly two hundred dollars," Mei-fu whispered. Her small nostrils flared as she savoured the words. "And soon the two will be four and then we will start our own business, and the four will become eight and the eight, sixteen." Her eyes sparkled as she slammed the cashbox shut and looked at Wu Lee. "I am sorry that I offend you, my son, but we are strangers trapped in a strange land, a harsh man's-land not fit for lone women and children. We have no one here. No one but ourselves. But we will eat winter rice yet, my dragon." Mei-fu clenched her fists and scowled at the dirt floor. Her voice cracked and she punched her fists against the straw mattress. "By all the gods, we will."

Again the drums of the potlatch filled the silence. Mei-fu pressed her hands to her eyes. "Why don't they stop?" she cried.

"Because they have something to celebrate." The boy's voice was dull and flat.

Mei-fu glanced at him and saw the tears, like melting ice, drip from the corners of his dark eyes. Quickly, she pulled him to her and cradled his head against her breast. His quiet sobs shuddered through her body and she felt the wetness of his grief seeping into the folds of her yellow robe. She held him tight against her and rocked back and forth. "Yes, my dragon," she murmured, "we will yet eat winter rice."

On the last day of the great potlatch Sitka stood in front of the longhouse and held tightly to Eva's hand. The large crowd around them jostled and chattered excitedly, anxious for the scramble to begin so they could pack their presents and start the long journey home before the rain fell. The sky was black and sullen.

The potlatch had gone well; everyone had participated and everyone had received and accepted a small British flag on a stick and a toy cane with a gilt top. Tcaga would be the new *beekw siem*. Chief Chaythoos had been honoured with a fine new canoe, lesser chiefs had received cedar chests, hunting equipment, and valuable scraps of iron and copper, and one old noble had been given a hand-cranked sewing machine which was a wonder to everyone. Even Eva had been recognized; she had won a laughing contest by staring implacably at her opponent for an hour and a half before the other girl withered and collapsed into fits of giggling. She had been awarded a waterproof basket woven from spruce roots, and she wore it proudly on her back as they waited for the scramble to begin.

A large platform of split cedar stood five feet off the ground and stretched across the front of the longhouse; it was piled to roof-level with thousands of Hudson's Bay blankets, hundreds of bolts of gaudy calico and gingham, metal wash-basins, iron pots and pans, steel hunting knives, woven baskets, leather boots, boxes of buttons, coils of rope, and more flags and toy canes. There were even a dozen velocipedes with large front wheels and small back ones, although no one knew how to ride them and the nearest road was five miles away. The crowd was amazed at Tcaga's wealth. Ordinarily they would have their knives drawn, ready to cut strips from the blankets as they were flung into the crowd, but today it would not be necessary; everyone would get at least one complete blanket.

The speaker stepped into view on the roof of the longhouse and addressed the crowd. He thanked them for attending, then spoke at length about the greatness of Tcaga's ancestors and how, with the acceptance of these gifts, Tcaga would take his place as *heekw siem*. At last he finished and stepped aside.

Tcaga appeared on the roof of the longhouse and, puffing and grunting, lowered himself carefully onto the huge pile of blankets. The speaker followed, and five more men climbed onto the platform. Tcaga picked out a bolt of crimson gingham, raised it ceremoniously over his head, and flung it into the air. The crowd roared as it unravelled like a streamer and floated down among them. They devoured it. Within seconds it was torn into pieces and the pieces were wadded into bundles and bags.

The speaker set to work on the enormous pile of blankets, hurling one after another into the air, where they flapped and billowed, then crumpled over the heads below. The crowd shrieked with joy as they elbowed and pushed. The velocipedes were rolled off the platform and snatched away. Coloured buttons rained down as boxes of them were tossed far into the crowd. The knives and heavy iron pots, too dangerous for throwing, were passed into the anxious hands of the men and women crowded against the platform. Pairs of boots, joined at the laces, were torn apart, the left going to one household, the right to another. No one cared: the black sky was gaudy with coloured cloth, buttons, and blankets. The crowd was ecstatic.

Sitka scratched half-heartedly in the dirt for buttons. She was more interested in watching Tcaga as he puffed and laboured over the bolts of cloth. Sweat was trickling down his face. He had not yet spoken to her, but she was certain he would today. Many times during the potlatch she had seen him looking at her out of the corner of his eye when he should have been watching the spirit dancers or listening to a legend. There had been a curiously wistful look about him. Today he would ask her to stay.

She braced herself as Matchakawillee shoved angrily past her and hobbled to the front of the crowd. The old woman stopped a few feet ahead of Sitka and rapped the *siem* of a small household on the shoulder with her stick. "He sold it," she shrieked. "All of it. From the creek with the beaver lodge to the old mill boundary. He sold all of our summer land to that slimy white fungus, Tyee Cains." The people around her stopped and listened.

A shower of coloured buttons struck Matchakawillee in the face and she swatted furiously at them. "Stop it!" she shrieked. "Stop that!" She slashed her stick onto the edge of the platform and the men throwing the gifts stopped immediately. Tcaga was white; he clutched the end of a bolt of yellow cloth which lay limply in the dirt, untouched by the crowd.

The old woman pointed her stick at him and hissed, "You are no *heekw siem*, you traitor." She whirled to face the crowd. "He has sold all of our summer land, from the creek with the beaver lodge to the boundary where the mill begins. I have just been there gathering herbs for my grandniece. Men are cutting down the trees. They are cutting them now. They ordered me off their land. Their land! Where do you think he got the money for all . . . this?" She kicked at the yellow fabric lying on the ground. "He sold our land, that's where. The land we have hunted on and cut the wood for our houses from since the dawn of the first man. Our land. He sold it. He sold it all!"

Tcaga twisted the yellow cloth in his hands. The First People stared at him and waited. "I had no choice," he said. "The white men appointed me chief. They would have taken the land anyway. Someone had to deal with them." The crowd shifted and groaned. "But I had no choice," he pleaded. "And look at what I got you for it." He pointed at the huge pile of gifts that remained on the platform. "Someone had to deal —"

"Yes," Matchakawillee shouted. "Look at what he got us for our land" — she kicked a velocipede held by a young woman and it clattered to the ground—"Vel-o-cee-peds," she sneered. "Where are the roads to drive them on? Toy flags and toy canes." She whirled to face Tcaga. "For this you have given away our land to be stripped of its trees? Land we have held for generations? You had no right! It was not yours to sell. You did it for yourself. For your own foolish pride. You did it so you could buy the respect of the First People. You are no *heekw siem*, Tcaga. You are a fool!" She screwed up her face and spat on the bright strip of yellow cloth.

Matchakawillee turned and stormed through the crowd towards her house. The *siem* she had first spoken to dropped his gifts and walked after her. The young woman with the velocipede did the same, and the people of the village followed. Slowly, one by one, the guests turned their backs on him and unpacked the cloth and blankets and buttons from their packs.

"Wait," Tcaga said. "No, I did it for you, for all of us. The world is full of trees to build our houses with. What does one small piece of land matter?"

But it was too late. The ears of the crowd were closed. The guests were heading for their canoes. Tcaga slumped down onto the pile of blankets, still holding the strip of yellow cloth.

Only Sitka and Eva remained. They stood among the vast jumble of the morning's havoc: torn fabric, crumpled blankets, broken flags, and canes. Sitka watched the tears rolling down Tcaga's fat cheeks. She took Eva's hand in hers, turned, and headed slowly towards the beach. As they walked, she bent and whispered in Eva's ear. The little girl wriggled free of the shoulder straps on her basket. It skidded down her arm and slipped softly from her fingertips.

END OF THE DOG DAYS

WILEY BURGESS stalked through the swamp, glaring at the black water rippling over his knees and the thin crust of pale green scum drying on his pants. His teeth were clenched in a slow-burning rage as his thoughts twisted brutally around the image of his father. "I'll show you." The words rumbled through his head like thunder, one at a time, with each step he took through the brackish water. "Bastard. I'll . . . show . . . you. . . ."

He marched into the sun, which was slung low over the flat horizon, deepening to orange as it settled into a thin veil of smoke. Far to the south a grass fire raged like a blood-red sea, rolling away from him in crimson waves, driven by the wind. His guide had taken the rest of the pack horses and gone ahead to set up camp; the fellow would probably not return to look for him until tomorrow. His own mount, a skittish palomino mare, had finally broken an hour ago, driven mad by the thick swarms of mosquitoes burrowing into her ears and the corners of her eyes. She had reared up in a frenzy, screaming, lashing out at the clouds of insects with her hooves, twisting and lurching, until he had tumbled into the marsh and watched helplessly as she galloped away, a grey cloud of mosquitoes streaming from her flanks.

The swamp ended. The ground rose. He waded through hip-high grass, oblivious to the small scuttlings of snakes and mice hurrying out of his path, obsessed with the hatred driving him on. The trickles of sweat under his leather shirt slowed as the sun sank lower, tinging the vast sky pink and mauve.

At sunset he found the palomino mare stretched on the ground, her left front leg broken, her golden hide black with mosquitoes and flies. The grass around her was beaten flat from hours of frantic thrashing, but now she lay still, her sides billowing softly with each shallow breath, her flanks quivering occasionally, sending up clouds of insects. He stood over her and watched as her eyes opened; they were frightened, soft brown, pleading, the eyes of Lady Chadwick's young cousin whom he had met at Chadwick Hall. Theresa, that was her name; they were Theresa's eyes.

"It will make a man of you." His father's voice cut through his mind like a razor. He stripped off his leather shirt, brushed away the flies, and draped it over the horse's side. "It will make a man of you."

The mosquitoes swarmed over his bare skin, feeding on him. He tilted his head back, shut his eyes, and concentrated on the dozens of stinging pricks. His lips parted. He ran his hand through the thick mat of hair on his chest and down to the bulge in his crotch. "Theresa . . ."

As the sky deepened to purple and vermilion, the horse's flesh glowed as though it were ivory, fine, sleek, smooth, like the girl's skin under her mounds of black cloth. He crouched by her head, his legs spread wide, and stroked her neck. Her nostrils flared, her muscles quivered, and the soft brown eyes widened with fear. *Her* eyes had looked like that, when his hands had touched her throat. She had thought he was going to strangle her. "Ridiculous," he had said. He was not a murderer.

His large hand closed over the mare's warm, velvety muzzle. He tightened his grip, digging his long fingers into the soft flesh. Her billowing sides stilled for a moment, then she jerked her head away. . . . Not a murderer.

He stood and slid his Enfield rifle from the mare's saddle, checked it, rested the cool metal against his chest, and waited. The mosquitoes swarmed and bit. The long fingers of colour pulled back across the sky to the western horizon, until he could see only the whites of the horse's eyes. His hand slid down to the buttons of his pants.

He swung the barrel down and pressed it against her ear. She struggled. She knew. The girl had struggled like that. "Too rough," she had cried. "You're hurting me." Her small hands beating against him. Her breasts squeezed flat against his chest. He cocked the trigger. The whites of her eyes. The whites of her eyes. Her teeth like fire on his neck. And then she was falling, falling, her raven hair fanning about her, her arms twisted behind her back — falling, falling . . .

"Father! . . ."

The gunshot rumbled like thunder across the black prairie, while far to the south the sky over the grass fire glowed blood-red.

Gassy Jack's bulk shifted awkwardly from side to side as he trundled down the grassy path past the ragged collection of shacks and stores which had fallen haphazardly into place along the waterfront east of the Globe Saloon. People had taken to calling the tiny village Gastown in honour of its founder. Gassy Jack smiled proudly. The summer evening was warm, the colours were vibrant. At last a cool breeze was blowing up from the inlet and the poplar leaves rustled over his head. He puckered his fleshy lips and began to whistle: a delicate silvery sound trilling magically up and down the scale to the tune of "Bonnie Mary".

When he had first heard that a New Westminster constable would be in Gastown on Sunday to investigate reports that his saloon was operating on the Lord's Day, he had been furious, but now, as he swung idly home with his fingers curled under the gills of two five-pound trout and the promise of a glorious sunset tickling the clouds to the west, he was grateful for the holiday. For several months the pain in his legs had been getting steadily worse, so it was a relief not to have to stand behind the bar all day. Besides, the fishing had been good and he had even managed to sell three cases of whisky on the sly, at double the usual price. Yes, he thought, it's been a grand day.

He stopped at the edge of a small clearing and leaned against a tree to rest his legs. Ahead was the Globe Saloon, nestled amongst the trees, looking out over the inlet. The original structure, with its grey-white clapboard and low, tilted walls, was still there, but he had improved upon it in the last two years with wooden struts, baling wire, and moss. He had even added two rooms: one for the hard-working, salacious little Chinese woman who attracted so much business, the other a small space at the back with a potbellied stove where he and Martha could sleep undisturbed by the grunts and moans of Mei-fu's late-night customers.

A rabbit darted across the clearing and disappeared into a thicket. Perhaps he should build a new saloon, he thought. Or even a hotel, a big modern one with two storeys and a verandah. The sun was setting. Smoke puffed out of his chimney, glowed pink, and shredded on the cool sea breeze.

The yellow dog did not bound out of the thickets to greet him as he usually did, wriggling and whining in a paroxysm of delight. He had taken to staying in Martha's bedroom. As Jack reached for the door, it opened, and he was startled by a tall, ugly Indian standing in the doorway. It was Martha's brother. Behind him stood his wife, and behind her his daughter, a small, pretty girl named Quahailya. "How is she?" he asked.

The pockmarked face of Martha's gloomy brother sagged. "Worse than yesterday." Gassy Jack held his breath; the man reeked of fish and whisky. "We go now. Come see tomorrow." The sombre trio filed out of the saloon, their eyes focused respectfully on the ground. As the little girl passed, she looked up at him with her small, elfish face, and he instinctively smiled.

He closed the door and shuffled across the sawdust floor of the saloon. The back room was dark, and it stank of whisky and of Martha's relatives. The stone woman lay on a cot by the one small window, wheezing and puffing. The burlap curtain above her stirred in the breeze, causing a delicate pattern of shadows to shift across her face. The yellow dog sat on the floor, his head nestled in the blankets, his tail thumping on the floorboards. Gassy Jack shuffled painfully across the room, unpinned the curtain to let in the soft glow of sunset, and kissed Martha on the cheek.

She stirred, and woke with a wrenching cough that shook the bed. She pushed herself up on one elbow and retched into a pail on the floor. Her face was grey.

"How is it, my love?" Jack asked.

Martha lay back, her mouth gaping and her lungs bubbling as she sucked in air. She reached for his hand and held it. He noticed that her grip was softer. "You see Quahailya?" she asked.

"Yes, and your drunken brother and his wife. What were they doing here?"

"I buy her for you."

"Who?"

"Quahailya. My niece. For when I am gone."

Jack turned his head away. "You planning on leaving soon?"

"No. I no want to go. I like it here."

"Then, why —"

"She young. She can wait. I just want to know who take my place, that's all. Quahailya good girl. She look after you real nice. You like her."

Jack got up from the cot. He stoked the fire in the stove and began preparing soup. "How old is she?"

"Twelve. But she grow into fine woman. She have big breasts, like me. I no bigger than Quahailya when I twelve."

"How much did you pay?"

"Oh, Jack . . ."

"How much?"

"Two cases whisky." Again Martha coughed and gasped for air. Jack held her head while she leaned over the bucket. "But she worth every drop. She take care of you good, Jack."

He fed her broth from the pot, scraping the sides of her mouth with a tin spoon, but she could eat little. Her enormous bulk had shrunk to loose folds of flesh which draped her like a shroud.

Martha closed her eyes and listened while Gassy Jack talked of his plans for the Deighton Hotel. Long after she was asleep he sat up, holding her hand, listening to her breathing, and thinking of how he had bought her to carry loads, cook, and clean for him. He tried to remember when he had stopped treating her as a workhorse and begun thinking of her as his wife.

He woke with a start. It was dark. His hand had fallen over the arm of the chair and the yellow dog was whining and nuzzling against it. The burlap curtain rustled in the breeze. The air smelt like rain. He leaned forward and listened for Martha's breathing. Silence. He lurched closer, his ear almost against her mouth, listening, listening, until at last he heard a faint bubbling deep within her chest.

He bolted from the room, stumbling over his chair as he ran. The saloon was dark but he crossed it in three steps, the pain in his legs forgotten, and burst into Mei-fu's small cubicle. She was sitting cross-legged on her mattress, her large black eyes watching him over the brim of a rice bowl, her chopsticks frozen midway to her mouth.

"It's Martha," he blurted. "I'm going to New Westminster for the doctor. Will you watch her?"

Before she could answer, he was running from her room. "Stop at George Black's and get horse," she called after him. "He's fastest around." The saloon door slammed against its frame and bounced open; a cold breeze scuttled across the floor, stirring small eddies in the thick piles of sawdust. Through the black rectangle she could see the sky, dark and starless. From across the inlet, on the other side of the mountains, came the faint rumble of thunder.

Slowly Mei-fu placed her rice bowl on the packed-dirt floor and crossed her chopsticks against its rim; then she turned to Wu Lee, who sat in a corner of the small room, staring through the open door at the black shapes of poplars thrashing in the wind. "Surely," she said, "if the Stone Woman passes to the Eternal Yellow Springs, it is an omen. With change comes change. In the last two years we have saved a great deal of money, and I have sent a letter to Wong Foo in San Francisco. Perhaps it is time we left this place."

The boy turned to her and Mei-fu smiled. For the first time in many years, there was joy in his eyes.

Gassy Jack grunted with each heavy lurch of his body against the tired horse as he galloped past the shacks of Gastown towards the Globe Saloon. The grey light of dawn seeped weakly through the treetops and rain streamed down in heavy straight lines, turning the path to mud. He twisted on the horse's back to urge on the doctor, who trotted cautiously behind, his thin frame bent into the storm.

At the edge of the clearing he abruptly reined in his horse and listened. "Awoo-o-o-o-o-o-o-o-o." It was a thin, mournful sound, barely audible over the hiss of the rain. It stopped. The hair on the back of his neck prickled. He jumped down from the horse and ran ahead, legs burning, soaked with rain, to the grove of poplar. There, by the open door of the Globe Saloon, the yellow dog squatted in the mud, his muzzle thrust up at the rain, and howled. For a brief moment he drowned out the storm, then his voice quavered, diminished to a whine, and died.

Wiley Burgess inched along the narrow ledge—in places it was only a foot wide—with his back pressed tight against the mountain of rock behind him. Six hundred feet below, the feathery tops of pine trees swayed in the wind and the sound of it rushed up the cliff and over the ledge like the roar of a river. He felt dizzy and faint. For three days he had eaten nothing but rubaboo, a thin, watery stew of boiled pemmican. There were only two fists of dried meat left, and he was still somewhere in the wild western ranges of the Rockies.

Cautiously he swung his right arm across his chest, passed the stout pole he had fetched from the campground to the guide, then quickly pressed back against the rock wall. He spread his fingers wide over the cold, rough granite and watched as the half-breed wedged the lever under a large boulder that blocked their path. He thought of the Thompson River, out there somewhere in the vast tangle of green below them. He thought of the raft they would build if they found the river, and of the treacherous descent to Kamloops, the Fraser, and finally the Pacific. He tried to remember how much longer it would take—the guide had told him. A month? Two? The numbers blurred in his mind. All he could recall was the March day, nearly five months before, when he had tramped defiantly out from Fort Carleton in a light snowfall with the voice of his father ringing in his ears: "Make something of yourself."

He tried to remember the exact point at which his spite, his rancor, his lust for vindication, had gone. Had they leached away in some icy northern stream? Had they dropped into some bottomless mountain chasm? Or had they merely faded away, bit by bit, during the hot, grinding tramp across the prairie? He could not remember. But at some point he had resigned himself to the fact that his father would never relent. He would not return. And just because the girl was dead.

Now, each morning, he creaked, dirty and stinking, from under his blanket and faced the west, only because it was shorter than going back. And each day he dully picked up the endless, brutal march to a futile goal for a reason he had forgotten.

Pebbles scrabbled over the ledge and clattered down the rock wall. He turned his head and watched as a large boulder teetered on the lip of the precipice, then tumbled over the edge, and he saw it as if in slow motion, floating down through space, falling, falling, and he was back in Lady Chadwick's guest room, with the naked body of her young cousin falling, falling, her raven hair fanning about her as her head floated down to the jagged stones of the fireplace hearth.

The lights of the car are winking, winking, as the train careers around a corner, up, up, from the dark prairie and into the rigid upthrust arms of the Rockies. Amor De Cosmos stands looking out the window, the drink in his hand frozen midway to his mouth; he knows that the blackness beyond drops into unseen chasms. He listens to the rhythmic jolt of the wheels, like the beating of a giant bird's wings on the hollow drum of the car.

The reflection of the occupants is thrust glaringly back upon him by the black square of glass. Sir John A. Macdonald, Prime Minister of Canada, sits in the upper left-hand corner, small, pale, ghost-like. Cartier is there, as is Doctor Tupper, President of the Privy Council, Sir Francis Hincks, Minister of Finance, and Hector Langevin, Public Works. There are others: Anthony Musgrave, Governor of Newfoundland, poor Seymour — although De Cosmos knows he is dead — representing British Columbia. Jonas Cains is there.

Cains stands to speak but De Cosmos cannot hear him. He watches the man haranguing the politicians in the black square of glass, but all is silence. The drumming of wings on the roof has stopped. The train has taken flight. For a moment there is only the whisper of rushing air. Then the whistle shrieks, the car tilts in the clutch of the giant black bird, and they are falling, tumbling through the cold night into the bottomless black chasm.

Macdonald is flung doll-like against the window; the glass shatters, he slips from the train. The others lurch and pitch about him like broken puppets. De Cosmos revolves slowly, surrounded by the grinding screech of metal, as the train slides down the cold granite arms. A coal-oil lantern crashes into the small of his back, explodes, bursts into flame. The car cracks open, splinters apart and he is falling free, a fiery comet, with the roar of the wind in his ears as he tumbles through the blackness.

Amor De Cosmos, born William Alexander Smith, sat bolt upright in bed, gaunt and haggard, and buried his face in his hands. His nightshirt had twisted up around his midriff, and it hugged him like a cold, clammy hand. Sweat glistened in his tangled beard. He threw back the covers, padded across the floor to the liquor cabinet, and poured a drink. His hands shook.

He gulped it down and leaned his back against the frame of the open window. Why, he wondered, why will they not let me be? It had been so long since he had slept peacefully, he could not remember when. Always it was the same: the train — the *confederation* train — the thunder of wings on the roof, the silence, the falling, the blackness. It was the *people* who wanted confederation, he told himself, not he. He had seen the vision time and time again — a single nation, mighty and sovereign, from coast to coast — but only because he had been chosen; it was still the people's dream, the people's wish . . . the people. "I am their messiah," he muttered, "their saviour."

He filled his glass again; his hands shook less. Jonas Cains, he thought, has corrupted my vision with his schemes and treachery because he smells money like a wolf smells blood. He shut his eyes and took a deep, shaky breath. And now Macdonald lusts after my province as a prop to shore up his sagging political career. Even England will only act, finally, out of fear, fear of losing the Pacific to the Yankees.

He stared sadly at the dishevelled bed; the thought of returning to its cold, damp sheets to be haunted again terrified him. He shut his eyes and pressed the empty bottle tight against his chest. "Only *I* act for the people," he muttered quickly, running the words together like an incantation; "my hands are clean, not a penny, not a penny; it is me they cry out for to lead them through their darkness, for I am their Saviour, I am their Christ, I am —

"God-damned devils!" He flung the bottle against the wall, whirled round, and leaned far out the open window over the empty street below. "I am History!" he shouted. A dog at the far end of the road began to bark. He turned his bloodshot eyes up to the black chasm of the night sky, his pale face shaking, a thread of saliva caught in the tangle of his beard. "*I* am *History*!"

Mei-fu closed the door of her room in the Niantic Hotel, listened for the sharp click as she twisted the key in its lock, then nervously jiggled the doorknob to ensure it was secure. As she hurried down the dark, musty-smelling passageway, the bustle under her barbarian costume of olive-green silk twitched uncomfortably across her backside. San Francisco. So little had changed. Even the Niantic Hotel, where she had spent her first anxious nights after pawning her silver fingernail sheaths so many years ago, was still the same. It was a dingy two-storey affair, built atop the hulk of a prospectors' ship beached on the ash-grey sands of the San Francisco waterfront.

"Good evening." She smiled primly at the grim-faced proprietor, who glared after her as she crossed the lobby and stepped out into the orange glow of a California sunset. Her heart beat fast against the tight walls of her corset as she dug her fingers into the folds of her numerous petticoats and cautiously descended the gangway to the busy street below. A tough-looking Chinese in a black coat and bowler hat, his hand tucked suggestively, menacingly, in his jacket pocket, stepped out of the shadows. She nodded in his direction and hurried down Francisco Street, conscious of his footsteps following behind. He was Sue Yop, the *boo how doy*, or personal bodyguard, of the Mandarin Wong Ching Foo.

As she entered Chinatown it was twilight, the Hour of the Dog. She bustled through the maze of narrow streets, shouldering her way arrogantly past the knots of men who clogged the corners; they growled angrily after her but kept a respectful distance from the *boo how doy*.

At Li Po's Herb Sanatorium, she turned into a narrow unlit corridor called Highbinder's Alley. The rising moon was blotted out by a sagging patchwork of overlapping balconies, sprouting like branches from the high walls. Tattered laundry rustled softly, like grey ghosts, in the breeze over her head. She peered at a small unmarked door, then glanced at Sue Yop. He nodded. She knocked three times, paused, then knocked twice more. The door opened a crack, throwing a narrow band of yellow light across a startled rat in the street. A pair of black eyes studied her a moment, then the door slammed shut.

Sue Yop pushed her gently aside and rapped out the code. Again the door opened. He thrust in a small square of ivory engraved with black characters: the personal calling card of the Mandarin Wong Foo. The door opened wider and Mei-fu brushed haughtily in, past the suspicious black eyes of the doorman and down a narrow flight of stairs. At the bottom was a beaded curtain and beyond it a dark passageway. Her heart thumped against her chest as she felt along the wall to another stairway. Lifting her skirts, she proceeded cautiously. The stairs snaked around a corner and ended at a small black door. As her hand reached for the latch the door crashed open and two drunken Chinese, bent double with laughter, stumbled past and wound erratically up the stairs. Mei-fu winced at the sudden flood of light, took a deep breath, and marched into San Francisco's notorious slave market.

All around the hall, conversations stumbled to a halt. Heads turned, and the clatter of bamboo tiles at the fan-tan tables stopped. Mei-fu did not lower her eyes. She swept defiantly across the room and seated herself in silence at a small green table by the wall. Sue Yop sat beside her, his hand still tucked menacingly in his coat pocket, and glared from one group of men to the next. Each gradually returned their attention to their own table, and slowly the babble of conversation resumed.

Mei-fu began to breathe again. She had done it — she was the first woman ever who had dared to enter the flesh market as a customer. She ordered a glass of rice wine from a nervous boy and sat back, chuckling proudly to herself, to take in the scene.

It was a curious mixture of opulence and squalor: red lacquer columns rose fifteen feet from the packed-dirt floor and disappeared into gaudy clouds of yellow silk banners and tasselled paper lanterns which wafted in the thick palls of smoke. Behind them shreds of black tarpaper sagged from the ceiling. A lanky wolfhound prowled the floor in search of scraps, muzzling his way through the hundred or so men who milled among the tables, drinking and betting on the games of Mah-Jongg, *paijiu*, and fan-tan. In the centre of the room was an empty platform supported on the backs of four carved dragons. The neck of each beast curled over a corner of the stage, and two steps led up to a small pedestal on each dragon's head. One wall was covered with a faded red-velvet curtain, the rest were bare planks spotted with mildew and decorated with pictures of naked Chinese girls.

Mei-fu waited, sipping her rice wine and glaring back at the passing men. Half an hour later a gong sounded, the Chinese rushed to their seats, and all eyes turned to the dragon stage. The curtain parted and four dour-looking men in different-coloured robes mounted the stage and bowed, then each ascended the neck of a separate dragon to his designated pedestal on the monster's head. They bowed again, then each addressed the crowd in turn: the man in yellow was from Changchun and was pleased to speak to his countrymen in Mandarin; the one in blue was honoured to represent all brave persons who spoke the noble language Min; the third, robed in green, humbly offered his services in Cantonese to the people of Guangdong and Kwangsi; the last, a sour-looking fellow in black, said he talked Hakka, that was all.

The gong sounded again, the curtains parted, and the chief auctioneer, an obese man in a gold and crimson robe, paraded in, the eight-inch nails of his right hand circled round the thin wrist of a young Chinese girl. He dragged her through the crowd and onto the stage and tugged at the gauzy white sheet she clutched around her. The girl was horrified and pulled away, but the shroud came off and she stood naked and trembling before the crowd, her head hung in shame. She attempted to cover herself with her hands, but the auctioneer grabbed her wrist and paraded her around the edge of the platform, holding up her arms, poking her small breasts, slapping her buttocks, rolling his eyes, and joking with the men in all four languages as he assured them she was a virgin and had just turned fourteen.

With the next crash of the gong the room exploded into frantic bidding. Men jumped up from their tables, pushed to the stage and gathered under the four dragon heads, shouting up at their representatives and tugging at the hems of their robes. Twice the gong sounded and the auctioneer consulted with the four harried men; the highest bid was revealed and the room erupted again into pandemonium. On the fourth and final blast the best offer was accepted, the sale was ended, and the frightened girl was led away. Mei-fu puckered her face in disgust; the scrawny child had gone for the outrageous price of $500. Her new owner swaggered proudly through the red-velvet curtain to pay his money and collect his property.

Mei-fu shook her head in amazement. She had not known what to expect, but the carved dragons, the sudden explosions of one hundred men shouting in four languages, the stripping and parading of the girls, were both frightening and exhilarating. She glanced at the wolfhound, who was watching her from the floor under a nearby table, and set down her drink. She would need to keep her wits about her.

The second girl would not do; she screamed and cried until tears dripped from her breasts. The third had a face like a monkey, the fourth was too old. Mei-fu waited patiently, studying the bidding, noting the prices, consulting with Sue Yop. Earlier in the day she had acquired two Chinese girls — one she had bailed out of prison, the other she had bought from an old Mandarin who was desperate for cash — and both were prettier than the specimens she had seen tonight. These, together with the three white prostitutes she had obtained from the San Francisco Women's Prison, made an adequate stable, but what she wanted now was something rare and outlandish, something exotic to tickle the curiosity of the oafish timberbeasts and lure them in like bears to the honey tree — and this the Mandarin Wong Foo, proprietor of the slave market, had promised as the final offering of the day.

She sat back in her chair and waited, letting the bizarre scene before her drift and blur as she daydreamed about the grand two-storey brothel — the Palace Royale — she had built this summer on the banks of Burrard Inlet, just a few hundred yards from the boundary of Jonas Cains's mill. Granted, even with the money she had talked Gassy Jack into investing, there was still not enough to make the place truly fashionable, but that would come. There had been so many unexpected expenses, like the pearl-handled revolver she had bought today for Wu Lee so he could guard the girls while she attended the auction. Not that she expected they would try to escape, but still, one could not be too cautious when it came to an investment. She thought of him sitting with his chair propped against the door of their room in the Niantic Hotel, his arms folded sternly across his chest, his gun tucked proudly in his belt, his fierce eyes glaring at his charges, and she chuckled. He was a wonderful boy.

Yes, money had been a problem, but she knew this was to be expected with any new venture. The saloon she had decided to install in the big room on the main floor would help tremendously. It was true that she had neglected to tell Gassy Jack he was investing in a business that would be in direct competition with his Globe Saloon, but she was more pleased with her shrewd business sense than she was worried about her scruples. After all, she rationalized, he had begun construction on the Deighton Hotel shortly after the Stone Woman's death, so he would have income from his lodgers, and, besides, Gastown was growing daily and needed a second saloon. Yes, she assured herself, it was the proper thing to do; it was sure to make her very rich.

She pressed her lips into a thin line. And the money, all of it, would go back into the business. For now the girls would have to make do with bare rooms and rough plank beds, but as the money poured out of the barbarians' pockets and into her cashbox, she would make the Palace Royale live up to its splendid name. She dreamed of satin quilts on goose-feather mattresses, of red-velvet drapes with gold tassels, of a chandelier to hold fifty candles, leaded-glass windows, carved screens of ivory and amber, china washstands, a long mahogany bar polished like glass, and brass spittoons for the ill-bred barbarians.

Sue Yop nudged her and nodded towards the platform as the gong sounded. The curtains parted and a woman marched through the crowd ahead of the startled autioneer and mounted the dragon stage unassisted. The crowd hushed. Mei-fu's jaw dropped. The woman was a Negress!

Quickly Mei-fu leaned across the table and whispered in the *boo how doy*'s ear. He nodded, slipped from his chair, and made his way through the stunned crowd as the Negress flung off her sheet and paraded naked around the edge of the platform with her hands on her hips. She was big-boned and strong, with long, tightly curled hair flowing over deep-brown shoulders. Mei-fu studied the handsome, angular face with its fleshy lips, the firm cambered breasts, reddish-brown with large black buds, the sensual curve of her back arching down to sleek rounded buttocks. She was perfect. Granted, she had the feet of an ape, but Mei-fu knew from experience that white men had no appreciation for the grace and delicacy of prettily bound feet.

The crowd around the dragon stage thinned as the Chinese backed away, exchanging disgusted looks; a few gathered their money from the gambling tables and pushed towards the door.

Mei-fu was delighted. Of course, the brazen black woman would be abhorrent to the refined tastes of civilized men, but for the rough and wild timberbeasts of Gold Mountain she would be a rare and exotic delicacy who would have them swimming down the mighty Fraser for the right to pour their silver dollars into her cashbox. She smacked her lips and chuckled softly to herself.

The auctioneer finished exhorting the crowd, and the gong crashed, its ring fading away like ripples in a pond. The room was silent. Sue Yop spoke softly to the green-robed man atop the head of one of the dragons. All eyes turned to Mei-fu. She stared straight ahead, her gaze fixed on the sullen Negress.

An old Mandarin with a mischievous smile swaggered up to

the stage, teetering from too much whisky. Mei-fu watched coldly as he made a boisterous offer. The *boo how doy* glanced in her direction and she curled her right index finger slowly, imperceptibly, towards herself. He turned his back on the stage and started towards her table.

The Mandarin's face whitened. He looked frantically from Sue Yop to the Negress and back again, horrified that his bluff had been called and he was to be stuck with the monstrous black woman. He scuttled back to his table, waving his hands over his head and pleading that his eyes were dim with age and that what he had thought to be a gazelle, upon closer inspection proved to be a devil ape, and never would he have such a vulgar creature in his house. The men chuckled respectfully into their sleeves.

Mei-fu nodded. The *boo how doy* returned and made a final offer. As the gong sounded, she picked up her purse and swept grandly across the floor towards the red-velvet curtain. The black woman was hers for seventy-five dollars.

It was the end of the dog days. The air was still and heavy with the scent of cedar. Deep in the bowels of the mill Matthew bent over the new shingle saw; a dark V of sweat tapered down the back of his shirt and disappeared under his belt. He glanced at the hornets flitting silently in and out of the shadows, where they had come to escape the heat. The buzzing of their wings was drowned out by the roar of machinery from the floor above.

He mopped the congealing blood from the saw with a rag, reached behind the blade, pulled a finger from where it lay curled among the gears, and flung it on the ground with the other two. Their owner, a high-strung youth from Canada, was on his way to the doctor in New Westminster.

"Ship's coming." The bearded face of Johann, the foreman, appeared over Matthew's head, framed by the trapdoor that led to the floor above. "Looks like the *Isabel.*"

"Cains?"

"Reckon."

"How's Charlie?"

"Fainted. Sent him to Stump Town on the *Cariboo Fly*. The boys will fetch him back when the doc's finished, though I don't know how much use he'll be with only two fingers on his right paw."

"Lots of shinglers are missing fingers," Matthew said. "We'll find something for him, Johann. We owe him that much."

"Reckon."

The steam whistle of the *Isabel* shrieked in the distance. Matthew scooped up the fingers with the rag and clambered up the ladder to the main floor. "See if you can get someone working that shingler again."

"All right."

Matthew swung through the mill past the howling Chinee trimmer and the clattering lath mill, past the pony saw and the great trimmer, which screamed as it sawed across the grain, cutting planks into lengths. He paused at the big hoe, the main saw. Bull Thompson, the wedger-off, a huge, nimble man, stood perched six feet above the floor, riding the back of a giant Douglas fir as it moved through the saw. He reached into the open cut, pulled out a loose wedge, and danced along the moving log, his spiked boots gripping the bark like claws, until his head was a foot from the whizzing blade. He jammed the shim into the narrow cut to keep the saw from binding, hefted a sledgehammer over his head, and drove the wedge into place, the heels of his boots lifting off the log with each swing of the heavy iron hammer.

"Good work," Matthew shouted.

At the mouth of the chute he stopped to listen to the groan of the bull wheel as it hauled logs up from the floating boom below. A wiry little man from Oregon skipped over the bobbing raft, jabbing with his pickaroon as he coaxed a large log onto the chute. It lurched, slipped backwards, then lurched again as the jagged teeth bit in and dragged the heavy timber up the ramp and into the mill.

"Zeke," Matthew yelled. "Tighten up that chain and you won't get so much slippage." The little man waved and hurried to make the adjustment.

The sun was high, and hazy yellow; somewhere, far to the east, a forest fire raged unchecked through the wilds, sending vast sheets of thin grey smoke drifting for days on the high mountain currents. Matthew winced as he stepped from the shadows of the mill into the bright day, and his nostrils burned with the hot, dry smell of cedar and smoke. He shook his head sadly at the thought of the good timber — thousands of acres of it — blazing out of control, but there was nothing he could do about it, except wait for the rain. It was like this in the hot, dry dog days at the end of every summer.

Through the glare reflected off the inlet, he saw the *Isabel* squeezed in among the numerous big ships that were loading lumber. Two horses appeared on deck, shimmering in waves of heat as they clattered down the gangplank and onto the wharf. A woman mounted one of them and sat sidesaddle, arranging the folds of her white dress over the horse's rump. She trotted the mare to the end of the dock and waited on the beach. Matthew recognized her as one of Jonas's daughters.

"Caroline. Hello."

"Why, Mr. Galer. How do you do." She bent low over the horse and extended her hand. Matthew noticed she had affected a slight southern drawl. He wiped his bloody fingers on his pants, but Caroline hastily withdrew her hand. "What's that?" She pointed at the gory rag.

Matthew grinned and raised it impishly over his head so she could get a better look. "Fingers. We got a clumsy shingler." Her eyes widened. "You going for a ride in this heat?" he asked.

"Why, yes." She was flustered. "I . . . I've never explored your side of the inlet before and Wiley has kindly offered to ride with me."

"Wiley?"

"Oh, of course you've never met Mr. Burgess. He just arrived on the inlet last week." She twisted in her saddle, her red hair falling over one shoulder, and waved to her companion. "His father is the Earl of Downsview," she added in a whisper.

Matthew glanced at the handsome, overdressed man in his late twenties who ambled down the wharf leading a dark stallion. He was tall and husky, with a square, tanned face, black hair parted in the middle, blue eyes, and a trim moustache. He extended a grey-gloved hand.

"Wiley, I would like you to meet Matthew Galer; Mr. Galer, Wiley Burgess. Wiley is going to be Father's new assistant at the mill. He came overland all the way from Canada, if you can imagine, though he's originally from England." The creases at the corners of Wiley's eyes puckered as he smiled.

"You don't say," Matthew said. "Well, pleased to meet you, Mr. Burgess. Say, that's a mighty hefty load of lumber you've got stacked on your wharf." Wiley turned to look across the inlet.

"Looks like about two hundred thousand feet."

"Yes, two hundred and fifty actually, and we'll be adding another fifty tomorrow. It's bound for Australia. We should be loading it next week."

"I know it's none of my business," Matthew said, "but I don't think that wharf can handle it. I rowed past there yesterday on my way to Brighton and noticed that half the pilings on the east side have been knocked loose by the rip-tide. I'd hate to see any man lose three hundred thousand feet of good lumber—even the competition."

Wiley's smile vanished. "Well, that's very sporting of you, Mr. Galer. I can't say that I agree with you, but thank you for your advice. I shall certainly take it into my consideration. Caroline, shall we go?"

"Certainly. It will be a relief to get into the forest and out of this heat. Oh, I almost forgot. The new governor is going to be here next Tuesday. He's been touring the interior, you know. Father's giving a grand dinner party for him and he asked me to invite you and Mrs. Galer. De Cosmos will be there, and we've asked old Sir James, although he wouldn't commit himself. He's gotten quite crotchety, you know," she added in a confidential whisper. "Will you and Mrs. Galer come?"

Matthew shifted awkwardly from foot to foot and rubbed the back of his neck. He was amazed at Cains's gall. The thought of sitting down to dinner with the man who had rustled his logs and nearly killed him rankled, and Abby would be furious, but still, the new governor . . . Perhaps he could do something about the timber leases he had applied for. "We'd be happy to," he said.

"Good. The *Isabel* will pick you up at sunset."

"No need to trouble with that, Caroline. We can take the *Cariboo Fly*."

"Oh please, Mr. Galer. Father gave me very specific instructions and he gets so angry when I don't arrange things the way he said."

"All right," Matthew conceded. "The *Isabel*, Tuesday at sunset."

"Fine. See you then."

Caroline took a last frowning look at the bloody rag dangling from Matthew's fingers, then spurred her horse to a gallop so suddenly that he had to leap back. Wiley grinned and hurried after her. They galloped across the clearing, dust clouds boiling behind them, past the mill and up towards the forest. Caroline perched on the precarious saddle, the reins resting lightly in her right hand, and leaned into the animal's stride, her head bent low, her elbows hugged close to her waist, her white dress and red hair billowing behind her.

Abby slammed the door of the house, grabbed her six-year-old son by the hand, and marched angrily into the forest.

"Where we going?" the boy asked as he hurried to keep up with her long strides.

"To see Sitka."

"How come?"

"Because, Martin, your father has accepted a dinner invitation at Mr. Cains's next week; someone will have to look after you while we're gone."

"Oh." They marched on in silence. "I could look after myself," Martin ventured. There was no answer. "Ma, are you mad?"

"No."

"You sure look mad. Your face is all red and you're walking —"

Abby stopped abruptly and took a deep breath. "Yes, Martin, I'm angry."

"How come?"

"Because your father has a distorted vision of morality and the acquisition of material wealth."

"Oh."

They continued on at a slower pace. Abby tried to imagine herself sitting in the big brick house across the inlet, chatting blithely with the man who had had her husband shot in the arm and left to drown in Burrard Inlet. She could understand, much as it disgusted her, how the new governor could be an important ally in acquiring the new timber leases, but she couldn't understand why they needed the leases in the first place. Business was thriving, yet Matthew seemed to be gripped by a reckless, obsessive drive for expansion. They still had plenty of uncut timber on the inlet; as well, in six different camps, two on the Fraser and four on Vancouver Island, men were hauling their trees out of the forest and floating them to Galer Mills. Between the old water mill and the new steam-powered one, they were cutting 130,000 feet a day. As well as the *Cariboo Fly*, they had two three-masted schooners, the *Matilda* and the *Delaware*, which carried Galer Mills' lumber to Hawaii, Argentina, Australia, and China. They had a beautiful home, a healthy son; they had each other. But still Matthew was not satisfied.

The hot summer sun blasted in her face as she stepped out of the cool forest onto an exposed ridge. Her anger began to drain away as she stopped to take in the bright colours of the inlet spread below her: the startling blue of the water, the hazy yellow sun glinting off the brass fittings of the *Isabel*, the black scar of smoke from the stack of the *Cariboo Fly* as it churned towards New Westminster, and the billowing white sails of Joe Da Costa's schooner slipping through the narrows to chase grey whales in the open ocean. In the centre of the inlet she could see the violent red of the rubber aprons worn by the workers on Spratt's barge, where oil was being pressed out of tons of herring. And everywhere were the infinite variations of the forest — the silver-green of poplar, the yellow-green of cedar, the blue-green of spruce, and the olive-green of pine and fir.

"Hey, Ma?"

"Yes, Martin?"

"Do you have to go?" The still air shuddered as the sound of an explosion echoed off the mountain behind them; Spratt had thrown another load of dynamite into the water to stun the herring so he could scoop them into nets as they floated to the surface.

"Yes, I have to go."

"Then it's not going to do any good to get angry about it, is it?"

She looked down, nonplussed, at the worried green eyes peering at her from under the small wrinkled brow, and was amazed, as she so often was these days, at how sombre and wise a six-year-old could be. She bent down and wrapped her arms around his small body. "No, Martin; I guess it's not." As she tried to kiss him, he wrinkled his nose and pushed her away, but when she started down the steep path that led to Sitka's house, he reached behind him and took her hand.

Dry twigs crackled underfoot. It was not really necessary to ask Sitka, Abby thought. There were other women at the mill with children of their own who would be happy to take Martin for the night. Indeed, Galer Mills was a small community now with a store, a library, a church, and twelve families living in the white cottages Matthew had built in a wide arc under the big cedars at the edge of the clearing. The daily classes she taught in the new schoolhouse, which had begun with just Eva, were attended now by Martin and nineteen other children, all from Galer Mills. But the women of the mill had husbands to provide for them; Sitka had no one.

Having her mind Martin gave Abby an excuse to bring her gifts of food and clothing. The first time she had returned from New Westminster with a dress for Eva, Sitka had refused to accept it. Abby pouted and told her it was a custom in white society to give a gift to the person who looks after your child, and that it was a great insult if the gift was refused. Sitka had stared at her hard, shrugged, and finally taken the dress.

The trail snaked through a stand of poplar, their silver-green leaves limp and wilting in the heat. In a meadow at the base of the hill, Abby could see Sitka and her daughter working in the small garden at the side of their one-room house. At the sight of the tiny cabin, the last of her anger at Matthew melted away, and she smiled; the walls were of rough cedar planks split by hand and chinked with moss and mud, but the roof was of fine sawn lumber and cedar shakes.

Two years ago, when Matthew had heard that Sitka would spend another winter in the keekwilee, he had cut wood for her roof, loaded it into a narrow wagon, and waited for the great potlatch at Snauq. When she was gone, six men and a pair of oxen lowered the cart down the steep path, their breaths forming clouds in the chill morning air. Matthew installed a cast-iron stove and connected the lengths of chimney pipe while the rest worked on the roof overhead. At dusk they had climbed back up the path, stopping occasionally to turn and look at the red glow of the cedar shakes as they caught the evening sun.

Sitka had been grateful, in her solemn, expressionless way, but Abby was disappointed that the joy she had expected to see in the woman's eyes was absent. It was obvious that something had gone wrong at the potlatch. Sitka refused to discuss it. The next day the children of Abby's school had stared and tittered as Eva strutted proudly into the classroom wearing a white frock and bonnet Abby had given her the previous year. It was the first time anyone had seen her without her cedar-bark cloak.

A garter snake slithered across the path at the edge of the meadow and disappeared into the dead grass. Abby shaded her eyes against the sun and stared at the women working in the small dirt plot. Something was wrong. She let go of Martin's hand and ran ahead.

The vegetable garden was a shambles: corn stalks and potato plants were crushed and scattered on the ground, small white carrots lay exposed to the hot sun, the intricate trellis of poplar and string with its load of climbing peas and beans was shattered, and everywhere were the deep prints and upturned clods of a galloping horse.

As Sitka rose and turned to face her, Abby realized how much the woman had aged in the past year; her coarse black hair had greyed and her face had withered; her blunt features had become sharp and crabbed.

"What happened?"

"A man and a woman on horses. They galloped through the garden side by side and tore it apart."

"Did you try to stop them?"

Sitka shrugged. "I yelled at them. We were gathering berries over by the path."

"But they kept on going?"

"No. The man said something to the woman. She stayed at the edge of the forest and he came back and rode through twice more — once that way, once this way. I threw a rock and hit him in the shoulder. It made him laugh."

Sitka returned to her work. Abby knelt beside her and began shoring up the plants that could be saved. "Was he a handsome man with a black moustache and grey suit?"

"Oh yes," Eva said. "Very handsome."

Abby looked up, surprised by the admiration in the little girl's voice. Eva was tall, with a pretty round face, an extravagant head of copper-coloured hair, and the long, thin limbs of a fast-growing eleven-year-old. She wore a ruffled dress Abby had bought for her, but it was already too small.

"You know them?" Sitka asked.

"Not really," Abby said. "I've never met them, but they live at the mill across the inlet." She decided not to ask Sitka to look after Martin while she went to dinner with the people who had trampled her garden.

"Why would they do this?"

Abby shook her head.

"She was so pretty," Eva said. "She had red hair and rode with both legs on one side of the horse, like the fine ladies in the picture book you showed me. She wore a long white dress and—"

"Enough," Sitka snapped.

"Have you memorized your nine-times table?" Abby asked.

Eva groaned. "I'll bet the lady in the white dress doesn't have to memorize the times table. What use will I ever have for arithmetic?"

Mei-fu arranged the cumbersome bustle at the back of her new olive-green dress as she settled herself on a coil of rope at the stern of the fishboat and pulled a notebook from her purse. She could recite all of the calculations by heart, but it delighted her to look at the numbers as she thought them through. Six girls capable of earning $20 per night ($30 for Clarissa), minus the necessary seven days' holiday per month, equals $35,880 per year. With the agreed 80/20 split I retain $28,704. Added to this is the $4,000 I so graciously loaned them for bail, passage, dresses, and pocket money, and which they agreed to repay within twelve months at five per cent interest per month, out of their earnings—leaving me with $35,104 for the first year.

Mei-fu paused to consider this. None of the girls had an ounce of business sense; she could easily have gotten ten per cent, but eventually they would have realized that every night they worked left them deeper in her debt. It would have been a clever financial manoeuvre, she thought, very clever . . . but one must consider the emotions of one's employees. Only a fool would continue to work under such circumstances, and my girls are not fools.

She tapped her long fingernails on the notebook as she stared vacantly ahead at the tall pillar of rock that marked the entrance to Burrard Inlet. Of course, she thought, some may find husbands willing to repay their loans, some will run away, and some will get pregnant, but if I plan carefully, collect what debts I can, and accept minor losses as inevitable, then all of my days will be profitable and joyous. She smiled and resumed her calculations. Then there is the whisky: approximately 150 glasses per night at 25 cents each, minus my cost of 25 per cent, gives me $10,260 from the saloon in the first year.

Of course, there will be expenses for food, linen, and building maintenance, and surely I will have to pay the government for the lot once they realize its value, but the town is booming, growth will be furious, and the Palace Royale will blossom with it. Everything considered, with the income from the girls and the whisky, I can conservatively expect to earn over $40,000 in my first year of operation.

She sucked in her breath and stared hungrily at the figure. "By all the gods," she whispered, "such a vast sum." No matter how many times she did the calculations, the result still made her dizzy. Of course, she quickly added, all of it must be reinvested in the business — well, almost all, for surely an important business-woman must look the part if she is to be respected by her customers. She should have proper dresses, fashionable western dresses, a little jewellery; perhaps she should replace her silver fingernail sheaths. . . . No, she hissed. No, I must reinvest it all; if I am frugal, if I keep my eyes open and my fists closed, if I take on just a few private customers — only the important ones who will pay much money — I can make the Palace Royale fit for a Manchu lord and still buy out Gassy Jack in the first year. She snapped her notebook shut, slipped it into her purse, and rested her chin in her hands. Even the rank smell of the fishboat baking in the hot sun could not diminish her joy.

She glanced up at Wu Lee as he came and sat beside her. Even he was smiling. She was curious to know what logic had convinced him that a mother who pillowed for money brought shame to one's ancestors, whereas a mother who ran a stable of pillowers was honourable indeed, but she knew better than to pose such a ticklish question to a child. It was enough that the boy was happy.

She turned to watch the girls who were clustered at the bow, roosting on nets and trunks and packing cases. Each spun a coloured parasol in a different rhythm — some clockwise, some counter-clockwise — and the effect was dizzying. The fastest twirlers were the two fifteen-year-old Chinese girls: Jade and Lotus Blossom. She had bailed the first out of the San Francisco Gaol, where she had been awaiting trial for stealing a basket of oranges. Mei-fu had been careful to impress upon the young girl the enormity of her crime, and was convinced that Jade would be eternally grateful. Lotus Blossom, however, was a different problem. She had been purchased from a wealthy Oriental merchant who had made such a series of foolish investments that he had to sell his concubines or face having his fingers broken at the hands of his creditors' *boo how doy*s. The girl had been pampered as though she were the Empress herself, and, on top of that, she was bright and ambitious. Lotus Blossom would need careful watching.

The parasols in the centre belonged to three prostitutes from the San Francisco Women's Prison. In return for loaning them the money to pay their fines, she had extracted a promise from each that they would work at the Palace Royale for a minimum of one year. All were pretty and under nineteen, but she had carefully selected each one to satisfy a different taste: there was the jovial and athletic Theresa, who was a curious mixture of Portuguese, Swedish, and Scots; Yvette, a sultry Frenchwoman with pouting lips and seductive eyes; and Susan, a husky, strapping English girl, handsome in a robust way, who, Mei-fu was certain, could withstand a hug from the most oafish of timberbeasts with little damage to her spine.

But the most precious treasure of all was the Negress Clarissa, who paced behind the group, revolving her parasol in a painfully slow circle. She was obedient, but aloof. She had refused to say how she had arrived upon the dragon stage, yet everything the small Chinese woman had told her to do, she had done quickly and obediently.

Mei-fu was still not convinced — the woman was far too secretive and proud. Her head began to ache. Oh well, she thought, the gods will do as they please. So far she has cost me little; if I get a week of work out of her, it will be a bargain.

As the fishboat approached Jonas Cains's wharf, its whistle sputtered and wailed. Mei-fu rose and minced delicately on her small feet over the sticky deck. At the engine-house she stopped and looked in at the incredible jumble of rusted gears, bailing wire, and hissing steam. She had inspected it several times during the short trip, yet she still came away shaking her head apprehensively. What worried her most was the long coil of rope fastened to the engine at one end and to a red buoy at the other. She was certain its function was to help locate the machinery for salvage in the likely event the boat sank. Thank the gods we did not have to travel all the way from San Francisco in this worm-eaten fish-bucket, she thought. Even the short trip from Victoria had taken twelve painful hours, three of them spent drifting at night in the silent, black strait as the skipper wrestled the demon engine back to life.

She gripped the rail and picked her way over the slimy deck to the bow. The girls clustered around her, jabbering in English and Cantonese as they pointed at the jumbled collection of shacks east of the mill. Seagulls circled the fishboat, screaming and swooping low over the deck. Mei-fu smiled at them: a good omen.

As they approached the wharf, which was dwarfed by its huge stacks of lumber, she chuckled. Jonas Cains was running along the beach, in the heat of the day, wrapped in his inevitable frock-coat, waving his arms and shouting. By the time he had scrambled down the narrow passage at the edge of the pier he was out of breath. "I won't have . . . the likes of you . . . on my wharf!" he sputtered. "This is private property. . . . Get out!"

The skipper jammed a wad of burlap into the running gears of the engine. The ship lurched violently and the women screamed. "Sorry, ladies," he said. "Ain't got no reverse. It's the only way I can stop her." The small boat wallowed to a stop in the low tide, with Jonas Cains glowering down at it from the dock.

"You can take your bunch of trollops and go to the devil, Madame Lee. They'll not set foot on my wharf."

"Oh, pretty boy," Yvette cooed. "Come to the devil with us trollops?"

Theresa threw open her arms, ground her hips in a slow circle, and shimmied. Jonas gasped. The women broke into raucous laughter.

"But, Mr. Cains . . ." — Mei-fu's voice was silvery and musical — "Considering what you do in the past, I did not think your squeamishness would be so easily offended."

Jonas's face quivered. He reached into his coat pocket, pulled out a silver revolver, and aimed it at Mei-fu's head. The girls were instantly silent.

"Get away from my land," he snarled.

The fishboat creaked as it rubbed against the dock. From behind came the dull sound of an underwater explosion near Spratt's Oilery.

Mei-fu turned to instruct the skipper, but he was already busy, pushing frantically on a long pole to ease them into deeper water. Slowly, foot by foot, the boat retreated. Jonas remained on the wharf, gun in hand, until the engine started and the fishboat chugged away from the dock.

As they edged along the shore towards the chaotic collection of log houses, shacks, and tents that had grown up around the Globe Saloon, Mei-fu began to shout: "Hey, Jack. Gassy Jack! You got rowboat, please?" A man appeared on the beach, then a second and a third. The girls took up the shout, waving their arms, blowing kisses, and calling for a rowboat. Again the skipper fed the tattered burlap back into the engine and they wallowed to a stop twenty yards offshore. The steam whistle sputtered and hissed.

By the time Gassy Jack hobbled down to the shore on his sore legs, leaning heavily on a cane, the beach was crowded with whistling, shouting men and a rowboat was halfway to the ship. He stood off to one side, watching, and marvelled at how the timid little Chinese woman who had clung tentatively to the fringes of the small crowd he had collected on this beach two years before now commanded a mob of her own.

Late in the afternoon, with a crowd of whistling men lined along the shore, Clarissa hitched up her skirts and lowered a brown, stockinged leg over the side of the fishboat. Wu Lee grabbed it and directed it to a bench. One by one, with shrieks and laughter, the girls climbed over the railing and down to the tiny rowboat.

Susan was the last. There were only three benches and the boat was already awash with coloured dresses billowing up and over the gunwale. "Maybe I should wait till he comes back for the baggage."

"There's room in the stern," Mei-fu said impatiently.

The English girl shrugged, hitched up her skirt, and straddled the rail. Again a stockinged leg descended, its foot groping for the bench, and again Wu Lee grabbed it. But this one fought back. It pulled away and struck him in the face. His nose began to bleed. He grabbed the leg hard and pulled it sharply down.

Susan screamed. For an instant she stood poised in mid-air, one foot over the gunwale, her arms flailing like a windmill, while the girls shifted to the opposite side to counterbalance the rocking boat; then she whimpered and toppled into the sea.

She surfaced sputtering and shrieking. Her dress floated around her like the pads of a water lily and she thrashed at it frantically, then suddenly stopped and stood up. The water was only up to her shoulders.

"Well, you have to walk now," Mei-fu said. "You dump us all climbing in here."

Wu Lee took the oars and edged the rowboat towards shore, while Susan walked behind, head bent, hair dripping, peering into the water for obstacles. Mei-fu craned her neck to watch the crowd of boisterous men wade into the inlet and swarm around the boat. One by one they lifted the women from their benches and carried them towards the beach.

The handsome butcher, George Black, hovered over her, and she tried to ignore him, but his dark eyes chipped away at her stern reserve and his big arms reached down to scoop her up. Quickly she slapped at his hands and gripped the gunwale, realizing for the first time that she was no longer one of them. I am an important woman, she told herself; I must remain separate. If they are carried, I will stay in the boat. If they keep to their place, then I will be able to keep to mine.

As the bow dug into the beach, she stepped delicately, imperiously, onto the sands of Gold Mountain and snapped open her parasol. She watched as a gallant logger hefted Susan into his arms and struggled towards shore. Ten feet from the beach he slipped on a rock and they floundered back into the sea. The crowd howled. Susan snatched her hat from where it floated on the still water and marched furiously to the beach, leaving the clumsy logger sitting sheepishly in the bay. Hip-flasks and jugs of whisky appeared and the celebration began.

At dusk Mei-fu led the parade down the broad path that cut through the centre of Gastown. Dozens of men were strung out behind her, singing and laughing. Giggles and the occasional shriek of mock outrage sifted through the maple leaves. Periodic gunshots sounded near by. They passed the Globe Saloon with its British flag fluttering from the roof. Further on, Mei-fu paused to admire Gassy Jack's new Deighton Hotel, which was nearing completion; then they continued on past a general store, dozens of clapboard houses, scrap-wood shanties, log cabins, tents, and keekwilees scattered amongst the trees, connected by a maze of dirt paths. She knew them all.

At last, at the far end of town, was the Palace Royale; the front door of the sprawling two-storey building faced the path, while the back extended over the water on pilings. She stared up at its crisp white corners, its enormous verandah, and its false front, and felt that she was finally home. She had supervised the placement of practically every board, so she could picture each room with the intimacy of a lover, pursing her lips at the minor defects, never losing sight of the tremendous potential.

The crowd gathered around her, waiting. She picked up her skirts, marched grandly up the steps, and opened the door. Her door. She stood to one side and waved the men in. Again the girls were hoisted, shrieking, into unfamiliar arms and carried inside. George Black hovered solicitously near by, but Mei-fu held firmly to the doorknob and waved him in. At last she was home.

Gassy Jack puffed slowly up the steps, leaning heavily on his cane. He smiled at her. She brushed the back of her hand across her eye. "While you were away, the government surveyors were here," he said. "They measured and staked the whole town." Mei-fu nodded. "Soon they will auction the lots," he said. "Very soon."

The *Isabel* was late. Abby stood stoically by her work-table in the windowed tower, dressed in a blue-velvet gown, ready for the unavoidable dinner at Jonas Cains's. Around her the room was cluttered with canvasses, wooden crates, and packing material. She had spent the evening selecting paintings to send to San Francisco. It would be her tenth shipment.

Seven years before, when she was nineteen and Matthew had taken her to the great port city for the first time, she had been reluctant to show her art. In each gallery she visited, the manager had praised the quality and skill of her work, then asked to see something more traditional, more realistic. "Do you have any landscapes?" one man had asked.

"This is a landscape," Abby had said.

"Yes, but it's so dark, so threatening, so closed in. Why, the trees seem to weep."

"It's a rain forest," Abby said. "The trees do weep."

"Yes, I'm sure but . . . Wouldn't you like to do an English pastoral landscape? You know, cows and rolling hills? They sell very well."

At dusk Abby had slunk back to the hotel, simmering with rage, and refused to go to any more galleries.

The next day, after she had taken a large dose of laudanum and fallen asleep, Matthew had carefully packed the rain forest and a self-portrait and carried them to a small, dark shop set in an alleyway off Market Street. The manager, Magnus Oberheim, was an effeminate, wraith-like German with a goatee and a monocle.

He immediately took the two paintings on consignment. Matthew did not tell Abby.

When he returned two days later he found that the rain forest had been sold—for the remarkable price of one hundred dollars—and that several customers had expressed interest in the portrait. Mr. Oberheim requested more paintings.

Abby was astonished when Matthew presented her with the cheque. She gathered up the rest of her pictures and hurried to the gallery, anxious to meet the remarkable little man who appreciated her work. Abby liked him immediately. He prepared tea for her in a silver samovar which, he explained, his parents had carried with them to America as they fled Prussia before the advancing wall of Napoleon's forces. He examined the new pictures slowly, critically, praising the best and poking gently at flaws in the others with his little finger. Abby was delighted. Mr. Oberheim had treated her as a professional.

Over the years she had received numerous proposals from the largest and most reputable of San Francisco galleries—even the man who had suggested she paint pastoral landscapes had offered to sell her paintings at a lesser commission than Mr. Oberheim— but Abby remained loyal to the little German who had rekindled her enthusiasm.

As she hovered over her work-table with the soft night sounds of summer drifting through the open windows, she could imagine him moving proudly about his cluttered shop, pouring tea from the silver samovar and discussing art with anyone who would listen.

She shuffled through a stack of paintings; one more was needed to complete the packing crate, but she considered all of the possibilities inadequate. In frustration she decided to stuff the empty space with rags and send the box as it was. As she pulled a length of muslin out of a low cupboard, the old stone statue Sitka had given her so many years ago rolled off the shelf and bumped against her feet. She had forgotten it. It lay on its side, the rough-hewn child sitting on its father's lap, the frail stone arms reaching out to him. She had not seen it since she was pregnant with Martin. She picked it up, turning it gently in her hands, and carried it to the box seat by the open window. "I thought I had lost you," she murmured.

Outside, the forest rustled, whispering softly; her blonde curls shifted over the shoulders of her blue-velvet dress as a cool breeze drifted in. She stroked the cold, hard stone with her fingertips, tracing the thin arms, the upturned head, the transcendent, painful "O" of the father's lips. It captivated her. As the last slanting rays of a late summer sunset struck the statue on her lap, it glowed golden and white, and she knew it was magical, with a life of its own she would never understand.

"Abby?" Matthew stood in the doorway looking uncomfortable in his black frock-coat and turnover collar. "The *Isabel*'s on its way. Are you ready?"

She held the statue up to him. "Do you remember this? I thought I'd lost it."

He came and sat beside her, glancing out the open window at the *Isabel*, which looked delicate and motionless in mid-inlet, its pale lights glinting in the gathering twilight. "Of course I do."

"I hadn't seen it since the year Martin was born."

He reached out his hands and lifted the statue gently from her lap. "The year you stopped taking laudanum."

Abby shut her eyes tightly and lowered her head as the painful recollection tumbled around her: the icy chills, the constant shaking, the clammy sheets of her bed, the desperate struggle for breath, the tears, the vomit, the endless spinning visions of an orphanage peopled by demons that crawled in her mouth and clawed through her body searching for the terrified child huddled in her womb. After two weeks she had emerged from the bedroom, pale and gaunt, and vowed she would never take the drug again.

She heard the rustle of cloth on the bench beside her and felt Matthew's lips brush gently against her eyelids. She opened them and smiled up at him. He set the statue on the seat between them and she chuckled. "I remember when you stormed up to the house in a rage because I had left such an offensive object on your desk."

He grinned. "People change," he said softly. "We all change."

Abby nodded. Below them the steam whistle of the *Isabel* hooted mournfully. She rose and took his arm. "Shall we go?" In the hallway she turned and closed the door softly on the small stone statue sitting alone on the box seat by the open window.

The night air was warm and redolent with seaweed and pine. They stood at the bow, leaning against each other, watching the lights of Cains's house growing larger and brighter. Fiddle music and laughter flowed out of Gastown and flooded the still inlet. Above them the moon, full and orange, hung in an indigo sky thick with stars. Abby squeezed Matthew's hand and smiled up at him. From somewhere near the ship a loon called, and its chilling cry drowned out the music from the Palace Royale.

Ahead, Abby could see the dinner guests clustered on Cains's front steps, silhouetted by the bright orange square of the open door, watching the ship as it approached the dock. She thought of Wiley and remembered she had not told Matthew about Sitka's garden. She would deal with it herself.

The mountain of sawn lumber on the wharf loomed into view. The purr of the engine stopped and the steam whistle hooted. Abby pursed her lips as she saw Jonas Cains coming to greet them, strutting along a narrow walkway at the edge of the pier with a lantern in one hand and a cigar in the other, smiling magnanimously. The tide was strong. The skipper poked his head out of the wheelhouse and strained to see into the dark. He started the engine again and the *Isabel* angled slowly forward until her side bumped against the pier.

The pilings under the dock groaned and shifted. Timbers cracked. "Look out," Matthew yelled. The mountain of timber quivered. The cigar dropped from Jonas's mouth and his smile vanished as he flung the lantern into the water and fled towards shore, darting and leaping over planks. Someone at the house screamed. Planks clattered onto the deck behind Jonas as he ran; then, as he leapt into the shallow water at the edge of the beach, the huge stacks of lumber leaned away from the *Isabel*, hesitated, and collapsed into the ocean with a roar.

Abby gripped the rail as the ship tilted and rolled. Spray flew up around her. Then, as suddenly as the maelstrom had begun, it stopped. The *Isabel* bobbed gently and was still. Already boards were fanning out across the inlet, drifting on the tide.

Matthew and Abby leaned over the rail and peered into the dark. Once she saw the dim outline of Jonas Cains standing in water up to his knees she began to giggle. Figures were running from the house to the beach. "Did you . . ." — she struggled to get the words out through her laughter — "did you . . . see . . . the look on his face?"

"Hallo," Jonas called in a thin, shaky voice. "Mr. Galer. Hallo. Are you all right?"

"Yes, we're fine," Matthew shouted. "Are *you?*" Abby bent double with laughter, one hand braced against the rail, the other on the tight walls of her corset.

"Is Mrs. Galer all right?"

Abby hooted. Matthew poked her in the ribs. "I'm not sure."

"Hang on. We'll get a rowboat and have you off in a jiffy."

By the time Wiley Burgess appeared with the rowboat, Abby had composed herself. Cains's family and guests lined the beach and watched while the flustered captain rigged a rope ladder and Matthew helped Abby over the rail. As she descended, the hem of her blue-velvet dress snagged on a wood splinter and tore. She settled herself in the bow, examined the damage, and swore. The tear was a foot long.

Jonas began his apologies as soon as the boat touched shore. "I'm most awfully sorry, Mrs. Galer. It must have given you quite a fright. I honestly had no idea the wharf was so perilous."

"Didn't Mr. Burgess tell you?" Matthew said. "I mentioned it last week."

Jonas looked sharply at Wiley. "No, I don't believe he did."

"I'll get the men," Wiley said. "If we move fast, we should be able to salvage at least half of it."

"Yes," Jonas said. "Well, you will probably have to drag most of the blackguards out of that Chinee brothel — "

"Jonas," Madeline hissed. "You can't — "

He held up a hand to silence her. "So you'd best get a leg on, man, or my timber will be halfway to Japan by dawn." Wiley ran off towards the bunkhouses. As the group turned away from the beach, Caroline glared at Matthew and Abby.

Jonas snaked his arm around the shoulders of a tall, bearded man and led the way up to the house. "You see, Governor Musgrave, a prime example of the sudden quirks of fortune which make the position of industry so perilous in this colony. That is why we must have the co-operation of government if progress and prosperity are to be brought to this wilderness. . . ."

As they climbed the steps to the red brick house, lanterns swung through the darkness and footsteps pounded along the path from the bunkhouses to the beach. Over it all was Wiley's voice angrily shouting orders.

While Jonas went upstairs to change, Madeline, in a high-collared black dress, took charge like a stern white-haired major-domo, ushering them into the dining room, leaning heavily on her cane. "I'm afraid we will not be able to wait for Mr. Burgess. Dinner is already later than planned and will be spoiled if we wait any longer." Abby watched the thin, bloodless lips as Madeline snapped commands, ordering them to their seats as though she were directing a military campaign. "Mrs. Galer, you will sit here." Abby noticed Caroline staring at the tear in her dress and sat down quickly.

The dining room was windowless and dour, with heavy draperies and walnut panelling, and small brass lamps fastened to the walls. An imposing oak table, elaborately carved and polished, filled most of the room. Three slim white candles were spaced along its length. She thought the effect was funereal; the gleaming oak looked too much like a casket. A grandfather clock ticked erratically behind her chair.

As Madeline finished her orders, two uniformed Chinese boys began pouring champagne. Abby studied the guests. To her right was Matthew, and on her left, Amor De Cosmos was hooking his cane on the back of his chair and riffling through his pockets. Across from them was Caroline and an empty place for Wiley. Madeline presided at one end of the casket. To the right of Jonas's chair, the colony's first governor, Sir James Douglas, was rearranging his place setting and fussing over his spectacles; he was wearing an old uniform with faded gold braid. To the left was the guest of honour, Anthony Musgrave, the current governor of British Columbia. He was a trim, handsome man in his late thirties, with a broad smile under his full black beard, a high forehead, and bright-blue eyes. Sarah had been placed next to him; she sat primly with her hands in her lap, her small, pinched face blushing as she glanced at the Governor out of the corner of her eye.

Jonas swept smiling into the room, slapping his hands together and rubbing them with avuncular briskness. "Nothing like a minor crisis to keep a man on his toes. Don't worry, though. Everything's under control." He picked up his glass and waved it over his head with a flourish. "I should like to propose a toast to our honoured and esteemed guest: Mr. Anthony Musgrave, the new Governor of British Columbia."

Abby raised her glass and joined in the toast with the rest. Madeline rang a small silver bell by her plate and a dour Chinese boy paraded in a tureen of clear, watery soup. He was followed by three attendants who began filling the bowls.

"Governor Musgrave," Jonas began, "I hear you have just completed a tour of the colony as far north as Barkerville. What are your impressions of our little 'England on the Pacific'?"

"Amazing, Mr. Cains. Simply amazing. I was prepared for neither the immensity nor the diversity of the place. You have everything here: rugged coastal mountains, the fertile Fraser Valley, impenetrable rain forests, the grasslands of the Chilcoten, awesome rock canyons, even sagebrush — why, it is a veritable potpourri of geography. And the size of it! Do you know, it is seven times larger than England?" There were exclamations of surprise around the table. "Yet there are fewer than nine thousand inhabitants in the entire colony, excluding the Indians, of course."

Jonas grunted. "Just the sort of jewel the Empire would be anxious to keep in its crown, wouldn't you say?"

Governor Musgrave smiled non-committally.

"Well," Jonas pressed, "what of the future? Will British Columbia join Canada?"

Sir James Douglas winced.

"Actually, that's what I've been touring the province to find out. The Colonial Office sent me with instructions to ascertain the feelings of the residents on union with Canada. Certainly Sir John A. Macdonald is anxious to acquire the colony, and there seems to be growing acceptance of the idea."

"Of course there is," De Cosmos interrupted as he held his glass for the waiter to refill. "I've been advocating a coast-to-coast confederation for years. Why, I've done all the hard work for you."

Governor Musgrave stared at him for a moment. "Yes, I'm sure. And a good job you've done on the mainland, but there is still a faction in Victoria agitating for union with America."

Madeline clicked her tongue in disgust.

"They simply do it out of spite," Jonas said. "Ever since New Westminster was chosen as the capital, the islanders have done everything possible to thwart the mainland. But Victoria has her precious seat of government back now; they'll come around."

"Victoria should have been the capital from the beginning," Sir James snapped.

Abby turned to the other end of the table where Matthew was listening to Caroline. ". . . poor Governor Seymour," she was saying as she stirred her soup thoughtfully. "How do you think he really died?"

"Why, Panama fever, of course," Madeline said. "Everyone knew he had it."

"Some say it was drink," De Cosmos interjected as he pushed his plate away and tapped his spoon lightly on the tablecloth. "But I met a man at Langley the other day who knew his personal secretary, who was with him at Bella Coola when he died. He said the Governor was severely ill with nervous tremors and sleeplessness, and that Dr. Comrie had instructed him to administer a tablespoon of medicine every hour. The secretary fell asleep and later woke to find that Governor Seymour had drunk the entire bottle." He tossed the spoon onto the table and it struck a glass. "Suicide."

Abby peeked under the table and tried to pinch the torn hem of her dress between her ankles. When she looked up, Caroline was watching her.

"Will you be printing that story in your newspaper, Mr. De Cosmos?" Musgrave asked coldly.

"I would if I still had one. No reason why I shouldn't; it's a true story," De Cosmos snapped. "But I sold the *Colonist* to John Robson some years ago. I am, however, considering starting a new publication. It seems that the people of British Columbia are going to need an editorial Moses to lead them safely through the morass of cold-hearted politics if a fair and equitable union with the east is to be effected. I feel it no less than my duty to serve them at this important historical juncture with a publication which will voice the opinions of the populace. I believe I will call it 'The People's Paper'." Again, Madeline clicked her tongue.

"Confederation!" Sir James sneered. "You can rest your printer's ink, Mr. De Cosmos. It will be a rainless year in Victoria before the people of the west will throw their lot in with those North American Chinamen. Why, the Governor himself has said he's only here on a fishing expedition."

"Actually," Musgrave interrupted, "It's gone a little further than that: it seems England herself now desires the union." Everyone stopped eating. Abby was aware of the grandfather clock ticking loudly behind her. "On my return from the interior, a telegram from Earl Granville was awaiting me in New Westminster. The gist of it is that England wishes the entrance of British Columbia into the Canadian confederation more urgently than ever before. Immediately upon my return to Victoria I am to appoint additional members to the Executive Committee to draft the terms of confederation."

Everyone at the table burst into excited conversation. Sir James wiped his face with a handkerchief as the soup plates were removed and a platter of three stuffed canvasback ducks and a plate of poached salmon were carried in. "But that's absurd," he blustered. "The colony belongs to England and must remain under her sovereign rule—for its own good, of course—until the population is large enough and strong enough to govern itself."

"But you heard the Governor," De Cosmos drawled, a smug smile on his face. "England wants to be rid of us. Clearly the days of despotism are over."

Sir James's face reddened and his jowls quivered. "You dare to call me a despot? Me? Why, I—"

"Gentlemen, please," Madeline said. "Jonas, perhaps you could serve Sir James some duck."

"Don't patronize me," Douglas snapped. "I don't want any duck. I want to know by what right this upstart Yankee traitor calls me a despot."

De Cosmos jumped to his feet. "Traitor? Why, I did more to forward the cause of democracy and progress in your autocratic state than you could ever—"

"Excuse me, gentlemen," Caroline said, rising as Wiley came into the room, and going to stand at his side. She hooked her hand in the crook of his arm. "I hate to interrupt a political debate with such a frivolous announcement," she said, "but I think Mr. Burgess would like to say something." She glared hard at De Cosmos.

"Yes, Wiley, please do," Madeline said.

De Cosmos sank sullenly into his chair, sniffed, and crossed his legs.

"The Hudson's Bay never should have given up its royal charter," Sir James mumbled.

De Cosmos stiffened. "That was the first—"

"Wiley?" Madeline interjected.

Burgess smiled and tugged at his vest. Abby noticed a dangling circle of hair to the left of his part—the fashionable hyacinth curl — and wondered if it was a deliberate affectation or if it had fallen free of its own volition. "I am pleased to announce that Mr. and Mrs. Cains have graciously consented to offer me the hand of their daughter Caroline in marriage."

Abby applauded with the rest of the guests. Madeline leaned towards her, beaming, and whispered confidentially that Wiley's father was the Earl of Downsview. Abby wanted to ask if she had investigated the claim — after the incident in Sitka's garden she instinctively distrusted the man — but instead she smiled and nodded, trying to look impressed. The fellow is clearly a snake, she thought.

Governor Musgrave proposed a toast. "To the new couple." Abby sighed and picked up her glass.

The conversation eddied around Wiley and Caroline, and Abby drifted in and out of it: wedding plans, prospects, where to build a house, Wiley's trip overland from Canada. Abby wondered how she was going to talk to them about Sitka. To her left, Amor De Cosmos was strangely silent, concentrating on his duck and over-cooked carrots. She wondered why he had never married.

". . . so I had to shoot the horse and walk the rest of the way to Fort Edmonton." Wiley was talking to Matthew. "But she was good eating."

"Wiley, you didn't!" Madeline was shocked.

"Amazing country," he said. "You can ride for weeks and see nothing but grassland."

Abby shuddered at the thought of the flat, endless prairie, where a bush was a tree, and a lake a treasure. She preferred her horizon close up, where she could see it.

"Mr. Galer." It was Governor Musgrave, calling down the length of the casket; Abby watched his bright-blue eyes twinkle in the candlelight. "I've heard about the community you are establishing across the inlet. How many people live there now?"

"One hundred seventy-six," Matthew said. "Mostly single men, but there's twelve families now, each with a house; we've got a store, a church, a library of sorts, and Abby here teaches school."

"And how many saloons do you have?"

"None."

"No saloons?" Governor Musgrave glanced at Jonas.

"Well, all of the sailors from his wharf just slip over to Gastown," Jonas said. "That's why you've got to give us a constable. Why, do you know there's even a brothel here now?"

"Jonas," Madeline hissed.

"Well, it's true. A diabolical Chinee hell-hag has opened a brothel not more than one hundred yards from the boundary of my own mill. It won't go away just because we close our eyes to it. What we need—"

"I don't believe those lots have ever been sold, Mr. Cains."

"Of course not; they're squatters; all of them are there illegally. I applied myself for a timber lease to all that property some years ago. And, I might say, my generous offer was turned down."

"It seems to me that when I left for the interior, a survey of this 'Gastown' was under way," the Governor said. "If I remember correctly, it's to be renamed the township of Granville and, I daresay, an auction of the lots might separate some of the vagrants from the more desirable citizens. Then we'll see about a policeman." Musgrave turned back to Matthew and left Cains to consider the possibilities. "And what do you see as the future for British Columbia, Mr. Galer?"

"Well, it seems the most logical choice would be to join the United States," Matthew said.

Everyone stopped eating and stared at him. "Of course, you are an American, are you not?" De Cosmos said. "And so your loyalties naturally lie with the Yankees."

"I'm sure Mr. Galer doesn't really expect us to join the Americans," Madeline said.

"No, I don't," Matthew said. "Fortunately, or unfortunately, political boundaries are seldom dictated by the logical principles of economics, geography, or even common sense. Countries, like people, are born of passion, and clearly the passions of the colony are directed to the east, not the south. I have no doubt that British Columbia will join with Canada, and that it will be the best thing for the province."

"Provided we get a railroad," Jonas added quickly.

"Railroad or not," Abby said, "British Columbia is sure to be dragged into confederation." She was surprised she had spoken. The Governor was smiling at her down the length of the table. "The interests of the colony are really of little importance," she said. "Sir John A. has made a botch-up of this Riel business and so he needs some grand plan, like a coast-to-coast confederation, to stir up a national spirit and ensure that the Tories will be re-elected. It could be a good thing for British Columbia, but that is hardly of concern to the Prime Minister. There are no heroes in this confederation issue, just a lot of individual politicians and businessmen lusting after their own self-interest."

Sir James cackled over his glass of champagne. The men stared at her, surprised that she understood the situation so well and equally surprised that she had said it so plainly. Abby glanced at Matthew and saw that he was grinning. She turned to Governor Musgrave. "We do, of course, get newspapers here from Canada, very quickly actually. They come through the United States."

"And what terms of union do you think would demonstrate a sincere interest in the welfare of the colony?" Musgrave asked.

"A railroad, of course," Abby said. "Seeing that Macdonald has to build it to Manitoba to deal with Riel, he might as well bring it over the Rockies. And the province should be granted representational government, with a grant to support it and the legislature, an effective mail service between Victoria and San Francisco, salaries for postal officials and judges, a telegraph system, lighthouses, jails, and they must, of course, assume responsibility for the Indians."

Governor Musgrave leaned back in his chair and smiled. "Perhaps we should appoint you to the committee which will draft the terms of union." The men around him laughed. Abby sipped her champagne. Caroline and Wiley were laughing. Madeline was laughing. Even the Governor was chuckling at his own joke. She looked at Sir James, his face half hidden by his glass. He winked at her.

The conversation droned on, slipping in and out of Abby's consciousness: Jonas raged about the Nanaimo coal strike — "The ringleaders should be hanged" — Caroline retold, with embellishments, the story of a Miss Booth, who had drowned herself in the Mystic Spring because, as Caroline confided with a flutter of her eyelashes, her amorous advances towards a certain Victoria journalist had not been reciprocated. Amor De Cosmos cut her off with a declaration that a fifty-dollar head tax should be imposed on all Chinese entering the province. Sarah said nothing.

After dinner Abby endured a tedious half-hour in the parlour with the women, listening to Caroline play the piano and trying to divert Madeline from relentlessly pursuing the topic of cultivating roses. Sarah slouched silently in a chair watching a peacock scrabbling in the dirt below the window. At last Matthew came to rescue her; she could tell by his grin that he had succeeded in gaining the Governor's support for his timber leases.

She had still not found an opportunity to speak to Caroline and Wiley about Sitka's garden, and it wasn't until they were preparing to leave that she noticed the young couple alone in the parlour. She excused herself from the group in the foyer and slipped into the room. Caroline lay stretched on an ottoman, reclining on her side to accommodate her enormous bustle. Wiley stood behind her and, as Abby entered, he removed his hands from her shoulders. They had been laughing.

"Miss Cains, Mr. Burgess, my congratulations on your engagement. I am very happy for you."

Caroline raised her eyebrows and stared at Abby. "Thank you."

"I am afraid this is very bad timing on my part, but there is something I must discuss with you and it is unlikely I will be seeing you again soon."

Caroline watched her with an amused grin. Wiley's smile narrowed. "Yes?"

"It concerns a friend of mine, an Indian woman, who lives in the forest not far from Galer Mills. It seems that when you were riding there last week you . . . well . . . you accidentally rode through her vegetable garden. I wouldn't mention it except that those vegetables were all she had to see herself and her daughter through the winter. I tried to replace them myself, but she refused. However, I am certain that if you offered to compensate her yourself she would accept."

Caroline rose from the ottoman and stood in front of Abby, smiling defiantly. "There must be some mistake, Mrs. Galer. We have had no truck with the savages, either here or across the inlet."

Abby sighed wearily. "You are making this most difficult, Miss Cains." She glanced angrily at Wiley. He grinned back at her. "You were the only riders near Galer Mills that day. My friend described you: a handsome man with black hair, moustache, and grey suit, and a young woman with a white dress and red hair. There is no mistake, Miss Cains. If you are worried about your behaviour becoming known, you needn't. I have — "

"My dear," Caroline purred sweetly, "I am hardly concerned about *my* behaviour. After all, *I* do not keep company with *siwashes*. Perhaps you took too much laudanum and got the details confused."

Abby was stunned.

"Oh, dear," Caroline drawled, "have I offended you? Surely you are aware that everyone knows of your . . . addiction. I suppose the only reason it is never mentioned is out of respect for your husband." Caroline indicated the torn hem of Abby's dress. "Undoubtedly that is why you were unable to dress properly for this evening's dinner."

Abby's mouth fell open. She wanted to scream at the woman, tell her how she had stopped taking the drug years ago, confront her with her insolence, but she realized the futility of defending herself to such a creature. Already she could hear the condescending "Of course, dear; we understand" ringing in her ears. Wiley grinned at her over Caroline's shoulder. She turned on her heel and swept out of the room, brushed past Matthew in the foyer, and hurried down the steps into the enveloping darkness of night with the infuriating lilt of Caroline's laughter fading behind her.

Gassy Jack counted one hundred and thirty-five dollars onto the rickety table that had been set up in the centre of Gastown, took his land receipt from the sweating clerk, and limped back into the crowd. The shooting pains in his legs had been getting steadily worse, but today he didn't care. The new Deighton Hotel and the tiny Globe Saloon were legally his.

It was late afternoon, hot and humid. The crows watching from the nearby cedar trees were quiet and listless. Gassy Jack mopped his brow with his sleeve and grudgingly unbuttoned his moose-hide coat. The bidding on Mei-fu's lot had begun.

The girls from the Palace Royale, in light dresses of white and cream muslin, clustered about the small Chinese woman, forming a gaudy tent with their coloured parasols. George Black was bidding against her, but at one hundred and five dollars he dropped out.

"One hundred five dollars, once." The auctioneer stood on a podium with a small lectern in front of him. He looked tired and his voice was shrill. "One hundred five, twice — "

"One hundred twenty dollars." The voice came from behind the spectators and everyone turned to look. It was Jonas Cains. The crowd buzzed. Gassy Jack chuckled to himself; it was the first time he had seen Cains smile.

"One hundred thirty," Mei-fu yelled.

"One thirty-five," said Jonas.

Mei-fu turned and scowled at him. The girls around her hissed and booed.

"One hundred forty."

"One hundred fifty dollars," Jonas shouted.

Gassy Jack took a deep breath and raised his hand. "One fifty-five." Again the crowd buzzed.

"Aieee," Mei-fu shrieked.

The smile vanished from Jonas's face as he looked from Jack to Mei-fu and back again. Was it a trick? "One hundred sixty dollars."

"One sixty-five," Jack bellowed.

Jade and Lotus Blossom were crying. Mei-fu whirled to face Gassy Jack. "You motherless, dog-eating turd," she yelled. Jack winced. The few ladies in the crowd gasped and hurried away from the auction. Mei-fu buried her face in Clarissa's ample bosom and began to sob.

"One hundred sixty-five dollars, once," the auctioneer cried.

No, Jonas thought, it is not a trick. The bitch has clearly been outfoxed. A small plot of land in the ramshackle village was useless to him; he merely wanted to see the dangerous hell-hag driven out of town.

"One hundred sixty-five dollars, twice."

Slowly the sly smile returned to Jonas's face. If someone else was willing to pay the price of his vengeance, so much the better.

The auctioneer cracked his gavel on the podium. "Sold, for one hundred sixty-five dollars."

Jack beamed, and for a moment forgot the pain in his legs as the covey of white-clad women shrieked with joy and crushed about him, kissing his purple-veined cheeks and stroking his barrel chest. He was tempted to keep the deed for himself—he was still angry about the Palace Royale saloon, which was stealing much of his business—but a bargain was a bargain. He had paid for the lot with Mei-fu's money and he would transfer it to her for a dollar, as agreed, and then he would collect his promised reward—an entire night with the Rubenesque nymph, Susan. And this time the diabolical Chinawoman would not insist that he pay like a common customer.

As he stood in the cluster of excited women, like a bee in a gaudy flower, and watched Jonas's face redden, as he breathed in their heady perfume and listened to the soft bumping of their delicate parasols, like angels' wings, over his head, the weeks of plotting and the elaborate secrecy about his partnership in the Palace Royale were suddenly worth it. He felt like a hero. And on top of it all he was having the delicious satisfaction of seeing the obnoxious, pompous old man's stern British reserve crumble.

"Bloody whores!" Jonas shouted.

The crowd turned to stare at him. His jowls quivered with rage and his mouth opened and closed silently, then he wheeled round and stormed along the path towards the mill, stumbling over a broken branch and kicking at it furiously. Gassy Jack's booming laughter rumbled out from his heavenly nest.

At a quarter to twelve on the night of July 19, 1871, Gassy Jack's yellow dog stood shivering on the ground behind a covered bandstand, with fiddle music, firecrackers, horses' hooves, and gunshots whizzing around him, and began to howl. A brood of twelve four-month-old pups jumped to their feet and clustered around him. They were mongrels, spotted yellow and black, with long fur, short legs, and big heads, and their stubby bodies shook as they thrust their small muzzles up at the black sky and howled pitifully. Gassy Jack laughed as he watched them and slipped his big arm around Quahailya's thin waist. She turned her small face up to him and leaned her cheek against his heavy moose-hide coat.

The pianoforte on the bandstand had been donated by Mei-fu, who was dancing her fifty-fourth jig of the evening. Next to the fiddle player was Amor De Cosmos, considerably drunk, pumping on a concertina and capering about the stage with his frock-coat flying around him. Below him the outdoor dance-floor Matthew had provided was slick with mud from the light drizzle that was falling. Susan shrieked as her dance partner slipped and pulled her down on top of him. Another couple tripped over them and thudded onto the floorboards, and the throng of dancers hooted and giggled as they skidded past the fallen bodies. Pulling free from their partners, Yvette and Theresa waded through the tangle of limbs and hoisted Susan to her feet. In the confusion, Clarissa slipped from the dance-floor, nodded slightly in Wiley Burgess's direction, and ghosted softly, cat-like, into the forest. Wiley waited a moment, glancing furtively about him, then prowled into the woods after her.

Madeline clicked her tongue in disgust as a rough-looking logger grabbed Sarah by the wrist and pulled her back into the dance. Everyone from Jonas's mill was there, as well as over a hundred sailors from a dozen ships; some had loaded their lumber a week before, then anchored in the inlet to wait for the celebration. Most of Galer Mills had come across the inlet on the *Cariboo Fly*.

There were not enough women. Men danced with men.

Whisky jugs had been passing freely from hand to hand since dawn. Occasionally a reveller slipped unconscious to the ground, and Wu Lee dragged the body out of the way of the horses that were charging up and down the path next to the dance-floor to the shelter of a large cedar tree — a job he did with relish, checking pockets for money or valuables along the way. There was little room left under the tree.

Caroline shouldered her way angrily through a crowd of New Westminster businessmen, looking for Wiley. She felt foolish and humiliated that she was unable to find him the night before their wedding.

Jonas glanced at his gold pocket-watch; it was almost midnight. He marched onto the dance-floor, mounted the stage, and raised his arms. The music faltered and finally stopped. He had paid for the fireworks himself, so he would make sure that *everyone* watched them.

Abby stood at the edge of the dance-floor, snuggled against Matthew. Her belly swelled in front of her; she was eight months pregnant.

"Five, four, three . . ." the crowd shouted. Pots and pans banged together. Gunshots sounded. From the mob came a roar like the sound of a cresting wave. Horses reared up as the rockets screamed out over the black water of Burrard Inlet and exploded into sprays of red, blue, green, and yellow.

British Columbia had entered confederation.

TEXADA

ABBY STOOD AT THE BOW OF THE *Isabel* under the blazing sun, patting her face with a handkerchief, as the ship steamed through the narrows. The high rock walls of Thoos loomed sheer and close on the port side.

"Look." Amor De Cosmos approached her from behind, his arms held out to the side, his coat spread like a limp black sail; it billowed slightly and he sighed as the breeze tickled his sides. "Up there." He nodded towards an eagle high above them, spiralling downwards slowly, steadily, its black wing-tips spread like fingers feeling the warm air for currents. Two seagulls darted and jerked around it, screaming and shrieking in a flurry of white feathers, but the eagle descended irrevocably, unalterably, towards the nests of Thoos, like an implacable machine.

Abby turned and leaned her back against the rail, and pointed at the steward who was struggling with an armload of fishing rods and rifles. De Cosmos had carried the equipment on board himself and dumped it perfunctorily on deck. "You planning on doing some fishing?"

The Premier chuckled. "Course not. It's just a ruse. Walkem and I told everyone we were off on a sporting expedition. Land speculation can be a dangerous business for a politician."

Abby chuckled. "You're a sly one, Amor."

De Cosmos rocked back and forth on his heels. "Just cautious.

I shepherd a fickle flock." A rifle clattered to the deck as the steward struggled towards the hatch. "Guess I'd best give the fellow a hand." He touched his fingers to his brow and marched away.

Abby turned back to the ocean. English Bay spread before her as flat and green as polished jade, and the mountains of Vancouver Island shimmered hazy and purple in the far distance. Fanny Molroy. . . . That's where it started, she thought. She wanted to remember, to fix the beginning in her mind, because she had a feeling that somehow it would be important. Fanny Molroy. . . .

She had first seen the famous chanteuse the week before in Victoria. It had been a warm, muggy Friday, the last day she and Matthew would spend on the island. In the morning they had purchased three waterfront lots from which they could ship lumber to the east if Victoria was chosen as the terminus for the railroad. In the afternoon they had gone to Jason's Furniture Store and ridden in the city's first "rising room". Abby had closed her eyes and marvelled as the doors slid shut, the operator heaved on the pulleys, and the small closet rose; she was delighted. In the evening they had taken a carriage to the Royal York Theatre and heard the famous singer Fanny Molroy.

Fanny was a small Irishwoman in her late thirties. She had stood alone in the footlights, in a simple black dress, her square face thrust up at the balcony, singing song after song: "Kathleen Mavourneen", "Comin' thro' the Rye", and "The Last Rose of Summer".

At intermission, as they strolled through the lobby, Abby had seen Jonas Cains waving at them from a cluster of men gathered around him.

"Mrs. Galer. Hallo, Mr. Galer."

She had not seen him since the night of the confederation festivities, and, as she approached on Matthew's arm, the heels of her kid leather shoes clicking over the marble lobby, she was shocked by how quickly he had aged: his hair had receded to a thin white fringe, his face looked grey and sunken, as though the bones underneath were crumbling, and his heavy-set body with its barrel chest was paunchy and slack.

They had sauntered towards the group of men: Attorney-General George Walkem; William Dalby, the Mayor of Victoria; Wiley Burgess, dapper and grinning. Amor De Cosmos had stood with his thumbs hooked in his waistcoat, his bearded chin jutting proudly forward, swaggering with his own importance at having recently been appointed the province's second premier.

She had approached with her hand extended. "Congratulations, Premier De Cosmos. The people could not have been blessed with a better leader."

De Cosmos had beamed and fidgeted with his cane, hooking it first on his left arm, then on the right. "Well, we do what we must," he had said. "Of course, I have taken office at a most difficult, I daresay even critical, period in the growth of the province, what with Ottawa stalling on its promise to build the railway and—"

"A brilliant chanteuse, don't you agree?" Jonas said. "Fanny Molroy. Splendid woman. Splendid voice." De Cosmos sniffed and looked away. "And how is it," Jonas continued, "that Mr. Burgess and I must wait three years and travel to another city to enjoy your splendid company? A situation which must be remedied, yes indeed. And I believe I have the perfect solution. We were just discussing—oh, pardon my rudeness. Of course you know our new Premier, but have you met Mr. Walkem and Mr. Dalby?" Jonas introduced the Attorney-General and the Mayor of Victoria. "We were just making arrangements for a day trip up Malaspina Strait to an island called—what's the name of that blasted place again, Wiley?"

"Texada."

"Texada, yes. It's a disgrace the way we name every rock and tree after the cursed Indians."

"It's Spanish," De Cosmos said. "Named in 1775, I believe, after a rear-admiral, Felix de Tejada."

Jonas glared at him. "Yes. I'm sure. Anyway, rumour has it"—he glanced around and lowered his voice—"that Texada is rich in iron ore. Just a rumour, you understand, but from a most reliable source. Yes, most reliable. And of course it costs us nothing to look, does it? Indeed, it should be a most pleasant trip: late summer sun, cool sea breezes, good company, the beauty of the ocean. I've never been to that part of the coast myself. We were thinking of next Saturday. Will you and Mrs. Galer join us?"

Abby had noticed the sly smile on Jonas's face, the mischievous look, the twinkle in his eye, but had thought nothing of it until this morning when the *Isabel* had steamed across the inlet to pick them up—and Jonas Cains was not on board.

"Beautiful, isn't it?"

Abby glanced behind her at Matthew, who stood with his hands on her shoulders, then turned back to the ocean. To her right the rugged coastal mountains dropped green and sharp like feathery cliffs into the sea. Seals stopped their play in the deep black pools at their base to stare, their small, round heads swivelling in the water as the ship passed. To the left, sun points dazzled on the deep-blue waves, and in the distance the mountains of Vancouver Island were hazy and purple.

"Matthew, don't you think it's a little peculiar that Cains didn't come today?"

Matthew shrugged. "No. Wiley said he had business in New Westminster."

"Do you think he's going to invest in an island he's never seen?"

"He sent his son-in-law, didn't he?" Matthew said defensively. "Hey, what's this all about?"

Abby turned back to the ocean. "Nothing. I just don't trust him."

"But it's not going to cost us anything," Matthew said. "I've got it all worked out. Come on. I was just going to get the others and explain it to them. You'll see."

Abby followed him down the deck to where De Cosmos, Walkem, and Dalby were sitting at the stern, talking to Wiley Burgess. A steward appeared with champagne. Abby leaned against the rail and sipped her drink, and listened while the politicians leaned forward in their chairs, engrossed in Matthew's plan. Despite the blazing sun, she could not shake off the chill sense of foreboding that had gripped the back of her neck like an icy hand ever since they had left the protective rock walls of Thoos. Even at high noon, with the red hills of Texada looming off the port bow, it was still there.

The men lowered a skiff and, as Matthew rowed the party to the rocky beach, Abby sat stiffly in the stern and looked disapprovingly at the bottles of champagne De Cosmos had brought with him. It was obvious he had no intention of exploring the island.

On shore the politicians set deck-chairs under a cedar overlooking the strait and opened a bottle of champagne while Matthew, Abby, and the geologist they had brought from Victoria walked into the woods.

They tramped over red hills, splashed through streams the

colour of tea, and chipped at maroon rocks. Texada was obviously rich in iron ore. An hour later they returned to the beach with a box of samples. "The island is a gold-mine of iron ore," Matthew announced.

Late in the afternoon, as the *Isabel* steamed back across the straits, the men, exhilarated and tipsy with sun and champagne, gathered again on the aft deck. Abby sat behind them, her anger folded like cold metal hands within her, and listened to Matthew's excited voice.

"We will form a company, perhaps a syndicate. We need fifteen to twenty men who are British subjects. With that number we could pre-empt the whole southern end of the island for next to nothing. I don't think any of us want to venture into mining, but if we keep the iron secret until after the pre-emptions are filed, we can sell the island later at an incredible profit. Profit, gentlemen. Pure, clean, and simple. The railway is coming. They'll need thousands of miles of track, tons of iron ore, and Texada will supply it. And once the line is completed, ore can be shipped to the manufacturing plants in eastern Canada, or America. Why, Texada's value is inestimable.

"Granted, we would have to be cautious filing so many pre-emptions—if word gets out everyone will want a piece of Texada—but I know the registrar, Edmonds, and I think we should make him a partner. I'll be president; after all, as an American I'm not eligible to pre-empt land, but I'm a good businessman, I have enough friends and employees to raise the required number of pre-emptors, and I have the added advantage of being free from political involvement."

"Hear, hear," De Cosmos said. The other politicians chuckled and raised their glasses.

"I'll take care of everything. All you gentlemen need do is file your pre-emptions, sit back, and wait to collect your profits."

"You can count me in," Mayor Dalby bellowed. "I want a piece of Texada." George Walkem, the Attorney-General, waffled. "Assuming, of course, the analysis of the ore samples proves favourable, I see no harm in a small wager on the natural resources Mother Nature has stored in our munificent province."

De Cosmos, who lay sprawled in a deck-chair, his champagne glass sparkling in the setting sun, was drunk but cautious: "I don't know," he said. "The people have always frowned on politicians speculating in land. They deem it unscrupulous."

"Scruples be damned," Dalby roared. "They don't pay you a salary, do they? How, exactly, are you expected to earn a living, my dear De Cosmos? Smuggling?"

"I admit the island is attractive," De Cosmos said. "But I must not compromise my position as premier. I see nothing wrong, however, with purchasing, say, a one-third or one-half interest in a legitimate company. Nothing wrong with that, is there, Walkem? Or, if you choose to sell the mine, well, my position brings me daily in contact with important and wealthy businessmen. I could act as your agent. Why, I daresay even the Dominion government may be interested. God knows Macdonald will need my support if he is to extricate himself from this odious Pacific Scandal, and he must expect to do something in return. I think a commission of ten per cent would be only fair, don't you?"

At dusk Matthew and Abby stood alone in the bow, gazing at the islands of Georgia Strait, still and mountainous in the fading light.

"Matthew," Abby said, "why would Cains direct us to a secret iron mine and then withdraw, smiling and benevolent? He has no love for us."

"Well, maybe he hasn't the time to deal with it, my love. His business is lumber."

"And so is yours."

"My business is money," Matthew said tersely. "Profit. Pure and simple." Abby clenched her teeth to keep from saying more. They stood in silence, gazing out at the white moon sparkling on the twilight waves.

"You're too suspicious," Matthew said. "The land will cost us next to nothing, and it's all legal. What can Cains do?" He stalked away, leaving Abby alone at the bow.

"I don't know," she said softly. "But I don't like it."

It was midnight before the *Isabel* slipped into English Bay, the reflection of the moon glinting across her prow. A faint breeze was blowing. The air was warm and the sky shimmering with stars. As the ship edged past the steep walls of Thoos, feathers drifted down from the rocks above, scuttled across her deck, and tumbled softly into the still, black water. Across the inlet the lights of Cains's mill winked and flickered over the small, dark waves.

The old maple tree in the centre of Gastown shivered in the

damp cold blowing in from the sea. Long white whiskers of rain streamed from its branches and gusted along the boardwalk, rattling against windows and rippling over doorsills. Mei-fu hurried along the walkway, her head bent into the piercing wind, her heavy cloak billowing around her, her small black shoes snapping like gunshots on the slick, weathered boards. In her heart was the scent of plum blossoms on a summer afternoon. Today she would pay back the last of Gassy Jack's investment. Today the Palace Royale would be totally hers.

As she passed the Deighton Hotel, a window opened above her and a bucketful of sudsy brown water fanned out on the wind and slapped onto the boardwalk with a splash a few feet ahead of her. She froze as the foam splattered across the bottom of her dress, then glared up at the window in time to see the mole-like face of Gassy Jack's sister-in-law disappear behind a lace curtain. Instinctively she scanned the street for a good throwing stone, but as she reached for one she noticed the shadowy outline of Gastown's new constable watching her through the window of his office across the street. She pulled back her hand and straightened up. It was not a day for trouble. She shook her head sadly and marched on.

Gassy Jack's sickness has spread to his brain, she thought. He was a fool to invite such a she-devil to share in his good fortune. When the Deighton Hotel was completed, he had written to his brother in London to come and help run the place. The brother had arrived with his shrewish old wife, who immediately took over the hotel, prowling the corridors like a warden searching for a jail-break. The rooms reeked of the ammonia she washed them with daily. Few visitors came any more, and half the men of Gastown had been barred from the saloon: some for wearing caulk boots, others for swearing, some for spitting, and a few, as Gassy Jack had recently told her, for watching the brittle twitch of the old woman's hips with a licentious gleam in their eyes. Mei-fu chuckled as she recalled the pained look on his face as he had related this most recent complaint. The thought of anyone lusting after such a sour old cabbage was ludicrous. Why surely, she thought, her Jade Gate must be frozen as solid as the glaciers of Lungkiang.

She had driven the customers away, and finally Gassy Jack, too, had abandoned the hotel to her and fled with Quahailya back to the peace and comfort of the old Globe Saloon. It was there that

Mei-fu headed now, relishing the feel of her heavy purse thumping solidly against her leg as she walked. He should have come to collect the last payment yesterday, she thought, as they had agreed, but he had not appeared. Now that she thought about it, she had not seen him for seven days. She quickened her pace.

Her heart beat faster as she entered the poplar grove and approached the Globe Saloon, where she had spent so many days and nights with her pride shut tight against the endless battering of the men who had come to her with their silver dollars clutched in their hands. She could recall none of their faces, but she could picture every crevice, every dust mote and spiderweb, of her small cubicle behind the burlap curtain. The saloon had not changed. The walls leaned in a little more, but it still looked the same. She sniffed delicately at the strange scent in the air and decided it was skunk cabbage. Strange, she thought; I've never noticed it in the winter before.

As soon as she poked at the door with her fingertip and it swung loosely open onto darkness, she knew something was wrong. There were no customers. "Hallo? Gassy Jack?" A rat scuttled across the sawdust floor and disappeared into the shadows. She stepped inside.

The room was littered with broken tables and chairs and shattered glass. The shelves behind the bar had been ransacked. She sniffed the air again; the smell was stronger, rancid and foul, and it made her flesh crawl. "Hallo?"

From the small room at the back came a soft whimper. Mei-fu pushed the door open and clapped her hand over her mouth. The smell of rotting flesh caught in her throat, and she turned and sagged against the door-frame. By the sputtering light of a candle stub she saw Gassy Jack stretched on the small rope-frame bed by the burlap curtain, his half-naked body bloated and still, the flesh around his eyes and mouth already collapsing. For a moment she saw Quahailya huddled on the dirt floor in a corner by the potbelly stove, her large black eyes and dirt-streaked face staring up at her, then the candle flickered and went out. Mei-fu rushed towards the young girl, but she screamed and struck out with her fists.

"*Dew neh loh moh*," Mei-fu whispered. She backed away and scrabbled through the cupboards for a new candle. Her hands shook as she lit it. The light flared up and flooded through the room, showing the frightened girl pressed against the log walls.

"What happened?" Mei-fu asked. She stood with her hands on her hips. The panic began to drain from Quahailya's face. Mei-fu edged closer. "Where's your baby?" she said softly. The eyes darted to a woven cradle by the door. The girl began to push herself up, but Mei-fu moved in front of her and in a moment Quahailya was in her arms, sobbing on her shoulder, the words flooding out of her. "I try," the girl cried. "I try do something."

"When did it happen?"

"Six days past. I go to his brother at Deighton Hotel," the girl whimpered. "But *she* answer door." Mei-fu placed her hand on the young girl's head to still her chattering teeth. "I not know what do. No one come. No one help."

"You could have come to me," Mei-fu said softly.

"She spit in my face," Quahailya wailed. "She call me *klootch-man* and spit in my face."

Mei-fu rocked the girl gently and over her shoulder regarded the decaying hulk of Gassy Jack, the ingenuous quack, who, with a single keg of whisky, had founded the village of Gastown.

"Tea?" Abby asked. She nudged the door open with her hip and backed into Matthew's cluttered office. Outside, the sawdust compound shimmered in the first heat of spring and the masts of the half-dozen schooners loading at the wharf swayed gently in the lee of the warm mountain. As the wail of the lunch whistle reverberated off the granite cliffs and the scream of the saw faded and died, a flock of ravens dozing in the backyards of the tight ring of stark white cottages lifted into the air, then settled again, their heads cocked, their eyes blinking in surprise at the sudden silence. The door slammed shut and Abby registered the anger in Matthew's grunt, like that of a wild boar.

"Well," he announced accusingly, "you were right."

She turned, placed the tea tray next to the folded newspaper on his desk, and stared into the cold, bitter green eyes; they reminded her at once of the day on the *Isabel* when English Bay had spread before her as hard and smooth as polished jade, and she knew it had something to do with Jonas Cains. "Texada?" she asked.

Matthew poked the newspaper towards her with his index finger. "Cains leaked the story to John Robson's newspaper; they've done it up as black as a funeral, with enough damaging innuendo to turn half our customers against us." He slammed his palm on the desk and Abby jumped. "You were right," he repeated angrily.

She did not want to be right; it wasn't what she wanted at all. She picked up the folded paper and gingerly opened it to the blazing headlines of the *Colonist*, February 9, 1874:

TEXADA ISLAND LAND GRAB EXPOSED!
De Cosmos Deeply Implicated!

Are government and big business in collusion to defraud the people of British Columbia? So it would seem!

The Colonist has recently learned from a reliable Burrard Inlet businessman that Mr. De Cosmos, whom custom requires us to dub honourable, and Matthew Galer of Galer Mills, in league with other prominent political figures, have pre-empted an entire Island believed to be rich in magnetic ore.

Mr. De Cosmos then travelled to Ottawa where it is reported he attempted to sell the mine for $150,000 to Sir John A. Macdonald in return for his — De Cosmos' — political support during the recent Pacific Scandal. Fortunately for the people of British Columbia the Macdonald ministry fell before this heinous transaction could be completed. De Cosmos, undeterred by his unscrupulous actions, then travelled to London — at public expense! — to make yet another attempt at lining his own pockets with the province's resources.

Will the greed of certain politicians never be satisfied?

And what of Mr. Galer; who is not even a British subject? Is it not enough that he has grabbed up all of the timber land at one cent per acre? Must he now monopolize all of the province's resources for his own selfish purposes?

The people of British Columbia stand outraged. Nothing short of a Royal Commission can settle this af-

"De Cosmos! Hang him! Hang De Cosmos!" The shouts floated through the open windows of the Hotel de France in Victoria. Abby, tense and jittery from brooding over the forthcoming Royal Commission, bolted from her armchair and looked down into the street below. "Matthew, come and see. It's a mob."

Matthew lay in bed reading a letter from a San Francisco mining company that had offered to buy Texada. He kicked off the bedcovers and padded to the window in his nightshirt; he was dazed and feverish from the grippe, and he reeked of camphor and lemon.

Men were milling on the boardwalk below. A wave of protestors rounded the corner and flooded down Government Street. Abby could hear the rumble of their boots on the rough planking of James Bay Bridge.

> We'll hang old De Cosmos on a sour apple tree,
> We'll hang old De Cosmos on a sour apple tree.

The chant began softly, started by a single man with a reedy voice, and it skipped through the crowd like a pebble on a mountainside until the mob roared:

> We'll hang old De Cosmos on a sour apple tree,
> So he won't betray us any more!

Abby shuddered as the front of the crowd swept under the window, their black coats drab against the dull evening sky, their faces red, ugly, angry. They were still coming from around the corner. The men on the boardwalk joined them. "Is it us?" Abby asked. "Texada, I mean?"

"Partly," Matthew said. "I guess that was the final straw. But it's the railroad they really want. The newspapers are saying that De Cosmos is renegotiating the terms of union; that he's offered the federal government a six-year extension in return for the Esquimalt drydock. Obviously the people won't have it. They feel cheated by Ottawa and betrayed by De Cosmos. They want the railroad and they want it now. But, yes, Texada is a part of it. It's added fuel to the fire, convinced them that De Cosmos is a traitor, that he's used them, abused his position for personal gain."

"Well, he hasn't," Abby snapped.

Matthew was startled by the anger in her voice. "Of course not, but they don't know that. He's never here to defend himself, he's always in Ottawa, so the people believe whatever slander John Robson decides to print."

Abby watched as the mob — at least eight hundred men — twisted round the corner of Yates Street and marched towards the Parliament Buildings. "Well, they're fools to believe it. Granted, Amor is a drunk and an insufferable egotist, but he's done more for British Columbia than any single man, living or dead." She stormed across the room and grabbed her cloak from its peg by the door. "And it's high time someone told them so."

"Abby? You're not going out there. I forbid it. Abby —" The door slammed behind her. Matthew tore off his nightshirt and ran to the wardrobe for his clothes.

The Parliament Buildings stood red against the grey sky. Inside, the chamber was full; men leaned from the windows on the second floor and the crowd overflowed down the front steps, and stood shouting on the muddy lawn.

Matthew shouldered his way through, pleading an urgent message for the Speaker, and finally arrived, exhausted, in the high-ceilinged chamber of the Legislative Assembly.

The hall was in chaos: the double doors, built with lumber from his own mill, had been shattered; a delegation stood at the bar, shouting for attention, their legs braced against the pressing mob; the floor was tightly packed, the room insufferably hot; the shocked Speaker stood beside his chair, thundering for order; the crowd glared at De Cosmos, yelling "Traitor!" and "Tyrant!"; men leaned over the railing of the visitors' gallery shaking their fists at the members below; clubs were waved overhead. De Cosmos sat stiffly in his chair, his legs crossed, his cane resting lightly on his lap, and stared at the ceiling, his face grim and fierce.

Matthew scanned the hundreds of venomous red faces, gleaming with sweat in the orange glow of the gas lamps. He could not find Abby.

"We, the people of Victoria ...!" shouted a husky man at the bar as he read from a piece of paper. The din softened. "We, the people of Victoria, resolve that no agreement shall be entered into with Ottawa regarding the graving dock or the provincial debt until such time as the new federal government makes clear its intentions on the railway!" The crowd roared.

"Further, be it resolved, that we, the people of Victoria, oppose any amendment to the terms of union by the provincial government until they have been submitted to the people for adoption." The mob cheered. A group at the back of the hall began singing the refrain with which they had marched through the streets while the rest shouted "Traitor!", "Tyrant!", and "Land-grabber!".

The Speaker stepped from his platform and hurried through a side door. De Cosmos rose to follow. A man in the centre of the crowd pulled a pistol from under his coat. Someone shouted a warning. De Cosmos froze. People around the gunman leapt upon him and knocked him to the floor. The hall was in turmoil.

"Shut up! You bloody fools, shut up!"

The crowd hushed, startled that a shrill female voice could bellow such unfeminine obscenities. Everyone stared at the visitors' gallery. Matthew saw Abby leaning on the balustrade, her arms apread on the rail, her face enraged, and he rushed towards the stairs.

"How dare you threaten a man who has selflessly dedicated his life to serving you?"

"It's Galer's wife," someone shouted. "Course she'd defend him: they're as guilty of land-grabbing as De Cosmos!" The crowd rumbled.

"Sir," Abby shouted. "How do you know that? What are your sources?" The man was silent. "I can tell you: he read it in the newspaper," she sneered. "John Robson's newspaper. All of you did and all of you swallowed it as gospel without pausing to consider his reasons for printing such filth: his political aspirations. Well, you've been duped. I can tell you, categorically, De Cosmos did not pre-empt a foot of land on Texada, even though he had every legal right to do so. And why shouldn't he? God knows you don't pay him a salary. But I don't expect you to take my word for it, any more than you should take John Robson's. You will have your Royal Commission and, as his reward for years of self-sacrifice in your behalf, Amor De Cosmos will be dragged before it and suffer the degradation of being examined like a common criminal. So wait for your verdict; don't presume yourself fit to judge because you 'read it in the newspaper'." The crowd was quiet a moment as they looked from Abby to De Cosmos and back again. Matthew had reached the balcony and stood silently behind her, smiling.

"Texada or not," someone shouted, "he's still trying to sell our railway for a lousy graving dock!" The crowd rumbled.

"And so you have a right to be heard — but in a rational and civilized manner. Instead, you have roared into the Parliament Buildings — the Parliament Buildings! Our very symbol of democracy and order! — like a pack of wolves howling for blood, shouting threats and insults, waving guns like madmen, again without pausing to hear the other side, without giving him a chance to defend himself." Abby lowered her voice and sneered, "You make me ashamed to be a citizen of the Dominion.

"Well, fine. You have had your say. The people have been heard.

You have presented your resolutions. Now go, before you disgrace yourselves any further. And as you leave I would ask you to consider this: who fought hardest to bring you representational government, who was it that united Vancouver Island and British Columbia, and—most important of all—how have you shown your thanks?" Abby reached back and hooked her arm in Matthew's. "Gentlemen, I suggest we leave."

They walked slowly down the length of the gallery. The crowd was already funnelling out through the broken double doors. People pushed back to make a path for them. As they reached the bottom of the stairs Abby heard someone mutter "... could run for office. Pity she's a woman." She winked at Matthew and whispered, "Not bad, eh?"

The following day, Amor De Cosmos resigned as premier of British Columbia.

ALL FLESH IS GRASS

"... and all the goodliness thereof is as the flower of the field: The grass withereth, the flower fadeth: because the spirit of the Lord bloweth upon it: surely the people is grass...."

The Reverend Mr. Derrick, in a black cassock, stood on the hillside with his shoulders hunched over a Bible, his thin brown hair plastered to his forehead by the steady drizzle. Abby watched the droplets of rain collect on his chin and fall slowly, steadily, one by one, onto the open pages of the prayer book. Before her was a grave, like an open wound in the soft green field; beside it was a sleek polished casket.

The sky was black, the air windless and still. Around her the grim hiss of the rain blotted out the sobs of the mourners. Her own face was dry, cold, brittle.

She focused on the tombstone and quietly recited the inscription, over and over, as though it were a prayer, an incantation. "Fanny Molroy, 1835–1875. Fanny Molroy ..." Fanny does not want to rest here, she thought. Fanny wants to return to San Francisco, to her home, and cannot understand why it is too much trouble to send her waterlogged body back. Poor Fanny....
She remembered the last time she had seen her perform, on the

stage of the Royal York, with the dying echoes of "The Last Rose of Summer" reverberating off the upper balcony, and closed her eyes. She has taken her last ocean voyage, Abby thought, and cannot understand why she has been left at the wrong port.

Men gripped the ropes cradled under the coffin and swung it over the muddy hole. As it slowly descended, Abby watched the grim, grey face of Jonas Cains, made dark and soft by the thin mesh of her black veil and the heavy curtain of rain streaming from the edge of her umbrella, staring at her from across the polished casket.

> " 'The voice said, Cry!' — And why, dear friends, are we to lift up the voice and cry? Do not the living know that they must die? Is not every death a solemn cry? Is not every coffin an eloquent sermon?"

She did not hate him. Indeed, she felt nothing. Her heart was dead. Her eyes were stone. No more tears would come. A gust of wind whipped down the mountain and she leaned into it, her white hands limp at her sides, her black veil pressed tight against her face.

Next to Jonas stood Wiley Burgess, patting his hair in place with a grey-gloved hand. Caroline leaned against him, her body turned at an angle so that her right breast nuzzled his side. She was yawning. Abby watched with fascination as the pink tongue arched in the black hole of her mouth.

> "Does not every grave, with open jaws and with tongue, cry, 'Prepare to meet thy God'; and every funeral sermon proclaim as from the housetops — 'The grass withereth and the flower fadeth.' "

A seagull, with the muddy-brown feathers of a one-year-old, waddled across the cemetery and hopped onto a tombstone. Abby stared at him as he sat motionless, his head cocked to one side, his beady black eyes blinking rapidly.

"Set thine house in order; for thou shalt surely die."

She shuffled to the right to avoid a thin trickle of mud that was seeping down the hillside from the pile of black dirt where the coffin had rested, and noticed that several of the mourners looked relieved; they had been watching, fascinated, afraid to warn her, afraid it should touch her.

Among them was Quahailya, in a fine black frock and feathered hat, staring intently at Reverend Derrick. She had no reason to attend — she knew neither Fanny Molroy nor any of the others whose bodies littered the bottom of the Pacific — but she had become obsessed with funerals. Three months after the death of Gassy Jack her infant son, Richard Mason Deighton, had died of consumption. Quahailya never recovered. She became a funeral witch, a thin, feeble ghost, dressed perpetually in black, whose grief-stricken face haunted every funeral.

Beside her stood Amor De Cosmos, his black coat flapping about him as he braced his haggard frame against the wind, his arms limp at his sides, rain dripping from his tangled beard. Abby watched the piercing blue eyes staring at her out of gaunt sockets, and noted the pain, the sympathy, on his face. Amor, she thought, why did you not force Sir John A. to buy the island? You could have done it. I know you tried, but just a little more pressure, a little more, and we'd never have gone to San Francisco. She tilted her head back and her mouth fell open, her throat parched for the tears that would not come.

> " 'And the voice said, Cry' — And this cry sends its ringing appeal to all hearts and across every ocean, that neither position, age, nor sex can claim immunity from death. A voice to all the dearest relationships of life."

She scanned the dense line of trees at the edge of the cemetery, their tops shrouded in black clouds, their branches bowed, pushed by the wind, pelted with rain. Sitka would be up there, somewhere, watching.

She longed to turn and face the broad, flat inlet, to run down the hill, away from this scene and back to her home. She longed for it to end. She longed to forget.

A sudden gust swept down the hillside, bringing with it the smell of last summer's leaves rotting in the wet grass. Her eldest son, Martin, tilted the black umbrella into the wind.

> "... and the children came unto Him, cold and pale in death...."

The trees swayed and shook the rain from their branches. Yes, Abby thought, a rain forest does weep. It weeps for its dead, for the bodies which will never return to its embrace.

She glanced at her youngest son, Angus, who fidgeted, bored and restless, at her side; he was four. He stood with his back to the funeral, his attention riveted on the muddy-brown seagull that blinked at him from the tombstone near by. He took a cautious step towards it, but Abby reached down and placed her hand on his copper-coloured hair.

"'The voice said, Cry!' — and it was a voice from the sea."

She shut her eyes tightly to block out the image of the small gull and the memories it brought flooding back to her.

Seagulls. Abby braced herself against the jostling crowd on the Victoria wharf and watched them wheel and dive around the S.S. *Pacific*, screaming white streaks against the slate-blue morning sky. "Matthew, I'm worried; maybe I shouldn't go."

"Now, Abby; Angus is all right. It's just a cold, and God knows Sitka will mind him better than any doctor could. Forget it."

"Forget it?" Abby snapped. "Sometimes I don't think you care anything for that child."

Matthew took a deep breath and dug his hands into his pants pockets. A large Chinese family, laden with trunks and satchels, shoved past.

"I'm sorry, Matthew. I didn't mean it; I'm just worried." Abby felt a light tap on her shoulder. "Ah, damn it! Look at this." A seagull dropping trickled down her shoulder, white against the dark-blue of her velvet cloak.

Matthew smiled. "They say it's a good omen. This is your lucky day."

"Some luck."

"Look. They're loading the horses."

At the stern of the *Pacific* a section of railing had been removed and a special gangplank lowered. The sleek black Arabians and blonde Palominos of the Hurlburt and Rockwell Performing Horse Circus trudged indifferently up the walkway, bored by yet another ocean voyage. Everyone on the wharf turned to watch the magnificent animals, gratified to see that at least the last in line, an old albino mare, showed a normal fear of ships. She reached the end of the gangplank and braced her front legs. The trainer pulled down hard on her halter. She danced to the side and her right rear hoof slipped over the walkway as Hurlburt himself raced up behind her and cracked his whip. She leapt onto the deck whinnying and shivering.

Abby tapped Matthew on the shoulder. "What are they doing?" She pointed at the deck-hands, who were filling the starboard lifeboats with water. Bucket after bucket was being hauled up from the harbour, passed in relay from hand to hand, and dumped into the six wooden dinghies which hung from cables over the ship's side.

Matthew paled. "She's listing to port. I guess they're trying to balance her."

"Maybe we should wait and take the *Salvador* or the *Dakota*?"

Matthew chuckled. "I thought I was the one who was supposed to be afraid of water. No, the mining company's representative is expecting me Monday. We've got to get rid of Texada — now. I'm sick of it." He picked up their trunk and hoisted it onto his shoulder. "Shall we go find our cabin?"

Matthew and Abby walked up the gangplank, past the huge red paddlewheel, and onto the crowded deck. As they edged along the starboard passageway, the captain approached. "Good morning, Mr. Galer, Mrs. Galer." He was a tall, handsome man in his early thirties with wavy black hair, twinkling blue eyes, and a perpetual smile. "I can get someone to help you with that trunk if you like."

"Thank you, Captain Howell," Matthew said. "But I can manage fine. That's quite a crowd you've got."

"Yes, they transferred the *City of Panama* to the coffee trade in Central America, you know. Ever since, we've been carrying full loads."

"We saw your men filling the starboard lifeboats," Abby said nervously.

"Just a precaution, Mrs. Galer." Captain Howell smiled. "I'm sure we won't need them. And you wouldn't want us to tip over, would you?" He touched his hand to his cap. "We'll be sailing at nine sharp. Enjoy your trip."

Early in the morning, the S.S. *Pacific* — twenty-five years old, 876 tons, 225 feet in length — edged out into Victoria Harbour. Her twin side-wheels groaned to a halt, dripping water into the still, black bay, then the whistle hooted and the blades thundered forward, gaining momentum, until a fine white spray flew back from the ship in a silver arc and the smoke from the stack curled overhead.

Abby stood at the railing and watched the waking city of Victoria: carriages skimmed over the rotten planking of James Bay Bridge, and punts and bumboats weaved amongst the schooners anchored in the harbour. High on the hillside the tall spire of Christ Church Cathedral disappeared into the lowering clouds. As they rounded Laurel Point, the houses thinned and the land abruptly became wild and green. The open ocean stretched before them: flat, dreary, and gun-metal grey.

In the afternoon Abby pulled a chair up to the railing and settled in to sketch the violent granite mountains and frontier settlements of the coast as they edged past. She had brought her largest sketch pad: it would be a four-day journey, five if the weather turned bad. She had begun to notice a slight change in the coastline — an easing of tension, a bluntness to the hills, broader strips of sandy beach — when she sensed someone looking over her shoulder.

"That's not bad. Not bad at all."

Abby turned and looked up at the square, freckled face of Fanny Molroy.

"You're very good at that. No, don't get up, I'll just sit here." Abby stared, stunned, as the famous singer pulled a chair up to the railing. Her hands and feet seemed too big for her body; she looked older and thinner than she did on stage; she was dressed in black, and her auburn hair was tucked under a broad-brimmed hat.

"You're Fanny Molroy," Abby said. "I saw you at the Royal York two years ago."

"How was I?"

"Why, wonderful. You have a beautiful voice."

Fanny nodded. "And who are you?"

"Abby Galer."

"Do you do that professionally?" She pointed a long, bony finger at Abby's sketch pad. "If you don't, you should."

"I have sold a few paintings in San Francisco," Abby said.

Fanny's forehead wrinkled as she muttered Abby's name to herself. "Of course," she said. "Abby Galer. Magnus Oberheim sells your work. Why, you're all the rage in San Francisco now."

"You know Magnus?"

Fanny chuckled. "Oh yes. Magnus and I go back a long way, almost to the gold-rush. In fact, if it weren't for him I wouldn't be here today. You see, my parents died in a hotel fire in '52. I had no relatives or friends, but I'd always had a decent voice, so I got a job singing in a dingy bar on Sutter Street. Magnus heard me there one night. He pulled a few strings, got me into the better hotels, found me a business manager, and, well . . ."

"And you've been singing ever since."

"Well, almost. I did retire for two years, at the insistence of my second husband, Wilbur. He was fiendishly jealous and couldn't stand to see me surrounded by admirers. Of course, it was foolish of me to give up my career for a man," Fanny patted the hair at the back of her hat and smiled wistfully, "but Wilbur had certain personal attributes, if you know what I mean, which made the sacrifice seem small indeed. Once one has dined on caviar, it is difficult to settle for sausage." Abby chuckled. "He died of consumption in '65."

"And did you remarry?"

"No. I considered it, of course — God knows, when a woman has money and a reputation there are plenty of able young men anxious to share it — but Wilbur spoiled me. He was a wonderful man."

Both women fell silent, watching the darkening cliffs in the late-afternoon light. Only a few seagulls remained, trailing in the wake of the ship, exhausted, glancing anxiously at shore. A small swell had begun.

"So," Fanny said. "Magnus discovered you, too. He seems to have a knack for it — for finding talent in others." Fanny shook her head. "He's a funny man.

"I suppose he told you the story about his parents escaping from Prussia with the silver samovar?" Abby nodded. "Well, it's not true. His mother and father are both factory workers in Chicago. Lived there all their lives. Magnus followed the gold-rush west in '49 but he was too late to make anything of it. He bought the samovar at an auction in '52."

"Why?" Abby said. "Why would he make up such a story?"

Fanny shrugged. "Gives him something to talk about; attracts attention to himself; adds a little adventure and romance to his life — and God knows Magnus could do with more of that. He's really a very talented artist, you know. He — "

"Excuse me." Matthew was standing beside Abby's chair. "I'm sorry to interrupt; I just wanted to let you know I've invited someone to join us for dinner, at seven. A Mr. Charles Horetzky."

Abby introduced Matthew to Fanny. "It's an honour," he said.

"Perhaps you would be so kind as to join our table this evening as well."

"I'd love to," Fanny replied.

Matthew nodded and withdrew, and the two women sat on at the railing, talking, their voices growing softer as the grey November sky turned black and starless. The last of the seagulls cried wearily and veered in to shore. The sea rolled softly and the air became cold and quiet, except for the chug of the engine and the splash of the paddlewheel. At seven Matthew escorted the ladies to dinner.

The dining salon of the S.S. *Pacific* was old and dingy; the walls were hung with dusty red drapes and faded gold braid, the carpet was worn, and the tables were small and crowded close together. Matthew's party was given the last empty place, jammed against a wall next to the kitchen door. A coal-oil lantern flickered overhead, and the cutlery vibrated with the thrum of the engine.

At seven-thirty a bulky man in a black coat and wing collar appeared in the doorway, his shoulders hunched, his hooded blue eyes darting from one table to the next. Matthew signalled him over and he threaded his way to the table like a cat on a slippery tile floor.

Abby disliked him immediately. As he slavered over Fanny's hand, she poked at her salad and studied him out of the corner of her eye. He was insufferable: a giant, swarthy man with the hooded eyes of an owl and a vast black beard touched with boot polish. His nature was impossibly contradictory. When she praised the salad, he pronounced it inedible. When she admired his jacket, he sniffed and declared it a grubby cast-off suitable only for travelling. When Fanny pointed out Francis Garesche, the Wells Fargo agent in Victoria, and whispered that he was rumoured to be transporting $80,000 in gold-dust from the new mining district of Cassiar to the mint in San Francisco, Horetzky pronounced him a man of little consequence. Abby was about to rebuke him when Matthew caught her eye and shook his head. She slammed her fork down on the table and glared at her plate of oysters. Horetzky did not notice.

When the main course was finished and the dishes were cleared away, Abby realized why Matthew had befriended the obnoxious giant. Horetzky pulled a small stack of photographs from his breast pocket and spread them on the table. "And this," he announced dramatically, "is Bute Inlet."

Fanny snatched up one of the photographs. "Pictures!" she

exclaimed. "Look, Abby. Mr. Horetzky is a picture-taker. Isn't this a darling shot of trees and mud?"

Horetzky stared at her, his mouth open, his face red and outraged, but she ignored him.

"I do so love photographs; they're so ... frivolous, so decadently frivolous."

Horetzky took the picture in two fingers and pulled it firmly out of her hand. "Madam," he said, "these 'darling shots', as you so whimsically call them, will be instrumental in deciding the terminus of the Canadian Pacific Railway, the greatest structural undertaking mankind has ever attempted. I am not a picture-taker but an engineer, charged with a solemn and monumental task involving —"

"Well, Charlie," Fanny broke in, "I would dearly love to hear all about your choo-choo trains, but I'm very tired and I think I'm getting a sick headache." She pushed back her chair and stood up. "Mr. Galer, it's been a pleasure meeting you."

Abby stood quickly and picked up her cloak. "I'll walk you to your cabin," she said. As the two women hurried out, Abby glanced over her shoulder and saw Horetzky, open-mouthed, staring after them. Matthew had his hand over his face, pretending to cough, but she could see his shoulders shaking and knew he was chuckling.

As they stepped onto the deck, they burst out laughing. Fanny tried to imitate Horetzky's pompous manner — she thrust out her chest, half closed her eyes, puffed out her cheeks, and screwed up her mouth as though she had been weaned on a pickle — but she quickly broke down in giggles. Repeatedly Abby tried to speak and finally gasped out the words "choo-choo train", which again sent them reeling.

"Shhh. . . ." The sound hissed up from the shadows near by. Abby looked, and, through her tears, saw a large family huddled under coats and blankets, trying to sleep in the lee of the dining salon. She put her fingers to her lips and motioned for Fanny to follow.

Stifling their giggles, the two women tiptoed past the family and numerous other passengers who were sprawled on the deck, unable to obtain berths on the crowded ship. A light drizzle was falling, and an icy wind blew from the southwest; Abby pulled her cloak tight against it. They stopped at the bow and stared out over the railing into the cold, black night. The sea was dark, the land invisible, but she knew they must have passed through the

Strait of Juan de Fuca, and rounded Cape Flattery, and were well out in the open ocean. A heavy swell was running.

"I really must get some sleep," Fanny said. "It's been a long day. But could I join you for breakfast tomorrow?"

"Of course," Abby said. "I'd be delighted."

They said goodnight and Fanny hurried away, her hand on her hat, her thin frame bent into the wind.

"I'll knock on your door at seven," Abby called after her. She turned back to the ocean, held onto the rail, and stretched up on her toes. The fresh air smelled good after the smoky dining room, and she relished the feel of the wind tugging at her hair and clothes. She stayed at the bow for half an hour, thinking of Horetzky, Magnus Oberheim, and Fanny Molroy.

Captain Charles Sawyer, of the clipper *Orpheus*, lurched across the floor of his jumbled cabin and banged into the table, upsetting an open half-bottle of gin. The liquor trickled across a stack of crumpled charts. "Jeeesusss . . . !" he bellowed. With the bottle pinned under his armpit, he lowered his face to the table and sucked up the gin as it seeped across the eastern coast of Africa. He had been hired by Jonas Cains to ship a load of lumber to San Francisco and had become lost in the strange waters of the North Pacific on the return voyage.

He flipped angrily through the maps: "Timor, Tahiti, the Straits of Endeavour, Java. Charts for every God-damned, God-forsaken, stinkin' sink-hole on the face of this Christly, bloody earth — but no buggerin' Puget Sound." He took a long swig from the bottle, whirled to face the closed door, and raged: "If I catch the dirty, motherless whore-monger who stole pissin' Puget Sound, I'll keel-haul 'im." He staggered to the open porthole and glared out at the blackness of the North Pacific. There were no stars, no moon; nothing but the steady whoosh of the rushing sea, like laughter in his ears. "Mary, Mother of God, where are we?" he whined. "Where the hell are we?"

There was a sharp rap at his door. "Ship to starboard, sir."

Captain Sawyer whirled round, his mouth open, his eyes full of wonder. "Well, intercept her, you bloody fool! Hard to starboard! I want that ship stopped!" He slumped against the wall of his cabin and took another swig. His eyes rolled heavenward and he chuckled. "Why, thank ye, Mary. Ye always was a good ol' gal."

Abby was about to go when she saw a faint glimmer of light far to starboard. It winked and disappeared. She gazed into the black night and drizzle, smiling at the thought that other passengers, bound for Victoria, might be straining to see the orange glow of the *Pacific*'s pilot-house. The light appeared again, closer, brighter, then a second and a third. I wonder what kind of ship it is, she thought. She squinted into the blackness but could not see its outline. It was coming rather close.

"I said hold yer bloody course!" Sawyer shouted.

The first mate drummed his fingers on the wheel. "But we'll cross her bow, sir."

"How else do you plan on stoppin' her: send her a bloody tellygram?"

All hands stood ready to haul, clustered at the mizen-mast and clinging to the shrouds aloft; they glanced nervously from the brig to the side-wheeler. "Hundred yards off the starboard bow," yelled the boatswain.

The first mate glanced at the Captain, then spun the wheel defiantly to port. Sawyer gripped the gin bottle by its neck and raised it over the man's head.

Abby gripped the rail. The ship was coming too close. Within seconds the silhouette of a large clipper under full sail and moving fast loomed into view fifty yards off the starboard bow, her sails full and taut. She whirled to face the wheelhouse and saw the dim outline of Captain Howell standing with his back to the window. "No," she whispered. "It can't ..." The clipper was headed straight for the *Pacific*.

She backed away from the railing, her eyes wide, her heart pounding. "Captain Howell," she called. Suddenly she could see herself, as if from a distance, racing wildly away from the bow, her shoes skidding on the slippery deck, her cloak flying behind her. "Captain Howell!" she shrieked. Her foot struck a sleeping figure and she tumbled forward, scraping her elbows across the rough planking. "Captain Howell!" The clipper's jib-boom crossed before the *Pacific*'s bow and the nameplate reared up before her, stark and frightening in the dim light. The *Orpheus*.

"Howell! Howell! Howell!" A man's boot lay by her right hand. She hurled it at the wheelhouse window and the glass shattered. The steam whistle screamed. The side-wheels thundered and groaned as they ground to a halt and paddled frantically in reverse.

The *Pacific* struck the clipper amidships and shuddered as she ground along its side. The two big boats waltzed slowly around one another, creaking and groaning, then the *Orpheus* drifted off and faded into the dark. A piece of splintered railing dangled from the *Pacific*'s prow.

Abby lay on the deck, stunned, and for a moment the ship was eerily silent. The engines had stopped, and the only sound was the rasp of the ocean and the hiss of rain.

Shouting broke out below-decks. People streamed out of the dining salon. The deck was in chaos. Captain Howell strode towards the bow, and the first mate met him next to Abby. They spoke in low, hurried tones.

"How bad?"

"She's making water fast, sir. There's already a foot in the hold. The bow-planks have parted below the 'tween-deck."

"We've enough canvas to fother her; we could thrum a topsail and haul it under her bottom."

"Aye, sir, but without the reverse engines I doubt it would do any good; she's coasting forward at a fair clip and driving water into the hold."

"All right. Have the engineer meet me below; everyone else is to man the pumps." He took a deep breath. "And tell Jenkins to issue the life-preservers."

"Aye, sir."

Captain Howell ran along the deck and disappeared down the forward hatch.

Abby pushed herself unsteadily to her feet and found that the deck was sharply tilted; the bow was already low in the water. Her heart was pounding. She groped along the rail, edging through the panicked crowd towards the dining salon to look for Matthew. The rain had increased. The wind was strong and cold. Men in nightshirts and women in dressing-gowns pushed at her from all directions as they shouted for their wives, husbands, children. At midship she found a small girl, about six years old, clinging to the railing and screaming for her mother; her thin cotton nightdress was soaked and her blonde hair was plastered to her red face. She bundled the child in her cloak, picked her up, and hurried on.

On the aft deck she saw a mob gathered around a large chest marked "Life-Preservers", which a sailor was trying to unlock. A man pushed him roughly aside and shattered the padlock with an axe. The crowd surged forward. Abby held the child against her chest, shouldered her way to the box, and grabbed three of the vests with one hand. A thin, bearded man held onto the belt of one of them and tugged sharply. Abby whirled round and kicked him in the shins. He dropped the belt and she ran from the crowd, back to the railing.

With one of the vests hidden under her dress, she fastened one to the child, then put on her own. As she was wrapping the girl in the cloak again, she glanced at the nearest lifeboat and her heart sank. A frail old man stood in it, waist-deep in water, crying and bailing frantically with his hands. She whisked up the child and ran to the port side.

Someone had loosed the horses. Passengers dodged and pushed out of the way as they galloped through the crowd, wild-eyed and panic-stricken, their hooves thundering on the deck. The bow was under water, and black waves, white-veined, rolled and crested a third of the way up the ship. The *Pacific* lurched, and the old albino mare braced her legs and skidded down the steep incline; she ploughed into a frightened crowd at the edge of the water and floundered into the sea, sweeping the passengers ahead of her.

The first mate lay unconscious on the bridge of the *Orpheus*. Captain Sawyer gripped the wheel and glared down at the boat-swain below. "Neither ship was damaged, I tell yc; it was just a light blow," he bellowed. His mind was racing. He felt remark-ably sober. You've damn well done it now, Sawyer, he thought. Get away and get away fast before they can pin it on you. Bloody steamie should have stopped.

"We should at least go back and check," the boatswain said.

"Christ, Carter; you're worse than a bloody simperin' woman," Sawyer sneered. "Why, we barely scraped her."

"But —"

"I said we're goin' on! Now, loose out the topgallants. I want full sail. Haul out! Light to!"

The men, who had gathered on the aft deck, trudged, grum-bling, back to their tasks. Sawyer called after them, "The wind's freshenin'; we'll be in Puget Sound afore dawn;" then he mut-tered to himself, "if I can find the bloody place. . . ."

Abby clutched the third life-preserver tightly in her free hand

and searched for Matthew. She edged along the rail to a small lifeboat jammed with women and men. The tackle was loose and two sailors were heaving on the lines trying to raise her, but the weight was too great. They shouted at the people to get out, but none would budge.

A wave broke over the *Pacific*'s bow and swept a dozen passengers into the sea. The air was shrill with cries and screams.

Abby felt a hand on her shoulder and whirled around fiercely, ready to defend the third vest. It was Matthew.

For a moment she stared at him stupidly, then his arms were around her, the smell of his hair was in her nostrils, and she began to cry. He picked her and the child up and pushed through the mob to the largest of the lifeboats.

Captain Howell was there, shouting orders at the first mate, who slashed at the boat's canvas covering with his knife. As the skin peeled back, the crowd surged forward and piled in. Captain Howell pulled a revolver from inside his coat. "This boat is for women and children only. I'll shoot any cowardly man who dares to take a woman's place." The few men who had boarded climbed sullenly out. Matthew swung Abby over the gunwale and set her among the thickening crowd of petticoats and nightdresses. She handed him the third life-preserver.

As she settled the screaming child on her lap, she noticed a frail woman in a voluminous white dressing-gown struggling with a man next to the cabin wall. At first she did not recognize her — the woman was bald; then she suddenly realized who it was: Fanny Molroy. They were fighting over a single life-preserver. The man pulled back his fist and punched her on the jaw. Fanny reeled back, covered her face with both hands, and slid slowly down the wall. She huddled on the deck, weeping.

"Matthew!" Abby jumped to her feet and pointed. "It's Fanny." She began climbing out of the boat, but Matthew pushed her back and ran to the cabin wall. He fastened his vest around Fanny, picked her up, and carried her to the rail. Captain Howell stopped him. "The boat's too heavy already. We can barely lift her on the blocks." The ship lurched again and the women screamed. "She'll have to stay here."

"Wait," Abby shouted. She pointed at a prim-looking girl behind her. "There's a man under her dress. I saw him. Take him!" The girl leapt forward, exposing a strong young man, and began pummelling Abby's back with her fists. Captain Howell and a dozen men surged forward, grabbed the man, and dragged him roughly out, while the young girl clawed at his coat, weeping hysterically and screaming that they had just been married. Matthew quickly swung Fanny over the gunwale and set her in the boat next to Abby.

The bow of the *Pacific* was deep in the water. Waves curled around the pilot-house at midship. Over a hundred men and women had crowded onto the aft deck and scrambled up onto the roof of the dining salon. A few clambered up the mainsail rigging in a futile attempt to escape the sea.

"Loose the tackle!" Captain Howell shouted. The davit was swung out and the lifeboat hung in mid-air, ten feet from the port gunwale, swaying in the wind. "Lower away." The men struggled, but the boat did not move; the pulleys were jammed with rust. The women began to whine and cry.

"Mr. Perkins! Fetch two axes. We'll cut the lines as the water comes under her." When the axes were brought, Captain Howell stationed himself at the stern cable and ordered Perkins to cut the forward line on his signal. Everyone waited.

A wave broke on the aft deck, like surf on a beach, and swept away a cluster of passengers. The sea around the ship was dotted with men and women, some with life-preservers, some without, bobbing on the heavy swell, shouting for help.

The older women in the lifeboat sat stoically, holding onto the gunwales, life-preservers around their chunky middles, their chins thrust up at the storm, their grey hair flying in the wind. Howell and Perkins waited with their axes raised.

"Mrs. Galer!" It was Charles Horetzky. His vast beard hung in dripping ringlets and he was waving a small brown package over his head. "The Bute Inlet photographs," he shouted. "You must deliver them to Sir Sandford Fleming; they are of the utmost importance to the Dominion." Abby passed the child to Fanny, and Horetzky tossed the bundle across the gap. She caught it and stuffed it into her dress pocket. "Remember," he shouted, "Sir Sandford Fleming;" then, as an afterthought, "Guard it with your life."

As the water rose and swirled round the men's ankles, Abby sat quietly and stared into Matthew's eyes. She could see him clearly, at the back of the crowd, head and shoulders above the rest, flattened against the cabin wall. He smiled, raised his hand, and waved, and Abby could see that his face was white and his hand shaking.

"Now!" Captain Howell swung his axe and the lifeboat's stern banged into the waves, jarring Abby's grip loose. The front cable snapped. The bow ploughed into the water and the boat drifted free, pitching and rolling on the black waves.

Abby knew the end was near for the *Pacific*. She held her breath and watched as the side-wheeler split in two, exploding with the sound of cracking timber. Passengers fell to their knees, skidded along the deck, and floundered into the ocean as the ship sank from under them.

The lifeboat rode high on the swell, up and over the ship's railing, and slammed against the wheelhouse. Abby felt cold water at her ankles. The boat rocked as men reached out of the water to grab at its sides. A woman at the front jumped overboard. The boat tilted and the wind was drowned out by screams. Two men pulled themselves up on the port gunwale and water poured in up to Abby's waist. She half jumped, half fell, into the ocean, and its coldness took her breath away.

"Abby!...." The shout was near by, but everywhere was darkness. Abby twisted in the water and her dress wrapped around her ankles. She struggled to undo her bootlaces.

"Abby!...." Fanny's panicked voice was directly behind her. "I lost her. The little girl."

Abby tried to swim but her clothes pulled her down and she swallowed a mouthful of water. "Fanny!..." She could not catch her breath. Her feet tangled in her petticoats and a wave washed over her. Then Fanny's arm curled round her neck and she felt herself gliding through the cold, black water. The cries around her grew softer, weaker, then faded altogether.

Numb and exhausted, Abby dragged herself up on a piece of wreckage until only her legs dangled in the sea. She was vaguely aware of Fanny beside her, of a horse whinnying in the distance, of the rolling waves and the coldness of the water, then she lost consciousness.

When she awoke, Fanny was gone; she had slipped, unnoticed, into the ocean while Abby slept.

The sea was calm, the sky the colour of lead. She dragged her numb legs out of the water and pulled herself to the centre of the wreckage; it was a corner of the wheelhouse and a portion of its roof.

During the day she drifted with the current past splintered boards, a hatbox, a life-preserver. She shivered uncontrollably, though her clothes had begun to dry. She guessed the current was carrying her north, back to Victoria. Late in the afternoon she saw a woman and two men draped across the hull of an overturned lifeboat. She shouted, but there was no response. As she watched, one of the men slid from the boat and disappeared into the ocean.

At night, the moon appeared, glinting white off the black waves, and with it the barbed-wire cold of the North Pacific in November. Abby huddled under her damp petticoats, listening to the hiss of the ocean, and for the first time she realized fully that Matthew was gone. She remembered her harsh words to him on the Victoria wharf, and her body shook like the coming of an earthquake, her tears poured out, and her wail echoed through the night.

She awoke in the early pre-dawn, panicked by a dream of him tangled in the seaweed at the bottom of the ocean. She could hardly move; her legs and hands were numb. She raised her head and saw land far in the distance, but by late afternoon it was still several miles to the north. The clouds raked away in long, trailing wisps and at sunset the sky glowed red and orange. The blackness returned, and Abby slept.

Victoria Daily Standard

Amor De Cosmos   Monday, November 10, 1875.

At seven AM Sunday morning Mrs. Abigail Galer of Galer Mills, Burrard Inlet, was pulled unconscious from the frigid waters of the Pacific twenty miles south of Cape Flattery. The American Revenue ship *Messenger* found her clinging to the pilothouse of the *Pacific*, which has recently been reported overdue in San Francis-co. Mrs. Galer is believed to be the only survivor of an estimated 300 passengers, mostly British Columbians, who sailed from Victoria Harbour on the morning of Nov. 4th. Details of the sinking are not yet available, but a full investigation is pending.

I am sure all of Victoria joins me in extending condolences to the un-

"... the grass withereth and the flower fadeth. There are hearts today in British Columbia that, but for the power of God's grace, would not smile again on earth. Our hands have grasped a few days ago the manly hand that is now still and cold in death. We have not the mortal remains of many of our friends, so dear to our memories, to lay in the grave, but 'the sea shall give up her dead,' and we shall see them again. And God grant that it may be with joy."

Matthew was gone. Abby shifted her feet in the wet grass, closed her eyes, and tried to picture his face. She could remember a thousand insignificant details—the dark "V" of sweat tapering down his shirt, the gleam of his patent-leather boots in the lobby of the Royal York, the smell of his hair on the deck of the *Pacific*—but she could not picture his face. She could hear his laughter, see the half-moons of dirt under his broad, flat nails, picture him standing before the mirror every morning, vain as a woman, brushing his copper-coloured hair, but his face remained blank.

She remembered the day last summer they had hurried home from Victoria, hot and grimy, the sun blazing down on them, the words of the acquittal of the Royal Commission still ringing in their ears, and how they had run from the heat into the cool woods, past Sitka's house and far up the inlet to where there was nothing but forest and ocean. They had waded, naked, into the sea and floated like driftwood, letting the accusations, the fear, and the anger soak away.

At sunset they had carried their clothes up a hillside, hung them on branches at the edge of a meadow, and lain on their backs in a field of wild grass and fireweed. Matthew had taken a single blade between his two thumbs and blown it like a trumpet. She had showered him with petals of fireweed, and they had stuck in the hair on his chest. She remembered his hand on her breast, calloused but gentle, and the rich, sweet smell of crushed wild grass. She remembered the feel of his skin, soft and warm, with the iron-hard muscles rippling like waves underneath. She remembered him above her, supported on his arms, fireweed falling from his chest, his copper hair glowing like a halo beneath the blood-red sky, his brow furrowed, the look of wonder in his eyes, and then she could see him clearly—Matthew in all his beauty, strength, and passion—then the image faded, and his face was gone.

"All flesh is grass; the grass withereth and the flower fadeth. ...."

THE WHISPERING TREE

KUMKUMLYE, THE GROVE OF MANY MAPLES, blazed amber and crimson in the early autumn light. Mei-fu hurried by them, stopped to check the eggs in her wicker basket, then scuttled on, past the tiny joss house and down the narrow corridor of Fantan Alley, very conscious of the fact that she had come to Gastown's small Chinese quarter dressed in the latest San Francisco fashion. Startled men flattened themselves against the walls of the narrow road as she swished past in her glossy green silk; eyes peered at her from the shadowy doorways of gambling houses which were alive with the clatter of coins and bamboo tiles.

She loved this crowded, dirty place; it reminded her of Sundays in San Francisco when she and Chang would walk through crowded Chinatown. Here, dingy shop windows glittered with Chinese characters cut from gold paper; the air was redolent with the smell of rice wine, seaweed, soya sauce, and opium, and the tinkling sound of dozens of dialects clashed with the braying of hawkers who leaned out of their stalls to sell her home brews or aphrodisiacs.

Mei-fu swept on, nodding regally at customers and acquaintances, until she came to the one structure in Fantan Alley that she loathed—the crib. It was an outdoor whorehouse, twelve feet by fourteen feet, made from slatted wooden crates set in an alcove at the end of the lane. Inside, six women slaves, diseased, drugged, starving, worked on narrow cots separated by torn burlap curtains. A group of snickering boys peered through the wooden bars, and she could see the silhouette of a gaunt, naked woman shuffling slowly down the length of the crib towards them.

"Aiyeee!..." The shout came from the doorway of a nearby restaurant. The woman froze. The boys fled. Mei-fu spat in the direction of the fat pimp, swathed in yards of red silk and gold braid, as he waddled towards the crib, cursing in Mandarin and shaking his fist at the retreating boys, then she darted through the narrow doorway of the Armstrong Rooming House.

The stairs creaked in the darkness. At the second floor she removed her hat and cursed Sam Wong, the man who owned the building; it had originally been a one-storey structure with ten-foot ceilings, but he had divided it in half horizontally, so that each floor was five feet high. Mei-fu scuttled down the hallway with her head bent awkwardly forward, searching for the door of Yum-koo Shee, her second cousin once removed.

Yum-koo, a smiling girl of nineteen with delicate features, stood swaying in the doorway on her tiny bound feet. Her father had brought her to San Francisco as a child to tend him and remind him of the family that waited for his return in Xiamen. Five years before, Yum-koo had been walking through Chinatown with him, laughing at one of his droll jokes, when suddenly the Knights of Labor had rounded a corner and swept howling down the cobbled street, swinging clubs and knives in a violent racist purge. Her father had thrown her in a trash can, and there she had huddled until the screams around her subsided. At dusk she had crept out and found her father, a few feet away, dead, the hilt of a knife showing through his blue cotton tunic. Terrified, she had used the last of his savings to flee north to Gold Mountain and the only relative she had left on the continent.

Mei-fu handed the basket of eggs to Yum-koo and the girl's eyes widened with delight as she bowed numerous times and ushered her cousin into the small, windowless room which was lit with two candle stubs. Mei-fu carefully gathered up her green silk and lowered herself to the sleeping mat, while Yum-koo lit the coals in her tin firebox and began preparing green tea.

The room was a perfect five-foot cube. Although paint was peeling from the cardboard walls and the floorboards looked

dangerously thin, Mei-fu was impressed by the order and clean-
liness of her cousin's quarters. Fragrant blue smoke curled up
from a joss stick set in the lap of a carved wooden goddess of
mercy draped in a red paper dress; light filtered through a thin
silk fan hung over a hole in the wall which, Mei-fu guessed, must
look down onto the open roof of the crib below. The smell of
disinfectant mingled with incense.

Mei-fu watched the young girl preparing tea and thought again
how pretty she was, except for her small hands, which were red
from work in the laundry, and of how much money she could
make at the Palace Royale. "What is it, cousin?" Mei-fu asked in
Cantonese. "Have you finally come to your senses and decided to
take my offer?"

Yum-koo looked grave. "No, honoured cousin. I have asked
you here to beg a favour."

"And for this you send for me?" Mei-fu took her tea and noticed
that Yum-koo was blushing; she guessed the girl was too embarrassed to come to the Palace Royale. "All right. What is it; what
can I do?"

Yum-koo took a piece of folded rice-paper from inside her
faded blue peasant's jacket and handed it to Mei-fu. "I received
this last week from my mother in Xiamen," she continued in
Cantonese. "She has chosen a husband for me, Ho-sun Lee; I
believe he is the second cousin of your dead husband's sister-in-
law. His family lost their farm in the Taiping rebellion and now
he is landless and starving. He wishes to come here, to Gold
Mountain, to marry me and work on the railroad.

"So yesterday I went to the survey office to see if they would
hire my Ho-sun Lee."

"Good girl," Mei-fu said. "But does he have the passage money
to get here?"

Yum-koo smiled slyly. "I am coming to that, cousin. When I
arrived at the office, half of Chinatown was there, asking for jobs
for cousins and uncles and nephews, but I waited and at last I
spoke to the big boss himself" — Yum-koo screwed up her face at
the awkward occidental name — "Andlew Ondldonk, and he said
yes, he would hire Ho-sun Lee, plus any other strong Chinese
men I could find, at a dollar a day, provided they arrive by next
spring. Some people say he pays the barbarians $1.75 a day. Can
you believe it?

"Naturally I thought of you, honoured cousin, who knows so

many men, both in San Francisco and Hong Kong. I was thinking that the streets of those cities must be crowded with men who want to come to Gold Mountain and work on the railroad but haven't the money. It occurred to me that if a smart woman were to invest some of her wealth in passage fares, she would be in a most profitable position. Yes, most profitable."

Mei-fu's mind was reeling with the possibilities. "Did he say how many men?"

"Not exactly—you would have to talk to him yourself, of course, and he is leaving for Yale tomorrow—but I did get the impression that a thousand would not be too many."

Mei-fu sucked in her breath as her mind raced through the calculations: a thousand passages at seventy Hong Kong dollars each, with food. . . . The men could repay the money monthly out of their wages at, say, two per-cent interest? . . . no, two and one-half, yes, two and one-half per-cent interest per month— "Oh, yes," Mei-fu said excitedly, "that could be a most profitable venture."

"And would my cousin," Yum-koo asked, smiling, "perhaps have room on such a ship for one small Ho-sun Lee?"

Mei-fu chuckled. "Of course, my shrewd cousin. Of course."

"More tea?"

"No, thank you." Mei-fu scrambled to her feet, being careful not to bang her head on the ceiling. "I must go see this, Andlew Ondldonk"—she deliberately mispronounced the name, chuckling at the sound of it, then continued in Cantonese—"at once, before he escapes. But I thank you for a most enlightening morning."

Silence. Sitka's canoe glided past *Kumkumlye*, the grove of many maples, and she watched their twisted branches, knobby with spring buds, rake across the moon like claws. At night the inlet was like in the old days: still, quiet, empty. The saws stopped their hungry screaming, the belching steamships slept in darkened coves, and even raucous Gastown was hidden and mute. The only sound was the lap of the waves on the bottom of the canoe and the gentle whisper of wind in the forest.

She reached back and fed more wood into the fire that burned on a clay-covered board propped across the gunwales in the centre of her canoe. She had soaked the sticks in seal oil so they would burn bright yellow and would not sputter. The flames curled up, and through them she saw Eva glancing nervously from under her ribboned hat at the far shore, working the thin cedar paddle soundlessly under the water the way her mother had taught her. Sitka sighed. For twelve winters, since Tcaga's disastrous potlatch, she had dressed her daughter in the white fashion, but still the sight unsettled her. Bustles and billowing rustling petticoats were not made for hunting from a narrow dugout. Eva's paddle slipped out of the water and stuttered across its surface, startling her out of her daydream. What was wrong with the girl, Sitka wondered? For weeks now she had been clumsy and careless; she could not keep her mind on even the simplest of tasks. Sitka shook her head and turned quickly back to her work. They had killed only two mallards, and already the faint glow of dawn was seeping over the mountains to the north.

A small flock of Goldeneye, attracted by the bright yellow light, glided towards the canoe, their heads bobbing in a staccato rhythm. Sitka hefted a long, slender spear of fire-hardened yew over her head and balanced it lightly on her fingertips. The cry of a loon shivered eerily over the inlet, echoed off the mountains, and faded. The ducks stopped twenty yards away, startled, blinking stupidly in the firelight, then paddled on curiously, hypnotically, towards the silent flames. Sitka waited, holding her breath. Ten yards. Soon they would see her. Soon they would scream and scatter over the inlet. She gripped the gunwale with her left hand and sighted down the length of the spear at a plump drake whose delicate eye markings looked like fine white tears in the firelight. When he was fifteen feet away her hand whipped forward and the long spear flew over the water with a whistling sound. The spell was broken. The flock lifted and careered over the inlet, their short wings flapping in panic, their heavy bodies colliding, their webbed feet churning the top of the water. The drake squawked and spread his wings to fly; then his head lolled back, his body shuddered, and slowly the weight of the long spear in his breast pulled him onto his side and he floated limply on the small black waves.

At dawn Sitka stood knee-deep in the icy water, muttering to herself as she struggled to haul the heavy dugout onto her fine white beach of powdered clamshell. She was angry. As soon as they had reached shore, Eva had leapt into the water and run up the path to their cabin, leaving her to deal with the canoe and the three ducks she had speared during the night. What was wrong with the girl? She flung the protective cedar mat across the hull of the overturned canoe, snatched up her bloody spear, and crouched at the edge of the water to wash it.

As she looked out at the early morning mist curling and percolating over the still inlet, her anger slowly faded. It was her favourite time of day. The saws had not yet begun to chew their morning meal. The sun winked blearily through a thin layer of cloud. Spring robins called from the forest behind her. A scruffy heron waded in the shallows near by and Sitka chuckled at the awkward way his knees bent backwards. She watched the reflection of her iron-grey hair shimmering in the small waves as the tide whispered gently at her feet, and she smiled. Life has not been so bad to us, she thought. The ocean and the forest provide all we need, I have my own warm house, and, most important of all, I at last have a daughter who has lived long enough to grow into a beautiful young woman. No, life is not so bad.

Sitka jumped to her feet as Abby's mill screamed into life. The heron flew off, his long, skinny legs dangling behind him like sticks. A moment later the saw across the inlet sputtered, coughed, and howled in reply. Sitka grabbed the ducks and marched up the path to her house.

"Eva? Eva! I want you to —" Sitka stopped. There, sitting cross-legged on a cedar mat just inside her doorway, was a young Indian man. He looked up at her with a broad, friendly smile. Sitka stared back, her eyes wide, her heart pounding at the implications. The ducks slipped from her hand.

The visitor leaned forward to retrieve them, but Sitka quickly snatched the birds out of his reach, flung them on the table, and strode to the back of the cabin. She searched through a stack of woven baskets, found the largest one they owned, and thrust it at Eva. "Go get camas bulbs. Plenty of them." She took her daughter by the arm and ushered her to the door.

"But we don't need camas bulbs," Eva protested. "We already have enough for —"

"Well, get some more," Sitka yelled as she pushed her out of the cabin and slammed the door. Then she whirled to face the young man. He was still smiling.

I must not look at him, she thought. Ignore him, that is the custom, pretend he doesn't exist. She walked casually to the table and began tearing handfuls of feathers out of the largest mallard. Her heart was pounding.

Who is he, she wondered? He does look familiar, but how can I be expected to know all the young men of the village when I haven't been there in over twelve winters? She edged around the table so that she could peek at him out of the corner of her eye. She guessed he was about twenty-four. He must be conceited, she thought. Look at how he sits so straight and proud with his broad shoulders pulled back and taps his caulked boots with those large, rough hands. Yes, conceited, she thought, and too handsome, far too handsome, to be any good. Now, maybe if his face was dotted with the pox marks which so many of my people wear it would be different, but no, he must have a smooth, pleasant brown face with high, round cheeks, and look at that broad forehead and that incessantly smiling mouth. She flopped the duck over and banged it angrily onto the table; feathers billowed around her. His hair is too straight, yes, too straight and perfect and black — why it's almost blue — and so short it barely brushes the collar of his white man's shirt. She noticed that a cloud of duck down was settling around him. And worst of all — he's an Indian!

He nodded at her, smiling. Sitka quickly looked away. An Indian! — and how dare he sit in my doorway! Again she turned the bruised mallard and flung it onto the table. Well, we'll see about that, my handsome, conceited visitor. She whirled round, grabbed her best cedar hat, and, being careful not to look at the smiling stranger, marched out of the cabin and into the forest.

She found Abby in a clearing high on the hillside and was shocked to see her sitting atop a puffing iron monster. She wore a muddy brown dress, her face was streaked with soot, and her beautiful yellow hair was wrapped in a filthy scarf. Sitka hid behind a shattered stump to watch. A group of men stood near by, leaning on saws and axes, staring suspiciously at the noisy machine, their faces scowling. A dozen bulls were chained together at the edge of the clearing, bellowing nervously, pawing the ground with their enormous hooves and rolling their eyes. The man named Johann, whom Sitka had often seen shouting and cursing at the oxen as they dragged the fallen trees out of the forest, hurried down the line, fussing and cooing over them like a worried mother, occasionally glancing over his shoulder at the belching contraption with a look of disgust.

Abby's eldest son, Martin, fastened a cable to a log, then opened a door at the side of the metal ox and tossed chunks of wood inside. Sitka gasped: the monster's belly was on fire. The boy waved at his mother and Sitka watched, horrified, as Abby gripped the iron bull and it roared hideously. Smoke billowed from the top of its head and it lurched forward, its huge round feet spitting dust and rocks, and dragged the log out of the woods. It stopped and growled menacingly as Abby hopped down.

Sitka was terrified, but she thought of the smiling visitor in her doorway and forced herself to march into the clearing. The men stood aside, gaping, as she walked up to Abby. "There's a man sitting in my doorway," she announced, waiting for the full impact of the news to register. "An Indian man!"

Abby's eyes remained blank. "Oh? Who?"

Sitka glanced nervously at the growling iron bull and shrugged. "I don't know. But you must tell him to go."

"Martin," Abby called over her shoulder, "I think the tractor is going to work fine. Can you manage it?"

"Sure," Martin replied. Sitka shuddered as the tall, slim sixteen-year-old climbed up on the rumbling machine; then she turned her back on the clearing and hurried into the woods.

Abby followed, puzzled, watching the swaying folds of Sitka's cedar-bark cape and her large bare feet padding soundlessly over rocks and deadfalls. "Why don't you tell him yourself? What does he want?"

Sitka's shoulders stiffened. "He wants to marry Eva."

"Eva?"

"When a man wants a wife, he goes to her house and sits in the doorway. Everybody ignores him—parents ignore him, daughter ignores him, nobody talks to him—so he waits. He waits one day, four days, whatever it takes, no food, no water. Then, when parents decide to accept him, they must ask a neighbour to invite him to their fire. If the parents don't want him, they just wait. Usually after four days the man gets hungry and goes away." Sitka swatted angrily at a spiderweb stretched across the trail. "But I don't want this Indian sitting in my house. You tell him to go."

"But don't you even want to know who he is? What's wrong with him? After all, Eva is twenty. It's not as if—"

Sitka stopped and turned to face Abby. "He's an Indian."

"So, Eva is half-Indian."

"Eva will marry a white."

"Why? Have you seen the way most white men treat half-breed women?" Abby could see the cold, hard anger in Sitka's face. "Why must she marry a white?"

"Because the Indian is dying," Sitka hissed, sweeping her hand out towards the inlet, where they could see the town of Granville nestled in the trees on the far shore. "Because the whites have everything—all the land, all the wealth, all the power. Behind this white man's Gastown is Snauq, the ugly little village my people fled to when the pinkman first came here. Then we were maybe three hundred men and women; today there are not even a hundred, crowded onto a piece of land no bigger than one of my dead mother's berry patches. The black-robes have taken our culture, the whites fish our salmon streams, the farmers fence off our land . . . the lumbermen cut down our trees." Abby winced. "The oolichan don't swim here any more. The otter are all gone. My people have smallpox, measles, syphilis; they speak Chinook or English instead of our own language; and they wear white man's clothes. You want me to send Eva over to this 'reservation' at Snauq to swill whisky for the rest of her life and be called *siwash* by the whites? You tell him to go. Eva will marry a white."

Abby stared at the ground and nodded. "All right. I'll tell him." Sitka sniffed and led the way back to her cabin.

The man was still there, sitting by the doorway, smiling. Abby knelt on the cedar mat and spoke to him quietly in English while Sitka muttered to herself and rummaged noisily through a stack of cedar boxes at the back of the house. She tried not to look at the young man, but several times she glanced curiously over her shoulder to see if he was still there. They were talking much too long.

At last Abby stood up and walked over to her, her hands stuffed in her dress pockets, her face serious and thoughtful. "His name is Kitamqin; the whites call him Johnny Snauq. For the last three years he has worked at the mill across the inlet, where he has saved enough to buy a small piece of land near Gastown. He says—"

"Did you tell him to go?"

"Yes," Abby said, "I told him. But he says he will wait." Sitka stiffened and glared at Johnny Snauq, who smiled and nodded back at her. "He seems quite determined, and I think you will find that Eva feels the same. Apparently they have been meeting secretly for almost a year." Sitka took a step towards the young man, but Abby placed a hand on her shoulder. "There's one more thing: he asked me to give you a message." Sitka glared at Abby's soot-stained face.

"He says he's Tcaga's son."

Sitka awoke feeling tired and crabby; she had tossed on the wooden sleeping platform all night, haunted by a dream of a wedding feast peopled by ghosts: the Slug was there, painted red and black, sucking noisily on duck bones; her mother and father were there; Matthew, blue and bloated, sat smiling in a corner; and even Gustaf—dear Gustaf— had sat by the fire cradling his broken head.

She lay in the semi-darkness for a long time, rubbing her eyes and watching the early morning twilight gather on the window-sill. Slowly she rolled over to face the doorway and groaned.

He was still there. Johnny Snauq. She could see his silhouette slumped against the wall where he had sat for the last five days. His stubbly chin rose and fell on his chest, and the air was vibrant with his snoring. He's not like his father, she thought.

She lay back on the bed and chuckled as she remembered the morning, so long ago, when Tcaga had come to her own door-way. He had not even lasted a day. Throughout the afternoon he had watched the women at the cooking fire, glancing at her only occasionally, and by sunset he was restless and hungry. Her parents panicked when he gathered up his mat to leave and quickly found someone to invite him to their fire.

At least this one is determined, Sitka thought. I'll give him that much.

She hopped down from her wooden bed and draped her cedar-bark cape around her, and began preparing a pale-blue broth of mussels and clams. As it heated, she stood by her cast-iron stove watching a patch of sunlight from the open window creep across the dirt floor towards the sleeping Indian. When it reached him, his clenched fists opened like flowers and his rough fingers flexed in the warmth. There was a crackling noise behind her as the soup boiled over, and she lifted it impatiently from the stove.

She sat on the edge of Eva's bed and gently tickled her daughter awake. It was a ritual she had executed, lovingly, every morning since Eva was a baby; the girl would squirm away from her fingers, groaning sleepily, trying to ignore her, until she could stand it no longer and would roll over with shrieks of laughter, her thick auburn hair tumbled across the red blanket, her eyes dancing with excitement, her face as bright and smooth as polished copper. This morning Eva awoke sullenly and swatted angrily at her mother's hands. "Don't do that. I'm not a child any more."

Sitka held the bowl of soup while Eva propped herself up and pulled the covers over her breasts. "You will go to help Abby Galer today. Do whatever she says and stay there until I come for you. You are not to return here today."

"Where are you going?"

"To the whispering tree. I have business there."

Eva stirred her broth slowly while she contemplated this. "I want to marry him, Mother. I mean to marry him."

"You are still my daughter," Sitka hissed. "You will do as I say."

They sat in silence, Eva staring at the untouched soup, Sitka watching her daughter. For the first time she noticed that the girl's face was ashen, her eyes were bloodshot. "Are you pregnant?"

Eva glared angrily at her, then looked away. "No. Of course not."

Sitka stared and waited. The bedcovers began to jiggle. Slowly, Eva raised her head, her eyes welling with tears, her lower lip quivering, and she nodded. The soup bowl began to shake; hot broth dribbled over its rim and trickled onto the red blanket. Quickly Sitka set the bowl on the floor and took her daughter in her arms. She rocked her back and forth and stroked her hair while Eva sobbed. "There, there, my daughter, my child, my poor little Eva. You don't have to marry him just because you carry his child. Your wise old mother knows of many ways to get rid of it. Today I will collect the roots of tansy or the berries of mistletoe. I —"

"No . . . ," Eva wailed through her tears. "I want to marry him; I love him. Please, Mama. . . . Please. . . ."

"Shhh-sh-sh-sh. . . . It's all right, child." While Sitka rocked her daughter, she glared bitterly over the girl's bare shoulder at Johnny Snauq, who was awake and watchful. She was gratified to see that he no longer smiled.

When the crying was done, she pushed Eva away and brushed the tears from her cheeks. "There now. We will speak more of this tonight. Wash your face and get dressed. You will spend the day with Abby Galer." The girl wiped her nose with the back of her hand and nodded balefully.

Sitka replaced the uneaten broth in the pot and gathered up her hunting knife, walking stick, and a stout carrying-basket; then she hurried out of the cabin and down the path to the inlet. When she returned, she saw Eva crouched by the doorway; the girl jumped up at the sound of her mother's footstep on the path and leaned against the wall, staring anxiously at the basket her mother used to collect roots and herbs.

Sitka carried a three-foot length of kelp. She blew into the hollow tube, tied the two ends together, and solemnly hung the loop on a nail over the doorway. It dangled limply, dripping seawater a few inches from Johnny Snauq's knee. "My breath will guard this house while I am gone," she said loudly. "Eva, you are not to come back here or I will know of it. Go now."

"When will you return?" Eva asked.

"At sunset. Go."

Eva took a last woeful look at the root basket and hurried down the path to Galer Mills. When she was out of sight, Sitka turned to face Johnny Snauq and, although it was forbidden, she stared at him long and hard. She shook her head sadly, then turned and marched into the forest.

The air was warm and pungent with the smell of damp earth, sweet fern, and swamp tea. She hurried through a stand of dogwood, brushing absently at spiderwebs that tickled her face, oblivious to the waxy white blooms around her, and began climbing the foothills of Grouse Mountain. Further on she glimpsed a cluster of soapberries, a rare treasure which ordinarily she would have gladly gathered and taken home to be whipped into a frothy white dessert; today she ignored them. The path became steeper and she leaned into it. Meadowlarks darted and twisted through the thickets ahead, while mating grouse drummed in the thick underbrush. A raccoon peered down at her from the top of a broken stump, his black eyes blinking inquisitively as she jammed her walking stick into the earth and laboured up the mountain.

The trees thinned. The sun climbed higher and burned hotly down on her shoulders and back. Breathing heavily, she swung her basket down on a rocky knoll and squatted on the ground to rest. Her chest ached. She could not remember having such trouble climbing to the whispering tree before. "You're getting old," she told herself. The treetops below undulated like waves as the wind pushed up the mountainside. Sitka tried to calculate her age. Eva had explained the curious system the whites had for numbering their years and she knew this was 1880, but the information was useless without knowing when she was born. She was certain she had married Tcaga at twenty-seven; her mother had told her so. She placed two pebbles and seven small twigs on the ground at her feet and chuckled. "Five winters with the lazy fat man" — she added five more sticks, then sat looking at them, thinking of the raid on her village and the massacre of Cutick, Moon, and Daylight. She quickly added a pair of broken branches — "Two winters as a slave" — then held a third reverently in her hand. "Poor Gustaf," she murmured, remembering how he had taught her to waltz, his shaggy beard jiggling with laughter, his brawny arms tight around her as they lurched about the tiny cabin on the Fraser River. She placed the twig carefully beside the others. "One short winter with the affectionate bear." She knew her daughter was twenty; since Eva was born she had climbed to the whispering tree each spring and carefully carved another notch in its trunk. She added two stones to the pile, removed one twig, and sat gazing at the result.

Her cheeks puffed out and she blew loudly through her mouth. "No wonder my chest hurts. Fifty-four winters." She picked up the stick that represented her year with Gustaf and held it gently in her big rough hand. "Two husbands, four children, fifty-four winters — and now I am to give up my only living daughter." She flung the twig angrily into her basket and stormed on up the mountain.

She heard the whispering tree calling to her before she saw it. The ancient cedar stood alone in the vast meadow dotted with yellow lilics and the swaying white tufts of tall, fluffy bear grass. It still clung stubbornly to the edge of the bluff, which dropped six hundred feet to a river below. Wind from the southern lowlands swept across the inlet, collided with the rock wall, and rushed upwards, gathering speed until it whistled over the lip of the cliff and into the arms of the dancing tree.

She stood for a moment at the base of the trunk and peered up through the branches. The burial boxes containing her dead mother and father were still there where she had lashed them many years ago, safe and untouched, rocking gently in the wind, their small peepholes facing south so her parents could gaze out over the inlet below. Above them were still her grandparents, then her great-grandparents, and finally, as always, at the top of the tree, Skwinatqa, her great-great-grandfather, who had paddled south from the Squamish River countless winters before.

Sitka propped the decrepit old pole, which she had notched into a rude ladder when she was a little girl, against the lowest branch, climbed up, and settled herself in the crook of a thick limb. "Yes, this is my tree." She patted its smooth trunk. "And when I am dead, Eva will carry my bones up here and I will look out over this water forever."

Her eyes swept slowly from west to east and, although she had seen the panoramic view many times, the sight took her breath away. Directly across the inlet was Gastown, or Granville, and behind it Snauq; the last time she had been here they were the same size, but now the white settlement had eaten like fungus into the southlands and was easily four times larger. Far to the southeast, smoke curled over New Westminster, where, Eva had told her, more than two thousand people now lived. Sitka shook her head, unable to comprehend. Her daughter had also told her about a new clearing called Port Moody, at the eastern tip of the inlet, where some said the railroad would end. Yes, it was there. Sitka shrugged; it was very small. She had not wanted to ask what a railroad was.

She glanced at the tablelands and foothills below her. She had long since become accustomed to the bald brown land and zig-zag scars of logging trails as Abby's men knocked down the forest to the west, past Thoos and halfway up the mountain, but now a small new clearing had appeared a mile to the east of her own cabin. The extent of the devastation made her wince, but simul-taneously she was relieved to see that the woods around her home were to be spared; her berry patches were safe, the fields where she dug camas bulbs, the stream where she speared salmon in the fall — all stood out lush and verdant, like a thicket of willow on a burnt-out mountainside. She tried to imagine living there alone, without Eva.

The inlet shimmered silver in the sunlight, and thin columns of smoke wafted up from Snauq. Yesterday she had waited near the path behind the reserve until a young Indian woman strolled by, her berry basket on her arm, singing softly in the horrid Chinook jargon which all of her people now spoke. She had

stepped out of the bushes in front of her and the young woman
had backed away, wide-eyed and frightened; Sitka wondered if
an entire generation had been kept in check with horror stories
of a new Wild-Woman-of-the-Woods who lived alone in a cabin
on the northern shore, and she chuckled.

"Do you know Johnny Snauq?" she had asked.

The girl had been immediately interested. Yes, of course she
knew Johnny Snauq, everyone did; and yes, it was true he had
worked at the mill for many years and now owned a fine cabin in
the woods behind Gastown. He was such a good man, kind and
bright, very bright; as children they had gone to the missionary
school together at the mouth of the Homulcheson River, where
he had learned to speak English as good as the whites', and did
the Wild-Woman know how handsome he was? The girl's eyes
had sparkled. Why, she herself had longed to marry him — all of
the young women did — and she would gladly have given up the
rights to her great and only berry patch for the chance to do so,
for it was said that his father — who was a drunken and evil
man — had grown very rich from selling whisky to the men of her
village, and that Johnny Snauq would one day inherit this wealth.

Sitka had tried desperately to find a flaw in his character. Did
he himself drink? Did he have a temper? Did he beat people? Had
he ever spoken rudely to his elders? Was he vain, sly, deceitful?

"No, no, no," the young woman had said. "Johnny is a good
man; the best my village has ever produced." Sitka had stormed
away in disgust.

The wind blew, the ancient cedar swayed, and the branch
Sitka sat on bobbed as gently as a canoe in a rolling swell. As the
wind increased and the trunks ground together, the tree began
to whisper, then the whisper built to a deep, guttural groan.

Sitka smiled. She could find no fault with Johnny Snauq; he
was a good man, and she supposed it didn't really matter that he
was an Indian. "Bring your daughter up white," Lady Douglas
had warned — and this she had done. What Eva did now was her
own business.

She gazed at the swaying tufts of bear grass in the vast meadow
and for the first time she appreciated how alone her whispering
tree was. She patted its trunk. "If you insist on living at the edge
of a precipice, my friend, then surely you will lose your seed
cones to the river below." She shut her eyes tightly as she realized
that this was what she really feared: with Eva gone, she would

truly be alone. She tried to imagine moving through her silent house without her daughter.

"You are stronger than I am, old tree. You have been clawed by bears, bent by the wind, broken by lightning, and burdened with the bones of my ancestors, yet still you stand rooted to your ledge. At least I have had children."

She wrapped her arms tightly round the cedar's trunk. "Yes, Eva will marry her handsome Indian." The tree sighed and moaned in a deep, muffled wail. Sitka pressed her cheek to its smooth red bark and a single tear, caught on the wind, shimmered silver in the sunlight and spiralled down to the water below.

Eva glanced nervously at the late afternoon sun slanting through the grimy windowpane. She had not wanted to come here. When she had left the cabin for Abby Galer's this morning, she had hidden along the path as agreed and a short while later Johnny had appeared. They had made love in the shade of a willow tree while a woodpecker hammered overhead; she had counted his ribs with her fingertips.

"We must get you something to eat," she had said. "It's been five days."

"Later. Today we go to see my father."

Eva had been shocked. "No! No, Johnny, we mustn't. It's bad enough I'm here with you, but what if my mother were to return and find I wasn't at Mrs. Galer's all day?"

Johnny sat with his back propped against the base of the willow and dug in the earth with the heel of his great caulk boots. "Your mother is too stubborn," he pouted. "Too stubborn and too cruel; I think she means to starve me to death."

"Now Johnny, you'll not starve. It's just two more days. If she doesn't agree by then, we'll elope as planned. But, please, Johnny, give her time."

"All right," he grumbled. "Two more days. But remember, my little Swedish Indian, you are not the only one with relatives. Today you will come and meet my father; he too has feelings."

Reluctantly Eva had agreed. They returned to the cabin and she changed into her best dress of yellow taffeta; then they took Johnny's dugout, which was hidden in the bushes a short distance away, and paddled across the inlet to Gastown. Eva had been there many times, but she was surprised at how much the village had grown this spring. There were five streets now, branching off the main one and rambling over fifty acres of houses, hotels, saloons, and stores. The painful howl of the nearby mill was distorted by the rasp of handsaws and the banging of hammers from a site on a hillside behind the town where a score of new houses were being erected.

They had crossed the main street at a run, hand in hand, dodging between the carriages, wagons, and horses that bustled back and forth between Gastown and New Westminster. "Speculators," Johnny had said. "They are buying up land and praying that the railway will come here instead of Port Moody or Victoria. I hope they are right; my own house would be worth many times what I paid for it."

Johnny had stopped in front of the Deighton Hotel under a huge old maple tree whose branches arched across the main street. A small group of loggers had gathered to heckle a wiry redheaded man who railed against the oppression of capitalism, challenging them to burn their bindles, start a union, and strike for decent housing, shorter work days, and better wages. Eva watched nervously as the sun climbed high over Gastown. She tried to urge Johnny on, but he stood resolutely at the fringes of the jeering crowd, nodding his head, staring intently at the excited redhead. It was past noon when they reached Tcaga's cabin.

It was a large old log structure, collapsing at one end, that had been built by miners in the days of the gold-rush when Gastown was no more than a stand of maple bordering a thin strip of gravelly beach. Inside was a bizarre mixture of crudeness and elegance; elaborate coal-oil lamps with hand-painted shades and dangling crystals were nailed to the rough log walls; two armchairs and a settee, intricately carved and covered with tattered green brocade, rested on the bare earthen floor; and the collapsing end of the cabin was partitioned off with dozens of small British flags sewn together into a huge gaudy curtain. The room reeked of whisky and mildew.

Eva waited nervously by the door, adjusting her eyes to the darkness, while Johnny greeted his father. In the centre of the room was the massive figure of Tcaga, sprawled on an ottoman of faded red velvet, his bare feet propped on a greasy horsehair pillow. He appraised her slowly, critically, his lips pursed, his small black eyes sparkling as they roved over her body. She guessed he was in his sixties; he was bald and naked except for an old pair of trousers rolled up to the knee; his flesh looked grey and yeasty as it flowed over the edges of the couch in paunchy rolls, and his breathing made a soft bubbling noise in the darkness. He beckoned her forward. She tried to curtsey the way Abby had taught her, but he grabbed her hand and held it tight. His skin was cold and moist.

"I never have believe it, Johnny," he said. Most of his teeth were missing and he spoke the rough Chinook trading language with a lisp. "That lazy old bitch of mine, she whelp fine-looking *klootchman*." He smacked his lips with a loud sucking noise. "We drink your bride. Johnny, bring — "

"Thank you," Eva had said. "But we really can't stay. Actually, we're not even supposed to be here at all. We just — "

"You." Tcaga pointed a stubby finger at her. "Sit over there. Johnny, bring bottle. He's behind curtain."

Eva had perched hesitantly on the edge of a green-brocade chair and blushed as Tcaga leered and nodded at her, boasting to Johnny of the talents and merits of his various women as he drank cup after cup of whisky. She could feel the mildew seeping through her yellow taffeta. Twice she had stood up to suggest they leave, and twice she had been ordered to sit. Johnny drank cautiously, but after five days without food his words quickly began to slur together. Her own tin mug lay untouched on the dirt floor. Eva was watching the fading light through the one small window and listening half-heartedly as Tcaga told how he had fought valiantly to save her mother from the northern raiders when they heard footsteps on the path outside. Tcaga stopped in mid-sentence and everyone listened.

There was no knock; the door was flung open and there was Sitka, red-faced, puffing heavily, her eyes narrowed to angry slits as she peered into the dim room. She glanced at Eva and Johnny, then stalked to the ottoman and stared at Tcaga. Her hands began to tremble. "So, this is where I find my daughter," she snarled.

Tcaga extended a limp hand and spoke in Chinook. "So, my *klootchman* comes home. You have drink?"

Sitka whirled to face Eva. "Get in the canoe." Eva began to protest, but Sitka grabbed her arm and pushed her roughly towards the door. "You make me ashamed; sneaking across the inlet behind my back to swill whisky in this traitor's shack. Like a fool I go to Abby Galer and she says, 'Your daughter has not been here all day, Sitka.' Then I run through the town like a fool from stranger to stranger asking, 'Please sir, have you seen my daughter?' "

Tcaga grunted and puffed as he pushed himself to his feet; Eva was surprised at how tall and massive he was. "Maybe you better listen why they here."

"I don't want to hear it." Sitka stormed towards the door.

"Woman!" Tcaga bellowed, his voice echoing like thunder in the dark, dirty room. "Shut up!" Sitka froze. He switched immediately to the old expressive Skomishoath language her people used to speak before the pinkman came. "That's better. After all, no matter how much you hate me, you are still, formally at least, my wife.

"My son and your daughter did not 'sneak' over here behind your back. It was I who sent for them. Yes, I engaged a messenger to inform them that I was dying and wished to meet your beautiful daughter, my son's future wife, so I could die in happiness." Sitka watched him suspiciously. He coughed weakly and sank back onto the ottoman, his meaty hand resting on his chest. She waited by the door, her face cold and hard, her eyes glinting like black obsidian.

"I have not been a good husband. This I know, and I am sorry for it. But it is too late for that. I can see in your eyes that the wounds in your heart have scarred over with bitterness and hate — and for this I am sad." Sitka looked away. "But, no matter how cruelly I have twisted the lines of our own lives, I will not allow your hate for me to destroy the lives of our children. They are good people. They are of the First People, and they are very fond of one another, as we once were." Sitka sniffed and refused to look at him. Tcaga laughed. "My wise old mother once told me that love was the poorest of all reasons to marry. I think perhaps she was wrong." He was silent for a moment. "My son is a good man; he is not like me. He will treat your daughter well. Where lies your heart? Will you allow them to marry?" Eva held her breath.

Sitka glared at the rough log wall, sighed heavily, then looked at Tcaga, her eyes soft and sad. "I have been to the whispering tree," she said. "They will marry on the day of the next full moon."

Tcaga reached for the bottle on the floor and immediately slipped back into loud and boisterous Chinook. "Good. You have drink. We celebrate, heh? You plenty smart *klootchman*, good *tenas klootchman*. Go get cup; he's over — " The door slammed. Sitka and Eva were gone. "Woman!" Tcaga bellowed. "You come back drink! Woman!..."

Sitka marched down the path towards the beach with a smiling, laughing Eva in tow and a reluctant twinkle in her eye as Tcaga's shouts faded behind her.

The days warmed. Clouds scudded in from the west, snagged on the mountains, and hunched low over the inlet, wet and brooding. At night Eva stood alone on the beach and watched the waxing moon as it flickered and winked eerily behind the trailing black wisps. She felt strangely sad, quiet, almost old. Her mother had withdrawn into herself, grown moody and silent, spending her days in the forest, ostensibly grubbing for yampah roots, returning each evening hunched under an empty burden basket, shaking her head sadly and muttering to herself. She had never been a joyful woman, but now her long stride withered to a shuffle, she wandered aimlessly, and her bright black eyes dimmed as though a great door had slammed permanently behind them. Eva had tried to arouse her with talk of the wedding, but Sitka was cold, sluggish, and indifferent, and would say no more than, "You will be married in the white fashion; I know nothing about it. Abby Galer is making the arrangements; talk to her." As the day approached and still her mother showed no interest, Eva began to worry that perhaps she would not even attend.

On the morning before the wedding, Abby appeared in the doorway, her arms full of packages, her face beaming, the excitement in her voice slicing through the gloom that had settled over the cabin like torpid dust. Sitka ignored the two women, banging noisily through her storage cupboards while they gathered excitedly round the table. The first bundle they opened was the finished wedding dress. Weeks ago Eva had stood patiently in Abby's windowed tower while the basic shell was fitted to her, but she had not seen it since, and the sight of it now, glittering in the dark cabin, made her gasp. It was white satin, with a small sunburst of silver beads framing the bodice. At the back was an enormous bustle and overskirt of fine ivory silk.

While Eva tried it on, Abby unwrapped a second dress — pearl-grey watered silk with a handsome bustle of navy brocade — and presented it to Sitka. The old woman glanced at it, sniffed indifferently, and turned back to her cupboards.

Eva was furious. She glared at her mother, her face hot and violently red against the cool white satin. "Aren't you even going to try it on?" she yelled. Sitka stared at her dumbly. "How could you be so rude? Abby and the wives at the mill spent weeks on these dresses. Now it is my turn to be ashamed of you."

And there it was again, the wounded, dying look in her old mother's eyes, the grim, bitter half-smile on the sad, lined face, as if she had been expecting this moment all along—the moment when her daughter would turn against her.

Eva lowered her voice. "You *are* going to come, aren't you?"

Sitka shrugged, shouldered her burden basket, and trudged into the forest. She did not return that night.

Eva awoke at dawn, unsettled by the sight of her mother's empty bed. She dressed slowly, haltingly, stopping frequently to stand in the doorway and stare at the forest trail. Clouds boiled blackly over the treetops and thunder rumbled ominously in the distance. It began to rain.

When she was ready, she wrapped herself in a hooded cloak, gathered the beautiful train in her arms, and walked to the beach to wait for the rowboat that would take her to Galer Mills. She wandered aimlessly along the shoreline, picking her way delicately over barnacle-encrusted rocks in her satin slippers, scanning the woods hopefully, her stomach churning with joy, fear, and pain. When the boat finally arrived, Eva did not hear it; she stood listlessly at the edge of the old keekwilee-house where she had spent her childhood, staring down through its broken roof at a lone salamander which blinked languidly up at her. Sitka had not come.

Reluctantly she settled herself in the bow, nodded to the grizzled old man who worked the oars, and huddled into her cloak to protect her dress from the rain. The small boat slipped quickly away from the beach, rocking on the choppy waves, and Eva watched sadly as the small cabin shrank in the distance, blurred, and disappeared behind a bend.

The deck of the *Cariboo Fly* was in chaos; Abby had publicized the event well. Umbrellas bumped and jostled down the passageways, and excited women giggled and shrieked as they darted from one cabin to the next. The men, in sombre black, had gathered at the bow, out of the way, champagne glasses clamped awkwardly in their chunky hands, chatting jovially as they gazed at the rain-soaked town looming into view. A few of Gastown's leading families had rowed across the inlet in the early morning rain so they could arrive in style as part of the grand party, but the crowd was made up mostly of millhands and loggers. They normally shrank from formal ceremonies, but Abby's offer of the day off — with pay — to everyone who attended, plus the added promise of plenty to drink, and dancing afterwards at the big house with most of Gastown's precious single women in attendance, had made the wedding irresistible. They stood awkwardly in the black tuxedos and shiny top hats Abby had ordered from Victoria and New Westminster, twisting at the waist to look to the side, their stiff-winged collars clamping their throats like neck braces.

Abby ran down the port passageway, searching for her foreman, Johann, who was to give the bride away. His was the only position she had found it difficult to fill. The bridesmaids had been easy: three were daughters of Galer Mills families and the other three she had culled from the prettiest of Snauq's maidens; they had been delighted to be included in the ceremony, and when they found they would be allowed to keep the beautiful grey-silk dresses that the wives at the mill were making, they had been ecstatic. Johann was more of a last resort. Abby had not known who to choose — Eva's father was dead, and she had no male relatives, so finally Abby had settled on Johann, knowing that he could be trusted to carry out his part with solemn dignity. And at least he's Swedish, as her father was, Abby thought.

The side-wheeler was in mid-inlet when Abby, running across the aft deck, stopped abruptly and peered through the rain. "Well, I'll be . . . ," she muttered. She gathered up her dress and hurried back along the passageway, her shoes clattering like hammers on the slippery deck.

The bridesmaids' cabin was awash with grey silk and white satin, and it reeked of roses and perfume. Eva looked anxiously up at her from where she was hunched on the floor wiping the mud from her slippers. "She's coming!" Abby cried.

The bride tore through the door in a flurry of white satin and Abby ran after her, trying to hold her umbrella over the precious wedding dress. The two women stood at the aft rail and peered through the rain. Although it was too far to identify the paddler,

Eva knew instantly from the powerful strokes and the way the paddle whisked from one side of the dugout to the other that it was her mother, and she was in a hurry. Eva beamed. They stood for several minutes watching the tiny canoe pitch violently on the choppy waves. "Should I order the ship to go back and pick her up?" Abby asked.

Eva laughed. "Oh, no. She wouldn't like that. Besides, knowing the way my mother can paddle, she might just beat us there." Abby was amazed to see that, indeed, Sitka was gaining on them. "What's that on her head?" Eva asked.

Abby squinted her eyes and leaned forwards. "It looks like a turban."

As the *Cariboo Fly* approached Cains's wharf, her steam whistle hooting, the little iron bell in the tower of Gastown's one small church began to clang. Abby stood at the rail with her guests and waved at the waiting crowd. Most of the reservation had turned out to greet the ship; everyone knew Tcaga and Johnny Snauq. They stood barefooted on the wet dock, cedar mats and tattered umbrellas over their heads, the women in calico print dresses and coloured head scarves, the men in faded white shirts and wool pants. Among them were the people of Gastown, mostly men: loggers, drifters, surveyors from the C.P.R., curious onlookers.

Abby was surprised to see Mei-fu's carriage—a black-lacquered landau with a chubby, smiling "God of Wealth" emblazoned on the door—parked on the beach at the foot of the wharf, but word spread quickly through the cluster of guests at the rail that today the Chinese labourers would arrive from Hong Kong. The dock was crowded with wagons, dozens of them, slick and shiny in the downpour—ox-carts, wains, drays, and farm-carts—spaced in a long line down the wharf and along the beach at the edge of the mill, their drivers waiting impatiently, hunched into oilskins, to take the labourers over the long, bumpy corduroy road to New Westminster. There a temporary tent city had been erected well outside of town.

Abby groaned as she listened to a Gastown merchant describing how the ships had tried to land at Stump Town yesterday and had been turned back by the city's brick-throwing, club-waving, anti-Chinese society. Ever since Onderdonk's plans to use Chinese labourers had been leaked to John Robson's newspaper, the ranks of the city's racists had grown steadily. She had read the virulent editorials demanding the exclusion of all Orientals from work on the railroad, but it had never occurred to her that a confrontation might occur on Eva's wedding day.

The gangplank was lowered. The passengers disembarked and blended with the crowd, which swirled along the wharf, hurrying through the downpour, the Indians following excitedly behind. Abby waited on the deck and watched as Sitka jumped into the shallow water further down the beach and dragged her canoe onto the wet sand next to the church. She shook her head; the woman was wearing an enormous hoopskirt, twenty years out of date and violently coloured in red, bright orange, and lemon yellow.

The church was a small white structure, only six years old, but already rust stains streamed like blood from its nail-holes, and moss grew green and wet in the chinks of its clapboards. Abby and Eva ran up the rickety front steps and into the vestibule, the bridesmaids giggling excitedly behind them, shaking rain from their cloaks. Sitka was waiting inside the doorway.

"I'm sorry. I—" Eva flew into her arms. Sitka rocked her. Over her daughter's shoulder she watched Abby, staring wide-eyed at the incredible red and orange dress with its yellow petticoat and matching turban. "This is the dress I wore the day Eva was born," she explained, her words thick and heavy. She pushed her daughter away and held her at arm's length. "Your father liked this dress."

Through the doorway Abby could see the Reverend Thomas Derrick, Old Hoisting Gear, taking his place at the head of the aisle, and she winced involuntarily as the memory of Matthew's funeral flooded back to her. The sound of the rain drumming on the cedar roof was drowned out by the church organ. "Martin's saved two seats at the front for us," she said.

Sitka hugged her daughter once more. "Johnny is a good man," she said, then whispered in the old Skomishoath language, "Today I am proud. May you have only sons." She marched stiffly down the aisle with Abby in her wake, the congregation whispering and giggling behind her, and sat rigidly in the front pew.

To Sitka the ceremony was awesome; she sat open-mouthed and stared at the beautiful woman in white and silver, so unlike her little Eva, who walked solemnly beside the dignified old man, her hand on his arm, her eyes on her husband, her long, slow stride keeping time with the mournful tune thundering out of the wondrous music box. Johnny watched her proudly, standing tall and handsome in his black coat and shiny shoes. Sitka was surprised and impressed by Tcaga—he looked almost dignified, despite his vast rolls of fat, in his swallow-tail jacket and sleek top hat—and her mind drifted wistfully back to the look of joy on his face the day their son was born. She quickly forgot it, though, when she realized from his quiet hiccuping and the way he swayed on his small feet that he was very drunk.

And then there was the sorcerer himself—Old Hoisting Gear—deceptively small and wizened, commanding the people to stand, to kneel, to pray, his shrill voice splitting through the church like the scream of a *hamatsa*. "The fear of God, the fear and nurture of the Lord. . . ." Sitka knew nothing of God, but she knew enough of shamans to fear this one. She dared not look at him; she *knew* that the little flutterings and billowings of his voluminous robes were caused not by the cold draft scuttling along the floor but by evil spirits that dwelt and played in the black folds of his cloak.

And so she gazed at the picture hanging on the wall behind the pulpit, showing the round, sad eyes of the pinkman's god, who had been nailed to a cross. Such a small and pitiful god, she thought. What had he done to be treated so? But as she listened to the ceremony and watched the dark, faded painting, her heart went out to the sad, round eyes, the piteous face, the scrawny, sagging body, the tiny crimson droplets of blood, and she was ashamed at her own selfishness. How near she had come to destroying her daughter's happiness, to condemning her eventually to what *she* now feared—a life alone. Granted, it would be difficult to rise at dawn without the ritual broth and tickling, to gather roots and berries in the quiet forest without the comforting sound of Eva humming near by, to sit down at sunset to her evening meal, alone, in the still cabin, but her own pain would be as nothing compared to this small, tortured man whose sad, round eyes could still smile. "It is well they framed your picture in cedar," Sitka said softly, "for surely your spirit still dwells in the fibres of this wood." Abby glanced at her curiously.

And then it was done. Sitka grimaced as Tcaga's son kissed Eva full on the mouth in plain sight of everyone. In vain she waited for a sign from her daughter, a look, a smile, something to show her fondness, her concern, her understanding, but Eva, caught in the excitement, clutched her new husband's hand and hurried down the aisle, looking neither to left nor to right, breaking into a run near the doorway, and fled from the church, from her, out into the storm, and into a new life.

Sitka sighed, slowly rose from the pew, and shuffled down the aisle. At the door she turned and looked once more at the pitiful pinkman's god, then she smiled grimly, shrugged, and plodded wearily down the trail to her canoe and home.

Jonas Cains's wharf was in chaos. Eva stood on the deck of the *Cariboo Fly* next to Johnny Snauq and scanned the eager, laughing faces crowding up the gangway and onto the ship, anxious to attend the reception at Galer Mills. She could not see her mother.

A dozen of the anti-Chinese protestors had mingled with the revellers and slipped unnoticed through the harried line of Cains's guards. They stood on the wharf, red-faced, jostling the wedding guests and haranguing the drivers who hunched grumpily in their wagons. Mei-fu ignored them, standing stiffly at the end of the dock under her large umbrella of oiled paper, and peered up the inlet towards Thoos. A shout went up from the crowd. And there it was, the first of the two ships from Hong Kong, sliding silently, hazily, like a ghost, through the downpour.

Abby joined Eva at the rail. "Where's my mother? I haven't seen —" But as soon as she asked the question she saw the slim canoe lurch over the waves as it glided swiftly out from the beach at Gastown.

"She doesn't want to come to the party," Abby said softly. "I asked her, but she said she wanted to go home."

The rain increased, bouncing up from the deck of the *Cariboo Fly* in a fine white haze, and drowned out the snarls of the protestors below. While the wedding guests stared at the strange three-masted bark, ragged and windblown from its long ocean voyage, as it edged towards the wharf, Johnny, Abby, and Eva stood at the starboard rail and watched Sitka's canoe riding the waves, the ends of her long yellow turban trailing in the water behind her.

The steam whistle of the *Cariboo Fly* shrieked and the deck shivered as the ship edged away from the dock. The people from New Westminster stopped their shouting and fist-shaking to smile and wave at the wedding party. Eva waved back, her stomach queasy at the sight of the odd juxtaposition: the *Cariboo Fly* going in one direction, the mysterious bark in the other, the crowd on the dock milling in between. The last face she saw was that of Mei-fu, whom she had never met, smiling up at her and waving frantically while the angry crowd boiled at her back.

And Mei-fu waved and waved. Why shouldn't I, she thought. It is a good omen to witness such happiness on this day, and the girl is very pretty, in the big-boned way of barbarians. She thought of Yum-koo Shee, dressed in her best blue coat, waiting nervously in the carriage on the beach for her own bridegroom. And there will be another wedding soon enough, she thought. And this one will I gladly pay for, for the girl is my cousin, and I hope this Ho-sun Lee will be a good husband and not beat her. . . . And so her thoughts rattled on and on as she smiled and waved and waved and smiled at the departing ship, ignoring the angry crowd behind her, knowing that Wu Lee was near by with his pearl-handled revolver and that Cains's men had come with their rifles to stand between her and the ridiculous men from New Westminster. Best of all, she could hear the protective pacing of Boss Ondldonk behind her.

Mei-fu chuckled at the thought of his name; she was quite capable of pronouncing "r"'s but it amused her to watch Andrew Onderdonk turn red when she said "Ondldonk" to his face. She glanced at him over her shoulder. He was a big bull of a man, in his late forties, dressed in the latest Wall Street fashion, with a broad-brimmed fedora and a heavy topcoat edged with beaver. She thought of the tough, scarred body under the fine clothes, with its thick mat of hair fanning down from the shoulders to his small, hard rump, and laughed out loud at her own wickedness. She had admired him the moment she met him in the squat, dingy survey office. He had sat behind his rickety pine-slab table, with blue cigar smoke swirling through his beard, as grandly as if he had been interviewing her in a mahogany-panelled conference room in New York, and listened attentively while she proposed her scheme. Glancing quickly at her figures, he had adjusted her extravagant proposed savings from $5 million down to $3.5 million, checked the addition once, grunted with satisfaction, and immediately ordered two thousand Chinese labourers.

She had seen him seldom since then — he spent a great deal of time tramping the canyons of Yale, where his precious railroad must go — but their meetings had been intensely passionate, and as a result she now held a monopoly on the importation of all Chinese workers. She had not seen him for the last three weeks, but this morning he had appeared, unannounced, striding down the dock, a damp cigar clenched in his teeth, looking for all the world, Mei-fu thought, like a general taking the battlefield. Jonas Cains had been there to greet him. Mei-fu had chuckled. She knew how it must gall Cains to loan her his wharf, but she knew also how desperately he wanted the railway to come here. She had watched him trotting obsequiously behind Boss Onderdonk with an umbrella, trying, unsuccessfully, to engage him in conversation.

Mei-fu winced. More protestors were arriving. She could see their horses flickering through the trees like wolves as they moved along the muddy road from New Westminster. How they frightened her. She had seen the beginning of the Chinese race riots before she left California and had since heard countless tales, like Yum-koo's, of brutality and hatred from the numerous frightened Chinese who had fled San Francisco to escape the violent purges of the Knights of Labor. Now she could see it starting all over again in Gold Mountain.

It had begun in Victoria, like a thunderstorm on a distant horizon, the week after she signed the contract with Onderdonk, and she had nervously followed its progress in the newspapers: editorials, rallies, anti-Chinese societies, proposals, motions, resolutions. She had spilled scalding tea down her best white dress the day she read that Amor De Cosmos had presented a petition to the House of Commons demanding that the Chinese be prohibited from working on the railway. Fortunately the politicians in Ottawa who controlled immigration could see the good sense in saving $3.5 million. The storm increased to a gale when the province tried to impose a sixty-dollar annual tax on all "celestials". Every Chinese man and woman in British Columbia, from labourers to merchants, had gone on strike: laundries and markets had closed, Cains's mill had produced only a quarter of its daily quota of lumber, Victoria matriarchs had fussed angrily in their own kitchens trying to discover the secret of making tea, and even the Palace Royale had stood dark and silent for the first time, its doors barred, its windows shuttered. The law was repealed, but still the storm had raged on until it swirled into Mei-fu's own backyard. Business fell off, fights broke out, vicious threatening letters arrived with the mail; she hired an extra bouncer and a bodyguard, and finally, the night before, a jagged brick had crashed through the stained-glass window in the foyer, showering Mei-fu with coloured glass and nicking her ear as it whistled past her head.

Why can't the whites just work for a dollar a day, Mei-fu thought. It's a decent wage. But no, they must be mollycoddled with free food and lodging, a wage twice that of the Chinamen, and they must be treated like Boss Onderdonk himself. Mei-fu glanced at Andrew. "Hypocritical barbarians," she muttered. "They so desperately want their railroad, but they won't lift a finger to build it. Yet, when someone tries to do it for them, they howl like children. They're soft. They — " But the gangplank had been lowered and Boss Onderdonk was scrambling up it to the deck of the three-masted bark. Mei-fu hurried after him.

He disappeared into the captain's cabin, but Mei-fu was distracted by the groans and foul smells seeping out of the forward hatch, which had just been pried open. She looked down into the black hole and turned away gagging. With a handkerchief over her nose and mouth she looked again, and as her eyes grew accustomed to the gloom, she could make out hundreds of pale, white figures in the dark hold, wriggling like maggots in the belly of a rotting whale. The stench of excrement, vomit, and death filtered through her handkerchief, and again she turned away, her face ashen and bewildered.

Rude stretchers of wooden planks littered the deck, and a rough-looking sailor squatting at the edge of the hatchway was busy tearing strips from dirty sailcloth. "What is all this?" she asked.

The seaman continued to rip at the tattered cloth with his big, rough hands and did not look up. "Shrouds for the dead and stretchers for the dying," he grunted. "And glad I'll be to get rid of 'em. We'd a dumped 'em into the Atlantic 'cept for some fool heathen notion 'bout their bones gotta go back to China."

"Dead? Dying?" Mei-fu was stupefied.

The sailor glanced up at the note of alarm in her voice. "Beg pardon, ma'am. No disrespect intended. Reckon you'd know more 'bout Chinee buryin's than me."

Indeed she did. Through her horror, a part of her mind was already ticking off her responsibilities: expenses and losses. A dead-house would have to be built to hold the corpses. Within seven years she must pay to ship the bodies back, not to mention the wasted passage fares and the lost interest. "How many?" she asked, her voice quavering.

"How many what, ma'am?"

"Dead." The word exploded angrily from her lips.

"Oh, seventy-five on this ship I reckon, 'nother hundred on t'other; then there's at least 'nother twenty-five don't stand a chance. 'Bout an even two hundred I guess."

"Aieee...."

"You all right, ma'am?"

"How did this happen?"

The sailor shrugged. "The geek who paid their fares in China was a cheap old bastard—beg pardon, ma'am. He didn't provide 'em with more'n a cup of rice a day and no vegetables. Scurvy mostly. Some starved. Then we had storms most of the way. Had to keep the hatches battened; that didn't help none. Pretty foul down there."

Mei-fu stared at the groaning skeletons crawling out of the hold like demons out of hell; their yellow skins, oozing sores, hung like paper from their bones, their lips and tongues were swollen and purple, their gums toothless and black, their heads bald, and the smell of them hung about the deck like a miasma. She ran to the rail and vomited over the side of the ship.

I'll kill him, she thought. My uncle is an idiot, a dog, an *eta*, worse than an *eta*, not fit to wipe the bum of his lowest-born slave. There is no money to be made from the dead.

Andrew Onderdonk walked stiffly up to her, his face stern and impersonal, his eyes as grey and brittle as graphite. "Madam," he said, "your uncle is an ass." Then he marched away to supervise the loading of the wagons.

Mei-fu's heart sank. "Truly, I will kill him," she hissed.

The gaunt Hong Kong men sprawled and squatted on the deck, oblivious to the torrential rain, grateful to be free of the stinking holds, and stared—horrified—at the brazen rich woman who swept about them in her glossy green silk asking for Ho-sun Lee. They had all heard of the devil-woman-who-behaved-like-a-man who would meet them in Gold Mountain, but none had dreamed that any female could be so bold as to actually speak to a strange man. Each one she approached trembled, avoided her gaze, and waved her on towards the aft deck, praying that she would not cause them the embarrassment of having to speak to her.

She found Ho-sun Lee propped against the mizen-mast. He was

a small, shrivelled man with bulging eyes who looked closer to fifty than to twenty-four.

"I am Mei-fu. Your bride is waiting. Can you walk?"

The little man smiled and nodded. "Yes, I can walk." Mei-fu was gratified to see that he still had most of his teeth, although the front ones wiggled in their sockets as he spoke.

She helped him to the gangplank and pointed at her carriage. "Your bride is there. Go to her."

Ho-sun Lee was horrified. "Oh, no. I couldn't. We must not meet before our wedding day."

"This is no time for propriety," Mei-fu snapped. "You see those barbarians with their clubs and rocks? They will soon start trouble. You will not be safe in the wagons."

It was true. The men from New Westminster had been shocked by the state of the Chinese, and they had stood dumbly aside while the dead were loaded on wagons and driven peacefully away, but they were rallying now and beginning to crowd around a half-full ox-cart, hurling curses like bullets at the cowering yellow men.

"Wu Lee," Mei-fu shouted. "Put this one in my carriage." Her son bounded up the gangway and half dragged the protesting Ho-sun Lee to the wharf. The men on the dock shouted angrily at them but they kept their distance, wary of the pistol in Wu Lee's hand and the deadly look on his face. Mei-fu waited at the rail until her son shoved the reluctant little man into her carriage and closed the door behind him; then she turned sadly back to the job of loading the others.

Few would accept her help, but the semi-conscious ones did not resist as she dragged them to the rail, determined to salvage what she could of her investment. Most of the lifting and hauling was done by Boss Onderdonk and by one old seaman who did not seem to mind touching Chinese flesh: the rest of the sailors stood by and watched. Cains's men could not be spared from the tense job of guarding the wagons as they were loaded, one at a time, and were galloped through the crowd and into the forest, their wheels spitting mud, the terrified and haggard Chinese, bald from scurvy and bloody from rock cuts, clinging to the guard-rails and gaping around them at their fabled Gold Mountain.

Mei-fu moved mechanically about the deck, her mouth set in a hard, grim line, her rain-soaked clothes clinging heavily to her body. Her long black hair had pulled loose from its butterfly clasp, and as she straightened to brush it from her face she heard the tinkle of gay laughter floating over the inlet. The *Cariboo Fly* was nearing Galer Mills. Its steam whistle hooted, and as the sound died away she heard the opening strains of the Bridal March played raucously on a fiddle and a concertina.

"Ahheahh! . . ." The scream was shrill and piercing and it went on and on. Mei-fu whirled to face the beach. The men had circled her carriage. They rocked it violently back and forth. The horses pranced and fretted in their harnesses, and there, framed in the window, was the terrified face of the bride, Yum-koo Shee.

A shot rang out and echoed off the mountains to the north.

CHAPTER ELEVEN

HELL'S GATE

"CAINS! ALWAYS CAINS," MARTIN YELLED. "The bastard's stolen half our orders already."

"He's a smart businessman," Johann said.

"He's a crook," Martin snapped.

Abby sat wearily at her desk — Matthew's desk — in the small log office, half listening to the row between her foreman and her first-born son as she watched the blood-red sun bleeding into the coal-black clouds.

"So what do you plan to do about it?" Johann asked.

"Same as I'd do for a rabid dog," Martin said.

"That's enough." Abby's voice was low and tired. "We're here to discuss business. Johann, what orders do we have outstanding?"

While the old Swede listed them off, Abby rubbed the back of her neck, the calluses on her hands scraping her skin. Australia, Singapore, Honolulu . . . ; there wasn't a local order among them. It had been seven years since the Royal Commission had acquitted Matthew of any wrongdoing, yet the curse of Texada Island still hung like a vulture over Galer Mills.

For a month after Matthew's death the mill had floundered while Abby brooded, wandering vacantly through the huge empty house, oblivious to the silent saws. She would stand for endless hours at her tower window, glaring across the inlet at the brick house of Jonas Cains, growing bitter and hateful. In her mind it was he who had killed Matthew.

At the end of the month Cains had appeared at her door and offered to buy Galer Mills. "Madam, your mill is dying," he said. "I am willing to take it off your hands." Calmly, Abby had walked to a cabinet by the stairs, pulled out a rifle, and levelled it at his head. "Get out," she hissed.

"Now, Mrs. Galer, you cannot possibly hope —" Abby had cocked the hammer and sighted down the barrel. Cains had left at a run.

That afternoon Abby, aware for the first time of the silence around her, had marched to the office and begun poring over the books of Galer Mills. The date of the Texada Scandal ran like a bloody red scar through the ledger. She called in Johann and learned that there were no orders and that half of the employees were gone.

Together, they had travelled frantically to New Westminster, Langley, and Victoria, cajoling, begging, pleading for orders, but only a few of their best customers would admit to needing lumber, and those who did mysteriously cancelled their orders within a week. She was certain that Cains had bought them off. He had succeeded in making the name of Galer Mills synonymous with corruption and dishonesty; even now, so many years after the Texada Scandal, occasional references to it still appeared in John Robson's newspaper.

In desperation Abby had taken the steamer to San Francisco, where they had never heard of Texada Island, and re-established ties with Matthew's shipping agent. Orders had begun to trickle in, from Australia, Singapore, Chile, and Honolulu. She applied for new timber leases. She sold the *Matilda* and rehired some of the men. Slowly, inch by painful inch, she and Johann had dragged the corpse of Galer Mills out of its grave and brought it back to life. But they could not revive the local market.

Abby tapped the end of a pencil against her teeth. "What about the message we sent to Onderdonk?" she asked. "Any answer yet?"

Johann stared at his hands and shook his head. Martin slouched moodily in his chair, picking at the tree sap on his tin pants, brooding over Jonas Cains.

Abby sighed and slapped the pencil onto her desk. "We could

wait for hell to freeze over before Cains will let anyone forget about Texada." The two men sat quietly before her. "All right. Enough. Martin, what about this steam donkey of yours? Is it working?"

The young man's face brightened and he leaned forward, his green eyes sparkling in the dim light of the coal-oil lantern. The machine was his own idea. When Abby had purchased the lightweight steam tractor two years ago, he had cursed and sweated over it, hacking trails for it through the woods, wrestling it around stumps and deadfalls, watching furiously while its flimsy wheels spun uselessly in spring mud and summer dust. Recently he had hit upon the idea of making the tractor stationary and bringing the logs to it. He had spent a month making a shallow boat of huge beams; then he had filled it with rock and scrap iron, bolted the boiler and engine to it, and added a drum winch and one hundred yards of cable. Yesterday he had finally dragged the contraption to the site where the loggers were working. He snaked out the cable and fastened it to a log. He fired the boiler, tapped the steam gauge, and waited. When the pressure was high enough, he jammed the lever forward and the huge log skittered in like a matchstick in half the time it would take a team of oxen to manoeuvre through the brush.

"Damn right it works."

"Watch your language," Abby said mechanically. "Has it improved production?"

"Doubled it, I'd say. I spent half the day on the donkey and the other half helping the crew catch up."

"Good. Could you make another if we could get a boiler and engine?"

"Of course; there's a winch over at Spratt's Oilery. We could—" Martin stopped. "But what's the point?"

"The point is, we're going to need all the lumber we can cut," Abby said. "I'm declaring war on Jonas Cains—a price war." Martin whooped with glee and Johann groaned. "I know, Johann, you've warned me against this before, but it's the only way. Cains must be driven out of business—now—and I mean to do it."

"But why?" Johann said.

Abby leaned back in her chair and looked out the window. The sun had set and the dark pane reflected her lined face. "Because I'm retiring. I'm going to turn the mill over to Martin; he's eighteen and quite capable of running it. I should have done it last

year, but there is still Cains to be dealt with and I know my son."
Abby glanced at Martin. "He's a hothead and would gladly — what
was your phrase, Martin? — 'do for him like I would a rabid dog'.
No. I will deal with Jonas Cains. And once it's done, the mill will
go to Martin."

"But there's no need to quit outright," Johann said. "The two
of you could — "

"No," Abby said curtly. "Look at me, Johann. I'm thirty-eight
years old; I look forty-eight and I feel sixty-eight. I'm tired, and I
want out. I've never told you this before, but I don't even like the
lumber business." The old Swede winced, and his face wrinkled
behind his bushy grey beard and Dundreary side-whiskers. She
looked at him fondly and lowered her voice. "The mill doesn't
need me any more, Johann, and I want out." She saw the dis-
appointment, the sadness, in his pale-blue eyes and quickly
busied herself rearranging the papers on her desk.

Her tone became brusque and clipped. "All right. Martin, you
look after the donkeys. With them and two extra shifts at the mill
we can triple production. Johann, I want you to start hiring
tomorrow. We'll need three more timber crews — fallers, buck-
ers, chokermen, the works — and I want a complete second shift
for the mill. Hire as many of Cains's men as you can — there's
plenty of them would rather work for us — but go to New Westminster if you need to. We're going to run the mill twenty-four
hours.

"I've already put ads in the local papers. We're selling at cost,
less if we have to." Abby paused. "This is a dangerous game we're
playing. Johann has warned me that a price war can hurt us as
badly as Cains, but we're prepared for it; he's not. I've saved most
of our profits from the last four years and I think that will cover
our losses, but just to be safe I'm cancelling all existing overseas
contracts. If we're going to corner the local market, we'll need
every stick we can cut." Johann began to object but Abby ignored
him.

"Even with all the building going on in this province, that's
only a small part of the market. The railroad is the real gold-mine.
I've done some ... investigating, and found that Cains is over-
extended at the bank. I'm certain he's counting on railway contracts to keep him afloat. If we can steal those away, he'll
flounder. I'm leaving for Yale tomorrow, and I won't be back
until I've convinced Andrew Onderdonk to deal with us instead
of with Cains."

Johann's mouth dropped open. "To Yale? By yourself? But, Mrs. Galer, you can't — "

"I can and I will."

"But, travelling all that way, and alone; why, you have no idea what's involved," Johann stammered. "At least let me go with you."

Abby smiled. "I appreciate your concern, Johann, but I need you here. You are to hire new men."

"But, Mrs. Galer — "

"I said you will stay," Abby snapped. She took a deep breath and shifted in her chair. "Well, that's about it," she said. "It's going to be hard. But it will be worth it. You're going to see a run on Galer Mills' lumber the likes of which you've never seen before." Her eyes sparkled. "Gentlemen, the days of Jonas Cains are numbered."

The office door banged open. Johann jumped and Abby lunged at her neat stacks of paper as an icy wind scattered them across her desk. For a moment the short, skinny form of Abby's second son, Angus, stood panting in the entrance, his wiry mop of copper-coloured hair fluttering in the breeze, his green eyes blinking in the bright light — "Hurry, Mama, it's all ready. Everybody's waiting for you. Hurry"—then he was gone, the door slamming behind him with a shudder. They sat in silence listening to his footsteps pounding down the pathway to the dock.

Johann chuckled. "I've never seen the little coot so excited. How old is he now? Twelve?"

Abby stood, rearranging her papers and weighting them with rocks, a proud smile on her face. "Eleven."

"Well, if he's going to make twelve without blowing a gasket we'd best get going."

Abby removed the glass lamp from the coal-oil lantern and turned down the wick. "Mrs. Galer?" Johann said. "Good luck." She stood for a moment watching the dull-red flame quiver in the cold breeze; then she smiled grimly, cupped her hand around it, and quickly blew it out.

The night was cold. She pulled her cloak tight against the wind and smiled. She loved early winter with its rich, earthy smells of rotting leaves and moist dirt, its cold nights and fast, violent storms. The inlet was dark, the sky black with clouds. The first fat drops of icy rain plopped onto the ground at her feet.

As she stepped onto the wharf, the crowd pressed around her.

These were her people, the people of Galer Mills, and even in the darkness she could recognize them all: plump Mrs. Roberts, who had recently given birth to twins; young Becky, who was being courted by a man from New Westminster; old Peter, who had been there since the beginning. As she walked among them, talking and smiling, laughing at their jokes, shaking their hands, she felt warm and secure. This was her home.

At the end of the dock she stopped and looked up at the tall pole with the shadowy ball on top, which was about to bring such a change to them all. It was an important moment, and she wondered if she should make a speech, but the rain was increasing to a downpour and she could hear the impatient jostling of children behind her. She put her hand on the cold metal switch. "Ready?" she called.

"Ready," the crowd chorused.

She slammed the lever down. An overhead cable buzzed and crackled. The carbon light flickered once, then blazed in a bright, white glare, flooding the dock. The crowd gasped, their wide eyes and startled faces, streaming with rain, thrust up at the dazzling bulb. A second later Johann pulled a switch by the office and six more lamps, ranged around the sawmill, flooded the clearing with light. The people of Galer Mills whirled round, holding their breaths in stunned silence. Never had they seen such a thing: every building, every house and shed, every rock and tree, was bathed in an unnatural snowy glare. A child began to cry, but his sobs were quickly drowned out by the buzz of the crowd.

Across the inlet, Jonas Cains's brow furrowed as he squinted in the darkness at the silvery sheen glinting off the black waves of the inlet.

Madeline glared at the quivering newspaper across the table, her lips pressed tight against the arthritic pain in her hand, then glanced out the leaded-glass window at the fine drizzle and the bleak morning landscape. "The trees are like bars," she announced as she extended a plate of kippers towards Jonas. There was no reply.

She grimaced, banged the plate onto the table, and rang a small silver bell beside her. As the Chinese houseboy slipped quietly into the room, she waved her hand at the dishes. "Take them away. And tell Cook I said she made too much again. I know she does it on purpose so you two can sit in that scullery and stuff yourselves at my expense, but I won't have it. Tell her, once more and she's fired. You understandee?" The houseboy looked at her blankly. "Oh, don't bother; I'll tell her myself. You'd only get it all wrong."

She sat stiffly, fiercely, waiting until the dishes were cleared. "Honestly, Jonas," she snapped, "I don't know how you can stand to read that shoddy little tabloid. I could never tolerate it myself; but then I was raised on the *Times* — a magnificent newspaper. Over fifty pages daily! — Why I still remember — "

"They've found a pass through the Selkirks," Jonas announced as he slapped the paper shut and slammed it onto the table. "It's to be the Kicking Horse through the Rockies and Rogers Pass through the Selkirks." He chuckled. "That's it. The last uncertainty is settled. The railroad will be here within five years and we, my dear, are soon to be rich."

Madeline stared dully out the window again at the grey, slanting rain and the tossing evergreens as Jonas poked a stubby finger at the newspaper.

"The line's in Regina now, and every prairie mudhole it passed through to get there has at least tripled its land values. Why, a common surveyor purchased a lot in Winnipeg last year for $1,500, then sold it a few months later for $10,000. And it was just resold last week for $40,000. Everywhere they've laid track the people have gone mad over land. And we, my dear, are sitting at the end of the line."

Madeline began drumming her nails on the table, ignoring the pain in her arthritic fingers. "And have you told Amor De Cosmos this? Apparently he is counting on Port Moody becoming the terminus. Mrs. Edwards, the land registrar's wife, told me just last week that he has purchased nearly half the townsite. Obviously he does not share your optimism, and it is rumoured he has a great deal of political influence in such decisions."

Jonas's cold grey eyes stared at her, clicking off the possibilities, then he began to chuckle.

The sound dragged Madeline back from the bleak window.

"My dear," Jonas said, "what do you do when an obstacle is blocking the path of your carriage?"

She stared down the length of the polished table and was startled to see the old ambition, the boyish excitement of the young man she had married. "Why, have it removed, of course."

Slowly her lined face puckered into a smile and she began to laugh. "Oh, jolly good," she said. "I never did like that man. Why, do you know he's fifty-seven and still single? And goodness knows it's not from lack of opportunity. Indeed, I daresay he's the most desirable bachelor in the province, yet he's never looked twice at a pretty woman. He even had plenty of opportunity with our own dear Caroline before Wiley came, although, of course, I would never have permitted her to marry an American. But I think it's all quite ... unnatural, don't you? Why, I have even heard that he dyes his hair with boot polish and—"

"Tell me," Jonas said abruptly. "What would you say to the suggestion that Canada sever its ties with England? Become a sovereign state?"

Madeline's eyes widened, her nostrils flared, and her lips pressed into a tight, angry hole. "Preposterous! Why, that's the most traitorous, blasphemous statement I have ever heard you utter. I will not permit—"

Jonas laughed and waved her into silence. "I didn't say it. De Cosmos did. My man in Ottawa telegraphed it at once. Just a passing reference in an otherwise insignificant speech. The local papers haven't picked it up yet, but if they did, now, with the federal election just two weeks away, I'd say the people of B.C. would react much as you."

"The blackguard would never win his bid for re-election."

Jonas snorted and pushed back his chair. "Good. I'll talk to John Robson about it today." He stood up and tossed the paper towards Madeline; it skidded down the long length of polished oak and slid into her lap. "You should read it once in a while. More gossip in there than in a dozen London papers." He winked and turned to go.

Madeline picked the paper up gingerly. "Jonas, will you be seeing Wiley today?"

"Reckon."

"Oh, Jonas," she snapped. "I wish you wouldn't use that vulgar expression; you're becoming as gauche as a Yankee." She smoothed the newspaper meticulously on the table and fished in her dress pocket for her spectacles. "Anyway, please ask him to pay me a call. I wish to speak to him about civic politics." She fitted the tight wire frames around her ears and gazed suspiciously at the paper.

"Civic politics?"

"Yes, I was thinking he would make an excellent —" She bent closer to the paper. "Jonas, have you seen this?"

The note of alarm in her voice drew him closer. "What?"

"This ... this ... advertisement. For the" —her lips curled in disgust— " 'The People's Lumber Store'? How utterly crass."

Jonas strode across the room and leaned over her shoulder, his mutton-chops tickling her cheek as he read. "Galer Mills —The People's Lumber Store. All grades of finished lumber — ½ price. Delivery to major settlements included." Jonas sniffed and snatched the paper out of her hand, his face turning pink as he folded it, turning it over and over, pressing the edges between his thumb and forefinger.

"Is it serious?" Madeline asked.

"No. No. Course not. Just a nuisance, that's all."

" 'Scuse me, Mr. Cains, Mrs. Cains." Carky tiptoed into the dining room, hat in hand, his oilskin dripping rain.

"You're dripping on my carpet," Madeline said frostily.

"Yes, ma'am. Pardon, ma'am. If you'll be excusin' me, Mr. Cains. But there's a wee spot of trouble at the mill. Half the men have just up and taken their leave. They're on their way to Galer Mills."

"Are those caulked boots?" Madeline threatened.

Carky began backing towards the door. "Yes, ma'am. To be sure. Pardon, ma'am."

"Then get off my carpets," she said wearily. Carky hurried out of the room, but Madeline was oblivious to his departure. She had already turned back to the leaded-glass window, to the grey rain driving down on the tattered remnants of her prim English garden. "Now, is it serious, Jonas?" Her voice sounded distant and muted as she watched the bare sticks of her rosebushes shiver in the cold wind.

"We can replace the men." He paced back and forth, scowling, thumbs hooked in vest pockets.

"And the customers?" Madeline asked. "Can we replace them?"

"Damn the customers. We've got Onderdonk in our pocket. The railroad will buy all the lumber we can cut."

Madeline's voice grew softer. "And what if the railroad were to decide to buy from the ... the People's Lumber Store?" she asked. But she could not wait for the answer, for she was thinking of her daughter Mariah, who had run away seventeen years before with the First Officer of a British man-of-war. She had not heard from her since. What has happened to her, she wondered. But the thought trailed off and she was suddenly back in England, in her own comfortable home in Chelsea, looking out through the window at the hummingbirds and butterflies in her immaculate summer garden, where the roses were full and whole and perfect. And she was crying, for there, at the edge of the flower-beds, where the weeping willows had stood, someone had placed bars.

Jonas stopped pacing and glared at her. "Andrew Onderdonk is well aware of Galer Mills' reputation. I've seen to that. She'll never get an order from him."

Abby shuffled down the gangplank of the *William Irving*, bent under the weight of her enormous bearskin coat, and stepped onto the rickety dock at Farr's Bluff. Behind her the broad, black Fraser hissed over shallow gravel beds. The ship could go no further.

Chinese labourers filed down the gangway and swirled noiselessly around her, groggy with sleep after the all-night journey from New Westminster. It was four in the morning, and the rain had just stopped. A jagged sliver of moon poked through the dirty black clouds. Abby stood on the dock, her oilskin cap dripping onto her forehead, clouds of steam roiling around her head as her warm breath hit the cold air, and watched the *William Irving* slip silently into the wide, dark Fraser and disappear into the blackness. A whistle hooted behind her. She turned and trudged after the crew, which was straggling into the tiny camp.

A lantern swung sluggishly through the night, illuminating three shabby tents that flapped and billowed like ghosts in the cold wind. Around her the black forest pressed tight against the small clearing. At one end was the locomotive, puffing steam furiously, its bright white eye glaring at the long ribbons of steel stretching ahead. Unable to turn around, it had backed all the way down from distant Hope to the end of steel, here, in the middle of nowhere. The end of the world, Abby thought. And the beginning of the railroad.

She waited impatiently for a crowd of white men to clamber down off the open flatcar, wondering what they were doing at Farr's Bluff. They didn't look like labourers; they had the well-fed, settled appearance of farmers, ranchers, and townspeople, and the mocking grins of trouble-makers. She threw her carpet-bag angrily onto the car as they circled around her, poking one another in the ribs and leering at her shapeless bearskin. The air reeked of whisky. She strained to reach the lower rung of the ladder, but her clothes weighed her down. Suddenly, hands grabbed her from behind and she flew up in a gale of laughter and tumbled in a heap onto the hard wooden deck. Someone jumped up on the ladder, slapped her rump and squeezed it. Her hand moved instinctively towards the revolver in her bag. But the men were moving off, arms around one another, laughing and staggering into the darkness.

The train lurched forward with a metal clang and a gush of steam. Abby grabbed at the iron lugs in the floor. The wheels screeched over the rails, gaining momentum; the boilers chugged as they built up steam; the flatcar shivered and sparks spiralled up from the smokestack, winked, and faded in the cold black air. The rain began again, icy, piercing, like a flurry of pins, slanting at an angle, driven by the wind. Abby pushed up the collar of her dirty bearskin. The train whistle hooted, faltered, jumped an octave, and blasted out an ear-splitting scream that rang in her head. A moment later it sounded again, far in the distance, thrown back from the mountains to the west, then the east, across the Fraser; again and again, the mournful wail echoed through the canyon.

Ho-sun Lee bolted up from his bedroll, panting, his wide eyes staring at the billow of grey canvas crackling overhead. And there it was again, further away, the eerie howl of the train, distorted by the wind into a painful shriek. He slumped back on his elbows. Every morning it is the same thing, he thought. Every morning I am woken by the train whistle a full hour before I must crawl out of this warm bed, and always just as I am dreaming of bears. He shuddered, pulled the grey blanket up around his nose, and listened carefully to the night sounds: the echo of the train whistle floating through the canyon, the whoosh of the trees in the wind, the patter of rain on the tent roof. He sighed. No bears.

Every country must have its dragons, he thought, and in Gold Mountain it is surely the grizzly. He had never actually seen one, but he had heard countless stories about the huge, snarling beasts with fire-red eyes, and he had seen the body of Lee Kwong carried into camp on a plank, his back broken, his face torn away from the eyebrows down. Grizzlies terrified him.

Ho-sun Lee forced the thought of bears out of his mind, unhooked his big toe from the hole in his top blanket, and snuggled
into the bottom one, happy and smiling. He thanked the gods of
his ancestors again for directing him to Gold Mountain. Granted,
he thought, the voyage was more terrifying than a thousand
dragons, but I have survived. My body has fleshed out and my
legs and back are strong again. Ho-sun Lee poked his tongue
around in his mouth and sighed. It is a great sadness, he thought,
that I have lost most of my teeth. Very sad. But if that is the price
one must pay for a wife like Yum-koo, I would gladly lose them
all. He smiled. Besides, I still have three strong and healthy teeth
with which to gnaw dried salmon and rice. It is not so bad. And I
am in Gold Mountain. . . .

He snuggled into his blanket and listened happily to the patter
of rain on the canvas roof. It is true, he thought, that this incessant wetness is rotting my feet, and my body crawls with lice, but
never again will I eat from garbage cans in the back alleys of
Hong Kong. Never again will I starve. Why, no one starves here.
No one. It is truly remarkable, he thought. Truly remarkable.

And then there was Yum-koo. He thought of her asleep on the
narrow mat in their tiny room in Fantan Alley, and the corners of
his eyes puckered into crow's-feet. He could picture every crevice of the delicate rosewood comb he had slipped from her hair
on their wedding night; he could smell the jasmine in her scented
hair as it tumbled over her pale-opal skin, her small round
breasts; he remembered the feel of her tiny fingers raking delicate red lines across his back.

Ho-sun Lee rolled over and groaned, pressing himself into the
warm mat. Soon work would stop for the barbarian festival of
Christmas and he would rush south to the small room in Fantan
Alley, where, with the luck of the gods, he would distribute
red-dyed eggs to celebrate the birth of his first son.

Such a rich and fertile land, he thought. Why, with the hard
work of my wife in the laundry and my work here we have
already saved—he squinted his eyes in the darkness while the
sums revolved slowly in his head; he was not good with numbers—eighty dollars! He sucked in his breath and beamed. Eighty
dollars! Truly a great sum. And when the railroad is finished, we
will surely have enough to return to Hong Kong a wealthy family.
At the thought of leaving Gold Mountain, the crow's-feet withered and faded from the corners of his eyes. His three remaining
teeth clamped tightly shut.

Ho-sun Lee began drifting back to sleep, thinking sadly of China and his small ancestral home in the province of Guandong, where the bones of his parents rested in the ground under faded red umbrellas with little silver bells tinkling in the wind. Suddenly he heard a sucking noise in the mud outside the tent. Immediately he was awake, wide awake, straining to hear through the thin canvas wall. Bears. He was certain of it. He could hear them breathing, he could hear their great shaggy paws shifting through the mud near his head. He held his breath. A man near by rolled over and began to snore. Ho-sun Lee turned his head slowly, his eyes dilated with fear, and scanned the six men sprawled in quiet heaps, oblivious to the giant grizzly on the other side of the thin cloth wall.

There was a scratching noise on the canvas near his head. The hair on the back of his neck prickled. Suddenly the side of the tent crashed in with a loud whack and he rolled away from the wall and screamed. Canvas tore. Ropes sprang. The tent billowed down on the frightened men and he felt the sharp crack of a wooden club on his back. He scrambled and pushed towards the door on his hands and knees, panicked as much by the screams and jostling around him as by the painful blows from above. At last he found an opening and tumbled out into the cold, dark night.

He lay sprawled in the mud, dazed, staring up at a tight ring of leering faces, grizzled faces, the huge, ugly faces of angry barbarians. Above him he saw fingers fumble at the buttons of a man's crotch. Laughter. A vile hot stream splattered across his face and chest. He began to push himself up, but a club cracked across the back of his neck and he felt a cold nausea in the pit of his stomach as he slumped down.

"Fuckin' yellow niggers."

Ho-sun Lee struggled to his feet, shaking the confusion from his head, vaguely aware of the dark shapes swarming around him, of the yellow lanterns swinging drunkenly through the night, and of the rough hands that gripped his arms. Most of the Chinese lay in a groaning heap at his feet and a burly man kicked his way among them, swinging a long steel knife like a sickle, slicing off queue after queue; the thick ropes of braided hair swung from his arm like coiled snakes.

"Hey! Over here." A man with a lantern stood at the edge of a steep gravel bank, his foot propped on the rump of an unconscious Chinaman. "Back to China," he shouted, and the inert body flopped over the edge, making a sickening crunching and crackling noise as it rolled down the near-vertical slope towards the cold Fraser. The men from Hope roared with laughter. More bodies were dragged to the edge and pushed over, some unconscious, some struggling, some pleading.

Ho-sun Lee stood at the edge of Farr's Bluff, shaking his head violently, while the man with the knife circled behind him. "Hey, hold up a minute," someone called. "Here's another hidin' in the tent. We could tie 'em together by their pigtails. . . ." Men rushed towards the voice and Ho-sun Lee glimpsed the struggling body of Kun-Lau, a quiet, frightened boy of fifteen who had arrived only a week before and since then had said no more than, "I hate Gold Mountain."

Ho-sun Lee's head jerked back. Hands swarmed over him. Gold Mountain . . . , he thought. He could feel the thin body of Kun-Lau shivering against his back. Cold rain roared down, numbing his bare skin. The queues were tied, the men stepped back, and then he felt the sickening shove.

They raced down through the blackness, skidding over loose gravel and broken shale, fingers clawing at the steep bank. The boy snagged on a bush. Ho-sun Lee's head snapped up and he screamed with pain, then the bush ripped free and Kun-Lau tumbled past him, ploughing through the gravel, face down. The boy's forehead thudded into a large rock, then he rolled limply, unconscious. Ho-sun Lee grabbed him and held him in his arms to stop the awful tugging and ripping at his scalp. Together they rolled and clattered over the sharp stones towards a narrow outcrop that hung over the cold, slow Fraser. As they struck the ledge he dug in his heels and for a moment saw the dim outline of a man clinging to the rock. A hand reached out to him. Their fingers brushed, then he and Kun-Lau whizzed past, tumbled over the edge, and plunged into the river.

Ho-sun Lee gasped for air. The shock of the icy water burned his skin. Slowly his head pulled back and down as the boy sank below him. The river closed over his face and he panicked, thrashing his arms and legs. He dived, feeling blindly down the lengths of hair to Kun-Lau's head, grabbed the boy around the neck, and struggled frantically to the surface.

With his arm hooked under Kun-Lau's chin he turned on his back and floated, numb and dazed, barely conscious, moving his legs slowly, thinking of Yum-koo, drifting aimlessly on the current which snaked through the canyon like an icy dragon.

The river widened and curled round a shallow bend. His feet bumped on the rocky bed, and with a final effort he hauled himself up and fell onto the shore. Kun-Lau lay on top of him, with his pigtail wrapped tight around his neck. The boy was dead.

Ho-sun Lee rested on the prickly gravel, pinned under the cold dead weight, unable to shift it, and stared up at the black and rainy night. Gold Mountain. . . . He poked his tongue around in his mouth. His three remaining teeth were gone.

For the hundredth time Abby flattened herself on the deck as the train thundered through a poorly drained hollow and another sheet of muddy water flew over her, soaking those on the back of the flatcar. From here she could see for miles, and everywhere was rain: sheets of it wreathed the tops of dark granite crags, shadowy black fingers poked down into dark, wet valleys, brown streams boiled through gullies into puckered green lakes, and the downpour in the canyon dissolved on the slick black rocks into a fine white mist.

For hours she had been thinking of the train as some sort of demonic, steam-powered Noah's Ark. She looked at her fellow passengers: all men, all tired, all wet and grumpy; they sat at a distance with their backs to her, ignoring her, ignoring the rain and sprays of water that flew up from the wheels and down from the sky. There were a dozen Chinese, four whites, six — no, five — Indians; the sixth had flown off somewhere north of Hope when the flatcar derailed and bounced over the ties like a runaway buggy on a corduroy road, rattling and banging the passengers over the wooden deck before it jumped back onto the tracks. Abby had watched, stunned, as the Indian rolled off the car, bounced on the gravel bed, and jumped up. He had run after the train for half a mile, shouting and waving his arms. No one had moved, the train had raced on. Finally the Indian gave up and sat down on the tracks, a small, lonely speck shrinking in the distance.

She reminded herself again to tell the engineer about him when she got to Yale. Perhaps someone would go back. . . . "But I'll be damned if I will," she muttered to herself. "I'll never travel this rail again." She pulled her bearskin coat tight around her throat and tried to stop shivering. This is madness, she thought. I could have taken a shallow-draught steamer all the way up the river, or, better yet, a warm, dry coach along the Cariboo Road. But no — I had to see the railroad first hand, count the ties, tot up the board feet of lumber in the bridges and trestles, see the line shacks and shoring timbers . . .

The train whistle shrieked. Abby automatically rolled onto her knees and buried her head under her hands as the engine roared into a tunnel and spears of ice splintered down from the roof and showered onto the open flatcar.

The roaring and clattering stopped. She struggled back to a sitting position, shoving and pulling at her waterlogged coat. The men sat stoically, impassively, in the same positions. A thin trickle of blood threaded its way down a crevice in an Indian's cheek. Another sheet of muddy water splashed over the back half of the car and the trickle of blood was gone.

The train puffed painfully up a steep mountain grade, threading higher and higher through the canyon walls; the river squeezed into narrow gorges below; the snow-line loomed a hundred feet above. Abby looked behind her at the Fraser, snaking darkly for hundreds of miles through wet, brooding valleys. On either side of it was the tangled rain forest, an impenetrable jungle of cedar, spruce, fir, and pine, stretching endlessly, mysteriously, over the murky horizon. It was awesome, limitless. Truly, Abby thought, it could never all be cut. For a moment she wished she had brought her sketch pad. But it had been so long since she had used it . . .

The rain gelled into a thick, wet slush. She tightened her grip on the iron lug as the train crept out onto a spindly maze of boards and struts propped high above the river against a jutting wall of rock. Spray flew up from the canyon and whipped like geysers through the spaces between the cars. The train gathered speed; its wheels thundered over the delicate bridge, its trail of smudge shredded on the wind. Faster, faster. The whistle shrieked. The men stirred. They flattened themselves on the deck and gripped the metal lugs. Abby sat up and craned her neck to see past the engine. "Get down!" someone shouted. A hand grabbed her ankle as the train shuddered violently to a stop with a muffled thud and the screech of wheels. Abby slid forward until her head extended into the empty gap between the flatcar and the coal car. Far below, between the ties, was the boiling water of the Fraser. A flurry of fine powdered snow settled around her.

"Snowslide." The man let go of her ankle. He was grim-faced, dour and lean. "They're tryin' to bust through." The train began to back up.

Abby edged back onto the car. Her hands were shaking. "Thank you."

Again the whistle screamed and the train lurched forward, gathered speed, and charged at the snowbank, roaring round the curve and thundering over the trestle. Abby braced herself, her nerves jangling. "Oh dear God," she whispered. "I'm not ready. Not yet, Matthew. I—" The engine slammed into the snowbank. Abby screamed as she skidded forward.

The train backed up. "Please, not again," she whimpered. She stared at the snow settling on her trembling hands, which were clamped around the iron lug. The train stopped. Abby held her breath.

"Everybody out." A pair of black boots were planted in the snow by her face. "Have to dig your way through if you ever wanna get to Yale. Shovels are up front." The men clambered onto the engine, stepping over Abby as they went. The black boot poked her ribs. "You too there, Bearskin, move yer butt." She looked up into the grizzled face of a toothless old man. He bent closer and his eyes widened. "Well, I'll be . . ."

Yale was a narrow, muddy scar. A double row of weathered clapboard shacks, overrun with moss, huddled under dripping branches and faded into a white haze of rain. Behind them, mildewed tents sagged limply in the downpour, squeezed into the precious empty spaces at the edge of the tangled forest. Abby lowered herself gingerly from the flatcar, wary of her bruised hips and numb feet. There were no sidewalks. She trudged along the main street, picking her way over the muddy ruts. Men swirled around her: tall Swedes, wiry Italians, Englishmen in bowler hats, turbaned Hindus, Indians with salmon slung over their shoulders, and tight knots of Chinese, their faces hidden by woven hats. They stared at her. A few nodded and smiled, but most just turned and gawked, open-mouthed, clouds of steam swirling round their tobacco-stained beards, bewildered eyes squinting through the rain. She was the only woman on the street. Aside from the prostitutes, women did not come to Yale. Why should they?

Abby dodged to the side as a skookum dray thundered past,

splattering her with mud. The tune "One More River to Cross", played frantically, raucously, on a player piano, flooded out of a rotting two-storey structure marked "Long Kelly's", where drunks littered the front verandah and gaudy feathered and painted hurdy-gurdy girls leaned out of upstairs windows.

A long line of bellowing oxen threaded through the crowd. Men pushed out of their way and Abby was jostled onto the porch of an inn called "The Last Rest". She stood for a moment watching the chaos in the street, then turned and trudged inside, trailing mud behind her. "I'd like a room, please."

A skinny old man sat perched on a high stool behind the rude pine-slab counter, squeezing a lock of stringy grey hair. He squinted down at her, the wattles of his neck flowing loosely over a tight wing collar. "And where is your husband, madam?"

"He's dead," Abby replied.

The proprietor frowned and brushed at the dandruff on his black frock-coat. "Surely, madam, you are not travelling ... alone?"

"Yes, I am."

"I'm sorry, but we run a Christian hotel here. Very respectable. There is only the common room left, and that is out of the question. We could never allow a single woman ..." Abby rummaged in her carpet-bag and slid a five-dollar bill onto the counter. The old man smiled, rubbed the tips of his fingers together, and curled the note into his pocket. "Of course, if sharing your bedroom with a dozen men is of no consequence to you, who am I to protest? Top of the stairs, first door on the left."

Abby picked up her carpet-bag. "Where can I find Andrew Onderdonk?"

"Not here. He left a week ago."

Abby froze. "What?" The proprietor glanced at her, his lizard eyes blinking indifferently as he picked at his fingernails. "Where is he?" Abby asked.

The old man shrugged. "Up north of Tunnel City, I guess. Tryin' to force a boat through Hell's Gate. Damn-fool notion, if you ask me."

"When will he be back?"

The old man examined his fingernails. "When the boat sinks, I suppose."

Abby leaned against the wall and sighed. "How do I get to Hell's Gate?"

"Train leaves at dawn."

"Train?" Abby shivered.

"That's right. Work train."

"Is there any other way?"

"I suppose you could get a horse. It's only twenty miles." The old man smiled wryly. "Course it's not very lady-like to go traipsin' through such country on yer own. . . ."

Abby turned to go up the stairs, then stopped on the lower step. "I'd like a bath."

"Bath's twenty-five cents. Fifty if you want clean water. Seventy-five if you want it hot."

Abby leaned into the warm steam wafting up from the mare's neck, shut her nostrils to the rangy smell of wet horse, and pushed gingerly at the spruce bough blocking her path. Slush splattered onto the back of her neck. She tucked her bearskin coat over her brown-wool britches and thought of the crisp black skirt and the starched white blouse in which she had planned to confront the notorious Mr. Onderdonk. They were folded neatly, uselessly, in her carpet-bag back at the hotel. She chuckled as she remembered the shocked looks on the faces of the men of Yale as she had cantered past Long Kelly's at dawn, watching the drunks who were stacked like cordwood out of the rain, listening to the sound of a lone concertina floating behind her. In Victoria or New Westminster a woman in pants would have been front-page news. Here the wonder was that a lone woman had come to Yale at all.

Abby followed the twin lines of new rail, leading her horse into the woods when trains, loaded with ties, thundered past. Handcars shunted urgently back and forth. Gangs of men appeared along the right-of-way: Indian ballasters, tamping loads of gravel into the spaces between the ties; Chinese with crowbars, lifting the completed track for spiking; whites gauging the rails and screwing down the fishplates. Then the steel disappeared and the knots of men grew thicker, swarming over the open grade, spacing ties and levelling the road. Huge scrapers, pulled by teams of oxen, lumbered ponderously over the gravel like dinosaurs. Wagon-loads of shattered rock clattered down into gullies, and blast after blast of dynamite rolled through the canyon like distant thunder. The gravel bed disappeared. The gangs of men thinned, then vanished behind her, and Abby rode on through the dripping brown and green scar that would soon be a railroad.

At eleven o'clock she heard the roar of Hell's Gate and worked her horse towards it, through the thin white fog that curled under the trees. At the edge of the canyon she was shocked to see hundreds of men, mostly Chinese, lining the cliff, staring down at the Fraser. She tied her horse to a tree, walked to the edge, and peered down into the gorge. A blast of cold spray hit her face and she gasped.

Two hundred feet below, the river squeezed and boiled through a narrow crevasse. Chinese dangled from ladders, shrouded in mist, fastening ring-bolts to the walls, their bare feet gripping the slick black rock. A maze of taut ropes hummed in the wind, criss-crossing down to a long white boat, half-hidden by spray, rolling and bucking in the white eddies at the mouth of Hell's Gate.

"Excuse me," Abby shouted over the roar of the river as she tapped a navvy on the shoulder. "Onderdonk? Where is he?" The man jerked his head towards a great bull of a man in a glistening black raincoat and fedora hat. Mist billowed around him as he leaned over the edge of the canyon, yelling at the men dangling from ropes below him.

"Mr. Onderdonk?" Abby shouted.

"What?" He glanced at her, then looked again. Cigar smoke swirled through his neatly parted beard. Abby was startled by the intensity of the light-blue eyes peering into her face. "Who are you?"

"I'm Mrs. Galer, of Galer Mills." She extended her hand.

Onderdonk waved her aside and shouted over her shoulder. "Space the men out along them ropes. Thirty men per rope. Wait for my signal."

"I've come to talk to you about —"

"Lumber. I know. I got your letter." He turned to face her, a curious half-smile on his face. "How'd you get here, anyway?"

"I took the *William Irving* to Farr's Bluff, an open flatcar to Yale, then a horse from Yale to here.

Onderdonk's left eyebrow arched up and Abby noticed a sly smirk lurking under the parted beard. "Have a nice trip?"

"Hideous," Abby said. "Bloody hideous."

Onderdonk chuckled, and the chuckle billowed into a full-bellied laugh. For a moment Abby was furious, but then she saw the absurdity of her situation, and she too began to laugh. "You're the first woman ever to travel here by rail," he said. "And on an open flatcar—in winter. Even my own wife came by coach. Shame you wasted your time."

Abby stopped laughing; her teeth clenched and her eyes narrowed.

"I already have an adequate supplier of lumber."

"Cains?"

Onderdonk nodded.

"Cains is an ass."

Onderdonk's eyebrow shot up again and he looked at her coldly. "An ass, madam? Well, that may be, but his ties and trestles are sound—a bit pricey, perhaps, but then he has never been involved in land-grabbing, has he? Now, if you'll excuse me ..." Onderdonk turned towards the rows of men, who were watching with interest.

Abby grabbed his arm and yanked him back to face her. "Nor has Galer Mills," she shouted. "My husband was framed by Jonas Cains and cleared by a Royal Commission!"

"Madam, this is hardly the time to discuss it. I—"

"Oh yes it is! I took your bloody train from—"

"Did you pay the conductor?"

"There was no conductor," Abby shrieked.

Onderdonk's eyes twinkled. "Just a joke, Mrs. Galer."

"Forgive me if I lack a sense of humour, Mr. Onderdonk, but I have been bumped and bruised, I have been drenched and half frozen to death on your beastly railroad; I have been ogled and groped by sex-starved bullies; I have been speared by icicles, and I have shovelled my way through snowslides to get to this god-forsaken wilderness—and all because you hadn't the courtesy, the common decency, to answer my letter. And now you dare to make accusations against my husband and then refuse to discuss any possibility of a lumber contract? Well, you will discuss it, Mr. Onderdonk. You bloody well will."

Onderdonk frowned, dropped his cigar butt into the mud, and ground it under his heel. "Very well," he said. "I suppose I owe you that much. But at the moment there are six men clinging to a pitching boat at the mouth of Hell's Gate. Do you mind if we pull them through first?"

Abby let go of his arm, chastened by the thought of the six men. "No, of course not," she stammered. "I . . . I'm sorry. Please, go ahead."

"Thank you." Onderdonk marched to the lip of the canyon and Abby followed. The navvies stood in rows behind them, the ropes dangling loosely in their hands. The last of the Chinese scrambled up over the edge. Far below was the boat, wallowing and pitching between sheer walls of grey basalt. Thick black smoke billowed up from her stack and men scurried along her deck, checking ropes and winches.

"The *Skuzzy*," Onderdonk announced proudly as he lit another cigar. "She's two hundred and fifty tons. I had her built at Tunnel City. One hundred twenty-seven feet long, twenty-four feet abeam, and she's got twenty bulkhead compartments."

"Can you pull her through?" Abby asked.

"We'll see in a minute." Onderdonk waved his hands over his head. The ship's steam whistle shrieked, a faint, plaintive wail, barely audible over the roar of the water.

"Pull!" Onderdonk shouted. One hundred and fifty men braced their feet in the mud, took up the slack, and leaned into the ropes. The lines snapped tight. Droplets of water scattered on the violent currents. The ship edged forwards, poking her bow into the narrow throat of Hell's Gate.

"Pull! Pull!"

Abby watched as the *Skuzzy*, caught in a spiderweb of ropes, twisted sideways in a whirlpool and struck the rocks with a grating crunch. Water boiled over her prow. Men scrambled along the deck and jabbed at the wall with poles. Slowly, painfully, she swung back to the centre of the channel. She was halfway through.

"Pull! Pull!" Onderdonk shouted.

Abby's heart pounded as the ship edged forward, rolling from side to side, froth bubbling over her gunwales, her long white length pinched in the middle by the sharp black rock. "Pull," she shouted. "Pull! Pull!" The Chinese beside her heaved on the line, which hummed in the wind; their arms shook; their feet skidded in the sticky gumbo.

A squat man at the back shouted as he slipped in the mud and ploughed into the legs of the man ahead. The line lunged forward and the navvy at the front skidded to the edge of the cliff, white-faced, and flopped onto his belly, his legs dangling into the canyon. For a moment his hands ripped frantically at bunches of green moss, then he screamed and disappeared.

Abby watched, stunned, as the body thudded off the slick rock, bounced onto the gunwale of the ship a few feet from the startled deckhands, and slid into the boiling river.

The *Skuzzy* drifted away from the loose rope. Her stern struck the far wall of the canyon and she began to slip backwards through Hell's Gate. Abby grabbed the rope and heaved. The men were on their feet behind her, yarding in the slack. "Pull!" she shouted. In a moment Onderdonk was beside her, his cigar and fedora lost in the confusion, his neatly combed hair flying in the wind. "Pull! Pull, you bastards!" he roared. Abby jammed her boots against a rock and yarded on the rope. Her fingers cramped. Her back ached. Her arms quivered. But the line payed in, inches at a time, then a foot, two feet, four. Abruptly it went slack, and she catapulted backward, tripped over Onderdonk, who lay sprawled in the mud, and fell on top of him. She looked around, stunned. All along the cliff navvies lay scattered on the ground in a tangle of ropes. The lines were slack.

"She's through!" Onderdonk yelled. The crowd roared, and up from the canyon came the triumphant hoot of the *Skuzzy*'s steam whistle.

"You're quite a woman, Mrs. Galer," Onderdonk said.

Abby stared down at the piercing blue eyes and realized she was lying on top of him. The warmth of his body seeped through her bearskin coat. His hand rested on the small of her back. "Does that mean you will buy my lumber?"

"Mrs. Galer, this is hardly a fair way to do business—pinning me to the ground."

Abby heard sniggering and looked up at a group of navvies who were standing near by. She jumped up, blushing, and walked quickly to the edge of the canyon. Onderdonk followed, brushing mud from his coat, and they stood in silence, watching the *Skuzzy* chug around a bend in the river, the shriek of her steam whistle fading in the distance.

"Mrs. Galer, you must understand my position."

"Cains must have done quite a job of poisoning your mind against me," Abby said.

Onderdonk took a deep breath and puffed out his cheeks. "I admit that I have heard a great deal of muck-raking and slander against Galer Mills, most of it from Mr. Cains, but—"

"And is it not patently obvious why?" Abby turned to face the tangled jungle of green on the far side of the canyon. Rain streamed down her face. "Galer Mills was the grandest logging show in the country before Cains declared war on us." She shook her head sadly. "I would never have believed that one man could bring so much grief. He cheated us out of the best timber leases. He rustled our logs, embroiled us in the Texada Scandal, smeared our name, turned the public against us. You probably know that my husband died when the *Pacific* sank seven years ago. It was Cains's ship that caused the accident. It's funny, but I've never been able to shake the feeling that maybe he sent it out deliberately, to murder Matthew; I don't know. But now he has turned the railway against me." Abby scooped up a handful of moss and tossed it into the canyon, where it scattered on the currents. "Tell me, Mr. Onderdonk, why does everyone believe him?"

"I don't."

Abby turned to face him. "Then why?"

"Because the public is on his side." Onderdonk jammed the fedora back on his head. "Mrs. Galer, I am a pragmatist. Believe me, I would like to help, but a railroad is not built on charity. You are asking me to take a great risk, with no incentive. The people already hate this railroad because I've hired nearly seven thousand Chinese to build it while there is fourteen per-cent unemployment amongst the whites. Practically every month there are incidents of violence against my labourers — whites against the Chinese — and there has even been some sabotage of completed rail. To buy lumber from a mill which the public believes to be corrupt would only compound the problem. And God knows I have enough troubles already."

"Mr. Onderdonk, you knew the problems that would result from hiring Chinese long before the first boatload arrived, yet you continued to bring them in by the thousands, and what's more, you contracted for them with a woman who hasn't exactly the most saintly of reputations. Mei-fu Chang runs the biggest brothel on the mainland. And you dare to quibble with me over public opinion?"

"That was different."

"Why?" Abby shouted.

"Because I saved the people three and a half million dollars," Onderdonk yelled. He jammed a cigar in his mouth and looked out over the canyon.

Abby smiled. "I see. Well, Mr. Onderdonk, what would you say to saving half a million dollars on just the trestles and bridges in one thirty-mile stretch?"

"I beg your pardon?"

"I checked with your operations manager in New Westminster before I left and found that you need forty million board feet just for the bridges above Yale. If you award that contract to Cains, you will pay thirty-five dollars per thousand board feet. I propose to sell you the same- or better-quality timber for twenty-five dollars. You could save half a million, and that's not even taking into account ties, shoring timbers, lumber for line shacks, and whatever else you need. Half a million dollars, Mr. Onderdonk. Would that soften the blow of public disapproval?"

Abby watched as he carefully lit the cigar, his cheeks puffing like bellows. He blew out a stream of blue smoke and smiled broadly. "Yes," he said. "Mrs. Galer, I believe it would."

Abby folded the newspaper, placed it on her lap, and stared vacantly out the office window. The rain had stopped. Black clouds scudded across the lower half of the moon and raindrops dripped slowly from the eaves of her office. Small waves on the inlet shone silver under the glare of electric lights. "Poor De Cosmos," she muttered.

There was a knock at the door and Johann walked in, stamping mud from his boots and shaking the last of the rain from his slick oilskin. "The first shipment of ties is just about loaded," he said. "They'll be on their way to Yale with the morning tide."

Abby nodded and continued gazing out the window.

Johann grunted. "That's not exactly the reaction I expected," he said. "That first shipment will bring Cains to his knees."

Abby smiled. "I'm sorry, Johann. I was thinking about De Cosmos. The paper says he hasn't come out of his house since he lost the election. I was just imagining him, holed up in his room with a case of whisky, drowning in self-pity."

Johann hung his coat on a hook and frowned. "Aye. He'd take it pretty hard. Course that's to be expected when a man's got a head on him as big as De Cosmos. Probably feels the whole world's turned agin him."

"He's a great man, Johann, a visionary." Abby chuckled. "Granted, he is insufferable, egotistical, and a drunk. But look at what he has accomplished. Can you imagine what it must feel like to be treated so cruelly by the papers after giving twenty years of your life to a province?" Abby shrugged. "And the sad part is that I'm certain he's right. One day Canada *will* be a sovereign state. It's just too early."

Johann grinned and put his finger to his lips. "Shh ... there might be some British about." Abby smiled weakly. "You and Matthew were good friends with De Cosmos, weren't you?"

Abby rearranged the paper on her lap and nodded. "We've been through a lot together."

"So why don't you bring him over to Galer Mills?"

"What?"

"It'd get him out of his room and away from the whisky. He just needs to feel needed, that's all."

"Do you think he'd come?"

"If you asked him he would. Make up some story about being desperate for his advice, or something. Make it sound like only he can save you. That'd fetch him over quick enough, and do him a world of good, too."

Abby slapped the top of her desk and stood up. "You're right, Johann. I'll do it. I'll send him a letter right now."

"Good. But before you get started, I've some news for you. We hired six more of Cains's men today and got some inside scuttlebutt on what's going on over there. He's got only one railway contract left, and it's already a week behind. He hasn't the men to cut it."

Abby's lips tightened into a thin smile and her eyes sparkled. "Has he gotten any local orders?"

"Not one since we dropped our prices. You've done it, Mrs. Galer. Cains's mill is grinding to a halt."

CHAPTER TWELVE

1886

ELECTION DAY JONAS CAINS STOOD AT HIS OF-fice window, staring at the wharf across the inlet. Black waves gleamed silver under the glare of electric light as they danced around the keel of a heavily laden steamer. Men swarmed over the stacks of lumber piled high on her decks. The howl of Galer's saw echoed painfully off the mountains to the north; it would go on all night, slicing into his dreams, making sleep impossible. His own mill was dark and silent.

The door opened and Carky stepped into the office, a battered slouch hat in his hand. His eyes were bloodshot, his grizzled beard stained yellow with snoose. "Ye be wantin' to see me, Mr. Cains?"

"Ah, Carky." Jonas smiled grimly and continued to stare at the mill across the inlet. "Yes. Yes, indeed. There's a job I want you to do for me."

Mei-fu set the lantern on the table, unlatched the window and pushed it up. Thunder echoed off the mountains to the north. The night was cold, black, and windy, and the rain drumming on the walls of her room set her nerves on edge. She paced back and forth, the short train of her tightly tailored dress flicking behind her like a cat's tail. From the front of the Palace Royale came the sound of music, dancing, laughter; from overhead the thump and creak of bedsprings — sounds that usually made her smile, the sounds of money being made. But tonight they were a distraction, a painful, rankling irritation.

Setting a tinfoil cylinder into her new Edison phonograph, she cranked the machine up and then perched on the edge of a delicate armchair. Firelight danced across the rich mahogany panelling as the sound of "The Blue Danube" waltz swirled around her. She folded her hands meticulously on her lap and forced herself to think of the new property she had bought today west of Gastown. "A wise investment," she told herself. "If the railroad comes here, it will be worth a fortune." She thought of the gold hidden in her walls, of the cash in the tin box under her floorboards, of the new sapphire necklace that had arrived today all the way from New York, but she could not focus her thoughts and her eyes kept drifting to the open window.

Angrily, she snatched a five-month-old copy of the *British Columbian* newspaper from the table beside her and flipped to the third page. She had read the article so many times she knew it by heart.

The British Columbian   Dec. 10, 1885

CHINESE KILLER SPOTTED

The Chinese outlaw, Wu-Lee Chang, who five years ago brutally shot and killed an unarmed New Westminster citizen before scores of witnesses who had gathered in a peaceful demonstration against the unnecessary importation of celestial railway workers, was seen last night in the vicinity of Williams Lake. Mr. Hortweiler, a longtime cattle rancher in the Williams Lake area, reported that around midnight last, he detected a disturbance in his henhouse and, rifle in hand, rushed to the defense of his chickens. When he arrived upon the scene the surprised Mr. Hortweiler found the culprit was not the expected wolverine or lynx but rather the deadly yellow murderer, Wu-Lee Chang, whom he recognized immediately from wanted posters at the local trading post. As the killer attempted to flee, a chicken in each hand, the courageous Hortweiler raised his rifle and shot him in the arm, but failed to wound the villain sufficiently to prevent his escape. This, the first break in the case since the brutal slaying, has launched an intensive manhunt in the area. I am certain that all of British Columbia joins me in wishing our valiant guard-

ians of peace godspeed in appre-
hending this dangerous criminal so
that he may soon meet the end he so
richly deserves upon the gallows of
British justice.

Mei-fu bent over the paper, her chin trembling. Five months, she thought. It had taken her so long to find him. The phonograph needle scraped painfully over the edge of the tinfoil cylinder. She snapped the paper shut and flung it onto the table. But tonight it would all be settled.

A sharp knock set her door rattling against its frame. Mei-fu bolted to her feet, ran to the window, and leaned out into the rain, looking left and right. Nothing. She whipped the curtains shut and blew out the coal-oil lamp. There was shouting in the hallway. She hurried to the door and flung it open.

Caroline Burgess lunged into the room, a burly, sour-faced bouncer tugging at her waist. "Where is he?" she screamed. "Where is my husband?" Mei-fu reeled back from the smell of whisky.

"I'm sorry," the bouncer said. "She sneaked in the back before I could stop her."

"Mrs. Burgess," Mei-fu said calmly, "I can assure you your husband is not on the premises. Now please go quietly."

"I know he's here," Caroline shrieked. "He's somewhere in this bloody little whorehouse of yours. Wiley . . ."

Mei-fu smiled as the faint creak of bedsprings filtered down from the floor above. She knew exactly where Wiley was. He was Clarissa's most regular and valued customer. None of the other girls would tolerate the rough games he demanded of them, but Clarissa had the stomach for it. And it's amazing, Mei-fu thought, what a man with cruel tastes will pay to accomplish his little death. She glanced nervously at the window and her smile faded. "He's not here. Now go." She waved her hand at the bouncer. "Get rid of her."

"I'll get you for this," Caroline yelled. "I'll get you. Wiley! . . ."

Mei-fu flung the door shut and waited, twisting her fingers and shaking her head, while the screaming faded down the hallway and the back door slammed. Silence. She rushed to the window, opened it, and peered into the dark forest. Rain clattered through the brittle salal that grew between the brothel and the woods. She relit the lantern and turned up the wick.

In the distance the sound of drunken laughter tumbled out of

Deighton House. She held her breath. Yes, there it was, a faint, low whistle from the bushes below. Thunder rumbled overhead as she leaned out the window. "Wu Lee?" she whispered. "Wu Lee?"

Slowly, cautiously, a man rose up out of the salal, his face shadowed by a large bowler hat. She grabbed his arm and pulled as he scrambled through the window, then she whipped the curtains shut and turned down the lamp.

"Wu Lee. . . ." She had not seen him in two years. How different he looked, how alien, in his high leather boots and black frock-coat. He was so big, so big and strange. His queue was gone, his hair clipped short around his turnover collar, and his left arm dangled in a sling, but it was his face that had truly changed. Gone were his laughing eyes and boyish grin and in their place was the gaunt, angry look of a bitter man. "Oh, Wu Lee." She buried her head in his chest. His arms wrapped lightly around her and she felt a shudder run through his body. Suddenly it all seemed so foolish — the gold, the cash, the property — and all that mattered was the hard, desperate look in the eyes of her son.

She touched his wounded arm gently. "You must agree to leave the country now, Wu Lee. It's too dangerous. This is no life. Look what they've done to you."

"They shot me for stealing chickens." Wu Lee's voice was brittle and distant. "It was not an unreasonable thing to do."

Mei-fu pushed away from him. "Unreasonable? . . ." She walked to the fireplace and stared into the flames. "You will go to San Francisco. I have booked passage for you under the name of Ho-Chee. The ship leaves a week from today. You will be safe in San Francisco and you can help me there by finding new girls. They turn over so fast here that —"

"No," Wu Lee said quietly.

"What?" Mei-fu stormed across the room and glared up at him. "Remember," she hissed, "I am your mother. You will do as I say."

"I will not go to San Francisco."

Mei-fu's hand darted out and slapped him hard across the face before she could stop it. Her mouth fell open in shock, then she turned her back on him and began to cry. "How dare you defy me?" she sobbed. "Your own mother, who cares only for your safety?"

Wu Lee shook his head slowly. "I am sorry, honoured mother," he said. "But I remember San Francisco too well from when I was a child; it is no different from here. I remember how my father walked in the mud to make room on the boardwalk for white men; I remember how my heart pounded with fear as we raced through the white neighbourhoods, terrified we would be caught; I remember the hatred, the brutality; I even remember the taunts of children in the street." He closed his eyes and chanted in English as though conjuring up a vision:

> "Chinky, chinky, Chinaman;
> Smokes a pipe of opium."

"Stop it," Mei-fu shrieked. "Stop it!" She covered her face with her hands and slumped into a chair.

"Please, honoured mother," Wu Lee said softly, "lower your voice or you will have me caught and hung."

"What do you want?" Mei-fu sobbed. "To spend the rest of your life hiding in the forest? Being shot for stealing chickens?"

"I want to go home," Wu Lee said. "Back to China."

Mei-fu looked up. "To China?"

Wu Lee nodded.

"But it's so far," she said. "In San Francisco I could visit you every year. But China . . . I would never see you again."

"You would if you came with me," Wu Lee said.

Mei-fu stared at him blankly. "Me? Go to China? But —" The brittle salal below the window crackled. Mei-fu froze. "You must go," she whispered. The rustling stopped. "Return here a week from today at eight o'clock. A ship will be waiting in the inlet. The barbarians are electing a mayor then, so the town will be too drunk to take notice of who boards here. You, at least, will sail to San Francisco and then, if you still wish it" — Mei-fu shut her eyes — "you may go on to China."

Wu Lee bowed deeply, then rested his hand lightly on his mother's shoulder. "And will you come with me?"

Mei-fu touched his wrist without looking up. "I don't know," she said. "But I will decide before you return. Now go."

Wu Lee bowed again, then pulled away and scrambled through the window.

Outside, as the thunder rolled on to the east and the rain clattered through the salal, Caroline Burgess ducked around a corner of the building, her red hair and white dress plastered to her skin. She pressed against the wall and grinned as Wu Lee hurried past and darted into the forest.

Carky swung the heavy leather bag with its load of eighteen-inch iron spikes over his shoulder and trudged moodily along the dark path towards the beach. Treetops rustled overhead and ragged black clouds scuttled through the moonlit sky.

"Filthy business," he grumbled. He walked with a slight stoop and a rolling gait, so that his white beard swung freely from side to side. Bloody filthy, he thought. And I'd no be doin' it if it wasna for the partnership. He chuckled and scratched at his crotch with his free hand. A full quarter share. Cains had promised it. Course, Carky thought, a quarter share of a dyin' mill isna worth spit, but that'll be changin' quick enough.

He placed the spikes in the bottom of a small white rowboat and straightened up, rubbing the small of his back. A sleek finger of moonlight stretched over the inlet, wavering and shifting on the light chop. "Fuckin' Cains," he mumbled. " 'Tis a sorry man who canna do his own dirty work." He eased the rowboat off the gravel beach and climbed in. The spikes shifted at his feet as the boat rocked on the small waves. He fitted the oarlocks into place and turned the boat around until the prow pointed to the bright white glare of the electric light at the end of Galer Mills' wharf.

Abby winced as the nails of her interlaced fingers bit red crescents into the backs of her hands. It was a mistake, she thought. A terrible mistake. She shifted uncomfortably in her chair, which listed to the right as its legs settled in the mud of Gastown's main street. Rain drummed on the canvas tarps overhead and storm lanterns swung eerily from the roof, making the bearded faces around her soft and fire-orange. Johann sat next to her, his arms folded tight across his chest.

"Gone, ladies and gentlemen, is the name of Gastown." Wiley Burgess stood slickly, confidently, under the tent on the raised platform at the front of the outdoor rally, his arms braced on the edges of a lectern, a white carnation in the lapel of his frock-coat, and shouted to be heard by the overflow crowd huddled under the dripping tarpaulin behind the last row of chairs. "And with that name go the rude and bumbling ways of our past. Today we have a new city with a new name and new responsibilities." His hyacinth curl fluttered loosely across his forehead as a gust of wind lifted the canvas roof, emptying puddles of rain into the street. Delicately he poked his index finger at the waxed and curled tips of his upturned moustache. "Vancouver: a city born to greatness, a city to rival San Francisco, a city, ladies and gentlemen, in need of a firm hand at the tiller, a mayor of substance and position, who will guide her safely into the magnificent future which is her birthright."

Abby was not listening. Her fingers twisted together as she watched Amor De Cosmos sitting stiffly, rigidly, at the rear of the podium next to Malcolm MacLean. His cane was braced across his lap like a shotgun. His hands trembled.

Five days before, she had rushed to catch him as he staggered down the gangplank of the *Cariboo Fly* and fell onto Galer Mills' wharf. He was gaunt, grey, and haggard, and he reeked of whisky. Johann had put him to bed and he had slept for two days. When he had finally emerged and crept gingerly down the stairs, clutching the banister with both hands, he was no longer the great confident statesman Abby had known. He raved constantly against the ingratitude of the public — "They could have offered me the post of lieutenant-governor, or at least a senatorship," he whined. "But no, not a blessed word of thanks. They've all turned against me. They hate me. Why, I wasn't even invited to the Governor General's party. Ah, how sharper than a serpent's tooth" — then he would abruptly break off and look blankly around him, his eyes blinking in bewilderment and confusion.

Each night Abby watched him slip furtively up the stairs, candle in hand — he refused to use the new electric lights, declaring them an abomination against nature — then listened to the slow, painful scrape of furniture being dragged across the oak floor above as he barricaded his door.

Yesterday he had rushed up to her like an excited child, waving a copy of the speech he would give on election night written on crumpled paper in his tortured script, and stared at her with piercing blue eyes, his hawk-like face only inches from hers, his mouth open, his lips trembling. Then, inexplicably, his shoulders slumped and his face crumbled into a hurt, bewildered expression that made Abby shiver. Tears welled up in his eyes, rolled slowly down his cheeks, and vanished into the tangle of his bushy black beard.

The wind whipped through the huge old maple tree in Gastown's square, pelting the canvas roof with rain and twigs. A mistake, Abby thought. A terrible mistake. She touched Johann's arm and whispered in his ear. "We should never have talked him into running for mayor. Look at him."

De Cosmos sat with his head craned back, a wild, questioning look in his eye as he watched the tarps billow and crackle overhead. His beard trembled and his lips curled into a painful grimace. He looked distraught, savage, mad.

The crowd applauded as Wiley Burgess finished and took his seat. Amor De Cosmos shuffled to the rostrum and fussed with his cane, hooking it first on the edge of the lectern and then on his arm, and finally laying it on the stage floor. He meticulously pressed the crumpled piece of paper with the palm of his hand and looked out at the rows of faces. The canvas rippled and snapped in the wind. His hands fell limply to his sides and his mouth opened. The crowd waited. He licked his lips. Abby held her breath.

"Yankee," someone shouted. De Cosmos flinched and his eyes darted from face to face, searching for the heckler. The audience rustled ominously. De Cosmos stood frozen at the lectern, his hair fluttering in the wind, and stared at the crowd, his face blank and puzzled. The patter of rain overhead was drowned out by hushed whispering. His beard began to quiver.

John Robson jumped up from his seat in the back row. "Come on, De Cosmos," he shouted. "I bought an extra case of capital I's just so's I could print your traitorous speech; so let's have it." The crowd roared. Thunder rumbled in the far distance. De Cosmos whirled round and looked behind him, his head cocked to one side, listening. Slowly he turned back to the audience. His mouth opened. The crowd quietened. Silence.

A thin trickle of the boot polish he used to dye his hair dripped from his temple and threaded its way through the maze of wrinkles in his cheek. He raised one hand to touch it and froze. Sheet lightning flickered over the forest to the east. De Cosmos closed his mouth and stood silently on the platform, rocking slightly from side to side, his brow furrowed, his eyes blank, glassy, bewildered. A nervous whisper in the back row spread through the crowd like wind through the trees.

It was Malcolm MacLean who ended the torment. He quietly picked up De Cosmos's cane, took him by the arm, and guided him, unresisting, to the edge of the platform. Abby took his hand

and, with Johann on one side, led him gently, like a docile child, through the chattering crowd.

At the back row De Cosmos stopped abruptly. As he glared at John Robson, the fog lifted from his face. His eyes blazed and he leaned over the editor until their faces were inches apart. Robson smirked up at him and opened his mouth, but before he could speak, De Cosmos's cane whizzed overhead and slashed across the back of his neck. Robson lurched forward, slumping to his knees in the mud. His head lolled forward and struck the back of the chair ahead.

De Cosmos gripped the stick in a frenzy with both hands, his teeth bared, and swung it to strike again, but Johann grabbed his arms and wrestled the cane out of his hand. As he broke it across his knee, De Cosmos's body sagged. His lips closed. His face softened and the blank, hopeless expression returned. Quickly Abby and Johann ushered him out of the billowing tent and hurried along the dark, wet beach towards the old *Cariboo Fly*, which was waiting to take them back to Galer Mills.

Jonas Cains leaned back in his chair and took a slow, deep breath. Gas rumbled painfully through his stomach. It was so sudden, so unexpected. Even after all these years, after all his scheming and conniving, he had not been prepared for the great man himself — William Cornelius Van Horne, General Manager and Vice-President of the mighty Canadian Pacific Railway — to come banging on his office door, personally. Jonas glanced nervously at the clutter of paper on his desk and the bits of broken machinery scattered across the floor. Rain dripped through the roof and plopped noisily into a tin bucket behind him. "Are you sure you wouldn't rather go up to the house and have a drink?" he said. "It's so much more — "

"No time," Van Horne blurted as he peeled the wrapper from a Havana cigar. "It's a simple matter, Mr. Cains. The Premier has agreed to extend your lease to 1890. In return, you are to give the railway five thousand acres now and an additional fifteen hundred acres each succeeding year. Yes or no?"

A simple matter, Jonas thought contemptuously. He leaned across the desk and held a match to Van Horne's cigar. His hand trembled. He resented the fact that this man knew exactly how deep he should gouge to take the edge off his triumph. He also resented Van Horne's age. Couldn't be more than forty, he thought. It didn't seem right that a man at least thirty years his junior should wield such power: the power to decide the terminus of the world's greatest railroad, the power to make him the richest man in the province.

Oh, he acts the part well enough, Jonas thought, with his blunt manners, barrel chest, and ice-blue eyes, but he's far too young to be a shrewd negotiator. He leaned back and rested his chin on steepled fingers. "Please forgive me if I seem a bit of a tomnoddy, Mr. Van Horne, but your proposition has quite made my head swim and I should like some time to consider it. The fact of the matter is that I must leave for San Francisco the day after the mayoralty election to conduct some business with my shipping agent—you have probably heard that my mill has suffered a temporary setback—but perhaps we could discuss—"

Van Horne snorted. "Oh, I heard all right. This Galer woman's really got you on the run, eh?"

Jonas reddened. "Hardly, Mr. Van Horne. Hardly. Now, if I could arrange to meet you when I return, perhaps—"

"You can do all the arranging you like," Van Horne said. "But it won't do you no good. I'm makin' you an offer now and it stands for about the next five minutes. Now look, Mr. Cains, if I bring the railway from Port Coquitlam right to your backyard, not only will you have a direct link to the eastern markets, but the land you retain will increase in value hundreds of times over. But you gotta make it worth the company's while."

"I see," Jonas said. He tapped the tips of his fingers together. "You require an immediate decision then. Very well, I'll offer you two thousand acres now and five hundred each succeeding year." There, he had said it, without the slightest quaver in his voice.

Van Horne jumped from his chair and whisked his hat off Jonas's desk. "Mr. Cains," he barked. "I did not come here to waste my time quibbling over a couple of thousand acres." He strode across the room, opened the door, and jammed his hat on his head. "After all, Mr. Cains, the railroad does not *need* you. Port Moody will make an adequate terminus."

"Wait," Jonas cried. Van Horne stopped in the doorway, his face calm and stern. "All right, all right," Jonas growled. "Four thousand acres now, one thousand each succeeding year—and that's my final offer."

Van Horne smiled. He touched his hand to the brim of his hat and nodded. "Sounds fair. I'll cable our lawyers to draw up the papers immediately. Good day, Mr. Cains."

Before Jonas could move from his chair, the great man was gone. He winced at the pain boiling in his stomach. "Blackguard," he muttered; then he leaned back and a smug smile spread slowly across his face. He chuckled, and the chuckle billowed into a full-bellied laugh. "Well, my high and mighty Mr. William Cornelius Van Horne," he muttered, "you are not so shrewd. I'd have gladly paid your five thousand acres — more — if that's what it took." Jonas snorted. I knew it, he thought. The fellow is simply too young.

Outside, Van Horne slammed the door of the black phaeton and spoke into the grill by the driver's head. "The Palace Royale," he said; then he settled back on the plush red velvet next to Andrew Onderdonk. As the carriage lurched forward, the two men puffed on their Havana cigars, filling the small compartment with blue-grey smoke.

"Well, how did it go?" Onderdonk asked.

"He agreed. And at four thousand acres." Onderdonk whistled in amazement. "I know," Van Horne said. "Incredible, isn't it? I started at five, thinking we would settle around two, but the old boy panicked and offered four, plus a thousand acres per year."

Onderdonk laughed out loud and slapped Van Horne's knee. "Well then, we must advise Montreal. Vancouver will be the final terminus."

Van Horne smiled slyly and blew out a long, thin stream of grey smoke. Rain thundered on the roof and rumbled through the cab as if it were the inside of a kettledrum. "Already done," he said. "I told them a month ago."

"You knew he'd agree?" Onderdonk asked.

Van Horne shrugged. "I thought he might, but it really didn't matter. Port Moody is quite unsuitable; water's too shallow. I decided to bring the rail to Vancouver long ago, whether Cains agreed or not. As it is, his gracious gift of four thousand acres, plus one thousand a year, is simply an added bonus."

Amor De Cosmos tapped the new walking stick Johann had given him to replace his broken cane on the floorboards and waited for his eyes to adjust to the darkness. Abby leaned against the wall next to him and smiled. She had not been able to retire as she had planned. For months she had tried to devote heself to her painting, but Galer Mills was in her blood. She constantly found herself drifting, uncontrollably, back to the office to leaf through the ledgers and check on orders, and always the sawmill itself was like a narcotic to her, luring her into its warm, cavernous interior. She loved the shafts of sunlight angling through the dusty air, its small, grimy windows, its rich, spicy smells of cedar, spruce, and fir. This was her life now. Ahead she could see the dim outline of Johann crouched on the catwalk, dwarfed by the huge whizzing blade of the Big Hoe as it screamed painfully through a cedar log. Further back was her youngest son, Angus, his shirt-sleeves rolled up, sweat gleaming on his arms, as he struggled to tighten the iron teeth that would hold the next log in place as it moved through the saw. Abby looked away. Even with his slim fourteen-year-old body he looked like Matthew in the dim light.

As the blade howled through the end of the log and the huge cedar plank clattered to the deck, Abby hurried forward and tapped Johann on the shoulder. "We're ready," she shouted. Johann flipped a switch and the saw whined to a stop. Abby lowered her voice. "Most of the timber crews voted this morning, but Burgess had a few of them turned away because they couldn't prove their residency." Abby slapped a bundle of paper against the palm of her hand. "I've drawn up rental receipts for them, plus all of the millhands. Everyone's going to vote."

"You're certain they're not going to vote for Burgess?" Johann asked. Abby's eyes widened and Johann laughed. "Just kidding, Mrs. Galer. Half our men quit Cains to come work here; they're not about to side with Burgess." He wiped his hands on an oily rag and tossed it into a metal bucket. "I'll go round 'em up and shut off the boilers," he said as he hurried off.

Abby looked around for De Cosmos and saw him jabbing his yew-wood stick at the battered cedar log Angus had just secured to the saw-bed. A strand of thick black hair had jiggled loose, and it dangled across his face. Abby frowned. He had not spoken since the night of the rally. For hours on end he sat on the front porch, a glass of whisky by his chair, staring blankly at the curtain of rain pouring from the eaves and the grey inlet beyond, unreachable, inconsolable, lost in a world of his own. When Abby told him she had withdrawn his candidacy, he had looked up at her, bewildered, the veins at his temples bulging as he strained to understand, to recognize her, then slowly his eyelids closed and tears began to roll down his cheeks.

Yesterday, in frustration, she had marched onto the porch, grabbed the glass out of his hand, and flung it over the railing. Instantly De Cosmos had jumped to his feet and swung his new walking stick over her head. He had hovered there a moment, his face twisted in confusion; then he had turned on his heel, stormed down to the beach, and rowed across to Gastown. At midnight Constable Miller had returned him, unconscious, vomit splattered down the front of his black frock-coat, and together he and Johann had carried him up to bed. There was no question of sending him back to Victoria now; he could not look after himself.

"Martin goin' to vote?" Angus asked.

Abby turned and smiled weakly at him. "He's twenty-one." The boy jammed his hands in the pockets of his tin pants and kicked at a wood shaving on the floor. She wrapped her arm around his shoulder. "Life's too short to want to be hurrying it, Angus." He scowled at her doubtfully, then stared at his boots. "All right," Abby said. "Why don't you go get cleaned up and come with us? You can see how it's done, so you'll be ready when it's your turn."

The scowl vanished. "Jeezly spit, you bet," the boy cried.

Abby was shocked by her son's language. "Angus," she began. But it was too late. He had wriggled free and run out of the mill. Abby sighed and shook her head.

Slowly, one by one, the machines around her sputtered and coughed to a stop — the pony saw, the Chinee trimmer, the clattering lath mill — until the only sound was the "chug-phtt" of the little shingle saw deep in the basement; then it too stopped and the quivering floorboards under her feet were still. Abby looked around at the vast mill. A fine white dust settled over the machinery like snow. The silence left a ringing in her ears. It hadn't been this quiet since before the price war.

"Mrs. Galer," De Cosmos called. His voice was hoarse and reedy. He leaned closer to the huge cedar log and pried into a scar on its side with the tip of his walking stick. "Mrs. Galer . . . ?" He peeled back a small piece of bark and uncovered the battered head of a large iron spike.

Suddenly from overhead came a shrill screech. De Cosmos whirled round and looked up. A small crow was battering itself

furiously against a tiny window in the ceiling, talons outstretched, its black wings a frantic blur against the bright square
of light. De Cosmos's mouth fell open. He stared up at the panicked bird, mesmerized, and shielded his face with his arm.

"Mrs. Galer," Johann called. He stood in the entrance to the
mill with his hands on his hips, a black silhouette against the
harsh sunlight. "They're all ready. Better hurry."

Abby placed her hand on De Cosmos's shoulder and shuddered
inwardly at the look of anguish on his face, the blank, bewildered
expression in his eyes. "It's all right, Amor," she said softly. "It's
just a bird; he'll find his way out." She took his arm and led him
slowly, gently, out of the mill.

Behind them, in the vast, dark room, where rays of sunlight
criss-crossed through the shadows and the machinery hunched
in silence under its gathering layers of fine, pale dust, the small
crow continued to batter itself against the pane of glass and the
huge cedar log waited before the saw.

Abby squeezed through the crowd on the boardwalk, ducked
under the old maple, and smoothed the skirt of her new burgun-
dy dress under her as she perched on the edge of a weathered
old bench that circled the tree's trunk. She was glad De Cosmos
had insisted on following some friends to the Sunnyside Saloon;
it felt good to be alone. And at least he's talking again, she
thought. The shadowy pattern of leaves shifted over the dirt at
her feet as the huge maple rustled in the late spring breeze.
Unconsciously her foot began to tap to the rhythm of Malcolm
MacLean's brass band as it blared out "Hail to the Chief" from
the porch of the Deighton Hotel. Dust swirled in front of her as a
rickety old dray, overloaded with lumber, squeezed through the
crowded square and rumbled down Water Street.

She twisted on the bench to look at the long line of voters
standing in the street out in front of the tiny government cottage
that served as courthouse, jail, and the private residence of Constable Miller. Martin was third from the end. A large crock of
whisky passed down the line from hand to hand, and when it
reached him he looked up and down the street before taking a
quick swig and passing it on. Abby smiled; even at twenty-one it
still mattered to him what she thought. Across the road, Clarissa
leaned out of an upper window of the Palace Royale and taunted
the men below.

Abby glanced at the man next to her, who was busy peeling a

thick tier of paper slips from the bottom of a land lease. She recognized him as George Black, the butcher, an ardent MacLean supporter. She leaned closer. "How many men have voted on that one lease?" she whispered. The butcher gazed at her through reproachful, half-lidded eyes and nibbled at the ends of his bushy black walrus moustache. "Don't worry," she said. "I'm on your side."

George Black smiled and winked at her. "Eleven. So far," he said. He jerked his thumb at a lanky man on crutches who was leaning against the bench next to him. "Chester here'll be the twelfth."

Abby winked back. "Good work," she whispered.

An elderly man tumbled down the steps of the Deighton Hotel and lay still in the street. Abby shuddered. The crowd on the boardwalk ignored him as Constable Miller grabbed his coat collar and dragged him off to join the dozen or so other men who were already sleeping it off in the backyard of Government Cottage. Chester took the land lease with his name freshly pasted on the bottom and limped off to join the line of voters.

Abby gazed down the main street, past the new soda-water factory, towards the Regina Hotel at the intersection of Abbott and Water. How the town had changed. She guessed there were upwards of seven hundred buildings stretched along the beach and scattered up the hillside to the south: hotels, saloons, houses, shops, stables, offices, warehouses — and the boom was just beginning. Only yesterday Vancouver had been named the official terminus of the Canadian Pacific Railway, and already men in black coats and bowler hats were scrabbling over the dense jumble of shattered trees that blanketed the new clearing to the west. Smoke billowed up from huge piles of slash on the C.P.R. lot, shrouding the "For Sale" signs that were jammed into the tangle of debris ten feet above the ground. Nowhere was the earth visible, yet the lots changed hands like chips in a poker game. "Vancouver," Abby thought. She shook her head slowly and smiled. To her it was still Gastown.

The playing of the band petered out in a confusion of hoots and squawks as everyone in the street hushed and turned to the west. Silence. "Back to China," someone shouted. Silence again; then a low, menacing rumble swept through the crowd. Abby hurried to the raised porch of the Deighton Hotel to get a better view.

Carky and three men from Cains's mill marched slowly up the

street past the old maple tree, towards Government Cottage. Nearly one hundred Chinese in blue peasant jackets and black pants shuffled nervously behind them in single file. They stopped at the end of the line of voters. A large, burly man who had been checking papers at the door stared at the Chinese, his mouth hanging loosely open. "Hey, get 'em outa here," he shouted. Carky stared sullenly at the ground, his arms folded across his chest.

"I said, get 'em out," the big man roared as he charged down the line. From all along the street, the crowd gravitated towards the disturbance.

"Has every man no a right to vote?" Carky shouted.

"Votin' is for civilized men," George Black yelled. "Tell that to Wiley Burgess." The crowd roared their approval.

The burly man towered over Carky. "No Indians and no Chinks; that's the law." He poked a stubby finger at Carky's shoulder. "Now, move."

A green-glass bottle spun through the air and thudded against the side of a Chinese's head. He screamed and slumped to the ground. The crowd surged forward.

Abby gripped the porch railing as the men in the band dropped their instruments and stampeded into the road. Women scurried for cover. The frightened Chinese scattered and raced down the street, rocks whizzing through the air around them, the mob of whites roaring behind them, waving clubs and fists. Men poured out of the Sunnyside Saloon. Abby watched, horrified, as Amor De Cosmos charged down the hotel steps, his coat-tails flying behind him, and kicked at the legs of a panicked Oriental, who stumbled and skidded through the dust. Five men pounced on him. George Black ripped a dead branch from the old maple tree and chased after the mob as it swarmed out of town.

In a moment the square was empty. Abby stepped gingerly down from the porch of the Deighton Hotel into the strangely quiet street. Dust scattered on the wind. She felt cold and fragile. In the new clearing to the west she could see the angry crowd clambering and stumbling over the thick pile of debris as the first of the Chinese jumped down and disappeared into the woods. Women peered cautiously from store-front windows and a few men picked their way uncertainly through the street where a dozen Chinese sprawled in the dust, moaning and struggling to stand. A few lay still and pale, arms and legs twisted into unnatural positions, red blood against their blue jackets. "Back to China. . . . Back to China. . . ." The angry roar drifted on the light spring breeze from deep in the forest on the far side of the new city.

Back to China . . . , Mei-fu thought. Her fingers trembled as she dropped the last gold coin into the hem of her dress and picked up her needle. Firelight sparkled and glowed from her emerald ring. Back to China. . . . There I will be as nothing, she thought. Oh, I will still have money — what little I can carry with me — but that will not last long, and in China, even a woman with money must lower her eyes before a man.

She looked around the room at the precious belongings she must leave behind: the ornate grandfather clock from France, her floor-length oval mirror from Italy, her beautiful gowns from San Francisco, her new Degas painting, and her ivory statues. And then there was the Palace Royale itself and the precious land she had built it on, her black-lacquered carriage and fine white horses, the deed to three hundred acres of prime land on the very edge of the booming new city, her servants, her girls — over twenty years of hard work.

Even Andrew Onderdonk could not be told of her departure. Mei-fu's lower lip quivered as she bit through the thread. "He's married anyway," she muttered as she flung the heavy dress on a chair and stormed across the room to the big oval mirror. "Besides, there will be other Andrew Onderdonks, even in China." But she knew as she said it there would not.

She slipped out of her chemise and stood naked in front of the mirror. Her breasts sagged, and over the years her waist had thickened. She turned and looked over her shoulder at her buttocks. They too were falling. She studied her face. It at least has not aged badly, she thought, and my hair has not yet greyed; but that will come. She looked at the crow's-feet fanning out from the corners of her eyes and at the small cushiony pads which had begun to appear on her throat.

She picked up a heavy sapphire necklace from the table beside the mirror and fastened it round her neck. It helped. She twisted from side to side and watched the firelight dance over the stones. Yes, it definitely helped, but still, she thought, I'm forty-eight years old — too old to be starting over.

She frowned, and turned away from the mirror; then she began to dress quickly: chemise, stockings, drawers, waist petticoat, corset, money belt — she fingered its crisp padding of American cash, with which she would pay their passage to Hong Kong — bustle, petticoats, underskirt, and, finally, the heavy black travelling dress. Mei-fu wrinkled her nose at it. The wide, flowing skirt was ten years out of date, but its hem could hold much more gold than the modern tailored fashions. She pulled it over her head and groaned at the weight of it. For a moment she wondered if she had loaded it with too many coins, but she quickly forced the thought out of her mind and hurried to open the window.

The night air was cool and fresh and the forest at the back of the Palace Royale swayed in the light spring breeze. She could not see the front street but she could imagine the scene as she listened to the sounds of the election celebration drifting on the wind: shouting, singing, laughter, the thunder of horses' hooves charging down the road, the off-key braying of Malcolm Mac-Lean's brass band as the drunken musicians played "Hail to the Chief" for the hundredth time, occasional gunshots, and the distant tinkle of shattering glass. My girls will be busy tonight, Mei-fu thought.

An hour before, she had watched from an upstairs window as the drunken mob paraded MacLean through the street on their shoulders. He had demanded to be put down after he knocked his head on a branch of the old maple. The crowd had placed him on the porch of the Deighton Hotel, where he smoothed his ruffled clothes and announced there would be fireworks at eight o'clock. Mei-fu had cheered louder than anyone. She was certain it was a blessing from the gods that at the very hour she and Wu Lee were to escape, the entire town would be watching the sky.

Mei-fu tapped her fingers on the windowsill to the rhythm of the squawking band and smiled. She was glad Wiley Burgess had lost the election. If that slimy eel were mayor, she thought, surely he would work my girls to death and expect it for free. Her smiled faded. "My girls . . . ," she whispered.

Her fingers shook as she lit the lantern and placed it on the table by the window. She checked her small travelling bag once more, then paced around the room. It was almost eight o'clock. She stopped in front of the big oval mirror and studied her appearance yet again. A lock of hair had fallen loose from the gold-and-diamond clasp at the back of her head. As she lifted her hand to fix it, she stopped.

The weighted hem of her dress banged against her ankles as she ran to her chiffonier and rummaged through drawer after drawer, flinging the contents onto the floor behind her, until at last she found it — the old rosewood comb Chang had given her so many years ago. Yellow paint from its decoration of carved wooden butterflies flaked off in her hand.

As the grandfather clock began to chime eight o'clock, the first of the skyrockets whistled up into the night. Quickly she unhooked the diamond clasp, jammed it in her dress pocket, and worked the comb into her hair. She ran to the window and leaned out. "Wu Lee," she whispered.

The salal bushes below her rustled and a shadow loomed up. She ran to get her bag, and when she turned back to the window, Wu Lee had already hooked one leg over the casement. "No," she hissed. "There's no time for visiting. We must take advantage of this cover the gods have so graciously given us. Quickly now, there's a boat waiting on the beach to take us to Victoria, and from there I've booked passage to San Francisco."

"You mean you're coming with me?" Wu Lee said.

"Of course," Mei-fu whispered. "Surely you don't think I am about to lose my only son. Now help your poor old mother out of here."

She passed her bag to him and awkwardly straddled the casement as she dragged the heavy folds of her dress through the window and flopped down into the bushes. A blood-red starburst exploded overhead. "Quickly," she said. "This way."

She took his hand and ran behind the Deighton Hotel, then on through the jumbled backyards of stores and houses, dodging packing crates, lumber, stumps, and trash. At the back of the butcher shop George Black's old German shepherd lumbered to its feet and barked furiously. Mei-fu's heart pounded. She darted down a narrow passage that led to the main street and stopped, breathing heavily. Already she was regretting the extra gold in the hem of her dress.

She peeked around the corner. The crowd was at the far end of the street. When she heard the whine of the next rocket whizzing up into the sky, she squeezed Wu Lee's hand and they raced across the road and into a wooded lot next to Old Hoisting

Gear's church. Through a small stand of jackpine, a bright white starburst shimmered in the black waters of Burrard Inlet fifty yards ahead. As Mei-fu ran, she felt her dress snag and tear on a branch and heard the light tinkle of gold falling out. She stopped and dropped to her knees, groping in the dirt for the lost coins.

"Come on," Wu Lee hissed.

"But this is gold, damn you," Mei-fu cried. The sky lit up with a rapid-fire burst of staccato explosions.

"Come on," Wu Lee shouted.

Mei-fu clutched at the tear in her dress as her son lifted her to her feet and dragged her onto the beach.

She ran, holding the hem of her dress high to keep the gold from falling out.

"Is that the ship?" Wu Lee asked.

Mei-fu looked at the small white boat rocking on the waves and nodded. Her heart pounded. She could not catch her breath. The sound of the rockets echoed off the mountains to the north.

"Hold it right there," a voice shouted. Men appeared at the edge of the woods, guns drawn and levelled. "You're under arrest." Mei-fu recognized the hard, metallic voice of Constable Miller. Wu Lee tugged hard on her arm and she raced across the sand in a final effort, her eyes fixed on the small white boat, but as they waded into the water the engines roared and it sped away. She whirled round to face the men advancing along the beach: Jonas Cains, Wiley Burgess, the town's single police officer, a half-dozen others.

Wu Lee reached inside his coat, pulled out the pearl-handled revolver, and aimed it at Constable Miller. "No!" Mei-fu screamed. She dropped the hem of her dress, lunged at the gun, and pushed it skyward, where the sound of the bullet being fired was drowned out by the explosions overhead.

The men circled round and pinned Wu Lee's arms behind his back. Mei-fu heard the ringing sound of a woman's laughter, and through her tears she could see the white dress and red hair of Caroline Burgess, who was standing on the beach at the edge of the water. As the fireworks boomed and crackled overhead, blue and blood-red against the black night sky, their thin trails of grey smoke shredding on the cool wind, the gold coins trickled out of Mei-fu's dress and settled into the soft sand, a few feet from shore.

"You're fired," Wiley shouted. He swayed on his feet and

shielded his bloodshot eyes from the grey-yellow light of dawn as it seeped through the doorway of the silent mill. His detachable collar dangled across his shirt-front from one button, and the rooster-tail at the back of his head quivered in the light breeze. He had been up all night.

"But, Mr. Burgess —" Carky said as he fidgeted with the wrench he had been using to repair the boiler.

"A bloody simple little job," Wiley raged. "Seventeen votes! I lost the election by seventeen Christly, lousy, bloody votes. If even a quarter of those Chinks had voted, I'd have won. But no. You couldn't even arrange that."

"But, Mr. Burgess," Carky said, "they drove us off, don't you see."

"They drove us off," Wiley mimicked in a whining voice. "There's no place in this mill for a man who can't do a simple job. Now get out."

Carky stiffened and his face flushed as the first of the Chinese labourers tiptoed into the dark mill, staring wide-eyed at the two shouting men. "I think you should be waiting for Mr. Cains to come back from San Francisco. He'll be having something to say about this."

"I run this mill," Wiley shrieked. "I'm the manager and I'll bloody well fire whoever I want to."

"But you see, Mr. Burgess. I've been doing a certain spot of work for Mr. Cains, don't you see, and he's promised me a partnership for it. A quarter share."

Wiley roared with laughter. "Oh, I'm well aware of the filthy spot of work you've been up to, you stinking old buzzard. And if you truly thought he'd give you even a tenth of this mill for it, then you're an even bigger fool than I thought. Cains'd burn this place down before he'd cut in scum like you. Now, get out. Do you hear me? You're fired."

Carky threw the wrench onto the boards at Wiley's feet and stormed out of the mill.

As the morning sun rose over the backbone of Seymour Mountain, shadows slipped up its steeply wooded slopes. Abby stood at the end of Galer Mills' wharf and checked her figures again. The inlet sparkled crisply, silver and bright blue, as it lapped at the pilings below her. She shaded her eyes with her hand and looked up at the man on the deck of the half-loaded ship. "Looks like we're short two thousand feet of railway ties. I'll ask Johann if he knows anything about it." Abby turned towards the mill, then called over her shoulder, "And keep those men working as best you can; they're none too chipper after yesterday's celebration."

She hurried across the sawdust-strewn yard where bluejays chattered and darted through the thin wisps of steam wafting up from last night's dew. To her right the eastern sky faded from orange to pale pink as the first rays of daylight slid down steep mountain slopes into cool rain-forest canyons.

"Johann," she called. The cavernous mill was cold, dark, and only half alive. The lesser machines coughed and sputtered as men moved slowly through the shadows, coaxing them into life, but the main saw was already in full howl, ripping its first cut through the huge old cedar. Johann flipped a switch and the log stopped. "We're missing some ties down at the dock," Abby said. "Can you come?"

He nodded, and waved to Angus as he climbed up out of the catwalk. "Take over here, will you? I'll be back in a shake."

"Sure thing," Angus shouted. He grinned as he hurried around the great blade and clambered down into the narrow track before the saw. He loved to run the Big Hoe, and it was only recently that Johann had begun to trust him with it.

"Not too fast," Johann shouted. "It's a big block. Just keep it steady."

Angus waved over his shoulder and flipped the switch. The saw screamed as it bit into the moving log.

Abby stopped in the doorway and turned to watch her son crouched before the six-foot butt of the advancing red cedar, gauging the width of the board being sliced from its side. She could still not get used to the idea of him running the huge machine alone. How fast he has grown, she thought. How terribly fast. He spun a wheel to shift the rear of the saw-bed and inched back as the log advanced slowly towards him. She shook her head sadly, and was turning towards the bright morning light when she heard the deadly high-pitched squeal of metal on metal and whirled round, her heart pounding.

Men in every corner of the mill stood frozen at their posts, staring at the ribbon of sparks showering out of the Big Hoe. "Run," Abby screamed. The boy jumped to his feet and turned to flee. Abby charged towards him but Johann grabbed her from behind and knocked her to the floor. She heard the grinding buzz as the saw jammed, then the sound of the shattering blade. Fragments of steel exploded through the mill, punching holes in the walls and the roof. Angus crumpled as a piece of the blade sliced across the back of his right knee and another lodged in his side.

In an instant it was over. Abby kicked free from Johann's arms and ran to the body sprawled on the floor. Men scrambled out from behind machines and grabbed automatically at the fire buckets hung on the walls to douse the flames racing through the giant old cedar.

Deep in the basement, the shingle sawyer backed away from his saw in horror as blood seeped through the cracks in the ceiling and dripped onto the blade in front of him.

CHAPTER THIRTEEN

JUNE 13 1886 ABBY WADDED HER HANDKERCHIEF into a damp ball, dropped it onto her office desk, and walked to the open window. A strong wind blew from the west, rolling wave after wave of sultry air up the inlet. She had never seen it so hot. Indeed, no one in the area could remember it ever being this hot—and this early in the year! For weeks the temperature had hovered near ninety degrees until the lush green rain forest had been seared brown, dry, and brittle. Men moved slowly along the beach, stripped of their woollen shirts, their bodies sagging under the blazing sun as they rolled huge logs into the floating stockpile next to the mill. The mill. . . . How she hated it now. It hunched in its bed of sawdust like a sleeping wolf, still, silent, and deadly. It would take months to get a new blade from San Francisco.

She glanced up at the big white house shimmering in heat risers on the hill and thought of Angus thrashing on the bed in his sweltering room, the sheet underneath him soaked with sweat.

"Excuse me, Mrs. Galer?"

Abby turned round and stiffened. Carky stood swaying awkwardly in the open doorway, his grizzled beard stained yellow with snoose, a pair of red suspenders framing the small pot-belly protruding under his woollen longjohns.

"How dare you come here?" she snarled.

Carky twisted the brim of his felt hat nervously in front of him. "I've hear'd about your wee bairn," he said softly. His words slurred together. "Ah, I'm sorry. Truly sorry. Will he be gettin' better, ma'am?"

"Did Cains send you here?" Abby snapped. "Does he want to gloat over how he butchered my son? Well, the boy may never walk properly again. That should make him happy."

Carky shifted uneasily on his feet. "I dinna work for Cains nae more, ma'am, and I'm sorry 'bout your bairn."

"Sorry," Abby sneered. "Like hell you are. It wouldn't surprise me if you spiked that log yourself."

Carky burped and glanced nervously up from his hat. "Aye," he mumbled. "I did."

"What?"

"It's no what you think, Mrs. Galer. Cains ordered me to do it and I didna stop to think that anyone would be gettin' hurt. I—he—just wanted to break your saw—to put a stop to this price war, don't you see?"

Abby flew at him in a rage and slashed the back of her bunched fist across the side of his face. "You bastard!" she screamed. She hit him again and again across his head, shoulders, and chest. He stood stiffly under her onslaught without defending himself. "Get out," she shrieked. "Get out of here!"

"I can gie ye Cains's head, lassie."

Abby stopped, her fist raised over her head. "What?"

Carky sniffed and wiped the trickle of blood dribbling from his nose onto the back of his sleeve. "Do ye no see, Mrs. Galer? It's Cains has done you dirt all these years. If it hadna been me spiked them logs he'd a found someone else, right enough. It's Cains you want to thrash, no me."

"Oh, and I suppose you'd go into court and testify against him," Abby jeered.

"I would."

She studied him carefully and frowned. "You're drunk," she sneered.

"Aye. But not so's I don't know my own mind."

"And you know you'd go to jail for what you've done?"

"I'm sixty-eight years old, Mrs. Galer." He grinned. "Least, as near as I can figure. It's doin' Cains's dirty work I've spent most of my life—and I've nothing to show for it but a pocketful of promises, he's seen to that. I canna even buy a proper meal right now." Carky sniffed back the blood trickling from his nose and stared at his hat. "It was Burgess fired me and I reckon Cains'd be takin' me back now, just to keep me quiet. But I'll be damned if I'll go," he snapped. "He's the devil himself, Mrs. Galer; full of promises and temptations—but he never intended to pay. Never. I know that now. It's laughin' behind my back he's been doin'. He's used me awful, Mrs. Galer, and always kept me poor so's I'd stay in his hip pocket. Well, I'll no stand it nae more. He'll pay now; by the saints he'll pay."

Carky took a deep breath and lowered his voice. "I'll no go to jail if you dinna press charges agin me, Mrs. Galer, but even if you've a mind to, I'll still be doin' it. I didna want to hurt anyone, ma'am, least of all your wee lad—I've no the stomach for it. It's a sorry life I've led and I've only a short time left to set it right, and nary a penny in my pocket. Jail'd no be such a bad place, knowin' Cains was there with me."

Abby walked to the window and looked out at the pale-green inlet, shimmering under the hot sun. The wind from the west was rising, hot and dry, whipping the water into silver whitecaps. Dragons' breath, she thought, that's what Matthew called the hot summer winds. "Did he murder my husband?" she asked.

"Beggin' your pardon, ma'am?"

"Cains. The *Orpheus* was his ship. Did he order it to ram the *Pacific* so he could kill my husband?"

"Och, no, ma'am. I was with him when we were hearin' the news and it's as shocked as anyone else he was. Cains is a devil, to be sure, but even he would no do such a thing."

Abby sniffed doubtfully. All these years, she thought, and I've been certain it was him. He doesn't know; how could he? It had to be Cains. It had to be.

She turned and leaned against the windowsill, her arms folded in front of her. "Does anyone else know about the spiking of my logs?"

"None as'd help," Carky said. "Only Cains and Wiley Burgess know."

Abby bit her lower lip and considered his proposition. "I appreciate what you're offering to do," she said. "But Cains is a powerful and wealthy man. It would take more than your testimony to convict him. The judge will believe that you simply want revenge for being fired. It's your word against his."

"Aye. I was thinkin' the same thing," Carky said. "But it's a long list of crimes the man has committed, and there is one can be supported by more'n my word alone." He fished in his coat pocket and pulled out a yellowed piece of rice-paper. "Do you remember Jimmy, the boatman?"

"Yes," Abby said. "The poor simpleton that was murdered by the Fenians."

"It was Cains had him murdered," Carky snapped.

"What?"

"And there wasna goin' to be any Fenian invasion. It was all a hoax. I dinna ken fit he was after, but it had summat to do with scarin' the east into buildin' the railroad. He offered me three thousand in gold to kill the poor bastard — beg pardon, ma'am — and to pin a note to him makin' it look like them Fenians done it. But like I told you, I've no stomach for maimin' and murder. When I wouldna do it, he offered the job to a wily little Chink what worked at the mill. And it's a sharp wee fellow he was, too; didna trust Cains. He writ it all out, here." Carky handed her the piece of rice-paper.

"It's in Chinee, ye ken, but his widow's writ it down in proper English on the back. It's all there: how he was to be knifin' poor Jimmy and stringin' 'im up on the Governor's porch; how Cains was to pay 'im four thousand dollars; even the wee bit a verse he was to pin to the body."

Abby's eyes widened as she read the paper.

"Suppose it was one of them premonitions he'd been havin' — figured he might not be livin' to collect his money — and it's right enough he was too."

"Did Cains kill the Chinaman?" Abby asked.

"I dinna ken, ma'am, but more'n likely he did. It was supposed to have been an accident in the mill the very next day, but I was no there to see it. Chang was all alone at the time, but I'm sure Cains did summat to the saw to make it happen.

"'Twas a good two years afore his Chinee widow and her bairn shows up at the mill demandin' to see Cains, and I knew right enough what was up, so I hid by the office window and heard the whole thing. That's how I was findin' out about the letter. Cains snatched it away from her and tore it up, thinkin' that would be endin' the whole matter." Carky chuckled. "But she was a smart lass; she'd made a copy and hid the original, and she told him so, too, bold as brass. Then Cains starts to laughin'. He didna deny a thing. Said it was his own word agin that of a dead man, and if ever she was after causin' him trouble, he'd be throwin' her in jail for slanderin' and there she'd stay till her teeth rotted out. Scared the bejesus outa her, he did. She was a strange woman in a strange land and didna know what to do but let the matter drop.

"It's a sorry man I was, knowin' I had the proof to be backin' her up, but I've bin runnin' with the devil so long it was hard to turn my back, ye ken? Then yesterday I was thinkin' how to do the bastard dirt when I remembers the letter and goes to see the Chinee widow. It's full of hate she is still. Cains murdered her husband and now his daughter's turned her only son in to the police. They'll be hangin' him soon enough. Och, she's fair burnin' to tell her story to a judge."

"Do you know what this means?" Abby cried. "We've got him. By God, we've got him." She ran to the door and shouted at Johann, who was working in the yard. "Fire up the *Cariboo Fly*. We're going to see Cains. Martin," she shouted. "Over here."

"Cains, ma'am?" Carky said. "Do ye no think it's Constable Miller you should be goin' to see?"

Abby turned to face him, her green eyes glittering and hard as jade. "Johann will go for the Constable," she barked. "But I'll see Cains myself first. I've paid for that right — he butchered my son and tried to ruin my husband — and by God I'll see him squirm."

"No, ma'am," Carky whined. "It's no like that."

Abby chuckled as she gingerly folded the precious rice paper and slipped it into her dress pocket. Then she ran down the dusty path to the beach.

Ho-sun Lee wiped the sweat from his brow and squinted his eyes against the blowing smoke as he gazed out over Burrard Inlet. "*Dew neh loh moh*," he swore. "Too bloody hot." Ships skittered over the dazzling green water, their white sails billowing full and taut in the unusually hot summer wind. The reflection hurt his eyes.

He turned back to the huge pile of burning slash and hoisted another log onto the windbreak beside it. All along the beach, enormous fires burned behind their protective fences as a vast section of the rain forest was reduced to ash to make room for the new railway station. Long plumes of smoke curled up from the C.P.R. lot and drifted towards the new town of Vancouver. To the west he could see the small joss-house at the beginning of Fantan Alley, and he smiled, blessing the gods again for sending him to work so close to Yum-koo. But then, since the terrible incident at Farr's Bluff, his work crew had gotten all the best jobs. He no longer slept in a tent. At night he would shoulder his long double-bitted axe and march proudly down Fantan Alley to his own house, where his wife and his strong, healthy boy would be waiting for him with cold tea and warm rice flavoured with seaweed and dried fish. Life was grand.

On impulse he set his axe against a log, pulled out his new wooden dentures, and smiled. He never grew tired of looking at them; they were a great treasure, carved by the finest craftsman in all of Chinatown. Granted, they had cost an entire year of his savings, but as he watched the sunlight gleaming off the white paint, he was certain it had been a wise purchase. The teeth were smiling back at him. He popped the dentures back into his mouth and returned to his work.

Just after noon, as the sun slanted down, hot and blinding, Ho-sun Lee straightened up with a strange prickling feeling at the back of his neck. The wind had stopped. Flames from the clearing fires spaced along the beach towered straight up in the still air.

Then, in an instant, the wind came again, hot and fierce, this time from the east, roaring up the inlet and driving the flames into their windbreaks. Sparks showered out of the huge wooden piles and spiralled up, caught in the wind. Ho-sun Lee grabbed his jacket from a nearby stump and beat at the small fires springing up around him. They leapt from one spot to the next, feeding on the tinder-dry slash.

Further down the beach, men were throwing down their tools and fleeing to the inlet. Within seconds, two-thirds of the clearing was ablaze. Ho-sun Lee took one last look at the raging fire, then dropped his jacket as flames licked at his pant leg, and ran towards the water. Over his shoulder he could see the vast orange cloud of sparks and embers drifting towards the wooden homes of Vancouver.

Silver spray flew up from the prow of the *Cariboo Fly*, glittering in the hot sunlight, as the ship lurched over the crest of a large wave and rolled down into the next trough. The inlet stretched ahead of her, a pale milky-green studded with shifting whitecaps. Pleasure sloops and sailboats tacked effortlessly across the water, the small figures on their decks waving as the ship passed.

Abby braced her hand against the bow railing and turned to face De Cosmos. The hot westerly wind whistled through her hair, and her white muslin dress whipped about her legs. "We've got him," she shouted. "After all these years, we've got him."

De Cosmos stared blankly ahead at the thick coils of smoke billowing up from the C.P.R. lot.

"Don't you understand?" Abby shouted. "It was Cains who set us up for the Texada Scandal, then told the newspapers about it." The clang of the Sunday-school bell drifted over the water from Old Hoisting Gear's church. Abby placed her hand on De Cosmos's shoulder. "He ruined your career, Amor, but you can pay him back now." Sparks spiralled up from the C.P.R. lot, crimson and orange against the tinder-dry forest. "We've got him, Amor. We've got him."

Slowly De Cosmos raised his arm, his long thin fingers trembling, and pointed towards the beach.

Sitka closed the door of Johnny Snauq's cabin behind her, and wrinkled her nose at the thick pall of smoke wafting up the hillside from the C.P.R. lot. How can they stand it? she wondered. For weeks the fires have burned, and still there is not enough land cleared for the greedy pinkmen. What if it never stops? My grandchild will be smoked like a salmon.

She looked down at the chubby, serious face of the child beside her and smiled. He was the son of Eva and Johnny. He was short and plump, with fine dark skin, yet he had her daughter's curly auburn hair. "It is hard to believe there is any of the First People's blood in you, Thomas." The boy smiled up at her, pleased. "Except maybe in your eyes," she added. They were fine eyes, black, shining, unfathomable; they took in everything, revealed nothing. My little mystery boy, Sitka thought.

She took Thomas's hand and started down the forest trail that led to Gastown and the beach. Dry needles crunched under her bare feet and swirled around her ankles like dust. Huge fir trees creaked and swayed overhead, and the delicate sword-ferns lining the path lay limp in the heat, bent backward, their pale-green undersides tossing in the hot wind. Sitka loosened the spruce-root fastening on her old cedar-bark cape.

"Are we going to the whispering tree, Grandmother?" Thomas asked.

"Yes."

The boy glanced nervously at the midday sun, blurred and yellow-grey through the thick blanket of smoke. "Will we be back in time for supper?"

Sitka smiled as she brushed a strand of white hair back from her face. "No. We will spend the night on the mountain." The boy scowled. "Come, Thomas," Sitka said as she put her arm around his shoulder. "It will be a great adventure."

The black eyes stared at her. "Why do we have to

"You want to see it, don't you?" Sitka said.

"Yes, but why don't we just look at it and come back for supper? Do we have to stay all night? What are we going to do?"

"Maybe we will see a sign," Sitka said.

Again the dark eyes flashed at her. "What sort of a sign?"

"I don't know."

"Then how will we know what it means?"

"Enough," Sitka said. "You ask too many questions." She took her arm off his shoulder and pushed him roughly ahead. "Just walk."

The boy trudged along the path in silence, while Sitka marched sullenly behind, ashamed of herself for treating him badly. But it was all so confusing. Bring your children up white, Lady Douglas had warned, and this she had done, but now Eva had married an Indian and produced a child whose face looked so much like that of Cutick, her own son, who had been butchered by the northern raiding party a lifetime ago, that it was painful to look at him. Yet Eva and Johnny lived in a white man's lodge, with a wooden floor, pale-yellow curtains at the windows, and a stone hearth for their house fire.

Sitka stopped at the bottom of the hill, wracked by a dry, aching cough. The smoke was thicker than usual today.

"Are you all right, Grandmother?" Thomas asked.

Sitka nodded, took the boy's hand, and led him through the maze of stumps that littered the newest of Vancouver's streets. The sound of hammers rang out from the double row of clap-board houses lining the road.

What if Lady Douglas was wrong? she thought. Who will tell

Thomas the legend of Skwinatqa, his great-great-great-great-grandfather, who led the First People south from the Skomi-shoath River countless winters ago? Who will give him an Indian name and show him how to know his guardian spirit? Eva understands nothing of these matters.

The wind suddenly stopped, then roared up the road from the east, whipping the shreds of Sitka's cedar-bark skirt around her bony knees. I am sixty years old, she thought. My hair has turned white, my skin is like an old moose-hide, and my bones ache. I haven't time to wait for another male child. This will be my last journey to the whispering tree. Please let there be a sign, she thought. There must be a sign.

At the far end of town a vast cloud of sparks billowed up from the C.P.R. lot, hovered a moment on the hot smoky wind, then rolled towards Gastown.

Wiley Burgess slipped his hand under his black frock-coat and loosened the sweaty cotton shirt from his back as he hurried down Water Street, his head bent into the warm wind, oblivious to the smoky haze around him. The town was quiet, hot and still. A few men lounged silently on the steps of the Deighton Hotel, their eyes following him like magnets as he passed. Clarissa sat in her chemise in an upstairs window of the Palace Royale, fanning herself slowly as she listened to the reproachful voice of Old Hoisting Gear booming through the open church doors across the street.

It had to be rigged, Wiley thought. I bought enough votes to win by a landslide. He dodged around a group of picnickers trudging slowly, languidly, towards the beach, their woven baskets swinging loosely from their fingertips. But it can still be fixed.

The week after the election he had registered a protest before Mr. Justice McCreight, charging fraudulent registration. Today, he and the city clerk would take the ballots and the voters' list to New Westminster for the beginning of the investigation. He was looking forward to the long coach ride with the taciturn old clerk. If anyone knows about fraudulent registration, he thought, he does. All he had to do was persuade the man to talk. He tapped the three hundred dollars in his breast pocket and smiled.

As he approached Government Cottage, the wind veered abruptly to the west and he stopped, startled by the dust clouds scudding through the square. He heard a faint roar as sparks spiralled up from the C.P.R. lot at the far end of the street and mushroomed into a bright-orange ball, churning against the smoky yellow sky. He held his breath; men jumped up from the steps of the Deighton Hotel; Clarissa leaned further out her window. The angry red cloud hesitated a moment, then rolled forward, whipped by the wind, and engulfed a flimsy clapboard shack at the end of Fantan Alley. The wind increased to a gale. Flames curled up through the roof of the wooden shanty, which shimmered in the heat for a moment, then collapsed inward. Bits of tarpaper and burning embers pirouetted through the air and settled on the joss-house at the edge of town, then on a hardware store, a factory, more houses.

"Fire!" Clarissa shouted. A woman screamed. Men poured into the street as the bell in the tower of Old Hoisting Gear's church clanged frantically. In a moment the whole eastern end of Vancouver was ablaze and flames rolled down the boardwalk, driven by the sudden gale. The people crowding into the square panicked, pushing in opposite directions as they ran for their homes and shops.

Wiley darted up the steps to Government Cottage and paused in the doorway while his eyes adjusted to the darkness. The room was small and crowded with furniture: a roll-top desk, chairs, a wide oak table still cluttered with papers from the city's first council meeting, a pot-bellied stove, a gun cabinet, storage shelves. At the back, spiderwebs dangled from a silver crucifix, which hung from the ceiling over a long wooden counter, and behind it the prisoner Wu Lee crouched on a cot in his tiny jail cell. "Where do they keep the ballots?" Wiley shouted at him.

A plump red-faced woman in a calico dress clattered down a flimsy staircase from the floor above, crying hysterically. "My baby," she shrieked. "I can't find my baby's shoes; he's got to have his shoes; he—"

Wiley grabbed her by the shoulders and shook her hard. "Mrs. Miller," he shouted. "The voters' list and ballots—where are they?"

"His shoes," the woman shrieked. "Shoes, shoes, shoes."

Wiley let go of one shoulder and slapped her across the face.

Mrs. Miller stopped screaming and pushed away, startled, her left hand pressed to her cheek; then she turned and fled back up the narrow staircase.

Across the street, Old Hoisting Gear's church rumbled and collapsed with a crash, showering embers and burning wood onto the roof of Government Cottage. Wiley whirled round and stared through the open door into the street.

The fire raged through half the town. A woman leapt from the upper floor of Deighton House and thudded into the shocked crowd below as the hotel windows blew out, showering the square with shattered glass. A terrified horse charged through the throng, pulling a riderless dray, and screamed as the wagon turned over and flipped him on his side. The old maple tree in the centre of town was ablaze, dripping fire, like rain, from its branches. The street was in chaos; people ran towards the beach, pushing, shoving, tripping. Wiley shook his head as Clarissa sprinted past the open door in her chemise, grabbed a small girl who sat crying on the boardwalk, and ran to the well in front of the burning church. Her brown legs whisked over the stone ledge, and she jumped down into the watery hole.

He turned back to face the prisoner Wu Lee, who stood at the door of the small cell, his face pale, his hands gripping the iron bars. "Tell me where the ballots are," he ordered.

"Open this door and I will show you," Wu Lee said.

"Tell me first. Then I'll open the door."

From the floor above came a loud crash and a shrill scream. Mrs. Miller ran down the narrow staircase, her shoeless baby in her arms, and fled into the street. Smoke curled through the cracks in the ceiling, and flames crackled overhead.

"There." Wu Lee pointed at the roll-top desk. Black smoke billowed out from the wall behind it. "In the desk."

Wiley scrambled over the big oak table and heaved on the latch. Locked. He looked wildly around for something to open it.

"Wu Lee!" Mei-fu screamed. She hurried into the room in a dressing gown of pale-green silk, her thick black hair tumbling loose about her shoulders, and ran to the cell. "Get him out," she shouted at Burgess. "Get him out."

Wiley ignored her. He grabbed a hatchet from the pile of kindling next to the pot-bellied stove and turned back to the desk, but it was too late. Flames curled through the narrow wooden slats of the old roll-top. "Shit." He flung the axe onto the floor and stormed out of the building as bits of burning paper flaked from the walls and swirled through the room like giant fireflies.

"The keys," Mei-fu shouted. "Where are they?"

Wu Lee choked on the thick smoke, unable to speak. He pointed at the burning desk.

Mei-fu grabbed the axe and smashed it down on the oak roll-top. The flimsy wood shattered, spraying her with sparks. She thrust her hand into the flames and felt for the key. The front window exploded. The ceiling at the back of the cell began to collapse. "Get out," Wu Lee yelled.

Mei-fu's sleeve was in flames. "I can't find it," she cried.

"Get out. Get out!"

Amor De Cosmos poked his head into the burning office as a heavy chest of drawers plummeted through the weakened ceiling and crashed onto the floor at the back of the jail. Flames roared through the small cell.

Mei-fu ran to the iron bars and shoved her red and blackened hand in. "Wu Lee!..." she screamed. Embers swirled down around her.

De Cosmos leapt across the room, grabbed her round the waist, and dragged her towards the door. "Wu Lee," she cried. Behind them the small cell was a mass of flames.

"Get out onto the wharf," Jonas yelled. He grabbed Caroline's hand, took Madeline by the elbow, and ushered them across the sawmill yard. "Where's Sarah?"

Madeline pulled her arm free. "I haven't seen her since this morning. She went into the woods behind the house." She began to move in that direction, but again Jonas grabbed her arm.

"It's too late," he shouted. "Get Caroline onto the dock."

Madeline nodded and circled her arm around Caroline's waist. "Do what you can to save the mill," she said.

Jonas stopped and smiled at her. Only in her eyes could he see the fear. He leaned forward and kissed her lightly on the cheek. Madeline wrinkled her nose and pretended to scowl at him. "Come on now," she said. "Before the whole place burns up." She turned, gritted her teeth against the arthritic pain in her legs, and marched onto the wharf, her cane rapping out her steps with precision on the rough planks.

Jonas watched until they were halfway down the dock; then he turned and ran back to the mill. "You," he shouted. "Get that ladder over here and start dousing the roof." A dozen Chinese labourers scurried in opposite directions, running from the well to the mill and back again, precious water spilling from their buckets as they bumped into one another. "Start a relay," Jonas roared. A few of the Chinese stopped and stared at him blankly, jabbering in Cantonese. "Here," Jonas shouted. He grabbed a small man by the collar, planted him a few feet from the well, and pushed the next one into position. Within minutes buckets were swinging down the line from hand to hand and splashing onto the sawmill walls. "Douse it," Jonas yelled. "Flood the damn place. You" — he grabbed a short, stocky Indian by the arm as he hurried past — "Get the barrels from the storeroom. Load them in a wagon and fill them from the inlet. Hurry." He shoved the man towards the beach. "Louis. Get all the blankets out of the bunkhouse and soak them. Move it!"

He stopped to gauge the awesome wall of fire roaring through the narrow strip of forest fifty yards to the west, pushed by the wind, crown-firing through the tops of the tinder-dry firs at the edge of the mill. Beyond them a thick, dark cloud billowed over the new city. Vancouver was ablaze. Flames leapt and curled fifty feet into the smoky black air. Over the roar of wind and fire, Jonas could hear the distant shouts of the townsfolk caught in the blaze. "God help them," he muttered.

"Get those blankets over here," Jonas roared. "Lay them out on the roof." The trees at the edge of the yard were ablaze, but the soft red dust at the base of the mill was already turning to a sticky gumbo as bucket after bucket of water was passed up the ladders and sluiced down the walls from the roof. Men swarmed over the building, flailing at the burning twigs showering around them. An old cedar tree at the edge of the clearing groaned, crackled, and toppled onto the bunkhouse, shattering the roof and engulfing it in flames. Jonas glanced nervously at Madeline and Caroline, who stood at the end of the wharf, their arms about each other, their faces thrust up at the fire raging through the treetops.

As suddenly as the wind had come it veered again, pushing the blaze back on itself. The fire towered straight up from the tops of the fir trees, then slowly fell back, its long, fiery plumes flickering over the charred forest like red and orange streamers. "We've done it," Jonas shouted. "It's turning back." The men on the roof roared.

Near by, a hundred-year-old fir, weakened by the flames, shuddered and sighed as its charred wooden core crackled in the shifting wind. The trunk snapped eighty feet above the ground. Jonas looked up at the roar overhead and opened his mouth to scream as the burning tree plummeted directly towards him.

"Wait there," Abby shouted. The *Cariboo Fly* steamed towards Cains's wharf, while the town blazed fifty yards off her port side. Behind her the ship's single lifeboat rolled and pitched on the milky-green waves as Johann rowed towards the dozen boys and girls of the Reverend Thomas Derrick's Sunday-school class. Waves surged up around their necks as they floundered into the deep water, driven by the heat and smoke billowing over their heads. Old Hoisting Gear waded among them with a small girl clinging to his back, his black robe bobbing on the green waves, his deep, rich voice booming out over the water as he sang a church hymn.

Ahead, through the thick smoke, Abby saw the panic on Caroline Burgess's face as she stood poised at the edge of the wharf, ready to jump. Burning debris had showered onto the dock near the beach and set the planks ablaze. Madeline tugged futilely at a board, trying to loosen it, but it was hopeless. The flames ate their way steadily down the pier towards the two women.

The *Cariboo Fly* was fifty yards away. "Hold on," Abby shouted. The deck shuddered under her feet as the engines slammed into reverse. Across the short distance she saw the pilings twist and buckle as they burned. The shore end of the wharf collapsed with a roar and the pier tilted at an angle. Steam hissed up from the green waves.

Caroline screamed and jumped into the deep water. Madeline dropped to her knees. Her cane clattered over the planking and rolled into the inlet. As she began crawling up the skewed deck, flames shot up beside her. "Help," Caroline yelled. Water swirled over her head as Madeline swung her legs over the end of the dock, glanced back at the roaring blaze, and dropped down into the water.

Abby stripped off her white muslin dress, her petticoats and heavy boots, and climbed over the railing in her chemise. Madeline thrashed under the dock, bumping against the barnacle-encrusted pylons, her heavy woollen skirts filling with water and pulling her under. Abby swung her arms over her head and dived, her long white body arched and taut as she sliced into the pale-green waves. Beneath the surface it was cool, quiet, and still.

She surfaced a few feet from Caroline and flicked the wet coils of hair out of her eyes. Madeline was sinking. Abby kicked her legs and struck out towards her, but Caroline grabbed her round the neck. She winced as the woman's long nails raked red welts across her shoulder. A wave surged over her head, and her mouth filled with salt water.

"Lie still," Abby shouted. "You'll drown us both." She broke Caroline's grip and grabbed her from behind, her left arm circled under her breasts, and swam towards the *Cariboo Fly*. Caroline lay still, her long, thin body trembling on top of Abby.

Abby grabbed the rope ladder dangling from the side of the ship and swung the woman around to face it. Caroline snatched the ropes greedily, thrashing her legs under the water and gouging Abby's thighs with her high-heeled boots. Abby pushed off from the side of the ship and swam towards the burning dock. Under it she saw Madeline's grey hair fan out on the surface like seaweed and disappear.

Shards of burning wood spun on the wind and hissed into the waves around Abby's head. She dived, her eyes wide open, searching for the old woman. The water was green and murky with churning sand and bits of kelp. She could see only a few feet, then the light vanished as she kicked deeper, feeling in the cold darkness with her hands. Her arm scraped against the barnacles of a pylon as the current pushed her inshore. Her lungs ached. She turned and felt desperately behind her—nothing—then kicked to the surface.

Abby gasped, filling her lungs with the smoky air. The burning dock groaned and crackled overhead. She took a deep breath and dived again as the wharf collapsed above her, smashing against her heels. The water turned black as the hazy sun was blotted out, and Abby groaned, knowing it was too late. Madeline Cains was gone.

Wiley Burgess ran down Water Street, glancing nervously at the flames leaping from building to building on either side of him: the hardware store, George Black's butcher shop, the Palace Royale. He dropped to his knees as the soda-water factory exploded behind him and a large section of the roof sailed over his head and crashed into the front of Hartney's General Store. It was hopeless; the buildings on the north side of the street were a solid mass of flames, so he could not reach the inlet.

He scrambled to his feet and ran uphill along Abbott Street, then south towards the Indian village and the safety of False Creek. The town had gone crazy. To his left a man stood in his backyard dousing a pile of firewood while his house blazed. To his right a woman ran to a well with an armload of books and dumped them in. The street was in chaos; people ran in every direction, lugging boxes, mattresses, furniture, and paintings, leading white-eyed horses, frantic cows, goats, and dogs, pushing, shouting, shoving, tripping; and over it all was the roar of fire, goading them into panic, and the thick, black smoke, stinging their eyes and choking their lungs. Ahead, a frail old man perched on the roof of his newly built house sprinkling water onto the cedar shakes from two tin cups.

Wiley darted into the woods at the edge of the settlement and ran along a narrow trail towards False Creek. Rabbits scurried through the underbrush on either side while the fire raced through the treetops overhead. He was breathing heavily. Sparks showered down into a stand of dry birch to his right; the bark crackled and the small grove of trees burst into flame.

He staggered into a gravel clearing and stopped. Ahead, fire raged through a narrow strip of dry marsh grass, willow, and underbrush. Through the flames he could see the longhouses of the Indian village, safe on the far side of a broad belt of swampy land that opened to the west onto English Bay and the ocean. Dugout canoes skimmed over the bay, the reflection of the blaze flickering in their wake like iridescent seaweed.

It was hopeless. He could not reach the water. He turned and looked back along the wooded trail. A grizzled old logger in tin pants and undershirt was hobbling towards him, followed by a young dandy who ran crouched over, holding a valise over his head as sparks and flame showered down around him. Behind them the path was ablaze. Wiley whirled around, panicked, scanning the burning forest for an escape. Nothing. He dropped to his knees and stretched out in a shallow puddle.

The two men stumbled into the clearing, slapping at the sparks smouldering in their clothes, and looked around. The open patch of gravel was a hundred feet long, fifty across. The trees at the edge swayed in the wind, long tongues of flame streaming from their tops. "We're trapped," the old man screamed. A willow tree groaned and toppled into the clearing with a whoosh.

Flames roared up just a few feet away. The two men dropped to the ground and huddled on the leeward side of Wiley.

Thick, black smoke rolled over the men. They buried their faces in their arms, sucking air from the top of the water. Their clothes began to smoke. Wiley rolled in the puddle, wetting his back. Within seconds his coat was smoking again as the wind drove heat and sparks at him. The other two men cowered against him, using his body as a windbreak. He grabbed the young man's valise and held it over his head and back.

For five minutes they lay in agony, slapping at sparks, gasping for air, their skin searing in the heat. "I can't stand it," the old man screeched. He jumped to his feet. "We're roasting alive." He sprinted towards the marsh, then stopped and ran frantically in the opposite direction. Wiley watched, his stomach churning, while the old man danced wildly in a cloud of smoke, his arms thrashing the air, then dropped to the ground. His body shimmered in the heat and burst into flame.

Wiley cowered under the valise, shivering from the pain of the thousand tiny burns on his hands and legs as sparks settled around him. The smell of burning flesh caught in his throat and he gagged.

A loud bang sounded a few inches from his left ear and the valise shuddered on his back. "My revolver," the young man gasped. Another bullet exploded from the heat and whined through the clearing, ricocheting off a rock. Wiley dug his fingers into the gravel, paralysed with fear, while the suitcase thumped and banged on his back, shot after shot whizzing over his head and ringing through the clearing.

As the wind shifted, pushing the fire back on itself, he vomited into the shallow puddle and fainted.

Sitka gripped Thomas's hand tighter as a flaming cedar tree crashed onto the trail behind them. They had made it through the burning town and into the forest to the east, but still the fire raced beside them, blocking their flight down the steep bank to the safety of the inlet. Her heart pounded as she ran. Her chest ached. A hundred yards away, the pale-green ocean flickered through the flames.

"Wait," she cried. To her right a landslide had ripped a wide clearing down the hillside. Smoke curled up from the tangle of shattered trees and broken stumps, but there were no flames.

"There." She grabbed Thomas round the waist and half lifted, half pushed him over the first of the fallen logs. From the top of the bank she could see hundreds of men and women wading out into the inlet.

Offshore the *Cariboo Fly* rocked in the wind, her decks crowded with survivors, the water around her thick with people grabbing at the ropes dangling from her side. More ships were steaming towards the fire from Galer Mills' wharf. Dugouts and small skiffs darted through the shallows, picking up those who were floundering in the heavy waves.

Sitka scrambled around a smoking stump. Ahead, Thomas stood waist-deep in the tangled branches of a willow tree. They were halfway down the bank. Sparks showered around her as a gust of wind whipped down the hillside, igniting the dry moss under her feet. She leapt onto the back of a fallen poplar; it shifted under her and she waved her arms, struggling to regain her balance, but her foot slipped and jammed between two logs. "Thomas," she screamed. As she tumbled forward her leg snapped below the knee and she slumped to the ground, striking her head on a jagged stump.

She bit her tongue to keep from crying out again, but it was too late. The boy was standing over her, tears welling up in his black eyes. He shoved at the huge log pinning her leg, but it wouldn't budge. The top of the hillside was ablaze and flames shot up from the tangle of dry wood around her. Sitka took a deep breath. "You must go to the inlet without me," she said.

"No," the boy wailed. He jammed his arm between the logs and tried to pull her leg free. Sitka felt nothing. His hand came out covered in blood.

"Go," Sitka barked. She tried to push him away, but fell back and shut her eyes. Her voice softened. "The spirits will protect me. I will see you tomorrow, and we will go to the whispering tree as I promised. Then you will have a spirit to watch over you." Flames curled up from the far side of the log that pinned her leg. She felt faint. The burning trees at the top of the bank whirled and spun overhead. "You must go now," she whispered. "Your mother is waiting for you. Yes, and she needs you. Go to her, Thomas. She's on that big white ship in the inlet. Get into the water and swim, Thomas. Swim out to the ship."

She shut her eyes in pain, then opened them again. The sky had darkened. She looked up into his shining black eyes and smiled. Yes, she thought. They are Indian eyes — the eyes of the First People.

Dawn. As the first black storm cloud billowed up over the granite mountains to the north and fanned out across the clear blue sky, Abby stopped in the middle of the smoking street, sniffed the air, and sighed with relief. A light breeze was blowing from the east, cool and fresh. It smelled of rain.

Around her, Vancouver was a vast plain of fine black ash. On the main road, only the Regina Hotel remained, a fluke of the wind and the desperate efforts of the men trapped inside. At the fringes of the fire, Jonas Cains's mill and house stood out stark and rigid against the charred earth and pale-blue sky. Just forty minutes, Abby thought. And over eight hundred structures and every living thing for a foot below the surface have been destroyed. Behind her a charred timber of the Palace Royale quivered in the breeze and collapsed in a whirlwind of ash.

Dazed men and women moved slowly over the hillside to the south, picking their way through the columns of smoke curling up from the ground, poking cautiously amongst the ashes of their homes. Others wandered aimlessly up and down the main street, peering into faces, calling out names, stubbornly refusing to go to the improvised morgue at False Creek for fear they would find the relatives they were seeking.

Abby staggered and leaned against the still-warm stones of the church well. She felt light-headed and giddy. Most of the night she had walked the burnt-out streets, moving from one group of injured to the next, dressing burns in flour and oil and wrapping them in skunk-cabbage leaves. Once she had crossed the inlet to help with the injured who were flooding into her home, but she was not needed. The women of Galer Mills were moving quickly and confidently through the crowded rooms, treating wounds, making beds, preparing food. She had stayed only briefly to supervise the moving of Angus to the kitchen so that a badly burned woman could have his bed, and then she returned to the devastated south shore to help the doctors who were pouring in from neighbouring towns.

At sunset the thick cloud of smoke and ash that hovered over Vancouver had rolled up the Fraser Valley, and by midnight a steady caravan of wagons laden with food, clothing, bandages, lumber, and tools was rattling down the corduroy road from

New Westminster, Langley, Port Moody, Mission — all up and down the Fraser Valley the word had spread and communities rushed to the aid of the burned-out town. As the wagons rolled in, the refugees poured out, carrying the few belongings they had saved, searching for shelter in the neighbouring villages. Every door of every house in the valley had been thrown open to welcome the survivors.

Abby backed away as a young man climbed up out of the well and men shouldered their way in to pull on the ropes that hung over the stone ledge. They heaved in unison. The body of the little girl rose up out of the well first. Her face was blue and her head lolled back, her wet hair hanging loosely over her plaid skirt. Then came Clarissa, her long brown body glistening in the sunlight, water echoing in the deep pool below as it dripped from the lace cuffs of her white chemise. The bodies were laid out on blankets while a doctor held a stethoscope to their chests.

"Drowned," someone said.

The doctor stood up and shook his head. "Suffocation, more likely," he said. "The fire'd suck all the oxygen out of there."

Mei-fu pushed through the crowd, dropped to her knees, and cradled Clarissa's head in her lap. Abby recognized the tattered green gown and remembered how she had crouched on the beach the night before and wrapped the Chinese woman's fire-blackened hand in skunk-cabbage leaves while she talked woodenly of her dead son and of Caroline Burgess, who had turned him in to the police. As they had sat on the sand, watching the black smoke-cloud that hunched sullenly over the inlet glow blood-red in the summer sunset, Abby had asked about Jonas Cains and Chang's letter. Mei-fu's eyes had narrowed and her voice had become sharp and brittle. "You help me," she hissed, "and he will pay. We must make him pay."

Abby gazed down the long black street at the solitary house of Jonas Cains, and the anger welled up in her again. She thought of Angus and how he had winced and his face had turned grey when she had propped his butchered leg up on pillows before the kitchen stove, and she began walking towards the mill. She thought of Amor De Cosmos, who again sat on the front porch, broken, defeated, and mute, watching the parade of burnt bodies move in and out of her house, and she thought of the simpleton Jimmy, hanging from the Governor's porch with a knife in his shoulder. As she moved down the blackened street, she pulled

Chang's letter out of her dress pocket and quickened her pace.

Men from the town swarmed over Cains's yard, boldly loading the last pile of sawn lumber into wagons; no one was there to stop them. From the side of the house, Abby could see that Madeline's meticulous garden had charred and withered from the heat. Black roses quivered on long, thin stems. She marched to the front of the house and up the brick steps. The big oak doors hung open. She banged on them with her fist and stepped into the foyer. A thick layer of ash drifted over Madeline's rose-coloured carpet.

"Cains," she shouted. There was no answer. She walked through the parlour and into the dining room. A thin cloud of acrid grey smoke eddied round the ceiling. The house was silent. Two plates of cold salmon and potato salad were set on the table next to half-filled goblets of wine. Her hand fell onto the back of one of the chairs. She had not been in the room since the night of the dinner party sixteen years before. It had not changed. The oak table still reminded her of a casket, and she could picture Cains staring at her coldly down its long, polished length. She pulled her hand away from the chair as she realized that Matthew had sat there. Matthew. . . . She whirled round and faced the open doors of the parlour. "Jonas Cains!" she roared.

He's escaped, she thought. Someone has warned him and he's escaped. She ran back to the foyer and pounded up the stairs to the second floor. The first room on the left was empty, and the next, and the next. At the end of the corridor the last door flew open and she recognized the long grey pony-tail of Sarah, Jonas Cains's mysterious daughter, as she darted out of the room and clattered down a narrow staircase at the end of the hall. The door swung loosely open. Abby pushed it with her fingertips and stepped into the room. She stopped, shocked, her mouth open, one hand braced on the door-frame. Jonas Cains lay in a big mahogany bed, the covers tucked up around his chest, his piercing grey eyes watching her, watching. The left side of his face was red and puckered with burns, and his left hand lay on the white linen, black and blistered. She held Chang's letter in front of her and walked slowly towards him.

"He's paralysed."

She whirled round and saw Caroline sitting on the floor, slumped against the wall, still wearing her damp white dress. A large peacock hunched on the edge of the dresser next to her, winking his tiny yellow eyes, defecating on the smooth, polished wood. The smell of smoke was heavy and cloying. "What happened?"

Caroline didn't answer. She shut her eyes and began to hum tunelessly. Abby walked towards the bed. Jonas's pale-grey eyes followed her as she moved, watching her, watching. She leaned over him and whispered in his ear, "Did you kill my husband?" The covers on his chest rose and fell steadily. The sharp eyes did not change their expression.

"He can't talk," Caroline said. "Can't walk, can't talk, can't move, can't . . ." Her voice trailed off.

Abby shuddered and backed towards the door, shaking her head. "It's not fair," she whispered. The room seemed oppressive, claustrophobic; it reeked of burnt flesh, smoke, and medicine. Tears welled up in her eyes. "I finally had him." Her stomach churned. She stopped in the doorway and stared at the hulk of Jonas Cains in its bed of fine white linen. The eyes were still watching her. Slowly she opened her hand and let Chang's letter slip from her fingers. As the faded yellow rice-paper fluttered to the floor, she turned and walked down the hallway. It was over.

On the stairway she passed Wiley Burgess bounding up the steps two at a time. His clothes were torn and stained with soot, his face splattered with mud. "What the hell are you doing here?" he demanded. She passed him without answering. "Get out," he shrieked. "You've no business here. Get out." She barely heard him as she walked out into the cool, fresh breeze and strode towards the beach.

Black clouds stretched over the sky, and the rain forest to the south rustled in the wind. At the edge of the inlet she stopped and looked back towards Vancouver. Tents had mushroomed up out of the ashes on the hillside and the air resounded with the pounding of hammers as new wooden frames were hoisted into the air. Thunder rumbled over the granite mountains to the north. As the first fat drops of rain plopped onto the black ground, Abby stretched her arms up towards the sky, and smiled.

EPILOGUE

HIGH ON THE MOUNTAIN THE ANCIENT CEDAR TREE RUSTLED AND swayed, shaking off the first light snow of early winter. On its lowest branch a bright new burial box rose and fell as gently as a canoe in a rolling swell. Facing the panoramic view of the city below, a small round hole had been cut in the centre of a red-and-black crest.

Across the inlet, far to the south, hundreds of houses rambled up the hillside, past the shrunken village of Snauq on False Creek, east to the New Westminster road, and west to the sea. The town was crowded and sprawling, and in its centre were buildings of brick and stone.

The long finger of the new wharf at Cains's mill poked far out into the inlet, which shone bright-blue, streaked with grey and silver where the currents ran. Across from it was the vast complex of Galer Mills. Houses dotted the beach on the north shore and a few nestled in the cleared tablelands at the foot of the mountain. Sitka's cabin still stood alone in its vast swath of green forest.

The light dusting of snow began in the foothills at the base of the high granite cliff. Above it, the ancient cedar swayed in the wind.

A hand reached up with a tuft of dry bear grass and brushed the snow from the bright-red crests on the new box. The wind increased and, as the smooth branches of the old cedar rubbed together, the whispering tree began to sing.

W^{THE}EST COASTERS

Vancouver Island and the
Pacific Mainland Coast
1857–1886

British Columbia

Fraser River

Yale

Hope

Vancouver Island

Vancouver

New Westminster

Langley

Victoria

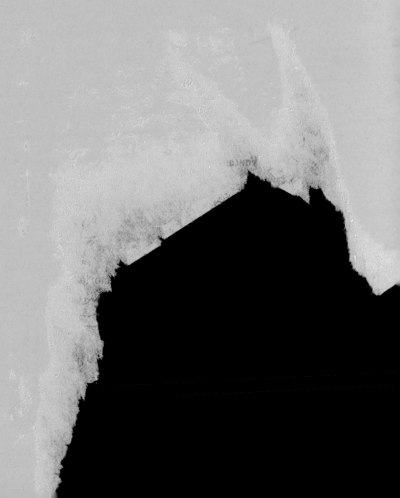